"How dare you force me abed? Get out!"

"Nay, lady. We both shall stay, and you will obey. The quicker you cooperate, the sooner you may leave."

"Fool! You know not what you are up against. You will never break me. No man has." Jehanne bit her lip at her own outburst. No man had broken her, but never had she spoken thus to one and not regretted it.

As he sat next to her, Fulk radiated heat and strength. Yet there was something more, she felt safe in his proximity. What an absurd idea.

Fulk leaned on one palm, his gaze boring into her. The firelight bounced blue sparks off his hair, and he seemed to fill her whole field of vision. "I have no wish to break you," he purred, a whisper of steel in his voice. "But bend you I will, and if it takes till summer, so be it."

* * *

Fulk the Reluctant
Harlequin Historical #713—July 2004

Praise for Elaine Knighton's debut

Beauchamp Besieged

"Sensational plot turns…gritty but vivid picture
Knighton paints of medieval times."
—*Publishers Weekly*

"Rich details create a strong sense of place in this debut."
—*Romantic Times*

"Raymond de Beauchamp is the sort of hero
not easily forgotten. He is tortured, brooding
and a slave to his passions."
—*The Romance Reader's Connection*

"A definite must-read for those who enjoy
a good medieval tale."
—*Romance Reviews Today*

FULK THE RELUCTANT

ELAINE ✝ KNIGHTON

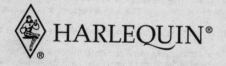

HARLEQUIN®

TORONTO • NEW YORK • LONDON
AMSTERDAM • PARIS • SYDNEY • HAMBURG
STOCKHOLM • ATHENS • TOKYO • MILAN • MADRID
PRAGUE • WARSAW • BUDAPEST • AUCKLAND

ISBN 0-373-29313-5

FULK THE RELUCTANT

Copyright © 2004 by Elaine Knighton

This edition published by arrangement with Harlequin Books S.A.

® and TM are trademarks of the publisher. Trademarks indicated with ® are registered in the United States Patent and Trademark Office, the Canadian Trade Marks Office and in other countries.

www.eHarlequin.com

Printed in U.S.A.

Please address questions and book requests to:
Harlequin Reader Service
U.S.: 3010 Walden Ave., P.O. Box 1325, Buffalo, NY 14269
Canadian: P.O. Box 609, Fort Erie, Ont. L2A 5X3

To my mom and dad,
who have always been there for me, no matter what....

Prologue

A tournament in France, 1230

Fulk de Galliard, the undisputed champion of that day's mêlée, lay facedown in the dust and wept like a child. Beside him sprawled his elder brother, his eyes still open to the hot sky. Proud, bold Rabel—witty and sarcastic and now utterly dead.

It had not been one of their usual arguments, for Fulk had thrown the first blow. A single, fatal blow.

Fulk raised his head and met his lord father's terrible, wounded eyes. He held up his bloodied right fist. "Cut it off," he begged.

The count shook his head slowly. "I will do nothing for you. You are an abomination...you are my son no longer."

Fulk sat up, wrenched his dagger free and sawed the blade against his wrist. If his father would not rid him of the offending hand, he would do it himself.

"Stop!" The count kicked the bloody weapon from Fulk's grasp. "I leave you to the mercy of Rabel's comrades."

As Rabel's body was carried from the practice grounds, the grim knights surrounded Fulk. He took a deep breath, but made no effort to defend himself. They laid into him with their fists and the flats of their swords. Fulk never uttered a sound. He took the beating as though he were made of stone.

But before the blackness took him, he had one last coherent thought. *I hope they've killed me.*

* * *

He eased his eyes open. It was dark. Freezing. Then he remembered. *Rabel is dead.* And if the pain and misery and cold were any indication, Fulk was not.

A pity. Rain spattered against his face. From the smell, he knew he lay in a mixture of mud, blood and horse dung. And would no doubt remain there, for the slightest attempt to move produced screams of protest from his limbs.

A squelching noise grew louder, accompanied by the sputtering of torches. Ah. They had come to finish him off. A good thing, and high time. He relaxed into the muck.

"Fulk...dearling, *mon pauvre ami!* What have they done to you?"

Fulk suppressed a groan and shut his eyes against this fresh humiliation. The beautiful Lady Greyhaven, his friend and advisor, arrived to rescue him. God bless her. And curse her.

She barked orders. "Come, get him onto the litter! Gently, gently now!"

Silk whispered across his brow, and the scents of violet, lavender, rose and musk came to him. Fulk reopened his eyes. The hands that lifted him were many, but did not belong to menservants.

Women. Fully a dozen of them. Dazzling gifts from God and yet the bane of his life. And all gazed at him with loving adoration.

"We know it was an accident, Fulk, everyone—"

"Shh! He needs a bed, bath and bandages, not talk!"

"God, he weighs as much as a horse!"

"Aye, you would know, Clothilde!"

"Ah, Fulk, with the good Lord's grace you will be well in no time...."

"Stop thinking of yourself, Pierrette, for I am certain that is your main worry—"

Fulk could bear it no longer. "For the love of God—my dear ladies—spare me your concern."

"Fulk, be quiet." Lady Greyhaven briskly bound his wrist with a cloth, laid his hand over his chest and covered him with a heavy blanket. "*Allez!* To the chateau!"

She is a commander worthy of any fighting force, Fulk thought fuzzily. Why did she have to come? The merciful thing would be to simply let him die. But he was too weak to do anything but submit, as blessed oblivion reclaimed him.

Chapter One

England, 1237

"With all due respect—a pox upon thee, milady!" The young man's voice cracked with indignation.

Fulk de Galliard wiped his sweaty forehead in the crook of his arm and glanced up from examining his charger's legs. Bryce, squire to the Duke of Warrick, was not normally given to cursing women. But then again, women were not usually found in the combatants' waiting area, especially at such a throat-parching tournament as this.

The apparent object of the lad's ire stood out of sight, on the off-side of the great-horse he attended. All Fulk could see was a pair of small, well-shod feet, their soft leather boots wrinkling at the ankles—with bronze spurs strapped thereon.

In a grim tone "milady" responded, "Squire, you made a promise, and now it must be kept. Else look well to your own arse, for I will not be denied." The small feet broadened their stance.

After a moment's hesitation, Bryce gave a resigned sigh and held out the charger's reins.

A gloved hand took them. "Many thanks, sir. I will care for him well. Rest easy, the duke will forgive us."

"You, perhaps, but not me." The squire sounded close to despair.

The young woman stepped into view. Garbed in a dusty crimson overgown, her skirts hiked into her belt, she led the restless white stallion away. Her thick plait of hip-length, sun-bleached hair swung to and fro as she walked, and with each confident stride, steely gleams escaped from beneath the uplifted folds of her kirtle.

She wears a mail shift? Fulk stared and wondered what to make of such a beguiling spectacle.

"Oh, Lord! I am dead!" Bryce groaned as girl and beast disappeared into the noisy confusion of the tournament grounds. "She has as good as stolen the duke's finest tourney horse. Why do I allow her to do this to me?"

"Why, indeed?" Fulk released his own mount's near front hoof, satisfied that none of the nails on the cleated shoe were loose. "Take the animal back. She is but a lass, after all."

The squire shook his head. "Sir, she has a veritable armory under her gown, for that, sir, was the Iron Maiden of Windermere."

"Ah." Fulk had heard of this golden-haired virago, who fought like a man and rode the hills heading a pack of armed young women. He did not approve of such goings-on. It was bad enough that men had to shed blood in the pointless and ignoble causes of their lords.

Women should have the good sense not to follow suit, but here was an obvious exception. "What is her intent?"

Bryce put a hand to his brow. "She means to fight in the mêlée, on my lord's charger."

"It is obvious the lady is deranged. If she is not slain, the horse might be."

"Aye, she must be stopped. She is a menace to all good men."

Fulk could not help but smile. He had never yet met a woman who was not, in one way or another.

The squire brightened. "If anyone can do it, 'tis you, Fulk de Galliard. I shall recommend you to my lord duke as soon as I recover from the beating with which he shall no doubt honor me."

"Leave me out of it. If I do well today, this will be my final tourney, for I'll have my sister's dowry in hand at last."

And high time, for Celine, fully ten and seven, was as comely and graceful a maid as ever lived. Once Fulk saw to her marriage he would be free of these endless, exhausting feats of arms.

"Ah, the Lady Celine." The squire's expression grew dreamy.

Fulk narrowed his eyes at Bryce. "My young friend, do not form a single carnal thought with her name upon your lips."

"Em, nay, I would not dare." The young man pointed at a sudden commotion. "Oh, the saints have smiled upon me after all."

He dashed off in the direction of the thoroughfare, where the duke's stallion trotted loose, creating havoc among the ale and pasty vendors, scattering musicians and jugglers. The charger allowed the squire to catch him, and as if to hide, jammed his great head under his captor's armpit.

The horse thief too had been caught. A defiant, unapologetic thief, if her expression and demeanor were to be believed. A tall, daunting knight propelled her from behind. One of his huge, gauntleted hands clamped the back of her slender neck. Only a father could maintain a look of such fury while handling a maid as fair as she, Fulk thought. But what manner of daughter behaved thus? He decided it was unkind to watch her humiliation, though by all appearances she was not perturbed. She held her head high, wincing now and again. Fulk knew exactly what such a neck-grip felt like, and had to admire the girl's fortitude, despite the sad evidence of her addlepatedness.

"It would seem the lady has surrendered to her parent."

"She drives Sir Alun mad, she does."

"So I gather." Fulk paused, not quite ready to turn back to his horse, after all. The maiden's thick, padded underjacket did not completely hide her subtle curves, and the lithe grace of her walk was all the more apparent for the lack of skirts.

Women. He never tired of looking at them. This one was certainly an eyeful, and probably more than a handful.

Or two, he amended, as she straightened her shoulders.

At this sign of resistance her lord father shoved her forward, and she stumbled. Fulk's chest tightened. No matter the provocation, a man of worth did not treat a woman thus, be she sane or otherwise. He had certainly never found it necessary. But he could not upbraid the girl's own sire, Sir Alun, Baron of Windermere.

"Beware that one, Galliard," Bryce cautioned. "The Iron

Maiden is an angel on the outside, and hellfire within. She might even try *your* sweet temper. Of course, chances are the lady will never be breached, so 'tis moot.''

Fulk shot the young man a quelling look. Sweet temper, indeed. If he only knew the effort it took to make it appear thus. But the lad needed a lesson in manners.

"I might suggest, Bryce, that you do not gossip about women. Especially ladies who have favored you with an intimate experience, but also those who have not. That would no doubt include all in attendance here, as well as the rest of Christendom and beyond.''

The knights and other squires within earshot chuckled.

Bryce's grin faltered and he turned away in silence.

"Best not to cross tongues with Fulk de Galliard, he's quicker'n the likes of you.''

Fulk looked up and nodded to his friend, Malcolm Mac Niall, a man alongside whom he had faced death more times than he cared to recall. Dark and hard as weathered oak, the Scot sauntered over and made a seat of an upturned bucket.

Fulk regretted his cutting words. He had long suffered the cruel wit of his brother Rabel, who had taken his example from their father, God rest them both. As ever, at the thought of them, Fulk's heart took an instant leap of grief and fury.

As ever, he soothed his pain with images of beauty. Rose petals on clean linen. Soft, white skin flushing pink beneath his hands. Shy smiles and ever-willing arms—and legs—opening to him. And now a new vision, of a fair, fiery lass with tangled, dark-gold tresses...

Fulk shook his head. The mêlée loomed ahead, and every detail of his equipment must be in order. He could not allow himself to be distracted by such an unlikely tidbit. Satisfied his stallion's legs were cool and tight, his bridle leathers uncracked, and every buckle snugged to perfection, Fulk's glance strayed to the contingent of Earl Grimald of Lexingford, his deadliest opponent in the upcoming fray.

"A plague on them and those tubs of lard they call horses,'' Malcolm growled, his big hands engulfing a pitcher of ale.

"Aye. Grimald's beasts eat better than we do." Fulk frowned. The earl and his pack were of grave concern.

Malcolm took a swig of the brew and smoothed his moustache with precise fingers. "There's the man to watch."

A big knight, known as Hengist the Hurler, busied himself with the girth on the earl's saddle. Hengist had a penchant not only for knocking heads, but for tossing them out of their owners' reach.

The blond knight looked up, and seeing Fulk's gaze upon him, straightened abruptly. Something glinted in his hand, then vanished into the folds of his tunic. Hengist stared at Fulk, hot menace slowly congealing in his ice-blue eyes.

Stifling an ugly urge to free the Hurler from his no doubt unsatisfactory existence, Fulk grinned and winked. The knight turned red and looked about to advance, but Fulk led his own horse away at a leisurely pace. There was no need to start the fight any earlier than required.

In the raised pavilion with the other young ladies, Jehanne of Windermere tipped her head and squinted against the glare of sun on steel, the better to view the dozens of knights and great-horses parading past.

Bright pennants and banners hung as limp as her own spirits in the still summer air. The grass of the tourney grounds had turned to yellow stubble, the noise and heat were stifling, and dust prevented her from clearly seeing any subtleties of technique the combatants used in the contests.

Not that such things mattered anymore. Hot anguish and bitter shame seethed within her. She had been so close to joining in the mêlée. Her father had dragged her off. But even that was not the worst of it. If not for him, today she would have fought her enemy—her *suitor*—the Earl Grimald. Aye, she might have slain him—or wounded him so he would have no need of a bride. Even if she had died instead, it would have been an honorable death, with sword in hand.

Forever free.

Jehanne squeezed wads of her fine linen gown in her fists and bit her lip. Lioba, the eldest of her handmaidens, sat beside her, frowning in concern.

"What's wrong with you, milady?" One violently red-hued curl escaped Lioba's coif as she leaned closer.

Jehanne released the crumpled fabric from her damp hands. "I am hot. You've tightened the side lacings of this infernal gown so I can scarcely breathe."

"Aye, you cannot run far when you cannot draw air into your lungs. There are other ways to best the Earl Grimald, Jehanne, besides meeting him in combat. Even in marriage, there are ways."

Jehanne stopped the protest that sprang to her lips. Lioba was good at reading her mind, but even she did not fully understand. She did not want to merely best the Earl Grimald. She wanted him gone from her sight, her mind, her life. But he had spun his web, tight and fine. She was trapped. And the last honorable means of escape had been denied her this day.

A soft peal of laughter emerged from a fashionable damsel seated beside her. *Aye, why not this vapid maiden?* The girl, jesting with one of her ladies, seemed quite an impossible creature. Such creamy skin, with suspiciously convenient touches of rose at cheeks and lips. Her hair gleamed in rivers of flaxen silk. Demure and graceful, she dimpled whenever a passing man of prowess acknowledged her.

What a lot of wasteful effort, just to be a proper lady.

The beautiful creature noticed Jehanne's scrutiny, and a wrinkle formed between her thin, pale brows. Jehanne returned the Creature's cold look with a polite smile. "Have you a favorite for the mêlée?"

"I do." She leaned forward, all coyness gone as she looked.

Jehanne followed her gaze, until it collided with one of the combatants, coming their way on a snorting, blood-bay horse. The man's surcoat was a plain blue, his outdated, flat-topped helm was unadorned, and his shield bore innumerable scars.

The modesty of the rider's accoutrements served only to emphasize the grandeur of his stallion. The big man handled the restive animal with admirable calm.

The chatter of the surrounding women died down. Putting her own misery aside, Jehanne looked about, baffled at the variety of expressions on the ladies' faces. Many were excited, wringing their hands, others blatantly lovelorn, and a few were plainly angry.

"Who is that?" she blurted.

As he approached, the fair damsel's knuckles whitened on the railing. "Fulk de Galliard. Fulk the *Reluctant,* you goose!"

Jehanne's jaw tightened. The lady was fast becoming intolerable. Then the object of so many eyes halted directly before them. No one spoke, no one moved. Galliard sat his massive charger and appeared to survey the ladies through the eye slits of his helm.

Jehanne stared. Never had she seen a lone man command the complete attention of so many women at once. But he did not lower his lance to receive any of the trembling, fluttering wisps of silk being offered him.

The heat rose in her cheeks. She felt his gaze as surely as if he had touched her skin. This—Fulk—looked at her. Her. The least likely of these worthy noblewomen to attract a man's attention, and no doubt the one least desirous of it. Jehanne had never yet given a knight her token, and she was not about to start with him.

His eyes gleamed from within his helm, then, in a brief, elegant movement of his hand he managed to salute the group of ladies as one before cantering away to join the fight. Sighs, strangled squeals, and sharp, indignant inhalations were the result.

"How is it that he cannot choose from among such a peerless group?" Jehanne took her seat again.

The lady smiled. "Oh, but he *has* chosen. The trouble is that he keeps *on* choosing."

"Fickle, is he?"

Another beauty, dark and glowing, raised her voice. "Ah, lady, with Fulk, it is more like generosity. He sacrifices himself upon the altars of our womanhood...."

At the melting look in the young lady's eyes, Jehanne had to smother a snort of scorn. "Is he named the Reluctant because he won't be faithful to any one of you?"

"Nay, not that. Some call him a coward because he is circumspect in battle. But we know better. Fulk is a sinfully dangerous man...and we adore his mystery." The Creature shivered. "You will see."

Indeed, as Fulk approached the fighting arena, a mixture of boos, hoots and wild cheers arose from the crowd grouped along the edge of the field. Whether nobles, grooms, cutpurses or ale-wives, all had an opinion of Fulk the Reluctant—and all stayed out of his way.

Jehanne's throat constricted and her heart pounded. How she would have loved to be a true knight, even if only for one day. To be resplendent and glorious and please her father by bringing honor to the house of FitzWalter. To live all the virtues of chivalry Sir Thomas had taught her in his endless stories of ancient kings and days of valor long past. And today, she might have become part of one of those tales....

No doubt Fulk the Reluctant was one of the new breed. Lusting after idle women and their riches. Squandering his might. Her thoughts were interrupted by the sound of approaching hoofbeats, which slowed and came to a stop. Jehanne did not turn her head to see who it was. From the rush of fear and revulsion that swept her, she knew, even as she prayed she was wrong.

"Lady Jehanne?"

Her heart sank at the familiar, gravelly voice. She tried to regain her composure, but her stomach only knotted tighter. Facing him at last, she could only manage, "My lord?"

Grimald, the Earl of Lexingford. Lord Grimald, the blight on her existence. In a full harness of exquisite, double-linked mail, he halted his sleek tourney horse near the gallery, a small army of squires and guardsmen forming a phalanx at his back. "Enjoying the spectacle?" He made the question sound like an accusation.

"Indeed I am." Jehanne avoided the earl's searing stare. Grimald's single-minded obsession with her—or rather, with Windermere, the estate she would inherit, was beyond frightening.

One way or another, the earl always got what he wanted.

Grimald drew himself taller as he sat his horse. "You, too, find Fulk the Reluctant irresistible, I suppose?"

"Certainly not."

"Honor me, then." He shoved his lance-tip toward her. Not a tournament head, pronged to diffuse the impact of a strike, but a regular war lance. Sharp and deadly.

Jehanne took a deep breath. She thought of saying she had given someone else her token. But telling falsehoods was not the way of a knight. Nor the daughter of a knight. She stood, her hands clutching the railing. "Nay, I will not."

The words hung naked and unadorned in the air, with nothing to soften their insult. Grimald purpled, from his beefy neck to his gray-streaked hair. A muscle twitched in his jaw. "Ah, *mais oui*. Jehanne, the Iron Maiden. You'd rather challenge a man to fight than lie with him and become a woman."

Jehanne felt her cheeks burn at his crudity. But the earl's statement was perfectly true. He eased the lance forward until its point just touched between her breasts, but she did not retreat.

She met his gaze. "I would rather lie down and be a dog than become *your* woman." A deadly silence fell, and Jehanne bit her tongue. To speak thus was not chivalrous, even if it were the truth. But so be it.

Grimald withdrew his lance. "Dog, eh? The proper term for you, I trow, is *bitch*." He snatched his black horsetail-plumed helm from his squire and spurred his mount toward the mêlée.

The young woman beside Jehanne fanned herself with a delicate, blue-veined hand. "Just what do you have that he desires so much?"

Jehanne studied her own hands, small and calloused. Of course no man would want her for herself. But nor did she want any man. "I have Windermere, lady. The best fief in all of England." With some satisfaction at the girl's surprised expression, Jehanne forced herself to watch the fighters churning in the dusty field below.

A blare of trumpets marked the start, and with a roar the charges began. The brightly caparisoned horses flew at each other, lances clashed against shields, swords rang, men bellowed and fell.

Squires led riderless horses away, wounded knights were borne out of danger on litters or staggered off, supported between friends. Some collapsed, overcome by the heat and dust in their airless helms.

If a man died in the course of a tournament he ran the risk of suffering excommunication—the Pope's penalty for such senseless slaughter. With a pang Jehanne wondered if the ruling would apply to a woman who died in a tourney. Which would she choose, damnation or Grimald? The difference was but slight, she decided.

As she watched, Jehanne could not help but appreciate Fulk de Galliard's style. He fought with unusual precision, rapidly unseating or disarming his opponents, but leaving none of them incapacitated. The small crowd of prisoners he had amassed waited in the shade for him to finish and come discuss the terms of their ransoms, as befit the demands of chivalry.

The mêlée drew to an end. Two champions had been chosen to finish the fighting on behalf of the exhausted opposing sides. Fulk and Grimald, with lances lowered, their mounts heaving. Winner take all. Fulk seemed unhurt, Jehanne thought.

Her stomach clenched as she remembered Grimald's lance-tip. She wondered whether the heralds had allowed it, or missed it. But, considering the earl's power, he could get away with most anything.

This man, Fulk, could not mistake the lethal lance-point. She held her breath. *What if he slays Grimald?* Her heart thudded faster. It could happen.... Fulk's powerful horse danced beneath him, then leaped forward, as if still fresh. At the same instant Grimald's charger lurched into motion. The earl listed to the left in his saddle, arms flailing, and Jehanne knew exactly where Fulk should aim. One blow to Grimald's right shoulder would send him flying.

What happened next brought everyone to their feet, as Fulk lived up to his dubious name. Grimald neared, and Fulk stood in his stirrups, calling something out to his opponent. He threw down his lance, reined to a halt and raised his right hand as if in surrender.

Shame on Fulk's behalf stabbed Jehanne, that he would dishonor himself thus in public, apparently only to save his own skin. But she could not hear his words over the noise of excited onlookers.

Grimald slowed, stopped, and nudged his opponent with his wicked lance-tip. Fulk leaned toward the earl as if speaking to him, and the heralds started to approach them.

Grimald shouted, the heralds shouted back, but in the end Fulk dismounted. The earl's knights seized Fulk's horse and weapons, and paraded him toward the women's gallery. Fulk's prisoners were now the earl's, and Fulk himself numbered among them.

A sense of helpless rage toward this useless knight filled Jehanne's being. He had thrown away his chance, failed himself, and though he knew it not, her as well. She stood and gestured toward him. "Why has he disgraced himself thus?"

The Creature sighed. "You *are* the innocent, aren't you? He has forfeited. And no one can ransom Fulk de Galliard, the earl will want a fortune for him."

"He is a churl to forfeit."

"Oh, no doubt he has a good reason. But we shall not hear of it. He has a beautiful way with words but never speaks of himself."

"Well, I have no desire to learn anything more about him." This was not entirely true, but Jehanne felt it necessary to close the subject of Galliard. Even as she awkwardly gathered her skirts to leave, the earl's men brought him nearer.

Folk heaped abuse upon him, hurling both insults and objects. He appeared completely disinterested, as though dishonor were a mantle he wore lightly. She wondered if during her own shameful march earlier she had looked half so detached.

Nay, not that...*empty* was a better word for how Fulk seemed. He looked drained of all feeling. And yet somehow, she knew he was not.

Already forgetting her previous declaration, Jehanne asked, "Why do any of you have the least regard for a such a knight?"

The Creature gaped. "How can you ask that? Just look at him. A magnificent animal, like none other! But even that is as nothing compared to being alone with him, up close. May the devil take him." She tossed her hair. "Besides, he is no knight. He walked away when the king wanted to honor him with knighthood. Needless to say, since then Fulk has been out of favor."

Jehanne took pause at this stunning revelation. That anyone might refuse knighting, and from a king, no less, was incomprehensible to her. As for him being an animal, magnificent or otherwise, that was merely a characteristic he shared in common with most men.

Why would anyone want to be alone with something so big and unpredictable? And certainly not...up close...as the Creature so delicately termed it. With a shudder, Jehanne continued to slip past the seated women. She had glimpsed Fulk's broad shoulders as he passed, and his barbaric, outrageously long hair. Black and wavy, it hung nearly to his belt. Such an affectation!

She firmly told herself she had no desire to look further upon such a travesty. If he *were* a knight, he did not deserve his spurs, so it was just as well he was not. She made her way to the steps leading down the side of the gallery. "Good day, ladies, I—"

Jehanne fell silent at the sight of her father striding toward her across the practice field, fury in his every movement.

"My lady," Lioba began in an urgent whisper.

"Go ahead to our pavilion, Lioba. Stay out of his way. I will be all right." But Jehanne's mouth went dry as she hurried alone to meet Sir Alun. He caught her arm, twisting it in a painful grip and pulled her along, faster than she could walk.

"Willful, obstinate female!" Her father stopped and whirled about to face her, his blue eyes snapping with rage. "You have insulted the Earl Grimald yet again! But this time you've gone too far."

He drew back his raised hand. A hard hand, she well knew. Jehanne's knees wobbled but she forced herself to hold still. Concentrating on the hot summer whine of the cicadas in the trees, she tensed her legs. A passing couple stopped to watch. Glancing at them, Alun drew a shaky breath before lowering his arm. "What am I to do with you?" he hissed.

Jehanne opened her eyes as far as she could. Never would she let her lord father see her weep. Not as long as she lived. She had already failed him, by not being the son he had desired so much.

But had she been, that son would never break down before his sire. It was the least she could do to spare him further anguish— short of marrying Grimald. "Let me be your right arm, Father."

"Be silent. No more tourneys. By the Rood, I regret having ever put a sword into your hand!"

Jehanne stared at him, her sense of betrayal complete. Her fa-

ther, the perfect knight, had himself brought her to this. For years
he had encouraged her to act the part of a lad, so he might avoid
the ugly truth of her sex. Now that she had honed her martial
skills as befit any son and heir, he wished her to abandon them
and use her womanhood—or rather, for the earl Grimald to use
her womanhood.

"Aye, well you might, my lord. For he will never touch me.
One of us will die first." With these words she braced herself for
the blow sure to follow. But Alun's fist remained at his side.

"We are going home. I will deal with you there."

Jehanne breathed her relief in spite of her despair. Home. Windermere. The place she loved more than anyone or anything.

Chapter Two

Three months had passed. In the earl's private chapel, caught between two Danish guardsmen, Fulk stopped struggling and stared at Grimald as he approached along the nave. The earl's smug, rapacious expression was smeared on his face like a handful of lard.

Fulk wanted to throttle him with his bare hands. The humiliating memory of the mêlée had burned deep into Fulk's heart. *I should have knocked him from his horse. And then his head from his shoulders.* At the time, however, his conscience had prevailed.

When he had seen the earl's saddle go awry, Fulk had halted, to allow Grimald to recover his seat. But instead of continuing the course, Grimald had accused Fulk of cutting his girth before the contest, and bullied the heralds into granting him the win.

And of course all thought Fulk had forfeited because of the earl's lethal lance-tip. Fulk had spent the remainder of the summer and all autumn still unransomed while the others had long been freed. He had not been held in chains, but his honor—such as it was—bound him just as tightly. He could no more flee than if he had signed a blood oath to stay.

Grimald had taken Fulk's precious horses, plus the cache of arms he had won over the years, and still insisted they were not enough to buy his freedom. Fulk had refused to part with his few books.

They were dearer to him than gold, and now were all he had left for his sister's dowry, but in any event such things were relatively worthless in the earl's view. It had become apparent that the earl wanted something more, something Fulk truly could not afford—a piece of his soul, or of what little remained.

Grimald took a single step closer, and the small sound echoed in the freezing, vaulted chamber. "Hengist, here, tells me you stood up to him the other night. That you tried to stop him from seeing justice done to a common criminal." Grimald stroked his chin. "Why did you interfere? That flea-bitten village of Redware Keep has nothing to do with you, except as your disinheritance."

Fulk did not appreciate the reminder of his father having disowned him. The English lands would now pass to his sister.

"The place means nothing to me, but the people do." Fulk's anger flared, and he jerked his upper body.

The Danes levered his hands higher behind his back, until he felt his shoulder joints start to separate. He took a deep breath and willed himself to relax.

The earl tilted his head. "Tsk. You love the people. I am grateful that Hengist has no such problem."

Fulk's stomach tightened. Thick and greasy, Hengist the Hurler stood to the earl's right. He smiled at Fulk and nodded, his angelic curls making a parody of his cunning face.

Grimald smiled, too. "He is an obedient knight. And so shall you receive adubbement and be sworn to your duty, Fulk, so help me. You may have refused your spurs from the king, but you will not refuse me. I shall make something of you yet."

"What, a pillager? A slayer of innocents? That is all knighthood has come to mean." Fulk met Grimald's gaze, letting all his loathing for the man burn through his eyes.

The earl's grin widened. "You will cooperate fully, Galliard. Else your precious village will burn to the ground. I command it and I command you. Do you understand?"

"Aye." *Too well.*

"Good. Deacon!" The earl pointed at Fulk. "He looks like a wild animal with that long hair. Cut it off. I would have him properly humbled, come the morn."

The cleric paled. "B-but, my lord, I believe his hair is part of a penance—"

"Cut it! Or perhaps, Deacon, there is something of yours you wouldn't mind having snipped, eh?'' Grimald grinned at the man, then stalked out the door.

Fulk's hatred chilled within his breast, and the icy shards pierced his heart. For seven years he had thought to keep the pain of Rabel's death fresh by letting his hair grow, as did his seemingly endless sorrow. But he did not need long hair to remind himself of the beast he was. Fulk looked at the deacon, who stood before him, trembling, his mouth agape.

"Do not distress yourself, friend. I will not seek vengeance from you when this is through, you have my word.''

The deacon smiled weakly and nodded, sweat dripping from his chin. Fulk closed his eyes. He would not go after the cleric.

He'd go after Grimald.

Jehanne hesitated, winced, then limped over the threshold into Windermere's dim chapel. She drew her hood lower to hide her throbbing face. The damp stone floor never gave way to warmth, no matter the season. This winter was proving exceptionally difficult, in more ways than ice and snow. Father Edgar, stingy with candles at the best of times, puttered in a gloomy corner.

"Father, I—'' Jehanne swayed and closed her eyes as a sparkling, black tide of dizziness raced toward her. She breathed deep, willing it away, and put her hand to the wall to steady herself. Fighting the pride that bade her keep silent, she swallowed her tears.

"What is it?'' The priest kept his broad back to her.

Jehanne ventured nearer, hugging her mantle tight, though the pressure of the rough wool made her bruises ache and her stripes burn anew. "I would ease my heart, and seek thy wisdom.'' Her voice was yet hoarse, so she cleared her throat.

Father Edgar turned, and narrowed his eyes. "'Tis not yet a year and you've come for absolution?''

Jehanne nodded, stung by his sarcasm. Why did he make it harder? He knew only desperation would bring her to him for confession before Easter, still months away.

"Tell me.'' He motioned for her to sit on the steps of the altar.

"I prefer to stand.''

Edgar's thick, tawny brows drew together. "So that's the way of it, eh? Yet again?'' The priest peered at her face, and she saw a flash of sympathy in his eyes. ''Mother of God!''

It was all Jehanne could do not to hide behind her hands. She knew she must look bad, but to cause Father Edgar to call upon the Virgin...

He caught the edge of her mantle and jerked it aside. She was all but naked in her thin shift. Held in place by her own sweat and blood, it clung to her in tatters.

The priest swallowed, then licked his lips. ''Behold what you have brought upon yourself.''

In an agony of embarrassment Jehanne snatched the cloth from his hand and pulled the garment back over her raw shoulders. She would suffer no man's gaze. Shivers began to wrack her body. ''And you think it just?''

Edgar's shiny face drew into hard, unforgiving lines. ''A woman must obey her betters. You should be ashamed. Especially since you have been given this lesson before, yet you force your father to go to such lengths to correct you, over and over—''

''I have done nothing wrong.''

''Have you not? In your arrogance you have defied not only your lord father but both the earl and God Himself. Expect no comfort from me.''

Jehanne stepped away, her eyelids stinging. She lifted her chin and straightened her back. ''So have I learned, Father. I will take no comfort. Not from you, nor from any son of Adam.''

Fulk knelt before the altar. The slate floor bit into his knees and the warm weight down his back was absent, for the deacon had indeed cropped his hair. He had been in the same spot for six hours, according to the great candle flickering to his right. And with each hour his simmering rage burned hotter. No peace came with his prayers, nor were they answered. Nothing happened that he might forego his fate. The guards set to watch him seemed drowsy, but lowered their pikes at him each time he eased his position in the slightest.

The chapel doors crashed open and Fulk jerked to attention, as did the Danes. A wave of icy air washed over him. A babble of murmurs and footsteps approached, including the click of a big dog's toenails.

"Out of the way, Deacon! Nay, Fulk's been at this long enough. I need him now. An excess of piety is not good for a knight—not one in my service. Hah!"

Fulk looked up. The heavy tread of the Earl of Lexingford preceded an even heavier hand upon Fulk's shoulder.

"Galliard, it is time. Arise."

It took Fulk a moment to force his numb legs to move beneath him and support his weight. He turned to face Grimald. Behind him were a half dozen of his favorites, waiting restlessly, like curs for a tidbit. A brindled mastiff skulked at the earl's left, to his right stood Hengist. The knight's lips twitched into a sneer when Fulk met his pale eyes.

Grimald looked Fulk up and down with a speculative, venomous gaze. "You need no more prayers. For the challenge I've set you, no amount of divine supplication will be of aid. Only brute strength and healthy lust will see the task completed."

Sweat trickled down Fulk's back. Whatever was in store, there would be no reprieve. No escape from a life of carnage, now that knighthood was upon him.

A snap of noble fingers brought attendants scurrying forward. Grimald twirled a pair of silver spurs about one thick finger, then tossed them onto the floor. "Get down again."

Fulk hesitated, and the pikemen encouraged him with jabs to his ribs. He sank back to his aching knees, fists clenched at his sides. With a clang of steel Hengist drew his sword. Fulk threw a questioning look to the earl. If this was a trap meant to end in death, Fulk would make damn certain he did not die alone, vows or no vows.

Then, from the silent exchange between Hengist and Grimald, Fulk knew why the knight was present. Not for murder, but purely for Fulk's humiliation. To be given the accolade by a lord of rank increased the status of the recipient.

Therefore the earl had brought one of the stupidest, most churlish knights alive to perform the ceremony in Fulk's case. It was fitting, in a way, Fulk thought, because even had he wanted the honor, he did not deserve it. He bowed his head slightly, and braced himself for Hengist's blows.

The flat of the blade pounded Fulk's right temple, then the left. He swayed as red burst into his vision. With each breath he steadied himself until he could see again, and thanked God the Hurler's aim was true.

The earl raised one hand. "Sir Fulk, I charge thee with the high purpose of our lord king: go to the hold of Windermere and wrest it from the hands of the traitor and conspirator against the crown, Alun FitzWalter. Relieve said Alun of his undeserved life. And take his devil of a daughter to wife."

"Wife!" Fulk could not believe he had heard aright. "I thought you had an agreement with her father—"

"Not anymore. Just make her wish she had said yes to me when she had the chance. And make doubly certain that the revenues from Windermere flow *into* my hands."

Fulk choked as the revelation sank in. Windermere. Sir Alun...the Iron Maiden. Unthinkable. He would not become another Hengist. A hired killer, a defiler of women, and in this case, a madwoman.

He waited for Hengist to sheath his sword, but instead the knight sidestepped, so the blade's cold edge pressed against Fulk's neck.

He held himself utterly still.

The earl leaned down, his hot breath at Fulk's cheek. "Listen well, Galliard. I have forgotten nothing of what your father did to me. And what the father owes, so shall the son pay. Or the daughter. Just as will Alun's."

Not for the first time Fulk cursed his late father's barbed wit. Grimald must have been nursing his hatred for years, letting it fester. *So shall the son pay.*

And the daughter? Alun's alone, or did he also mean his own sister...*Celine?* Fulk swallowed the fury that rose to stifle him. Now was not the time, nor was a church the place. He nodded, and the sword edge nicked his throat, sending a warm rivulet down his chest. Still smiling, Hengist resheathed his weapon.

The earl briefly thrust a piece of parchment before Fulk. "Here is the king's warrant. Dispose of Alun quickly and make certain the wench is humbled for her effrontery. The crown wants a secure succession at Windermere, so see that you get her breeding straightaway. If you survive, you will be a hero in the eyes of all the men she has refused. The maiden of iron-clad virtue, conquered at last.'' Grimald's laughter sounded as out of place in the chapel as a raven's cawing. Fulk remained silent. He had thought Sir Alun FitzWalter to be the earl's ally and loyal to the king. He had not heard of any treachery, but nor did he take interest in political intrigues. The pit of his stomach burned. Damn Grimald for dragging him here to be made chief fool in a farce like this.

''Overjoyed at the prospect, are you?'' The earl beamed. ''She cannot possibly find fault with a great strapping fellow like you, especially once you've sped up her inheritance. Do the ladies not swoon at the prospect of being bedded by Fulk the Reluctant?''

Upon hearing that name spoken aloud, Fulk forced himself to breathe, slow and deep. But his heart hammered and he ground his teeth. One of the leering courtiers shrilled, ''Oh, most assuredly, my lord. He's a veritable stallion, methinks. Just look at his flowing black mane!''

The others howled with laughter at Fulk's rough-shorn state.

Fulk swung his gaze toward Lexingford's sniggering lackeys, and their merriment died away. The earl slapped his back.

''You see? Fulk plans to vanquish Alun with but a single malevolent glance, so he need not risk himself in swordplay—except with the girl. Who knows what's under her tunic? She may have bigger ballocks than does he.'' Grimald guffawed and clouted Fulk again.

With an effort Fulk resisted the urge to grab Grimald's arm and twist it off at the shoulder. Apparently there was only the one child of Alun's, but Fulk knew nothing of her beyond her wild reputation and his own observation that she was headstrong and witless. Carefully he kept his voice low. ''Lexingford, what is the name of Sir Alun's daughter? And does she know of her father's treachery?''

''What she knows matters not. She is called Jehanne, and she has embarrassed me. Whatever she claims, you damn well better bring the little bitch to heel. Capture Windermere, keep the girl under control and I shall give you your freedom.''

Grimald backed away a step. "We leave you to contemplate your good fortune." He strode down the nave toward the doors, his retinue in tow. Before exiting, the earl paused. "Oh, and Fulk? The lady Celine. Where is she, these days? My people cannot seem to find her."

Fulk swallowed. She was with Lady Greyhaven, near the Scottish border. Grimald knew Fulk would never intentionally reveal her whereabouts. So he hedged. "Why do you ask?"

"I want to send someone to collect her...for safekeeping. I have a certain bridegroom in mind—Sir Hengist, a man known for his great prowess. After all, he is already in charge of Redware. And in light of today's events, who would be a more fitting addition to the great knights of the house of Galliard?"

Hengist bowed to Fulk, his mocking air turning the courtesy into an insult. Fulk leveled a stare at the big knight. The bloody Hurler and Celine, his pure, innocent sister? Never. He would not allow so much as Hengist's shadow to fall upon her.

Grimald smiled. "Of course, should you make quick work of Alun, I shall leave the choice of Celine's husband up to you."

So he had a chance, before Grimald ferreted her out. "I will not fail her, my lord." Fulk's words emerged as a growl. He might as well snarl, he felt like a chained animal. He caught a whiff of anger from Hengist at his and Grimald's agreement. Fulk bowed low as the earl and his retinue left. The doors slammed shut.

Echoes reverberated in the chapel, slowly settling into silence, like dust on a coffin. The bastard. Fulk's resolve hardened, cold and deadly. He would do the earl's bidding. Up to a point. Take the keep, aye, he would find a way, if it meant protecting the king's interests, and obtaining an adequate dowry for Celine. But nothing, and no one, would make him take a woman against her will.

Chapter Three

The practice field at Windermere was empty but for a few of the household warriors, walking their steaming horses over the chopped turf. Jehanne turned her face to the winter sunlight of late afternoon, and closed her eyes. Once more she visualized the target, saw herself hit it full center.

Gripping her lance, she put her horse into a gallop. She leveled the shaft at the proper angle over her mount's withers and aimed for the small disc at the end of the quintain's arm. A squeeze of her legs brought a final burst of speed from her horse as she approached impact.

Jehanne braced herself, her weight in her stirrups, and with a crack the lance slammed the target. The spiked ball swung behind her, close enough for her to feel it catch a few hairs from her plait.

Sir Thomas crossed his arms and shook his grizzled head as she trotted up to him. She thumped the lance-butt to the ground. "What? What, sir, am I doing wrong? I hit it, did I not? For the twentieth time in succession?" Weariness tugged at her limbs. For all her skill, she had to practice twice as hard as the men to keep up.

The master-at-arms looked up at her, his blue eyes surprisingly clear in his seamed face. "Jenn, it is not the hitting of anything you must perfect. Truly, you beat the quintain in fine form, and are faster than ever I was, even in my prime. Nay, 'tis the look in your eye of late."

"What look?"

Sir Thomas took the lance from her. "You're angry at your father, lass. I know it is hard to accept, but you are full-grown now. Were you his son it would still be your duty to marry when he wished it. What can you hope to gain by putting it off?"

Jehanne looked down at her hands, then out over the expanse of lake and field and forest that comprised Windermere. The motley green and orange hues of foliage still clung like tattered flags to the trees. The browns and grays of jutting rock were more subtle, but just as beautiful. The long, shimmering lake, the crown jewel of Windermere, reflected every color of both earth and sky, even as the mist gathered to shroud it for the night.

"I love this place, Thomas. I don't want to give it to a stranger. No one will care for it as I do, nor protect the land and villeins. These suitors the earl sends—upon his orders every one of them would bleed the fief dry within a few winters. I cannot let that happen."

"But, lass..."

To Jehanne's dismay, the old knight paused to swipe at his eyes and leaned on her lance for support.

"Sir?" Dismounting, she hurried to him.

"You have suffered, Jenn. I cannot bear to see it go on." Thomas's voice broke.

"Oh, Thomas." Jehanne could barely speak past the closing of her throat, and put her arm around his shoulders. "You are like a father to me. I wish you were, in fact," she whispered.

The old man pulled away. "Do not let me hear you say such a thing again. Sir Alun is hard, but he has more noble blood in his little finger than does that peasant-bred Grimald in his whole body. And you are of that blood. Never take it for granted. There are things that may be learned, and things that one is born to. Part of life is finding out which is which."

Jehanne smiled sadly and took back her lance. "I was born to this place, Thomas. And it, too, is in my blood."

After seeing her horse safely into the avener's care and soothing her pack of boisterous hounds, Jehanne took a rear stairway to her chamber. She did not want to meet anyone. As she slipped into her room, Lioba greeted her with a bowl of steaming water.

"You are wanted below, milady. Immediately. A messenger has come, they need you to read the letter."

Panic jolted Jehanne as she splashed her still-tender face with the arnica and mint-steeped water. The matter had to be serious, to merit parchment instead of simple memorization or a wax tablet. Lioba helped her peel off hose and tunic.

She dared not defy her father by remaining in men's clothing before strangers. She slipped into a fresh linen shift, hurriedly donned a loose overgown of russet wool, and snugged it to her hips with a fine, but unadorned leathern belt. Her sweat-dampened hair, still in its plait, would have to do.

Lioba gave her hand a squeeze before she left. Jehanne flashed a smile to the steadfast woman, and flew down the stairs.

Her father's men nodded to her but shuffled uneasily, glancing away as soon as she met their eyes. She swallowed hard and continued toward the center of the hall.

Gangly and fair, her cousin Thaddeus sat in the carved wooden seat usually reserved for her. His full lips curled into a sly smile. Her father stood by, arms crossed, his face stony.

Garbed in green and brown velvet, the messenger approached. "Mademoiselle." His eyes flicked her up and down, then fixed upon her face. Jehanne recognized the now familiar instant of shock at the sight of her livid scar.

"What are you staring at? Give me the letter."

The messenger sniffed, then produced a scroll and he slapped it into her palm. The wax which sealed it bore the imprint of Grimald's signet. Jehanne broke the seal and stared at the letter. The parchment shivered in her hands. The words she struggled to decipher were too awful to fully comprehend.

With a glance to her father, she cleared her throat. "Know ye this, Sir Alun, that insofar as I, Lexingford, have tried to p-prevail upon you, with all good intent and peaceful means, to achieve the purposes of Henry, our lord King, your refusal to c-convince your daughter of the wisdom of his choice forces him to send a lawful body of men, led by Sir Fulk de Galliard, to put an end to this rebellion..." Her voice trailed away. *Sir* Fulk? The coward was now a knight, on his way to steal her land!

"Is that it?" Anger burnished her father's handsome face, his eyes a cold, blue contrast to his sun-browned skin.

"It is all that is of note. The earl is ever flowery in his declarations of doom." Jehanne let the parchment fall from her fingers.

With a swish of silk the messenger scooped it up and rerolled it. "Your reply, sir?"

Jehanne winced at the man's arrogant tone. He knew nothing of her father. Alun grabbed the scroll from him and menaced him with it as if it were a dagger. "If thine arse were not so obviously too tight, I would send this back to my good friend the earl, permanently lodged between your cheeks, with my compliments."

The man paled and retreated. Jehanne had little doubt Sir Alun would make good on his threat should the fellow linger. "My lord, he is but a messenger, and honor requires that we allow him to leave unmolested."

As she expected, Alun redirected his anger toward her. "What will you have me say, then? That my daughter is beyond my control, that she defies me with her every breath, that she shames me before the world? He knows that already."

Pain gnawed at Jehanne's heart. A heart that had frozen stiff and numb around the cherished adoration she held for her father.

"Would you have me sacrifice my honor for the venal purposes of the Earl of Lexingford? He has not your best interests in mind. Is this threat not the proof of it?"

"Your idealism ever clouds your judgment, Jehanne. You fancy yourself a knight of old, on some noble quest for truth and beauty. Face it, girl, as I have done. You are a female. You must be wed and under a man's authority. For your own good, as well as that of Windermere. As much as it hurts me to not have a son, it will hurt me more to know there will be no grandson, either. God help us, you are the last of the house of FitzWalter!"

She was the last legitimate heir, Thaddeus being a bastard in every sense of the word. A derisive snort broke the quiet that followed. Jehanne scowled at the messenger, whose fear had apparently given way to a lurid interest. Manners be damned.

"Get thee gone!" she shouted.

"Wait." Her father's voice. Low, controlled and deadly. "Tell the earl to bid Fulk de Galliard to come ahead."

Once the messenger had scurried away, Alun cut his gaze to Jehanne. "Grimald must be eager to see this Fulk punished, if he sends him here. I shall determine what manner of man he is, and sway his purpose to mine. To that end, you, daughter, shall welcome him, and give him no reason to wreak havoc upon Windermere.

"But take heed. He is the last. If he is still willing after having seen you, and you yet refuse him, I wash my hands of you. I'll leave Windermere to the Church, to atone for whatever it is I have done to cause God give me so much grief. Even Grimald cannot take it from the bishopric, the way he could from you. I will go on a pilgrimage and you do as you like."

The ache in Jehanne's breast built to an unbearable agony. Her hand crept to her dagger hilt. "I know not whether to use this upon Galliard or myself. Please, do not push me further."

The look Alun gave her was one of rage and pain, of disappointment and exhaustion, but of love she could no longer see a trace. Alun raised his goblet of wine. "May Grimald be damned to hell." He drained it violently, then headed for the stairs. His gait was not the confident stride of a man in his prime, but hesitant and unsteady, as though he no longer knew his way around his own keep.

"Father!" A chill crept along Jehanne's limbs. Give Windermere to the Church? She could not believe he would carry out such a threat. Apart from that, he seemed unwell.

A fever had come to the village with a passing tinker. Father Edgar had taken to his bed, many others were ill, and already a few elderly folk had died. Alun, proud and stubborn, would never allow her to help him if he ailed. And she, hurt and bitter, did not much feel like insisting.

But he was strong as an ox. To put up with such a daughter he had to be, as he frequently reminded her. As if to prove the point, Alun waved her away without turning around, and trudged up the steps to his solar.

Jehanne drew a deep breath. He did not understand. No one did. Aye, Jehanne the Iron Maiden believed in the ideals of knighthood. They were what she had clung to in her efforts to

please her father, to make up for her failure in not having been
born male. But it was all for naught.

The long hours spent with javelin and bow, sword and buckler,
horse and hounds, everything she could think of to prepare herself
to defend Windermere once her father grew old—all wasted. He
wanted her to toss her inheritance to a man obviously unworthy,
otherwise that man would not be doing the earl's bidding.

Fulk the Reluctant.

Jehanne's fingers tightened on the edge of the trestle table, and
she set her jaw. She had refused the earl and paid dearly for it.
She would not give up now and wed Fulk.

She still had time to prepare. Jehanne called her dogs, a pack
of ever-hungry lurchers, and made for the armory.

Dawn topped the tree-clad hills, sending a bright shaft of sunlight into Fulk's eyes. His company of mercenary lancers, tired
from the long journey the day before, moved slowly about their
duties in the encampment. Fulk swung his sword to and fro, loosening his muscles, his breath creating puffs of white in the chill
air.

"It has been too long since you've borne arms, lad." Malcolm
relaxed against the shoulder of his skewbald palfrey. "You'll be
a lamb for the young lady's slaughter."

Fulk stopped swinging. "I have forgotten nothing of combat,
Mac Niall. Especially with women."

"Aye. Naught but the fact that you could have been your king's
champion, you could've had any baroness or countess or princess
you cared to crook your finger at."

"Stow it, Malcolm. Those days are long gone, and you of all
people should know better than to remind me. Besides, I *have*
had every baroness, countess and princess—"

"I meant to wed, and be landed thereby. But I suppose this
place'll be as good as any." Malcolm merely yawned when con-
fronted by Fulk's glare. "Och, I do hate to see so much muscle
wasted turning the pages of books. Sharpening quills, now that
takes special skill with a blade, I must admit. But you'll need a
mountain of feathers to get fit for battle."

"Malcolm, I refuse to fly into rages just to provide you entertainment. And should you doubt my skill with a sword, meet me on trodden ground, and we shall see who bests whom.''

"'Tisnae worth the bother," Malcolm said, futilely shoving his abundant, dark-red hair back from his brow. "Nay, I'd rather wait until we meet Sir Alun and his wee daughter, and you can meet *her* on trodden ground. How far off is Windermere?''

"Another day, if the ford is clear. The sumpter horses and wains will slow us a bit, but as the lanes are not knee-deep, we should make right good time." Fulk slammed his sword into its scabbard, and still fuming, headed for the picket line.

Windermere did not lay in the direction he would go, had he a choice. There was all the world to explore, knowledge to discover. A thousand places where he could happily spend his life as a scholar. Even were he not in this situation, though, Redware still clamored for freedom.

Fulk pushed his dreams back to the place where he kept them hidden. He mounted his newly purchased horse, a stout Frisian of good blood, and let the sight of the splendid beast soothe his heart.

The destrier's hooves crunched through the waning rime of ice in the muddy lane.

"I thought you didnae want a charger that cost twenty years' wages.'' Malcolm affectionately slapped his own palfrey's thick neck as he rode beside Fulk.

"I will not trust even these miserable remnants of my life to an inferior animal. The stallion is grand, and better schooled than I expected.''

The Frisian tossed his great head as if in agreement with Fulk's high opinion of him.

"But God's eyes, Malcolm, I'll never find the like of my books again. It breaks my heart.''

"Aye, a bloody fortune in books tied up in a pair of nags and a pack of mercenaries. Still, I believe 'tis a leap in the right direction. Now you may start entering tournaments again, once you have charmed the lady Jehanne out of her armor, and make up some of your losses.''

Fulk gave Malcolm a withering look. "Neither prospect appeals, Mac Niall. Besides, as you have so gallantly pointed out, I am out of practice. I will do what I must to keep Redware intact and Celine out of Hengist's hands, but not one thing more."

"You should find her a proper and grateful husband, right quick, then. Save yourself a realm of heartache." Malcolm stared straight ahead between his horse's ears as he said this.

Necessary though it was, Fulk's stomach lurched at the thought of little Celine wed. To anyone. "Her dowry, too, is on the hoof, between this one and my new courser. She can't inherit Redware unless she marries or comes of age."

He cleared his throat, and glanced again at the Scot, whose eyes had narrowed into the typical, over-vigilant gaze the man had, which missed nothing.

"There. See the birds flushing, beyond that rise?" Malcolm pointed. "'Tis trouble, coming at a gallop."

Malcolm was probably right, as ever. "Then I should go meet it. Embrace it. The devil curse Lexingford, pig's arse that he is," Fulk growled. He glanced down at his helm, hanging from his saddle. It could stay there. "Malcolm, kindly keep the men in good order." With a touch of Fulk's spurs the stallion bounded forward.

The countryside was cold, but not bleak, for even the gray stubble in the fields gleamed in the sun, and where the villeins had furrowed, the black earth put forth a rich smell. Beyond the uneven stripes of plowed and fallow land the forest loomed, dark even in winter, the trunks and branches interlinked and woven like basketwork.

There were few villages this far north, and towns were even more rare. The keep of Windermere lay at the southern tip of the lake from which it took its name, in the Cumbrian Mountains, two days' hard ride from Scotland. At a crucial point along the River Leven it was possible to cross at a bridge maintained by the FitzWalter, if he allowed passage.

Fulk thought of this, and other problems that might be presented to a man attacking the hold of Sir Alun. Especially a man who did not want bloodshed. There was only one course, and that was to wait outside until they surrendered. A slow, painful way, but at least it left the choice of life up to the defenders.

Up the road ahead a rider neared, the strange horse's blowing audible across the distance in the cold air. The Frisian's nostrils flared and his neck arched, the thin skin forming creases at his powerful jaw. The stranger approached, elbows and knees flailing, a white cloth tied to one arm. At the sight of Fulk the young man halted quickly and none too straight, nearly putting himself over his horse's side.

"G-greetings, milord, ah...g-good day and G-God bless."

Fulk eyed the youth. Yellow hair streamed from beneath a jaunty, brimless hat, his blue velvet jacket was well padded, and a fine short-sword rode at his hip. But his mount heaved, the foam at its mouth was flecked with blood, and its flanks bore raised welts from the lad's lashings.

Fulk said nothing, and positioned the Frisian to block the road. Let the varlet sweat and explain himself.

The stranger's eyes bulged. "I am Thaddeus, squire to Sir Alun, come in p-peace to meet the p-party sent by the Earl of Lexingford. And you, my lord, p-perchance you might be...?"

"Fulk de Galliard. What do you want?"

Thaddeus's eyes lost some of their fear and gained a cunning light. "To bargain, my lord. I would save you an argument, seeing how you—"

"How I what? Do I look as though I want to avoid an argument?"

"Well, I thought—"

"You did not think. Did you dream, *perchance,* that I am come merely to pretend to take Windermere?"

"Take Windermere? But, I thought you were another suitor!"

"I and all these men behind me—" Fulk waved over his horse's rump "—are indeed coming to pay suit to Sir Alun, to win his heart. And if he does not love us, we shall take his head, instead." Fulk bluffed, but he was good at it.

Thaddeus paled, then rallied. "The lady Jehanne shall not receive you kindly, in any case."

"Nor do I expect her to. Why don't you run along home, boy? There is no escape this way. Tell Sir Alun we will parley and offer him every courtesy—as long as he offers no resistance."

The young man began to turn his horse, and his expression darkened into surliness. "What do I g-get for sticking my neck out, then? I came all this way, and nothing to show for it. Every one knows your reputation, *Sir* Fulk. Why should we fear you?'

Fulk leaned forward slightly, and the Frisian hopped, startling Thaddeus. The boy's mount rolled its eyes, and the Frisian's ears lay flat back on his elegant head.

"You may know my reputation, but you do not know *me*, Squire Thaddeus, nor does any one of your bedfellows. It would be the wiser course for you to go. Now. And have a care for that beast. If I find you've brought it to grief on this selfish escapade, you will have me to answer to."

The young man's Adam's apple bobbed, and he kicked his horse around. He raised his riding whip, evidently thought better of it, and said, "She will be coming for *you* right quick! Hah!"

Thaddeus trotted off, his blond locks bouncing at his back.

Malcolm cantered to Fulk's side. "What pretty thing was that?"

"A young viper, my friend. But we may find him useful, ere we are done."

"Lioba, Beatrix, stay a half length behind, on either side of me. I would face Galliard as an arrow does its target."

Upon these instructions Jehanne's handmaidens, girded and armed as fully as she, dropped their mounts back to form a wedge of horseflesh, with their lady at the leading point. They used this formation to charge when routing out poachers and chasing troublemakers.

It was difficult, dangerous, and for Jehanne at least, as satisfying as warm bread and honey. Word had spread, and now often as not, thieves simply dropped their booty and ran rather than meet the Iron Maiden of Windermere's swift justice.

But this was different. She might lose her home, her freedom, everything she cherished. Soon, Jehanne thought, it had to be soon, and so it was. A speck on the horizon grew, winding ever closer, until she recognized her cousin, galloping his horse like a madman.

To her disgust he did not stop, but passed her company by as if they were invisible, ignoring her shouted greeting. She would need to check on Thaddeus's poor gelding when she returned.

If she returned. The possibility of a real fight, to the death, could not be dismissed lightly. She had always believed goodness and right could defeat wickedness and wrong. That was the whole point of knightly virtue, of trial by combat. God would grant victory to the man—or woman—most deserving.

But she was no longer entirely certain she was that woman. Perhaps her father was right...but she could not afford to doubt herself now, much less doubt God.

"There they are, see?" Jehanne pointed to a black line slowly wending its way nearer, pinpoints of reflected sunlight flashing from lance tips and helms.

"Jenn, that is a small army. Methinks we should make haste to get home and lock the gates," Lioba said, a tremor in her voice.

"I will meet him alone if I must," Jehanne replied, but inside she quaked. Never mind Galliard, Thaddeus would no doubt tell her father what she was doing.

If he had risen from his sickbed, a stout rod would be ready upon her return. But if that was the price of honor, so be it. It would not be the first time. She snugged her helm down and rode on.

Fulk saw the phalanx of riders ahead and signaled the column to halt. "Another greeting party. But this is a meagre welcome, for a keep supposedly so hospitable."

Malcolm grunted his agreement. "Just see there's no trap set in that narrow defile. 'Tis a prime place for an ambush."

Fulk ignored Malcolm's warning. "Here she comes."

"She? The wee lass herself?"

"Not so wee. And all three are shes."

"Well I'll be a bizzem's bastard."

"Let me do the talking, Mac Niall." Fulk pushed his mail coif back and rode forward, his right hand raised in peace. The three women halted several yards away. The one in front, presumably the Iron Maiden in person, bristled with sword, lance and shield.

She did nothing but stare at him through her helm's eye slits, much as he had done at the tournament so long ago.

"Gracious lady, it pleases me more than I can say to see you so lovely, hale and accompanied by such beautiful chaperones."

Speaking in the variety of Norman French used at Henry's court, Fulk paused to see if this elegant address served any purpose.

The lady of Windermere looked at her companions, then back to him. "Fulk de Galliard, you are trespassing. Get thee gone or suffer the consequences."

North country English, plain and to the point. Fulk turned to the Scot. "I do not think she understands my French, Malcolm. Nay, say nothing. I shall pretend my own bafflement." He shrugged his shoulders, raised his brows, tilted his head, and turned down the corners of his mouth, all at once. The gestures and expressions in themselves were purely Gallic, but he hoped quite obvious in their meaning.

Still using the court French, Fulk continued amiably, though on a slightly different path. "Ah, so you would seek to cast me off, without a single kind word between us. Believe me, lady, it would do my heart good to turn around here and now, and never lay eyes upon you again. But here I am come, and here I will continue, until I am done."

"Why do you go on so, Fulk? What is the point?" Malcolm grumbled.

"My dear friend, this valiant, though sadly demented creature will never formally challenge me if she believes I do not understand her terms. I have no intention of leaving, nor of fighting such a tender morsel of womankind. Mark me, she will ride off soon, rather than admit she has not the faintest idea what I am saying."

Jehanne cleared her throat. "Consider this warning, Sir Fulk. Make any attempt to breach my walls, and you will find yourself hanging from one of them."

With a curt nod of her steel-encased head, she reined her horse around and cantered off with her women.

"How unexpectedly delightful. The lady I am to wed owns a better helm than I, sports finer mail than half the knights in Lexingford, and has a burning desire that I become bird-food with which to decorate her curtain wall. Who could ask for more?"

Malcolm grinned. "She's a braw lass, all right. You are a lucky man, Fulk."

"One day I will remind you of that foolish sentiment, Mac Niall." Wearily Fulk waved the column into motion again.

It would be a long siege.

Chapter Four

Jehanne peered through the battlement loophole and strained to focus upon the curve of the road below. Her ears ached from the wind as it whistled around the frost-laden stones of the open turret.

It had been six exhausting, hungry weeks since Fulk de Galliard and his men first made their encampment in the practice grounds beyond the curtain wall.

She cursed the single entrance and the lay of the land which made the keep easy to defend, but also meant Fulk did not need a large army in order to besiege her. Today, for some reason, he was leading them within bowshot, and if it was the last thing she did, she was determined to give him a taste of her ire.

She blinked. Once, twice, and the indistinct cavalcade of armed men turned into individuals. Her heart pounded and her fingers clenched her bow grip. There he was. Fulk the Reluctant. Raven-haired and carrion-hearted, no doubt.

For the earl to send a man without honor to take the keep was yet a further insult to the strength of Windermere. Or rather, its former strength. As if he already possessed the castle, Fulk rode at ease, his lance casually resting across his shoulder.

Why did they risk drawing close now? No matter. Opportunity was at hand.

Jehanne straightened her arm and drew the bowstring taut. With her thumb she adjusted the arrowshaft's angle, squeezed the grip and aimed a bit to the left, as the bow tended to pull right. Her trembling muscles fought the power she held in check. She caught her breath and slitted her eyes. Galliard's chest made a broad target.

Three cold, stiff fingers on her right hand released the arrow. The bowstring sang and the steel-tipped, ashwood cylinder hissed forth. In an instant Jehanne had a second one nocked and ready. She looked down to see the result of the first.

Horses galloped and men shouted. Her heart waxed jubilant. "Flee, dogs, flee! Run before I skewer every last one of you!" Then her smile faded. Where was Fulk?

She scrambled toward the top of the battlement for a better view. The curtain wall's curve demanded a higher vantage if she wanted a good shot. The lip of stone bit her palms as she hoisted herself upon the ledge.

Lightly she jumped from one merlon to the next, her bow at her back, a sheer drop of more than thirty cubits at her feet. The height did not bother her—as long as she did not look down.

The murky moat below was half-frozen and clogged with decaying reeds. As Fulk hurried his men toward the gates, Jehanne paused, made certain of her footing, and loosed the second shaft.

He looked up, and even from that distance she saw the shock on his face at the sight of her skipping along the teeth of the battlements, so far above him. Then an icy gust of wind caught her. For one terrifying instant she wavered on the brink.

Jehanne let her weight shift backwards and landed feet first on the granite stones of the allure. The walkway before her undulated, snakelike, as she tried to focus. She scowled and willed the rippling flagstones to be still. Of late she grew dizzy every time she moved too fast.

"My lady?" Elly, one of her handmaids, stood forlorn, hugging herself, shivering in the breeze. The girl was too thin. And so was Jehanne. But she would not surrender this keep without a fight to any besieger, whether sent by the king or the pope or the devil himself.

"What is it, Elly?"

"Oh, you must come down straightaway. The gate is breached—we are taken!"

Jehanne caught the maid's shoulders. "How can that be? Look, they are still outside." She dragged the girl to the nearest battlement crenellation and peered down. No horses. No men. Only the rattle and slither of portcullis chains from the gatehouse. Her heart clenched.

Galliard was cunning. He had watched and waited, never once putting himself in harm's way until now. And why should he? The ravaging fever had done his work for him.

Grabbing her bow and a fistful of arrows, Jehanne raced to the corner tower. "Sir Thomas!" She looked left and right for the old man. He lay curled up on his side against the wall, sweating and gasping for breath, his sword still clutched in one hand.

"Oh, my wee Jenn, I must tell you something...."

"Shh, dear Thomas, save your strength." Jehanne's throat tightened as she stroked his brow. She had no tears left. In the last few weeks the fever had struck Windermere hard. The dead lay in frozen piles in the bailey, layered in quicklime. In desperation she had ordered some of the bodies propped along the battlements, to make the keep appear well-manned.

She cupped Thomas's hot, white-stubbled cheek with her palm and looked back to the walkway. "Elly, a litter!"

The girl reappeared, teeth chattering. At the sight of the ailing knight her face crumpled. "I'll fetch Corwin," she sobbed, and trotted off.

Jehanne returned her attention to Thomas. Apart from his collapse, his dusky color worried her. Just like her father, he had hidden his illness well. Stubborn old man! She slipped her arms around his body and held him close. Carefully, she covered the knight with her mantle, putting her empty quiver beneath his head.

"Rest here until the lads bear you to the hall," she whispered, and briefly his eyes opened in acknowledgement. Then the snorting of horses below reminded her of duty elsewhere. It was up to her, now.

Most of her father's men had deserted when the fever first ravaged Windermere. Alun had perished even before Fulk's arrival on Twelfth Night. After riding out to meet Fulk, she had come home to chaos. At the familiar burning sensation her father's memory provoked, she forced her eyes wide open. No time to dwell upon the past.

Bow and arrows in hand, Jehanne bounded down the stairs. As

she reached the entrance to the main ward, she shoved the arrows under her belt, then straightened her surcoat. Starved and without her mantle, she shook in the frigid air. But, taking a deep breath, she held her head high and passed through the archway.

At least a score of heavily armed, mounted men waited in the bailey. Her heart sank. Each one of them was the equivalent of ten men afoot. Snowflakes drifted onto the horses' wide rumps, and the breath and steam of the animals clouded the air. Once, she would have hurried to put her hand to the biggest stallion's silken, black coat.

But she was no longer a child.

And it was Fulk the Reluctant who sat the great-horse. His lance protruded before him, and hanging from its tip was the squirming figure of Thaddeus. Fulk had caught the back of the young fool's belt, and his lance shaft bowed and creaked ominously with the weight.

Fulk's shield bore her arrow. Silently, Jehanne cursed her aim, or his quick defense. She knew not which to blame for her failure to kill him.

Her enemy turned his dark gaze upon her, and she shivered. She had never stood this close to him, nor felt his presence so acutely. His short, jet hair was awry as if he had just pulled back his camail, and his face...the Creature at the tourney had not exaggerated.

Jehanne swallowed as her gaze drifted down his body. She had a weakness for clean-limbed, black horses. And if ever there were a man whose looks could compete with them, she beheld him now.

She deepened her frown.

Fulk dropped his lance-tip and Thaddeus tumbled to the ground. Jehanne ran to him. He jumped up and pushed her away.

"This is all your fault! Demented, idiot girl. I hope this one makes you g-good and sorry when he uses you—"

A mellow, lightly accented voice spoke in English. "Cease your filthy rudeness, knave. Collect your blood money and go." Fulk tossed a plump purse to Thaddeus, who stuffed it inside his surcoat.

Jehanne stared at her cousin. "Traitor!" She lunged after him, but he danced backward, cackling his glee.

One of Fulk's men slid from his horse, grabbed the now shrieking Thaddeus by the scruff of his neck, and threw him bodily out the gates. "Beetle-gnawed snake's tongue." The Scot straightened his plaid, a complex weave of muted blues and greens, and scowled at Thaddeus.

The young man clambered to his feet and gestured obscenely as Jehanne nocked an arrow and aimed at him. Before she could release it a big hand caught hers, and leather-clad fingers wrapped around both the bow grip and her white knuckles.

Ignoring her cry of protest, Fulk took the weapon and snapped it like kindling over his knee. Jehanne stared in disbelief at the ruins of her bow, then at the man who had destroyed it. She had never heard of anyone breaking a bow with his bare hands. And for him to shatter the elegant, powerful weapon she had shaped and polished herself was like having a piece of her heart torn out.

"That was mine," she whispered.

"It is over, Lady Jehanne. I would speak with you now."

Fulk's words were mild but his voice was low and tight. Slowly, she met his eyes. The warm, lustrous color of Norsemen's dark amber, she found them unexpectedly beautiful. His restraint was more difficult to bear than if he had twisted her arm or beaten her.

A momentary weakness rippled through Jehanne, a temptation to compromise. Her limbs were heavy with fatigue, her stomach knotted with hunger.

Nay. She would not be defeated. Not by treachery, not by force, and not by Fulk de Galliard. Rage at her conqueror and disappointment with herself surged in her gut. She slapped the hilt of her sword.

"I will not stand by and allow you to simply walk in and take my keep unchallenged. I demand a single combat between us, sir. To the death if it so pleases you."

Scattered laughter rumbled from the warriors. Fulk's eyes widened. A crease formed on his forehead. "You wish to do battle with me, hand to hand?"

"Aye." Jehanne squared her shoulders.

"Do you want to die so young?"

"If honor requires it."

Fulk's eyes seemed to glow from within, but his voice remained soft. "You will have to await some other form of death, my lady. I refuse to accept such a challenge."

"Why? Because I am not a man?"

"Aye, and you are unwell at that. It is an absurd notion."

Jehanne clenched her hands in a futile attempt to contain her temper. His gentle tone implied he thought her feeble—of mind as well as body, no doubt.

The bite of her nails into her palms only prodded her anger. All her pain rushed back. The sickness, the death, the starvation...the betrayal. "You do me no honor, sir." Her voice broke. She lashed out at Fulk with feet and fists and teeth.

His men guffawed, fueling her assault. Fulk himself was impervious. Her blows had no effect. Even had they the force of a man's strength, he was too heavily padded and too well muscled for them to do him damage. He caught her wrists in an inescapable grip.

"I said 'speak', not brawl, Lady Jehanne. I know your father is dead, that you grieve for him still. Young Thaddeus told us of the fever. You are without resources, without friends. You are alone, but for me. Do not abuse my patience."

Fulk released her, and she stood stiffly. At least she had not disgraced herself by weeping. But by speaking the truth so baldly, he had knocked a hole in her resolve. She raised her head. "I need no one besides myself. Why can you not leave me in peace?"

"The Earl of Lexingford says it is our lord king's will. You had best abide by it. To disobey me is to disobey him. And while I am a forgiving sort, he is not."

Fulk was right about that, too, God rot him. Once the king held her in disfavor, no one would dare help. Jehanne looked up at Fulk again, her vision blurred by despair. She had never seen anyone so tall and imposing. Despite the tales of his refusals to fight, he did not look the least bit reluctant.

He maintained a neutral expression, but faint lines, perhaps born of mirth, showed around his generous mouth. She met his gaze again, and for an instant found sympathy where she had least expected it. Jehanne sniffed and wiped her nose on her sleeve. Then she hiccoughed. Loudly.

Fulk flashed a grin, involuntarily, it seemed. She had to admit he was a well-favored beast. Spectacularly handsome, in fact. But she had rejected many a good-looking man. A fair face never changed a man's essential volatility, nor his lust, nor his greed.

Beyond that, however, and much more disturbing, Fulk had a compelling air of warmth. Most peculiar in her experience. Being near him gave her the oddest impression.

She sensed he was indeed a dangerous man, no matter how soft-spoken, but along with that came the unwelcome feeling that if she were in his good graces, nothing could ever go wrong again. And if it did, it would not matter....

Jehanne gave herself a shake. The greater danger lay with Fulk's charm. Or perhaps he had some sorcery at his command. From what she had heard at the tourney, he had beguiled a dozen women, perhaps a score of women, or even more for all she knew. He was here to use and betray her.

She was grateful for his smile. He did not take her seriously, his guard would be lax. And he could do nothing to embarrass her further than she had already done herself. He would not try to comfort her, nor offer his pity.

Jehanne did not want sympathy. She wanted Windermere free and safe, wanted Fulk the Reluctant to turn around and ride back to the earl's kennels or wherever it was he had come from.

But he was not about to depart. He kept his gaze on her, and she looked from his eyes to his broad shoulders, draped with a thick mantle of green wool. From his belted waist hung a hand-and-a-half sword, and his sturdy legs were endlessly long. He was like an oak tree planted in her courtyard. Impossible to sway. But...even if she could not uproot the tree, she could whittle away at it.

"Have you looked your fill?" he asked.

Jehanne jerked her back straight. "Aye. More than I can stomach."

To her mortification, at that moment an audible growl came from her midsection. Fulk's gaze darkened and he signaled his men with a small movement of his head. Within a few moments she heard the hollow rumble of wains crossing the drawbridge. Curse his efficient hide. He was moving in.

"I have brought thee gifts, my lady."

"I have no desire for finery, Sir Fulk. You can buy neither my loyalty nor my affection with useless trinkets."

One elegant black brow cocked upward. "Can I not? Come see." Removing his gauntlet with his teeth, he offered her his right hand. Jehanne looked at it, then at him and his calm, sure demeanor.

Beneath his courtly manner lurked a devious heart bent on taking all Windermere could give. What little was left, anyway. She clenched her fists and hesitated. Did she dare ignore him? Step past his outstretched palm to reenter the hall?

Fulk decided the matter by gripping her elbow and propelling her toward the gate.

"Unhand me!" Jehanne hated the sensation of her own helplessness against male brawn, and could not wrench herself free before the first wain halted in front of them. She glanced at Fulk over her shoulder and a jolt of fear rippled through her body. Lord God, he was big. He could snap her arm in two as easily as he had her bow.

What manner of woman could have produced an offspring capable of attaining such size? Yet he was perfectly proportioned. Still, he unnerved her. If he were fully human, he could only be the result of some outlandish mixture of—of she knew not what.

Frowning, Fulk released her arm and lifted a corner of the oiled tenting that covered the wain's crated contents. As the light penetrated, a cacophony of honks and flutters made Jehanne start. Geese. Dozens of them.

She stared at Fulk. Too late, she realized her mouth hung open. She ran to the next wain. Smoked hams, sacks of flour, crocks of butter and honey. Barrels of wine and ale. Dried fish and cakes of salt. Barley and oat-seed...life for her people.

Gratitude eroded Jehanne's bone-deep resistance. She would prefer to starve, had she only herself to consider. But calculated or not, Fulk's charity was a godsend, especially for the children. Gritting her teeth, she turned to thank him as courtesy demanded, but he was already overseeing his men as they unloaded the provisions.

The folk of Windermere emerged, gaunt and hesitant. They looked to her and kept their distance, ready to forego the bounty if she said they must. Jehanne closed her eyes briefly, then waved the people forward. With glad cries they hurried to carry the stores inside the keep.

She had rebuffed his messengers all these weeks. She would never have believed any offer of peace in return for opening the gates. Siege armies put their prisoners to the sword. Why should Fulk be any different? He was, though. Unlike any man she had ever met.

Though the words threatened to stick in her throat, she managed to get them out. "Sir Fulk, please accept the thanks of an ungracious woman on behalf of Windermere. Your Christian act puts me to shame. I have allowed my people to suffer far too long."

Fulk rested one booted foot upon a cask and leaned his elbow on his knee. "Nay, my lady. Had I any true Christian kindness I would have catapulted the hams over your walls weeks ago. But had you a full belly then, your aim would have been even better this day."

He must have noticed that the arrows in her belt matched the one caught in his shield. Jehanne swallowed and strove to keep her voice light. "It would have made no difference, I'm afraid. I am a poor shot under the best of circumstances." She would rather he did not know of her considerable skill with a bow.

"Not so poor." He pulled his mantle aside and showed her his left forearm. A wound oozed red, soaking his sleeve.

Jehanne clapped a hand to her mouth. The arrow had gone right through his shield. Her heart battered her ribs, but pride kept her from running away. No man suffered such an injury without responding in kind. She held her head high, ready to receive whatever punishment he might deal her. His pretense of friendliness was meant only to put her off guard.

Fulk snapped his mantle back over his arm and Jehanne flinched at the sudden movement. The knight's mouth tightened. "Forgive me, I forgot the sight of blood offends some folk. If you have a cloth, I can staunch it."

Was the man being sarcastic? "I—I'll find one," she stammered. "Come to the hall."

Jehanne breathed again, but not easily. He was posing, saving his wrath to deliver it later. Tonight, no doubt. In private. She shuddered at the thought of angry hands upon her body...tearing away her clothes, her pride. Apart from her virginity, he would rob her of all honor...of all hope.

And there was nothing she could do to stop him. Hunger and weariness had sapped her. She thought of the battlements. How easy it would be to fall... Nay. That was a coward's way out. She must somehow endure until her strength returned.

Jehanne led Fulk and his men to her father's great hall, now stark and echoing. Her father's warriors had taken their wages in tapestries and silver plate. They had looted the hall and fled during Fulk's approach, on the heels of the deadly fever.

As she hurried to the chest of linens, shame gnawed deep, that strangers should see her home brought to such a desperate condition. Worse, Fulk assumed he was now lord of Windermere, and of her, too.

He stood near the weeks-old ashes of the fire circle, giving orders to both his people and hers. Her battered pride revived. Anger warmed her anew.

As if he sensed Jehanne's shift of attitude, Fulk gazed at her from across the hall, his expression unreadable. With a catch in her throat, she found herself staring back instead of preparing to tend his wound. She inhaled deeply and strode to meet him.

Though he towered over her, the fear she expected did not blossom. Nor could she stop looking at him. Witchcraft. Magic. Nothing else explained the unwelcome ache in her heart.

His amber eyes grew opaque, and he pulled the bandages from her nerveless fingers. "Eat and take your rest now, lady. I shall explain my requirements to you later."

Jehanne did not reply. She could not, without spluttering her indignation. This—sorcerer—had *requirements?* Windermere belonged to her, and she would forever belong to it. Let him think he ruled, let him imagine that she might comply. Jehanne, daughter of Alun FitzWalter, would win her keep back.

Chapter Five

Fulk stretched, leaned back in his chair, and warily eyed his new acquisition. Lady Jehanne sat rigid and silent before the fire, with a half-dozen sated hounds of dubious pedigree asleep at her feet. In spite of the hour and more formal circumstances, she still wore the heavy men's tunic and plain surcoat of earlier in the day, her body all but lost in the folds of wool and linen.

A long, untidy fall of hair, the color of ripe barley, twined about her arms and down her straight back. Crowning her head was a circlet of silver, apparently her only concession to the occasion of his arrival. But, resting at a decided tilt, it lent the lady an unexpected air of vulnerability.

Her haughty gaze flicked to his eyes and away again. Her opinion of him was low, indeed. No doubt he would feel much the same, were their positions reversed. Shifting in his seat, Fulk crossed his legs and rested his chin on his palm. What a confusing bundle of contradictions. A mere woman, all alone, yet so bold as to openly defy him. To loose an arrow upon him and wound him, no less.

She possessed a degree of pride, unrelated to vanity, heretofore unknown to him in a female. He was used to women of delicate sensibilities, artful in their allure, soft of voice and skin.

This one was brittle in her righteousness, hardened by her devotion to lofty ideals, but especially to *things*. Land and cattle, serfs and profits seemed to be her main preoccupations, apart from her love of violence.

Nothing of any interest to him.

Nay, during the siege he had thanked God for each day that
passed without the necessity of a bloody fight. And thanked Him
even more that he had not been forced to do battle with his supposed future father-in-law. Now that he had met the lady, Fulk
knew she would never have forgiven him Alun's death, be the
man traitor to the king or hero to the people.

Jehanne's contingent of gentlewomen, three in all, surrounded
her like mother wolves defending their young. They would flay
him alive with their stares if they could, he'd warrant.

But they were vastly outnumbered. Malcolm sat next to him,
and all the rest of his men were present, speaking quietly among
themselves, though well apart from the women and the other
members of the household. Fulk had ordered it so, on pain of a
night in chains, should any one of them cause the ladies of Windermere a moment's distress.

Thus far his consideration to the resident females had met with
more resentment than gratitude. The men did not chafe much at
the imposed limitations, but the women seemed to take it as an
insult, yet another demonstration of the power Fulk held over
them.

He cleared his throat. "Lady Jehanne," he murmured.

Slowly, she turned her head toward him. "My lord?"

He might have been a toad, her tone was so dry. He gestured
toward Malcolm, off to one side. "This is Sir Malcolm, known
as the Fierce, son of Hunter of Clan Mac Niall. A man of both
honor and rare caution." Malcolm bowed and Fulk let her wait a
moment before he continued, and took a good look at her fresh-
scrubbed face.

She looked much the same as he remembered from the Duke's
tournament. Skin like a country maid, sun-kissed and quick to
blush. Grave, gray-hued eyes, startling in their depth and clarity.

But now a narrow, ragged scar marred her beauty. It slanted
and skipped from her right brow to her nose, then onto her left
cheek where it faded away. A pity. She made no effort to hide it.

He wondered how she had come by such a wound. Dueling
with her suitors, perhaps? Not altogether beyond the realm of
possibility. Their eyes met, and though Jehanne's gaze was un-
flinching, she clasped her hands so tightly the knuckles showed

white. Aye, she had changed. Still bold, but the wholly defiant manner of her exploits last summer had been replaced by wariness.

Nor was she as young as Fulk had first assumed—in her early twenties, he guessed. She must have spurned the earl and his candidates for ages.

Fulk smiled to himself. She had dodged marriage the way he had dodged his knighting. Well, she was welcome to her spinsterhood. He would not deprive her of it. But deal with her he must.

"My lady, there is much to be done on the morrow. My men will aid you in the burial of your dead. I should also inspect your demesnes. Will you accompany me and show me what needs attention?"

Her eyes widened. "*My* demesnes? Do you mock me, sir?"

Fulk suppressed his impatience. She was determined to take everything he said as an offense. He could hardly blame her.

"I would not bludgeon you with the truth. But I believe you would relish the designation 'our' even less, am I right?"

Though Jehanne tossed her head, the movement could not disguise the shudder his words provoked. "You are indeed correct in that belief. But as befits the vanquished, I will do whatever you wish—tomorrow. May I go now?"

She stood, chin raised, her small hands still clasped before her. Fulk rose and bowed. "By all means, lady. Sleep well."

No doubt she would—better than he, for his wounded arm ached from wrist to shoulder. As the women climbed the stairs to their quarters he took his seat again and turned to Malcolm.

"Vanquished? She would dagger me in a trice if she could."

Malcolm's sharp, almost sinister features were the picture of skepticism. He leaned in close, his voice low. "You're right there. I would watch my back, Fulk. The lass willnae be rolling over for you any time soon."

"An interesting choice of words, Malcolm. Aye, she must take after her father."

"And a more cunning plotter against your precious king you'd nae have found. So I heard ere we set out—the quicker Alun FitzWalter were brought to justice the easier his Grace would

breathe. 'Tis blessed we are he was taken before we arrived.''
Malcolm crossed his arms and stared at the fire.

The Scot's expression darkened, in spite of his last statement.
Fulk handed him a goblet of wine. "What is it, Mac Niall?"

"Och, Fulk, 'tis the state of this keep is causing me to fret."
Malcolm took a long swallow and twirled the cup between his
palms. "We will be here a right long time. And it would appear
there are not enough womenfolk to go round."

"Come now, they will be awaiting you in relays. It is the rest
of us will suffer."

"Lies, Fulk. Vicious rumors meant to sully my reputation as a
man pure of both heart and mind."

"You should not tell such falsehoods, or your fortune with the
ladies might change, even as has mine."

Malcolm sighed. "I would fain be in love with the woman I
wed, and wake with her beside me, day in and day out."

Fulk poked at a smoldering log and it rekindled with a burst
of yellow flame. "Though it makes my hair stand on end, I can
envision you bedded—just. But wedded? I think not."

The Scot sighed. "What's the difference? To give a woman
my body is to give her my heart and soul as well. Do you not
feel the same?"

Fulk ran his fingers through his thick hair. It was growing back
fast—as if it sought again to needlessly remind him of Rabel. He
replied truthfully to the Scot, "I have no answer to that, for never
have I given a lady any part of myself that I did not want returned.
Certainly neither my heart nor soul."

"Ah, that much is obvious, for if you had, you'd know 'tis
sheer hell, and to love is to suffer the tortures of the damned."
Malcolm stood abruptly. "Good evening, Galliard." The Scot
stalked off, muttering to himself and shaking his head.

Fulk stared after his friend. Malcolm was in a bad way. Scattered. Irritable. But surely not in love.

The hour was late, and the fire in Jehanne's chamber had dwindled to a smoking pile of red and black coals. She shook out the
gauzy linen of her shift, straightened her overgown, and finger-
combed her hair one more time. She checked to make certain the

dagger strapped to her calf was secure. She would not use it unless she had to.

Not unless he forced her to.

She felt like an impostor—pretending femininity. But she had made up her mind. Nothing could be worse than lying awake waiting for Fulk to burst in, punish her and take what the king said was his due. For him to overpower and ravish her would be far more humiliating, terrifying and degrading than if she went to him of her own free will.

This way, she retained her dignity. This way, it was her choice, not his.

"My lady, I beg of you, do not do this." Lioba, ever proud and protective, put a hand to Jehanne's shoulder. "We shall watch over you, this and every night. He will not come nigh without having to deal with us."

Elly and Beatrix murmured their agreement. They had already pushed their clothes chests near the door, in order to barricade it quickly.

Jehanne clasped Lioba's fingers. "You are brave, and I appreciate the protection each of you offers. But think upon it. This Galliard comes at the king's behest. He and the Earl of Lexingford plotted together and falsely accused my lord father of treason. We cannot stop Fulk's possession of Windermere. Nor can I stop him from possessing me."

She paused and stared into the red heart of the fire. The decision she had made had been the most difficult of her life.

"The earl's letter was quite plainspoken. It is best for the villagers that I surrender gracefully, as honor demands. But should this knight reveal himself as wholly a beast, I shall defend myself, for honor will then be forfeit."

"Let us accompany you to his door, at least. We will sit without the solar and be ready should you call for aid."

Jehanne could not help a small smile. "Very well. But it may be he who cries for mercy, should he provoke me."

Her words were bold, but her stomach churned as she approached Fulk's chamber. Partly because she had taken some food at last—and it did not sit well—and partly because deep inside, a tiny piece of her took interest in Fulk de Galliard. Came alive at the thought of him. And not in a way suitable to any respectable maiden.

Jehanne stopped before the entry of the solar that had been her father's private chamber. She took a deep breath and raised her hand to knock. The door flew open, and the Scot blocked her way.

Quick blue eyes, hair the color of a blood-bay horse, and a moustache of which any Saxon would have been proud. All in all, his face was a not unpleasing juxtaposition of lean planes and angles.

"Mademoiselle?" His French had a thick Gaelic overlay.

"I would see Sir Fulk."

"Would you, now? What say you, Fulk? Dare we risk admitting the lady?"

Jehanne heard a thud and a curse. Rubbing his head, Galliard loomed behind the Scotsman. He must have caught the low beam.

"Malcolm, kindly stand aside and let her in."

"I cannae do that, not 'til I've checked her person for weapons." The Scot's eyes raked her up and down.

"Malcolm...I thank you for your concern. But I will not subject Lady Jehanne to such discourtesy in her own father's solar."

Jehanne gripped her skirts tighter. Fulk had no way of knowing what discourtesies she had already suffered here. Even now it was not easy for her to cross the threshold, but she challenged Malcolm with her gaze. He narrowed his eyes, then the barest hint of humor glinted in their depths, and he allowed her to slip past.

She stood as she had countless times before, in the center of the room, facing yet another man who could break her as he willed—or make the attempt. With the sole of her bare foot she found the familiar, sharp edge of an uneven floorboard she had used over the years to keep her fear at bay.

To her surprise, Fulk bowed. "How may we serve you, Mademoiselle?"

There it was again, that way Fulk had of turning his voice into a caress, of putting her at ease when she needed to remain vigilant.

"I would speak with you alone, my lord." She curtsied to Malcolm by way of dismissing him.

Fulk's glance cut to the Scot. A whoosh of air billowed Jehanne's skirts as Malcolm closed the door, silent on its greased hinges. Galliard had jumped out of bed to greet her, it appeared, for he was but half clad, in a white linen tunic and footless chausses. The clinging gray wool that encased his long legs showed every ripple of muscle with shameless clarity.

He did not apologize, however. Instead, he stared at her as though she were a vision he had dreamed into reality—of what, she could not fathom. After a moment, and a swallow or two, he found his voice.

"Please, be seated, my lady."

He offered her the most comfortable spot—the bed. Jehanne was not about to refuse, out of either propriety or fear. Her feet barely touched the floor as she sat on the edge of the mattress, still warm from Fulk's body.

Slowly he approached, his languid eyes focused upon her breasts. A burst of panic seared her throat. He was not going to wait. He was going to take her...*now.*

It was entirely possible he might kill her, albeit perhaps unintentionally. He had to be at least four cubits tall. He must weigh more than sixteen stone. The very breath would be squeezed from her body, he would tear her in two—Jehanne clutched the bedclothes and with an effort stopped herself from uttering a small moan.

He was almost upon her. What had the wretch found to smile about? Did he enjoy terrifying women? She would wager his past conquests had been but games, played with willing partners. This was life and death, to her, at least.

Mere inches away, Fulk leaned toward her. A pulse throbbed in his neck. A beast, ready to pounce.

Jehanne held herself rigid. Disjointed thoughts raced through her mind. Why must he smell so good? Like cedar, or sandalwood, or—oh, God, she did not want to be hurt. She would have to raise her skirts to pull the dagger.

Even as she debated whether to grab for it, Fulk rested one hand on the bed, and reached behind her, feeling for something tangled in the sheets.

"Pardon me, I had best cover myself." He brought forth a garment of some sort and stepped back.

Jehanne trembled in her relief, angry with herself for giving way to fear so easily.

The robe he shook out was an amazing creation, ermine-lined, of deep red-and-purple-hued silk, thickly embroidered in loops and whorls of fantastic intricacy. As Fulk shrugged into it, wrapping himself in its voluminous folds, he paused at her frank stare. "Does it not please you?"

"Well, I—"

"Plunder, my lady. One cannot always pick and choose. Or can it be that you *do* admire it?"

He had the audacity to strike a pose, like a statue of some ancient king. Or warlock.

"Oh." She gulped. "It dazzles the eye. Surely it belonged to a great lord in some faraway land?"

"Aye. But it no longer fit him."

His tone made her wonder if the previous owner had lost some of his bulk in an unpleasant manner.

Fulk dragged a stool close and folded his legs in an attempt to sit, but gave up and chose a large, flat-topped chest instead. It put more distance between them, which suited Jehanne far better.

"Would you like some wine?" He dangled the flagon.

"Nay. I had best come to the point, Lord—er, what shall I call you? You are in truth a viscount, so I've heard?"

Fulk looked down at his hands, then met her eyes. "In France, perhaps, had my father not—well, that is another matter. Suffice it to say His Grace Henry has deprived me of any title I may once have expected here in England. But do not call me 'lord'. It makes me feel that I must refer to myself in the plural." He gave her a devastating, self-deprecating grin.

"I see." Jehanne cleared her throat and sat up straighter.

God's teeth and gums. As if his body and voice and eyes were not enough—but she would not let him sway her from her purpose.

If it were possible to die of shame, she would have done so gladly, rather than say what she had to say next. She stood, praying she could bear his lustful attentions without showing fear. "I am here, Sir Fulk, to offer...to offer myself—I am aware of what is expected of me, as the...the spoils of war, as it were."

To her astonishment, Fulk blushed. Right up to the roots of his black hair. He bounced up from his seat and turned his back to her.

"Watch the beam!" Her warning popped out before she could consider not giving it.

"The devil's own!" Fulk pressed his palm to his head again, this time to the opposite side, and glared at the offending timber. "Who built this place? Dwarves?" He slammed the flagon of wine down and the liquid sloshed onto the table.

Jehanne tried not to laugh. Bruised and bloodied, Fulk himself was the only casualty of violence so far in the taking of Windermere. He quickly regained his composure, however, and to her dismay, came to sit beside her on the bed.

His was a warm, vibrant presence. Discreetly she edged away from him.

Twisting at the waist, Fulk leaned back against the bedpost. Jehanne longed to run from his penetrating scrutiny, so much so that she barely heeded him.

"Be assured, Lady Jehanne, that you are a—a most tempting prize—were the situation different. I will not lie to you. I have been ordered to beget an heir for Windermere. On you. And the very fact that it is the Earl Grimald's desire makes it an impossibility for me to carry out such an act. It would make me feel like an animal. I could not subject you to the role, even were you willing. And that I do not believe for an instant."

Jehanne repeated Fulk's words to herself, to make certain she had heard correctly. *He could not beget an heir on her because it would make him feel like an animal.* She acknowledged his stammering attempt not to offend her. She understood. Here, indeed, he had just cause for reluctance. Her scars made her ugly, and there was no way around it.

Fulk rubbed his knees as if they were sore. Watching him, Jehanne frowned. She found she could not help admiring the shape of his powerful, tight-knit hands, and their surprising cleanliness. She pushed away the thought of the strength she had already felt in his long fingers and dragged her attention back to the conversation.

"Duty is not meant to be pleasant," she said.

His hands stilled. "Do you mean to say you *want* me to...?"

At the distressed look on his face Jehanne was unaccountably amused. So, perhaps she frightened him, too. Good. She bit her lip but a nervous laugh emerged despite her best effort.

"What? Do you now mock *me,* lady?"

As his color rose again, so did her mirth, born more from feeling overwhelmed than any humor in the situation. "Of course not Forgive me, sir, but—"

"I did not come to this Godforsaken place to be made an object of hilarity. Kindly take your leave. I shall summon you when next I wish your presence."

At his icy tone Jehanne sobered. "Very well. But do not count upon my attendance. This is the last time you will have the opportunity I have just offered."

"What you deem as noble sacrifice, I deem as cold-blooded manipulation. Leave me, mademoiselle." Fulk stood.

Jehanne stared up at him, her remaining composure ready to snap, her pride in tatters. "I cannot, sir."

"Why?" He crossed his arms, deepening the dark V of his chest where the tunic gaped open. In his royal-hued robe, he resembled nothing so much as a displeased potentate from Byzantium—or so she imagined, never having seen one.

She drew a deep breath. "The...the terms of conquest were made clear to me before your arrival. They are part of why my resistance lasted so long. But my duty is to my people. I capitulate for their sake. They have suffered enough. If I do not meet the earl's demands, he will punish me in some other, even more horrible manner—nay, sir, I did not mean that the way it sounded—'

Jehanne waited for Fulk's color to return to normal. When her own heart had slowed, she too got to her feet, crunching the rushes and sweetgrass beneath them.

"Grimald wants me thoroughly humiliated. That is why I come to you. To salvage something of my self-respect before the inevitable happens, and at the same time protect my people from future insult."

"The 'inevitable'?" Fulk's luminous eyes appeared wounded "Lady Jehanne, whatever you may think of me, I am not a rapist."

"It would not be rape."

"Would it not?"

"Nay...I—it is how these things are honorably accomplished when in a situation such as mine." Jehanne wound a strand of her hair about one finger. She had not sounded very convincing, but meeting the demands of honor did not make the prospect of being the object of a man's lust any less dreadful.

"A situation such as *ours,* milady. In a way I am a prisoner here as much as you. But, for a woman to submit out of fear, even if not on her own behalf, is a sin. And for me...to take you...take you to wife, with the slightest misgiving on your part—or mine, for that matter—is just as wrong, methinks."

Jehanne was dumbfounded to hear such a revolutionary attitude. And from a man, no less. If in fact he meant what he said. "What will you do to satisfy the earl, then?"

"I know not. But he holds my sister's life hostage. Among other things." Fulk swept up the wine flagon and drank straight from its mouth.

"Hostage?" The possibility of such goings-on between her enemies had never crossed Jehanne's mind. He must be lying, to gain her sympathy. But the pain she had glimpsed in his eyes looked real enough.

"Grimald holds her well-being as a club to my head."

"Then what shall we do?"

"What do you *want* to do?" Fulk wiped his mouth with the back of his hand and looked at her squarely.

Jehanne's mind raced with possibilities. To beat him in a fair fight and regain her honor. To watch his back as he rode away in defeat from her lands. Her gaze strayed to Fulk's sword, lying within easy reach, then back to the man, awaiting her reply.

He had the upper hand, his men were fit and well-fed. It would not be easy getting rid of him. She sighed.

"My people will be afraid if they see an ongoing quarrel between us. They fear a reprisal, should the earl suspect we are not loyal vassals. Windermere's immediate safety lies in your strength, and my cooperation. Your men-at-arms are all that stand between us and any marauder. At this crossroads, alone, I am easily conquered."

"Not so easily." Fulk cradled his bandaged arm.

"I am sorry for that." *I am sorry I missed a more vital spo* *Sir Fulk.* Nay, that was not true. It should have been, but it wa not.

"I am grateful you did not pierce my heart." He gazed at he not a trace of guile showing.

Jehanne felt her own cheeks bloom, but could not look awa "We must put up a pretense of mutual affection, or at least c tolerance." She examined her nails, bitten to the quick.

Fulk tipped his head to one side. "How grand a pretense woul you like to attempt?"

At the low, sensual timbre of his voice, the bottom dropped ou of her stomach. "As much as I can bear."

"I can be very convincing."

Fulk's growing smile was dangerous. Captivating. Much to appealing. Jehanne swallowed hard. An unfamiliar quiver in he belly told her it would not take a great deal of effort on his pa to make a pretense wholly unnecessary.

She must keep her heart steeled against him. It was merely lu she felt, nothing more. "No doubt. Just remember, the appearanc of amity is for the public's benefit only."

"Aye. In six months' time we'll tie a pillow round your middle And in nine months we will come up with a foundling—ou heir—is that the plan?" His grin became positively roguish.

"It is not! Who is to say you would be so potent—or I s fertile, or the imaginary babe so healthy?"

How had he turned the conversation into such a ridiculous fan tasy? Fulk's voice interrupted her thoughts. "Ah, but were th child to die, I would be prostrated by grief, and would have to g on a pilgrimage to cleanse my soul."

"What if the mother died? Would that not solve all your prob lems? You'd be able to take a bride of your own choosing." Jehanne glared at Fulk, until the growing look of strain on hi face caused her to soften her gaze. Her own mother had die giving her life. It would not be surprising to learn Fulk had kille his, too, simply by virtue of his size.

He began pacing before her, this time ducking the beam at eac end of his circuit as if he had grown up with it. "That is a wicked thing to suggest, lady."

He raked his hand through his loose black curls. "Besides, the father's death would be just as convenient, for you." He shot her a piercing look. "Windermere is a vast and beautiful fief, is it not?"

Jehanne blinked at the abrupt change of subject. "It is large, and was once a rich, productive place."

"One the earl might covet for his own?"

Where was he going with his questions? "Certainly."

"How did your father become Grimald's enemy?"

"My father has ever been true—faithful to both the earl and our lord king."

"You cannot expect me to believe that. Why then was I sent to confiscate this place? I was shown the king's seal upon the matter—" Fulk stopped in his tracks. He rubbed his brow and she followed his look toward the shield hung over the bed, blazoned with the FitzWalter arms.

A pair of lions, back to back. Fitting symbols for a family who would fight to the death.

"My lady, go, rest you this night, and on the morrow let us speak again."

Jehanne straightened her shoulders. "I do not wish to further discuss the plots and intrigues that have ensnared my family. You are here simply because I refused the earl and his henchmen, thus he has used other means to force our cooperation. The effect on me is the same, for I have no doubt you will go to great lengths to protect your sister. But since you appear to be a pawn just as am I, I intend to do something about this injustice."

Fulk questioned her with an arched brow.

"I shall petition the king. In person. And you shall be forever removed from the chessboard." Jehanne strode to the door, fully expecting Fulk to stop her with one of his big hands on her arm.

"Perhaps you should do, lady. But give me a month, ere you set my doom into motion."

"Why should I grant you any grace period?"

"Because you have not a chance in hell of changing the king's mind. And because I spared you."

Jehanne suddenly felt small and alone, no longer righteous. Despite what she would like to think of him, she had a feeling this opponent possessed a sense of honor. And that made it all the harder to hate him on principle, for being the one to take Windermere away from her. The question was, could he hold on to it? She might yet retake the keep, God willing.

"Agreed, Sir Fulk. We shall not act in haste. I bid you good night."

He opened the door for her. As she passed him, heat escaped from his open robe, licking at her back. Still, Jehanne shivered. She hurried toward her own chamber. Her women were nowhere in sight, and she risked a look over her shoulder. Fulk had retreated, and Malcolm was already in place, watching her for a moment before he ducked into the solar.

Jehanne shrugged off the sense of isolation that dogged her as she walked down the echoing corridor. The Scot had apparently chased her ladies away, damn him. She paused, her hand on the door of her own chamber, reassured by the murmur of her women's voices within.

Another thought occurred to her. If the earl did want Windermere for himself, why send a man who hated him, even under the pretext of her father's supposed treason?

She looked up toward the solar. The keep would still belong to Fulk, who might not share its potential, as the earl's other lackeys would have done. It was almost as though the earl had placed both his enemies into one pot.

Chapter Six

Fulk woke to the faint scent of mint, the only trace of Jehanne's presence the previous night.

But the herb's aroma also reminded him of hot nights and warm seas, of dewy, kohl-ringed eyes and veiled faces....

Fulk blinked away the erotic images, and instead studied the complex weave of the faded red and gold bedcurtains. After a moment, he sat up and thrust them aside. A milky sunbeam had found its way through the wooden slats at the window, and now seethed with dust on its way to the floor.

At the thought of his last encounter with Jehanne he shook his head. What in hell had possessed him? *I can be very convincing.* Lord God. He had smiled, knowing full well how it would affect her. Or how it affected most women. Fulk groaned inwardly. He was not treading lightly, nor taking steps to remain disentangled from this woman and her miserable keep.

And whose fault was it?

Hers. Hers entirely. He wanted nothing to do with her. Not with her, her haunted eyes, her eloquent, chewed-upon hands, nor her lithe, hungry body that cried out to be touched—Fulk's groan turned into a growling yawn.

He stretched and went to the window seat. Pushing open the shutters he looked out upon the tidy village, fields and white-clad forest now under his protection. The rising mist caught the sun and diffused its light, veiling the harsh reality of lingering disease and starvation below.

Just what he needed—more responsibility, when worrying about Celine was already an all-consuming occupation.

An energetic rap sounded at the door, adding to his foul mood. "Come."

Malcolm entered sideways, glancing left and right, checking for potential assassins behind the bed curtains and the door, as was his wont.

"I am quite alone, Hunterson."

"In your present state, Fulk, any number of malefactors could be hovering, daggers at the ready, and you would pay them no heed." Malcolm stepped to the window. "'Tis a lovely dawn."

"Aye. And with the coming of this day the yoke of Windermere falls securely about my neck. I will never get free of this place. It is a pit of quicksand, I know it."

"Why should you wish to be free? 'Tis every man's dream, handed to you gratis, both lady and land."

"Nay, Malcolm. I have already paid too dear for it—with every last one of my books, and to buy what? A ransom in fine horseflesh and foodstuffs. Land and warlording are not how I had thought to live my life. And now I've been tethered to the likes of a mermaid. She will take me down with her, to depths beyond my capacity, until I drown in a sea of tears."

"What rot! This is what comes of your bookishness, Fulk. You wax morbidly poetic instead of forging ahead." Malcolm sat opposite him and propped one booted foot on the window ledge.

"Leave me alone. I am unwell." Fulk leaned his aching head against the cold stone of the embrasure.

"Lovesick, you mean."

"You are the plague that ails me."

"Nay, Fulk. I know what cure you will be needin', right quick."

"Not another word. Why don't you find out if the girl intends to show me round, or if I should look for the bailiff?"

"Ah, 'tis 'the girl', now. You're so pitifully transparent, Fulk. You cannae hide your longing behind such disrespectful forms of address." Malcolm waggled an elegantly gloved and beringed finger at Fulk.

God have mercy on me should I strike the man dead. Some

times Fulk would like to have forgotten that Malcolm was of noble blood, and related to the Viking Earls of Orkney. He gazed at his friend's grinning, feral face.

"You, Hunterson, tread upon thin ice. And if my goodwill means aught to thee, you had best retreat to shore."

The Scot paled a shade but his voice ground out low and steady. "You're a bloody fool. Treasure in your grasp and you would toss it aside over a dead man."

"Watch yourself, sir." Fulk's heart lurched with regret. As ever, he was tortured by the image of Rabel, dying. Rabel, drowning in his own blood. "You know what I mean."

"Aye, Fulk, I do. But you are that blind, if true love were to clout you o'er the head, you would fight it off instead of embracing it."

"I cannot concern myself with love. I must find Celine a refuge, to keep her safe from the Hurler. I thought of bringing her here, but this place is not yet stable." And, he did not add, there were far too many men about. One look at his sister was often enough to bring lovelorn suitors crawling to him, begging for her hand. But none that he cared to have as a good-brother.

Malcolm did not reply.

Fulk stared at his friend. His silence was heavy. Full to bursting. "Oh, Lord. Nay, Malcolm. Not you, too. Not Celine. You have never even spoken to her!"

The Scot's eyes only burned more intensely.

Fulk stood. Blood roared through his chest and into his head. Nay. Such a thing could never be. Celine was fragile. Delicate. Not a maid for the likes of Hengist, nor even for Malcolm, wild and fierce as a northern gale. While his honor and bravery were unimpeachable, his passions ran too hot.

Fulk could not think of a single man of his acquaintance who would be suitable for his sister. It would only be a matter of time before she fell into the clutches of some unscrupulous varlet, if she were not close by that Fulk might guard her himself. Even were her dowry intact, the search for a properly civilized groom might take a long time.

Malcolm rocked on the balls of his feet. "You will not stand in my way, Galliard. Not you nor any man."

"I will protect her at all costs. Even against you."

"Nay, Fulk. My heart is set and no turnin' back." Malcolm took a belligerent stance, his thumbs hooked through his sword-belt.

Fulk took a deep breath. "I will see you dead ere I allow you to cause her an instant of pain."

Malcolm raised his chin. "And I would see to my own demise should I ever be guilty of harming her."

A terrible surge of deadly anger threatened to engulf Fulk. He struggled for control, shoving at the crimson wave until it began to subside. "Ah, Mac Niall. But to have you as good-brother? Who could imagine it and not tremble at the thought?"

"I may have to slit your throat for you one of these nights, and save you the fretting." Malcolm grinned wolfishly, accepting the truce in his own way.

"Don't be making promises you will not keep." Fulk gave his friend a wry look. "Let us not allow women to get in the way of our comradeship."

"Perish the thought, Fulk. And that of a warm, willing lass in your arms at night. The lady Jehanne is fair to beggin' for a good cuddle."

"Oh, indeed, Malcolm, so you have finally noticed. Never mind that, come with me on the tour of Windermere. Give me your worthy opinion."

"Aye, flatter me, Fulk. You know damn well you cannae do without me."

"Well do I know, Malcolm."

With a wink, the Scot slipped to the door. "I'll order up the horses."

Fulk strode into the bailey. The sharp, clear air made everything in sight appear unnaturally vivid, whether animal, human or the very stones of the keep. A cold breeze swirled the snow in little eddies over the cobbles.

Already mounted, Jehanne shivered as she waited. Fulk put a hand to her palfrey's shoulder. "Lady, it is freezing, you need not attend. Send the bailiff in your stead."

She gazed down at him, her face expressionless. "He is long dead, Sir Fulk. I will warm as we progress."

In Fulk's experience a sedate ride in winter was among the most chilling endeavors he knew, but he said nothing. He crossed the ward to his gray courser, held by a hollow-cheeked young man of the keep, who stiffened visibly at his approach.

Fulk circled his beast, noting its shining coat, the gleaming leathers, and the lack of even a shred of straw in its mane and tail. He ran his hand down the animal's foreleg and tapped its fetlock, leaning slightly against the horse's shoulder as he picked up its foot. A big ball of snow had collected in the hoof, but once brushed away, the foot was scrubbed clean inside.

"This is a surpassing fine job you have done, lad. Is it love of horses or fear of me that inspires you?" Fulk straightened and met the groom's eyes, which were nearly popping from his head as he stood, trembling.

The young man hesitated and looked to his lady. Fulk caught their silent exchange. She would protect the lad, no matter his answer. The other servants watched with apprehensive faces.

"B-both, milord."

Fulk smiled. "What is your name?"

"Corwin, sir."

"Then, Corwin the Truthful, I charge you with the exclusive care of my great-horse and this courser. You alone shall see to their well-being. That will suit you, am I right?"

Corwin swayed. "Aye, milord."

The boy was incapable of further speech, but the glow in his brown eyes fairly shouted his happiness. Fulk took the reins.

"Fetch me some butter, lad, then go break your fast properly."

Corwin trotted away, and Jehanne's palfrey stamped a hoof, dislodging the snow that had impacted within it. Jehanne gazed down at Fulk, her expression unreadable. "You have won him for life. Ever has Corwin yearned for grand horses such as yours. But what want you with butter? Surely your courser will not eat it?"

"Nay, it will simply make the way easier."

When the crock arrived, Fulk showed Corwin how to pack the

horses' hooves with the fat to keep snow from balling and im-
peding the animals' progress.

"It can save you a nasty fall, and your horse a pulled tendon
It keeps their heels supple as well."

"It is a waste of food, in my opinion," Jehanne said.

"You are no longer under siege, my lady."

"I still feel that I am. And will until you have gone."

Fulk swung onto the gray. "Tsk, what of our pact of pretense?"
He brought his mount to her side. "Would you have them think
us enemies?"

The bailey had filled with servants and villagers, apparently
come to see their new master, now that they knew he was not
about to put them to death.

"Give me your hand," Fulk ordered softly.

Jehanne frowned at him. "What for?"

Those daggered glances of hers would try the patience of a
Beguine, but Fulk kept his voice low. "Have you no experience
of courtesy? Give me your hand!"

She thrust her fist toward him. He dropped his reins to take it
and uncurled her fingers with some difficulty. When she tried to
pull away he held her hand fast and brought it up to his mouth
Fulk inhaled Jehanne's scent and looked at her as he kissed the
backs of her fingers. Even the leather of her gloves held a trace
of mint. Her eyes narrowed and both her scar and the tip of her
nose turned pink. With a final squeeze he released her. She
scrubbed furiously at her face with her wrist and jogged her horse
forward.

What was the matter with the woman? Had no one ever kissed
her hand before? She was skittish as an untouched yearling. Fulk
had an unbidden urge to gather Jehanne up, take her somewhere
warm and private, and get her used to being kissed in a variety
of places.

It was obviously what she needed quite desperately. Even Malcolm had seen it. But Fulk quelled the thought and followed her
out the gates.

Once they had passed beyond the village and crossed the bridge
over the rushing Leven, rolling hills spread in invitation before

them. On the forest edge oaks and yews stood guard over brilliant, snowy fields, and the lake mirrored the glowing blue sky.

With a sudden spray of white Jehanne galloped away from Fulk and the rest of the company. From where the lane curved she headed into an open field. Her hair streamed bright behind her, like hammered gold.

"Stay you, Malcolm, please."

At the Scot's nod of assent Fulk eased his horse into a canter, keeping Jehanne in sight without coming too close. He did not imagine she had succumbed to a fit of playfulness. Nay, the lady carried a heavy load of sorrow, and no doubt at times it was too much to be borne.

She disappeared over a rise, but the fading plumes of her horse's breath were still visible. Upon cresting the hill Fulk halted. Jehanne had abandoned her mount and now floundered on foot through the snow, moving toward the deep blue shadows cast by the forest.

"*Oyez!* Come back!" He hurried forward and came around, cutting off her approach to the wood. Jumping down from his courser, he allowed Jehanne to choose the distance between them. He sensed that she might bolt, should he press her.

"What is the matter, lady?"

Bowing her head, she hugged herself, then went to her knees. She curled up like a hedgehog and hid her face.

Cautiously, Fulk drew near, the new snow squeaking beneath his feet. "Have I offended thee?" He put a tentative hand upon Jehanne's shoulder.

She jerked and shuddered as though he had poured ice water down her back.

"Ah, lady, tell me true, I cannot bear to see you thus and think that I have caused such pain."

When she did not reply he knelt beside her. Panic rose within Fulk at the thought of this woman suffering alone. It cut him to the quick, for he knew she saw him as the source of her torment. He, who had kissed away many a tear from many a delicate cheek...

Without considering the consequences he put his arms about her. Jehanne cried out and struggled, but he merely tightened his embrace, though his forearm still hurt. He could feel her ribs through her clothing, and guilt panged at what he had put her through, under siege.

Slowly her resistance ebbed, though her trembling continued. She rested stiffly, her cheek to his shoulder, her eyes squeezed shut. A tear dripped onto his gauntlet, reflecting the bright sky for a moment before it soaked into the leather.

Silence lay thick about them, but for their breathing.

Jehanne looked up at Fulk, anguish shadowing her eyes. "Forgive me, sir, I know not what came over me. I am weary...and foolish. I—I thought when we agreed to a pretense, it would take the form of polite words and pleasantry. I did not expect to be kissed. I did not know how very little I could stand...." Her voice faded away into a whisper.

"I am sorry for my clumsiness. That was no properly executed kiss, lady. I touched not your skin, but that of some fortunate animal whom you allow closer than ever you will me, it seems."

The offering of comfort to women was ingrained in Fulk, a part of his nature he could not stifle, even had he wanted to try. It gave him pleasure to cradle Jehanne in his arms, to murmur soothing words. But when he smoothed a stray lock of hair from her cheek, she flinched as his fingers brushed her scar.

"You would not enjoy any intimate encounter with me, I am certain." She turned her face from him as if in shame, and Fulk knew she herself believed what she said.

"I will not ask why you make such a claim, for it must be false. Unless you are not what you appear to be...a maiden who has just lost her father, and any number of friends and vassals. One who, after weeks of suffering, has been betrayed into the hands of a stranger. One who does not want to be at the mercy of any man, be he king, or earl or knight...am I right?"

She went limp. "Aye. I cannot go through with this, sir. Tell Grimald I have gone mad. He cannot fault you for that. He will not abuse your sister knowing I have been brought so low. The news will bring him joy."

Fulk's chest constricted at the empty defeat he heard in Jehanne's voice. "I will give him no cause for joy." He ground out the words in a whispered vow.

The backs of his gloved fingers again hovered near her cheek, but this time he stopped himself from touching her. Fulk was certain Jehanne would not be glad of his comfort once she regained her pride and anger. This softening of hers was only due to pain and the wearing effects of hunger.

Then she looked up at him again, her clear, silver eyes large in her thin face. Her lips parted as if she were about to speak. She hesitated.

Fulk did not. He knew but one way to bring back her fighting spirit. He pulled her close and brushed her mouth with his. Her heat and sweetness set him alight. He deepened the kiss, tracing her lips with his tongue. His thoughts grew incoherent with an unexpected burst of desire.

Then and there in the snow he wanted her to burn with him. For the merest instant she did belong to him—he recognized her fleeting response, honest and unpracticed. He had a sense of urgency, that if he could not now touch her heart, if the moment slipped away, then she too would drift forever beyond his reach.

He parted his mouth from hers. "Jehanne..."

Even as her name left his lips she slapped his face, hard. She beat at him with her fists and abruptly withdrew, taking with her the spark of warmth she had shared, closing herself off once again.

It was as though he had held a drowning woman who had made a last effort to cling to life, but in the end was swept away by the current of a river too powerful and swift for either of them to combat.

An unaccountable anger filled Fulk, at what or whom, he was not sure. He had revived her hatred of him, that much was certain. And hatred went a long way in keeping one strong, well beyond one's limits. But he did not suffer blows lightly—from anyone.

"This is your second assault upon my person. Never strike me again, lady. Be well advised, for you shall rue the day."

"Aye. I have no doubt of that." Her level gaze was arrogant and unyielding.

Against her protests Fulk bundled Jehanne into his arms and put her on her horse. Fuming, he mounted his own and led her back to the road, where Malcolm and their escort waited. Upon reaching the others, Jehanne sat her palfrey, staring at nothing.

"What have you done to her, Fulk?" Malcolm's expression was a mixture of outrage and disbelief. "She is right as rain in one breath and fairly bewitched in the next!"

Fulk glared at the Scot. "She must be put to bed straightaway. She needs rest and some good red meat in her. Organize a hunt. Get word to the crofters they are to come to the hall in three days' time and present me their concerns, once they have feasted."

"Red meat, indeed. Nothing would be better for her than a hot oaty porridge."

"Just do as I ask." Fulk sidestepped his courser to Jehanne's palfrey, made sure she was securely seated, and brought her at a canter to the castle gates.

Someone was removing her clothes. Jehanne roused from her pillow, started to scream, to fight the hands peeling off her wet surcoat. "Nay, nay, nay!"

"Shh, dearling, 'tis only your Lioba here, no one but me, and naught to fear."

The woman's warm hand soothed Jehanne's brow, and her heart gradually slowed to a normal rhythm. "What happened? Did I faint?"

"That wicked Galliard was at you in the snowy field—nay love, he hadn't time to compromise your virtue, for the men caught up with him and put a stop to his pawing."

Jehanne pinched the bridge of her nose. What was the matter with her? She could remember nothing but a fast ride, cold snow on her legs, a warm kiss...and her palm smacking against the smooth contours of Fulk's clean-shaven cheek. Her hand went to her throat.

Heaven help her, she had struck Galliard yet again!

Shame seared her, that she had so little control, that he inspired such strong reactions. But she had never before been kissed—not like that, by a grown man, nor with the passion she had felt flowing from him. Jehanne swallowed and looked at Lioba.

"How know you these events?"

"One of Fulk's lot told me all about it. Mogg—a big fellow, built like a boar. He bears no great love for his master. You would do well to befriend him. He might keep us informed."

"Friendship with men is an impossibility. Besides, this Mogg is a hired mercenary like the others, not Fulk's own. He will not be privy to anything useful." Jehanne chafed her arms against the chill. She felt dizzy, tired and hollow.

Lioba rubbed the arnica-mint ointment on Jehanne's shoulders, then draped them with a bed-shawl. "Perhaps. But Galliard has only the Scot at his back."

Jehanne looked into Lioba's vehement eyes. "Please, love, do not think those thoughts. There is no honor in assassination, and Fulk is more clever than I expected. But where is he? What does he now?"

She reached for the dry garment lying at the foot of her bed, an old-fashioned bliaut her mother's mother had worn at court. The dark green fabric hung in loose folds upon her slender frame. She felt like a scarecrow, but there was nothing for it. Most of the few clothes she owned were too big for her now.

"Lord Fulk has gone a-hunting, milady." Lioba's spirals of red hair shook indignantly. "He will be away for days. If we had the men, we could retake the keep."

Jehanne hugged herself, surprised by an irrational pang of disappointment at the news Fulk was out. She firmly squashed the feeling before it could take root.

"All in good time. I should have known he would see to his own pleasure before attending the villeins. Would that there were more of me to go around, what with the lambing come spring, and the planting—oh, Lioba! How will we manage, with so few hands? I cannot bear the thought of famine in the wake of that cursed fever. I should have taken a husband long ago. One strong enough to manage the fief and dull enough to forego glory."

"But, my lady, that is not your nature. You were never meant for the callous bastards the earl and your lord father offered you! Forgive me...." Lioba put a hand to her mouth.

Jehanne smiled wryly. "Always speak your mind, for that is something I can rely upon. I had best go see what is happening downstairs." She headed for the door, still shaky.

"Nay, you must rest, my lady. Galliard ordered me to keep you abed, and for once I agree."

Jehanne swung around. "Ordered you?"

In silence she wrenched the heavy door open and swept out. Galliard had best keep his orders for his own people, not hers. She started down the stairs. The cold stone steps gave way to a section of wooden ones, easily burned in case an enemy tried to gain access to the upper levels.

In her haste Jehanne tripped, scuffing her foot. Her soft cry caught the attention of Mac Niall, who stood warming himself by the central fire in the great hall. He took the stairs two at a time and offered his arm for support.

She refused and the Scot frowned. "Have you stubbed a wee toe, then?"

"It is but a splinter." Jehanne limped to the hearth and took a seat.

"Where are your shoes?"

He sounded just like Lioba did when she scolded.

"If you must know, the dogs ate them, all but my ones for riding."

"Tsk. Let me see it." Malcolm held out his hand.

Jehanne stared at him. "Nay, I will see to it myself."

Malcolm made a sound of impatience. "I'm not going to fondle your limbs, milady, just pick out a wee bit of wood. I'd do it for a dog, do you think I would treat you worse?"

Jehanne pressed her lips together. His remark was reminiscent of what Grimald thought of her. But it was altogether too difficult to tell whether the Scot was jesting or serious. Slowly she extended her foot for him to take.

Propping it upon his hairy knee, he had the splinter out within moments. Before he released her, her skirt slipped to reveal the dagger strapped to her calf.

Malcolm narrowed one eye. "Lass, you had best be careful with a blade like that. If you must needs run, 'twill slip down to your ankle and trip you up. Put it higher, just below the knee."

He favored her with a conspiratorial grin, giving Jehanne time to recover from the surprise of his collaboration. Any other man in his position would have immediately disarmed her. Not to mention that he had indeed passed over the opportunity to stroke her leg.

"You have my thanks, sir."

"You're welcome to all my advice, lady. I had best be off." He put his hands to his thighs and stood.

"Why did you not go hunting with Sir Fulk?" Jehanne wrapped her skirts around her cold feet. Indeed, that was the only advantage to women's attire.

"Och, chasing deer over hill and dale is not a favorite pastime of mine. I much prefer small game and my falcons. But I left them all behind when I came away with Fulk."

From the look in Malcolm's eyes she decided not to ask what else he had left behind, or why. "You have been together a long time?"

"Aye. Longer than most." The Scot gazed at her pointedly.

"Why else he is called The Reluctant?"

"Well, he has forsworn killing." With thumb and forefinger, Malcolm stroked his moustache from the center outward.

Jehanne was indignant. No self-respecting baron should sit by and risk defeat for having taken such a vow. "How can he defend this place if he is not willing to fight off an enemy?"

"I'm thinking he will be leaving that bit for *you* to attend to, milady." Malcolm patted his own dagger, winked, and left abruptly, whistling.

Jehanne stared after him, too surprised to think of an adequate response. Let Galliard and Mac Niall laugh. An overconfident enemy was halfway to defeat. So Sir Thomas always said. Jehanne warmed at the thought of the old man. She would bring him something tasty, and speed him back onto his feet.

A rustle from above caught her attention. Lioba descended the stairs, determination emanating from her every movement. Jehanne sighed in resignation. There was no arguing with Lioba when she got this way.

"All right, Madame Nurse, I will go back to bed, as soon as we take some soup to Thomas. He needs tempting."

"Aye. He's not the only one. You are naught but skin and bone."

With so many of her people still hungry, the thought of food did not appeal to Jehanne, but neither did the prospect of suffering Lioba's ongoing wrath. "Very well. However much he eats, so will I. Will that satisfy you?"

The woman smiled triumphantly. "Good. I shall tell him that, and he will stuff himself on your behalf."

Jehanne smiled. She knew when she was beaten. Lioba crossed the hall to her, and hand in hand, they headed to the kitchen sheds.

Chapter Seven

The surly brindled mastiff ventured closer, and boldly put his nose right to the edge of the table where Hengist the Hurler dined. The knight looked up from his meal long enough to curse and kick at the dog, then he threw his own well-gnawed mutton joint precisely at the animal's retreating hindquarters. With a snarl, the mastiff snapped the bone up and loped with it to a far corner of the hall.

Opposite Hengist, Earl Grimald sat in an ornately carved oaken chair. Nearby, coals glowed in an iron brazier, in addition to the inferno roaring in the main fireplace.

"Have a care with my beast," Grimald drawled, startling Hengist out of his thoughts. Tenting his fingers, the earl looked at him with unreadable, black eyes.

Hengist stopped sucking his greasy forefinger and sat up straight. "You treat your dog better than you do me. Why did you not send *me* to take Windermere? Why give such pleasure, such bounty, to a useless, undeserving wretch like Fulk?"

"Bounty?" Grimald gave him a wintry smile. "Hengist, you have not understood my intent. Think you a decimated, starving fief is bounty? That the Iron Maiden—all gristle and scars—is a prize? Fulk will be fortunate to emerge alive from her clutches. And if he does, you will be awaiting him." The earl tipped his head back and raised his thick brows at a round-eyed page, standing frozen at attention by the door.

Hengist thought back to the one time he had seen the Iron Maiden, at the tourney where they had captured Fulk. Where by virtue of his knife to a girth he had falsely hoped he himself might at last be free of the Earl Grimald. The girl had looked a glorious creature, and even with her sunburnt cheeks and dusty plait, she had carried herself with a noble, pure air of dignity.

His heart lurched at the memory. He longed to possess some small measure of that golden, virtuous pride of hers...he shook his head. Such things were beyond his reach. But perhaps Windermere was not. "What of the keep? It still belongs to the FitzWalter's girl."

"Once Fulk weds her it becomes his."

"Aye! That is my point. He's done nothing to deserve it."

"Ah, but he has, Hengist. He was born to a devil of a French count who made my life a torment for years, with his bloody wit, his ridicule. I gave him aid amongst his enemies, and he rewarded me with scorn. I hated the father and I hate the sons. The one that remains, anyway."

"You speak as though taking Windermere were a punishment."

"I meant it to be just that, Hengist. And the plague that struck was a fortunate twist. The timing was a bit off, but in the end the little bitch was left defenseless, and even if she did not die, her father did. But no one has to know Fulk did not kill him."

Apparently not noticing Hengist's troubled frown, the earl snapped his fingers at the page and pointed to his goblet.

"Sir Alun was my ally, years ago. We committed several, shall we say, profitable indiscretions together. He knew a great deal more than was healthy. I feared one day he might have an attack of conscience. So, I asked for his daughter, hoping to bring a quick resolution to my problem. He doted on her so, he would hold his tongue were she in my hands."

"Sounds reasonable."

"But he knew what I did not—exactly how stubborn she is."

The page, in his haste to refill his lord's cup, dribbled wine onto the table. The earl caught his arm before he could retreat, and the child stilled, white-faced and trembling.

Hengist pursed his lips and stared uneasily at the fair-haired page. A vaguely familiar twist of anxiety assailed his gut. He himself had grown up in the earl's household. As a child, he had once seen his own reflection in a piece of polished steel. He had much resembled this boy...this terrified boy.

If Lexingford was in one of his moods, Hengist thought, there was blessed little he could do for the page—or himself—but try to keep talking. He cleared his throat. "Well, I did believe Alun loyal, until I heard you convince Fulk of his treachery. Why else send anyone to kill him? The king would not stand for an outright attack...oh, I see."

Grimald grinned without humor. "Do you?" He slid his gaze to the flames dancing over the brazier's coals, then dragged the boy's wrist closer to the red shimmer of heat.

Hengist knit his brow and wiped his suddenly damp palms on his surcoat. He tried to think, so he might speak more rapidly, but the effort of logic proved even more difficult than usual.

"So...King Henry will be angered to learn that one of his barons was murdered by a landless coward, who is already guilty of killing another of his favorites, eh? The king wants the keep secure, the river crossing in good repair, the daughter pregnant and out of the way...he'll want the killer hanged."

After a moment of bliss at the thought of Fulk dangling from a rope, Hengist's frown returned. He sniffed. "Still, I would have liked a chance at the girl myself." He meant to woo Jehanne, but dared not express such a sentiment to his lord.

Grimald ignored the page for the moment, and his toothy smile returned. "I am certain you yet will, my lad. But that vixen aside, what of the Lady Celine?"

Hengist nearly stopped breathing. *That* lady was like a fairy princess, or so he had heard. "But you told Fulk he might choose."

"Pah! Dead men have no choices. As you just said, he will have to be brought to justice for his unprovoked assault upon the FitzWalter—a cousin of the king's, I believe. Everyone will soon hear the tale of carnage being so conveniently spread by that vicious little weasel—what was his name—Theseus?"

"Thaddeus," Hengist said. "And good riddance."

"Relatives always make the most treacherous enemies. But imagine Henry's ire when he hears that Fulk—his former ward, no less—has gone berserk. An heiress refused him, so he put her father's head on a pike! Once Fulk is condemned to death, you will be free to use Jehanne, or get rid of her and have the lovely Celine instead. We will emerge as champions of the king, guardians of his interests. And you may be lord of Redware and Windermere both, as long as you channel the greater part of their revenues to me.''

Hengist had grown weak with desire at the suggestion of having not one, but possibly two women at the same time. Then the earl's final statement sank in. "The greater part?"

Grimald's lip curled. "We mustn't forget what you are not, Hengist. A man of consequence, of breeding, of intelligence. You have limits. And I am the one who has made it possible for you to step beyond what should have been your natural restraints. I alone.''

His dark gaze drifted from Hengist to the coals, to the page's hand, as yet unharmed, then to the mastiff. The earl's mouth curved into a dreadful grin, and the page gave a small whimper before he fainted.

Hengist's fist tightened around his eating dagger. He had endured a lifetime of insults. Enough was enough. He tensed his legs to rise, but Grimald lunged over the table, quick as a serpent. He pressed his own blade beside Hengist's nose. The slim piece of steel pricked the younger man's lower eyelid when he blinked.

The earl growled, low and deadly. "I have dealt with dozens like you, lad. I hate to think I've erred in my judgment of your potential, under my guidance." The point dug deeper into the soft flesh below Hengist's eye. "Empty sockets are ugly to behold.''

Tears mingled with the sweat trickling down Hengist's cheeks. He rolled his eyes in an attempt to move them away from danger, and saw the page, still in a heap on the floor. "Aye," he rasped.

"Good," Grimald crooned, easing the pressure of the blade.

The beast in the corner lifted its head and snarled.

"Slayer, he knows." The earl nodded in the direction of the dog. "He's dined on some of my...misjudgments. Haven't you, son?"

Slayer parted his lips and bared his fangs in a grin not unlike his master's. Hengist choked, and Grimald howled with laughter.

Chapter Eight

The hunt over, Fulk allowed his courser to walk the last mile to Windermere. With two days of warming, the snow had all but disappeared, and the horses' hooves sucked noisily in the muddy lanes. Though he was tired, Fulk appreciated the beauty surrounding him.

Long, rippling shreds of cloud swept the evening sky, stained a dusky pink by the setting sun. Far away, a black phalanx of geese winged along, their cries of mutual encouragement carried on the breeze. The naked trees upon the hillsides waited patiently for spring.

Dark limbs twined to form a dense canopy, the bracken beneath still kissed with touches of red amongst the brown, and here and there, a brave tendril of green reached for the light.

The mercenaries laughed and chatted as they rode, satisfied well enough with the slaughter of animals, since at Windermere there had been neither battle nor loot. It had been that sad imperative which had forced Fulk to sell his books in order to pay the men, as well as replace his horses. Grimald had ordered the siege, but he was not about to finance it. In part the arrangement had suited Fulk, for if their wages came from him, then so would the men's loyalty, such as it was, be his.

But the chase had been a great success. The huntsman and his helpers carried deer slung on poles, rabbits over their shoulders, and a variety of birds on strings. At every cottage and croft they passed, villein and freeholder alike, Fulk gave the inhabitants a gift of small game. He wanted them to know they need not fear him, but also to see that he had men and arms enough to keep order in the fief.

A show of force was usually all that was necessary to prevent the need of actually using it. A sword was a last resort, after negotiation and compromise failed. And, in the case of Thaddeus, bribery and intimidation had succeeded where common sense had not.

As Windermere's walls came into view, Fulk recalled the long weeks of siege.

Never would he forget the sight of Jehanne running along the teeth of that sheer wall. God knew how she had managed such a feat. Nor could he forget her deadly aim. It had been a pity to destroy her bow, obviously lovingly crafted.

But her perspective had needed quick correction, and besides, such things did not belong in the hands of angry women. Perhaps one day he could make it up to her. Should he ever actually wed her, some sort of gift was in order.

But he would worry about that when the time came.

If the time came.

Jehanne hovered restlessly at the foot of the stairs, awaiting Fulk's entry. Doubt pricked at her decision to approach her problem—*him*—from a different angle. She would treat her enemy as an honored guest. She would smother him in kindness, shame him by her exalted manners.

Though it felt a great deal like surrender, under the circumstances she could do no less. In all the tales of chivalry she had heard, there was no such thing as an excess of courtesy, whether dealing with friend or foe.

To that end, Lioba had brushed Jehanne's hair until it shone like burnished gold. Jehanne had even gone so far as to don a kirtle of blue wool, with a long-sleeved undergown of creamy linen. A belt of gilded, leaf-shaped links rested on her hips.

The hall was in order, beeswax candles lit, fresh straw and rushes upon the floor. In the once-cold fire circle, flames leaped, the finest, driest wood sacrificed in order to limit the smoke.

Her unruly dogs had been banished to the back bailey, and her kestrel rested upon a perch at the high table. All the serving men and women had been made to wash their faces and hands.

Jehanne gazed about, satisfied with what she saw. Her father's sword and shield hung gleaming upon the wall above the chair that had been his—and was now hers. The house of FitzWalter was nothing if not generous, and she, Jehanne of Windermere, was not about to let Fulk de Galliard see it otherwise.

She heard his deep voice, and Malcolm's answering burr amidst the murmur of the men-at-arms. A breath of cold air preceded them as the anteroom's door opened and closed. Ahead of the others, Fulk strode into the hall and stopped.

Jehanne hid her satisfaction at the look of surprise on his face.

"I see I find you well, lady." He rested his heavy bow and its quiver of arrows upon a trestle. His face was grimed and his clothes dripped bits of leaves and moss as he drew off his gauntlets. Throwing gloves atop weaponry, Fulk joined Malcolm and the lancers as they gathered about the fire.

Jehanne stood tall, doing her best to look queenly. "Aye, as I do you, Sir Fulk. You and your men must be hungry. Meat and ale are ready. And if you wish to relax, a hot bath awaits you in the solar."

Fulk raised his brows. He crossed his arms and gazed at her for a long, uncomfortable moment. "What brings this on?"

"Have you no experience of courtesy?" she countered, with the exact tone of irritation he had used in the bailey when he had kissed her hand.

"Not in a lioness's den."

He smiled, no doubt assuming his charm would soothe the barb. It did—a bit—but Jehanne was not ashamed. Lions were part of her family crest, and Fulk knew it.

He continued, "I thank you, my lady. I will not allow your servants' labor to go to waste." Turning, he started up the stairs.

Jehanne followed determinedly.

Fulk halted and looked over his shoulder at her, his smile gone. "You will not presume to attend me." His regal tone demanded obedience.

"It is my duty and privilege."

Fulk shook his head. "I want none of your duty, and I grant you no privilege."

Jehanne would have just as soon dispensed with the so-called privilege, but her duty as baroness, especially one without daughters of a suitable age, dictated that she personally bathe noble guests and see them comfortably to their beds.

"You dishonor me. You dishonor yourself, by being so churlish."

He seemed to consider this, then gave her a disarming grin, both wicked and appealing. "Well then. Come if you dare. But only under certain conditions."

"What are they?" Trepidation caught Jehanne square in the stomach, so confident did Fulk sound.

"We will not be alone whilst I am wet and naked at your mercy. Nor will I allow you to behold me in that state." He continued climbing upwards, as if the matter were settled.

Jehanne caught up her skirts, cursed them silently and hurried after Fulk, dimly aware that Malcolm was behind her.

"I welcome the presence of anyone who might assist me, but how am I to carry out my charge without looking at you?"

"By feel. Blindfold her, Malcolm," Fulk advised, without breaking stride. "It is the simplest solution. I would never trust a woman not to peek."

"Right-o, lad," the Scot replied.

"Do I have your solemn promise?" From the threshold of the solar, Fulk gazed at Jehanne, his amber eyes gleaming.

She could not back down now. "Aye. I will do as you wish. Though I do not see the point."

Fulk nodded, then disappeared through the doorway, shutting her outside the chamber as he went.

Jehanne rounded on the Scot and caught him grinning. "Insufferable, the pair of you!"

"Aye, I'll not argue with you, lady. Fulk has taught me that much in manners."

Pressing her lips together, Jehanne put her hand to the carved wood of the door to push it open. She gasped as thick fingers closed about her wrist.

Malcolm loomed at her back. "Nay, lady. Not 'til I've bound

your eyes. Fulk can shed his chausses faster than any man alive, I'll warrant.''

"A feat he is proud of, no doubt."

"Nay, just glad about, lady. Fulk takes no pride in his prowess, but he is grateful for it."

Jehanne did not dignify Malcolm's observation with a response. He made her wait while he felt about his person for the required material for the blindfold. When he came up empty-handed, she lost her patience and pulled off her rarely worn veil.

"Use my head-cloth if you must, for goodness' sake!"

Thrusting it toward him, she added, "At least I know it's clean."

Malcolm took the linen with a flourish. "You are unkind, mademoiselle, especially when you havenae offered *me* a bath!"

"Make his 'lairdship' share, then."

"Och, we would ne'er fit, and the water would be all outside the tub." Malcolm wound the fabric about her head, covering her eyes twice with a double layer.

"This is absurd! And you know very well I did not mean the both of you at once. Ah—not so tight!"

"A promise is a sacred thing, lady, and if Fulk doesnae want you to lay eyes upon him, nor shall ye, not as long as I am here to prevent it."

"It isn't as though I would be the first."

"Indeed not. But mayhap you are different from the others, in his mind. Have you thought of that?" The Scot put his big hands upon her shoulders, ready to guide her into the solar.

"Indeed not," Jehanne echoed, knowing full well Malcolm knew she *had* thought of it. "Let's get on with this. And hark you," she warned. "Don't allow me to accidentally touch him where I should not. I will not have the two of you making a fool of me."

Malcolm made a soothing noise. "Now that would be impossible, I trow, with one so steely as thee. But shall I call Mistress Lioba, just to ensure that we behave ourselves?"

"Nay!" Jehanne blurted, regretting her vehemence. "I need no more protection from him than the dagger at my waist and the one strapped below my knee—which advice I thank you for, by the way. I hope you do not have cause to regret it.''

"Nay, nay. Fulk's disarmed many a fiesty lass, I have no worry.''

That was not the reply she wanted to hear.

Gently, Malcolm pushed her into the solar, and Jehanne could hear the sound of belts and boots clumping to the floor. The steamy fragrance of rosemary and sage in the hot water eased her rapid breathing. She wished it were *her* bath, and that she was soaking in it, blissfully alone in her chamber.

Part of her was relieved not to have to look upon Fulk, and part was furious that he teased—acting as if the sight of his body could matter one whit to her, and pretending he had the smallest shred of modesty.

Fulk was most cordial in his greeting. "I bid you well come, lady, and my thanks, Hunterson, for escorting her.''

"You see, mademoiselle, Galliard is tame as a kitten. He will do ye no harm. Och, he's dipping his dagger in the bath, and now his finger, and now he is tasting it—"

"What tedious ritual is this?" Jehanne demanded, irked that she could not see for herself.

"In case of acid, my lady," Fulk drawled. "Or poison. Right, Malcolm?''

"Aye, I've finally taught you some small measure of caution.''

They both had raised their voices, as if being blindfolded meant she could not hear. "What an outrageous notion.''

"Methinks you would do just about anything to keep Windermere out of my hands, or anyone else's," Fulk said.

He was right enough about that, so Jehanne held her tongue.

There was a final dull thump, as of a bundle of clothes landing across the solar, then the plop and swish of a body entering the bath. Fulk's sigh of happiness was accompanied by the unmistakable sound of water sloshing onto the flagstones.

"Told ye," Malcolm whispered. "Here he is, now. All yours.''

The Scot led Jehanne forward. Without warning, he placed her hands upon Fulk's wet shoulders, a complex combination of heavy muscle and bone that felt alarmingly warm and alive.

Hastily she withdrew.

"Shirking already?" he asked.

"Certainly not. Malcolm, kindly provide me with a sponge and soap." She waited. "Malcolm?"

The scrape of the door's closing was the only reply.

"Of all the—" Jehanne stopped herself. They were trying to goad her into anger. She could play along just as well. "Your guardian has abandoned you to my care. Are you not afraid?"

"Oh, aye. Malcolm's warned me of your various prickly spots. But as you have pointed out, you are honor bound not to slaughter one who has broken bread in your hall."

"You have broken more than that." The thought of her bow still rankled. "Soap, sir?"

The wooden bowl settled into her palms as Fulk transferred it. "Here. Wash me as you will. There is a table to your right to set it upon."

"This is really most difficult. How can I bathe you properly unless I can see? I don't *want* to see you," she added, almost truthfully, "but I need to."

"My, that presents quite a contradiction. No matter. Just feel your way over me. Surely you know the significant landmarks?" Fulk splashed a bit, as if to give her a hint.

"Aye," she said grimly. "I will begin with your hard head." Jehanne reached for him. But did not find him.

There was a greater splashing, then the sound of Fulk's emergence from underwater. A slap of warm liquid hit Jehanne's chest and quickly grew cold. He must have ducked, then thrown his head back. Apart from a sharp intake of breath, she refrained from complaint. She would give him no cause to censure her manners. But then again...

Jehanne extended her soapy hands and met his head from behind. His wet locks curled around and between her fingers, thick and slippery. She rubbed the soap in, and found herself trembling with a riot of conflicting emotions.

To touch this man so casually, as though he represented no assault on her freedom, as though she accepted him as a new part of her life, was asking the impossible.

It would be easy to jerk his head back by the hair and slit his throat. Or throttle him with the blindfold. Or, easier still, to let her hands drift from his scalp, slide down his neck and begin to knead those broad, bare shoulders...

Fulk gave a little groan of pleasure, as if she were actually rubbing him. Jehanne brought her thoughts sharply under control. She would not harm him, for he had indeed eaten at her table, but nor would she touch him without the sponge between his skin and hers.

Where *had* that wretched sponge got to?

Fulk slipped down away from her and dunked himself again. This time she sidestepped to safety as he noisily resurfaced.

"What next?" he asked, sputtering.

"Give me the sponge, and your back."

He pressed it into Jehanne's hand, and gingerly, awkwardly, she began to scrub.

As she leaned over the edge of the tub, her foot slipped on the wet stone floor. Catching Fulk by one shoulder she held on to him briefly before finding her balance.

His skin was smooth and unmarked to her sensitive fingers. An untoward bitterness filled her throat, that a great hulking lout like him should be thus, while she—

"Sorry about the flood. But you have good hands, lady. My aches and pains flee with your every touch."

"Hmmph," Jehanne replied, working her way down his flank, over ridges of hard flesh and rib. She reached in the direction of the table, where she had left the soap bowl, then cried out as Fulk roughly pulled her arm against his neck.

"Unhand me!"

"You were about to pass your wrist through the candle flame. But as long as you are here—" Fulk pressed her palm to his breast, and urged her hand into small circles. He fed it soap and moved it over the silky hair on his chest, until it dipped between the muscles and rose to the opposite side.

"If I crook my elbow, you will choke, sir." Jehanne gritted her teeth in her effort not to do just that. That he would make so bold with her—

"If you crook your elbow, you will be in the drink with me, pate-first." As if to prove his point, Fulk tugged gently on her arm, until her breasts touched the back of his head.

She jerked upward, freeing herself, and hurled the sponge. It landed on the floor with a splat. "Have you no sense of decorum? Is everything a game of dalliance with you? I am soaked. This is ridiculous. You are unfair."

"Shall I release you from your promise not to look at me? Then you will not need my guidance." His tone was one of perfect reasonability, as if he spoke to a cretinous child.

It drove Jehanne mad.

"I have no desire to behold you! I do not need your guidance! I need no one's help, I—"

There was a powerful upsurge of water, and Jehanne cringed involuntarily at his sudden motion. She knew Fulk stood before her, though still in the bath, and instinctively raised her hand to sweep off the blindfold. She would not be his victim without a fight.

His firm voice stopped her. "Nay. I have not yet released you. Finish what you've begun, or leave. I asked for none of this. I will jump in the lake next time, and save you the trouble."

"I feel humiliated with my eyes bound," Jehanne admitted, angry at herself for being afraid, even for a moment. "Why do you insist?"

Fulk sighed. "Take the cloth off, then. But my reticence is difficult to explain. You will probably laugh." There was a discreet swirling of water. "There. I'm sitting again."

With both apprehension and relief Jehanne slid the linen from her eyes. She smoothed her hair and gazed warily at Fulk. He rested the back of his neck against the tub edge, his eyes closed, his long, muscular throat exposed.

The firelight spangled his wet skin with red-gold reflections, shimmering with each breath he took. His bent knees rose above the surface, and as the water retreated, the hair on his legs formed a line down the front of each shin.

Over the rim of the tub his right hand dangled, relaxed and empty. A well-made hand, powerful yet elegant. But Jehanne narrowed her eyes at the sight of a thick scar across his wrist.

It was the first sign she had seen of any serious wound he had suffered. Indeed, he bore remarkably few battle scars. She did not know if that was a result of skill, cowardice, or if by virtue of his size he merely frightened other men away. In any event, at the moment he was defenseless—at least relatively so.

It occurred to Jehanne that by allowing her to bathe him, by resting there with his eyes closed, Fulk trusted her with his life. His test for poison had been pure nonsense, but he did not discount her by assuming she had not the strength or will to kill him.

He paid her the highest compliment one knightly enemy could give another—that he knew he could rely upon her honor, even to her own cost.

"Go ahead and explain if you wish. I will listen," she offered gently.

He opened one eye and peered at her. "Is that Jehanne of Windermere? Or are you her long-lost, honey-tongued twin?"

Jehanne arched a brow. "Are you trying to resummon the one full of ire? She is yet close by."

He grinned conspiratorially. "Nay, let her listen at the door whilst we have a friendly chat."

Jehanne could not help but return his smile. She pulled a stool next to the tub and sat. Lord, who would have thought?

Fulk cleared his throat. "This will no doubt sound terribly vain to you, but here it is. You see, I spent the greater part of my boyhood at Henry's court, as a hostage, to ensure my lord father's cooperation. But I was well kept—a page, squire, all that. And at his court, being the place of elegance and refinement that it is, every youth is assigned to a lady.

"Apart from his achieving all the skills of arms and horsemanship, he learns from this woman the arts of chivalry. How to behave courteously, dine in a mannerly fashion, sing, dance, play an instrument, speak properly and develop enough wit to entertain demoiselles and grande dames alike."

Hesitating, Fulk rubbed under his jaw with the backs of his fingers.

"How charming. I never would have guessed," Jehanne murmured.

"Oh, I thank you for that, Baroness!" He growled and began to wash himself, as if the conversation were over.

Why did he assume she knew nothing of court life? True, she

did not, but that was no excuse. "It was merely a jest. You have the manners of a Saracen prince, I trow. Do go on."

"Well. I was a big lad."

She slapped her knees. "You don't mean it!"

"Do not interrupt." Fulk sniffed and frowned. "When I was but ten and five, I looked nearly twenty, so I was told. The court ladies liked what they saw. They pursued, and at first I fled, but...well, I began to learn a great deal more than table manners. It was heaven for a time, but they wounded me, more than once. Women of position and power looked at me—even touched me—whenever they wished, as if I were some great, well-favored beast without sensibilities. That's all," he finished lamely.

"You poor, poor thing." Hiding her smile, Jehanne shook her head.

From beneath black, water-clumped lashes Fulk gave her a slow, daunting look. Her mirth vanished and she wanted to turn her face away. His dark-gold eyes, his damp, glowing skin, the impressive parts of him that showed above the bath—hinting at what lay beneath—all these held a disturbing, overwhelming attraction.

Perhaps it was true that jaded, sophisticated women would not search beyond his animal beauty. Perhaps they would assume there was nothing more, and with such a spectacularly well-honed body, why would they wish to complicate their pleasure?

But, it was extraordinarily difficult for Jehanne to imagine any young man in that position caring that he was unappreciated. Whatever the case, the sooner he was dressed, the better. She stood and brought him some lengths of toweling. "The water is growing cold. Shall I turn my back?"

He gazed up—not at her face—and grinned. "I see you're wet, and none too warm, either. Aye, by all means, turn around."

Her cheeks blazing, Jehanne crossed her arms. She would not be intimidated. "There. No need."

"As you will." Fulk shrugged and gripped the sides of the cloth-lined tub, ready to rise.

Jehanne bit her lip. He *was* just another comely male animal, nothing more. If she looked upon him it would be no different from viewing a bull or a stallion or a ram, except—she was most assuredly not considering the selection of *this* male animal for breeding purposes.

Fulk surged out of the water, but at the last moment Jehanne averted her eyes. She wanted no memory of his nakedness to remain and torment her. The only problem was, her wayward mind insisted upon imagining what it had not actually seen.

She wanted to kick herself. And Fulk.

"You are a gracious lady, to be so considerate of my comfort," he murmured, the linen already wrapped about his lean hips. He reached for another towel and began to rub his hair.

His unexpected, soft words, which sounded sincere, diffused Jehanne's irritation. She recalled his look when he had first entered the hall that evening. Not one of triumphant homecoming after a pleasurable two days of sport. Just simple dog-tiredness.

"What did you bring down in the hunt?" she asked.

"Enough to feed this place the rest of the winter, if you are frugal."

That surprised her. "Thank you. I could not have done so well on my own, I must confess."

"Why should you have to? My men and I are here, therefore we must be of service."

Jehanne had no reply to that. She began to search for his royal-hued robe, just to cover her startlement.

But Fulk went to the bed, slid beneath the covers, and sent the towel he had been wearing sailing across the chamber.

She watched as he punched and arranged his pillow. "Are you not coming down to dine?"

"Nay." He turned on his side, his back to her.

"Do you want a trencher brought up?"

"Too weary."

Jehanne began to move toward the door. "Then you need nothing else?"

Fulk rolled to face her again with a languid smile. "I do have a need, at that."

She stiffened. If he wanted relief, it was best she found it for him, before he had his men drag in some hapless female. As long as it was not she herself he had in mind. "I imagine there is a willing wench about, if you will be patient."

His eyes widened. "Jesu, but you are quick to jump to conclusions. I merely meant to say my hunting tunic is torn, and if someone could mend it, I would be grateful. Truly, I need no procuress."

"Oh—of course not." At that moment Jehanne wished *he* were blindfolded, her face felt so hot. She found the wadded garment, identified its holes, and tucked it under her arm.

"Your hospitality knows no bounds." Fulk grinned and winked. "Worry not, I shan't tell a soul."

Her attempts at courtesy were a complete and utter disaster in the face of a slippery devil like him. "Good night," Jehanne managed to choke out, then hurriedly departed the solar.

From the corridor she could still hear his laughter.

A few chilly days later, for Jehanne had barely spoken to him since the bath, Fulk found his way to the keep's tiny scriptorium. Dust covered the small, slanted table and every other surface in the chamber.

Apparently the late Sir Alun had kept his records by notching tally sticks, for there was nothing useful apart from the simple furnishings and the fading afternoon light. Fulk had been putting off what had to be done, and he had best get on with it.

Flattening one of his last, precious sheets of parchment, he dipped his goose quill into the makeshift ink he had concocted, a dubious mixture of rusty water, oak gall, and wine.

He held the pen over the clean yellow surface, hating to make that first mark, which would commit him to finishing the letter. He bit his lip and carefully drew the vertical stroke of a *T*, precise and sharp-edged.

"What are you doing?"

"Shite!" Fulk jumped at Jehanne's voice, coming from behind. His knee knocked the underside of the table, and in its bowl the dark liquid shivered precariously. A large brown splotch now adorned the top of the page.

"Hmm. Can't you do better than that?" Jehanne peered over his shoulder.

"Nay! Not with you creeping about." Fulk found his bit of rag and frantically blotted the parchment, with little improvement.

Jehanne came around to face him and gazed at his effort with a critical eye. She was back to wearing a squire's garb, and had an exquisite little falcon perched upon her shoulder. "Have you any other colors? You might turn it into a nightingale, or a blossom."

Jehanne glanced at the sheet once more and tapped her lips with a slender finger. "Then again..."

"I am writing a letter, not illuminating scripture. Go away."

"A letter to whom?"

"My sister."

"Regarding what?"

Fulk looked up and scowled. "You make it impossible to concentrate." Didn't she just. Standing there, her mere breathing an act of grace, with that jewel of a kestrel nestled by her cheek.

She pursed her lips. "If it is a secret letter, I would not use parchment unless I had armed couriers to deliver it."

"Oh?"

"Send a wax tablet instead, so that it might be easily eradicated. Or make your messenger learn by heart what you wish to relay to her."

Fulk pushed away from the table. "What I wish to say will not fit upon a rude wax tablet, nor do I want any messenger to know what I would tell Celine in private."

"A delicate matter?"

"Aye."

"Something she will not be happy to hear, no doubt." Jehanne crossed her arms.

"Perhaps not." Fulk stood, his heart thudding for no discernable reason.

"Then you should tell her in person. It is a coward's way to send another with unpleasant news." A small crease formed between Jehanne's brows.

Fulk opened his mouth to make a rebuttal, then thought better of it. "I have no choice. I cannot be in two places at once."

Jehanne fingered the thin sheepskin. "It is spoilt, for your fine purposes."

"Do you wish to send a letter as well?"

"My petition to the king?" She gave him an arch look.

"Don't ask my help in composing it."

"I need no help. Not in this endeavor nor in any other."

"So you have told me before. Take a fresh parchment, then, and the ink, and my quill, and my seat, and go to it. His Grace will ignore your plea, as he has mine."

Apparently unperturbed, Jehanne slid onto the bench. The kestrel craned its neck and eyed Fulk. Jehanne picked up the pen, and Fulk resisted the urge to correct the way she held it, as if she were about to stab the parchment instead of write upon it.

She looked up at him. "Henry will appreciate my heartfelt sincerity. And he will want to see justice done."

"I doubt it."

"What did you do to offend him, besides refusing adubbement?"

Fulk retreated from her earnest look. How could he possibly explain such a monumental disaster? Slowly, he brought his hand closer to Jehanne's shoulder, offering it for the kestrel to examine.

Keeping his gaze on the bird's compact, elegant head, Fulk continued. "Henry had a favorite, a knight who excelled in all things. One day—a very long, hot day—this knight and I argued. I struck him. I killed him." *I killed him...I killed him...*the words echoed endlessly in Fulk's mind, like a bell tolling for the dead.

"How unfortunate. For him in particular."

"For many people."

"This knight was well-loved?"

"Aye."

"By you especially, I'll warrant, for him to have angered you so. But, I think you have left out the meat of the story."

Fulk stared at Jehanne. Her eyes were wide, clear, filled with sadness. She was too young to understand such things. Or should have been. "It is a story best left untold," he murmured, keeping his gaze on the kestrel.

"The difficulty lies in enduring the weight of such an unspeakable tale in one's heart, not knowing how long or how far one must go before the burden will be eased," she responded, her voice equally low.

With an ache in his throat Fulk regarded her stricken expression. She referred to herself. What horror had she survived, apart from the obvious tribulations of her life? He could not ask, for her pride would never allow her to reveal it, no more than could he fully speak of his sorrow. "For some, the weight will be there forever," he said.

Jehanne put the pen down and folded her hands, looking at him thoughtfully. "You smile like a condemned man who mocks the executioner."

Fulk had to admire her astuteness. "Well, I am no longer afraid. I merely wait for the axe to fall. The inevitable, as you once put it." He held his breath as the wee hawk lowered and tilted her head to eye his hand more closely.

"I don't understand."

"I am on the block and I am the axeman, in one."

"That is a heavy burden, indeed."

Without warning the kestrel stepped from Jehanne's shoulder to Fulk's wrist. He winced as the needle-sharp talons gripped his unprotected flesh, but was careful not to frighten the small bird. He made small kissing noises, and stroked her breast with the back of one finger.

"But she hates men!" Though Jehanne's voice was tinged with indignation, she made no sudden moves. It seemed she too preferred that he be spared further injury from her pet.

Perhaps she still wanted to inflict it upon him herself.

"Ah. If the falcon finds me acceptable, then it would be logical to assume either that I am not much of a man, or she has regained a proper sense of judgment." Fulk stepped toward Jehanne and saw the muscles in her jaw tense. "Stand and be still, and I will return her to you."

Jehanne's glance flicked to him and away again. She rose and stood before him. Straight-backed, her chin up, as might a son stand before his angry father—afraid, but too proud to run. Fulk brought his left hand closer to her face.

A muscle in her cheek contracted, a tiny flicker of motion. She fixed her gaze, looking out the window opening, where, on the horizon, purpled clouds were rapidly fading to blue-gray. A place far beyond his reach.

Awkwardly, Fulk smoothed Jehanne's gold-dusted hair out of the way. He brought the kestrel to the back of her shoulder. With a twist of his arm he encouraged the bird to step onto the leather patch on Jehanne's heavy tunic.

"That's a bonny girl...." Fulk lavished praise upon the falcon as he rubbed his punctured skin. "Why do you not have jesses on her?"

"If she doesn't want to be with me, I will not force her." Now Jehanne met his eyes, and her gaze did not waver.

Fulk swallowed. "But without them, no one knows she is not wild, that she belongs to you."

"I know. She knows. It is enough."

Something in her tone—certainty, or pride—told Fulk there was no chance of his inclusion in Jehanne's small circle of trust. But no matter. His first duty was to see Celine safely wed. To a wealthy, powerful, gentle man, preferably one past the age of wanting to run off to battle, but still vigorous enough to give her children.

Once that was done, he would help Jehanne train a force to defend Windermere. Then he would go back to the king, on his knees if necessary, and have Hengist replaced by a worthy baron. Perhaps he would never himself be lord of Redware. But he could beg on his people's behalf. He would give his head, if it came to that.

Jehanne coughed. "Sir Fulk."

Roused from his thoughts, he blinked. "Aye?"

"Do you have any familiarity with sheep?"

Fulk suppressed a grimace. "Good lord. Certainly not."

"What of manual labor? Also known as *work*." She tilted her head most charmingly, just as the kestrel had.

He found himself suddenly stupid. "Work?"

"A simple enough concept, but I see it is beyond you. Well." Her smile held a certain element of mischief, if not malice. "On the morrow you shall get to know my sheep. All three hundred and twelve of them."

Chapter Nine

Jehanne breathed in the scent of wet wool and sighed happily. Ewes bulged with lambs. The spring verdure sprang forth thick and fresh. Her sheep were in better condition than she had dared hope, but a busy season lay ahead, and Windermere was not a place where one could sit idly on one's pride. Everyone had to help. Perhaps a taste of menial drudgery would serve to convince Fulk this fief was best left to her.

She watched as the shepherd, Sperling, paced along the edges of the flock, his ragged mantle flowing, his skin dark from both dirt and sun. Half-wild, he rarely came to the keep even to receive food or wages. But Jehanne had always gotten along with him, and appreciated his knowledge and vigilance when it came to sheep.

"Well done, Sperling! You have kept the wolves hungry this year."

Unsmiling, the shepherd nodded his acknowledgment.

Jehanne glanced to see if Fulk paid heed and laughed aloud. He stood some distance apart, his back to a tree, still fending off the aggressive, long-horned bellwether that considered him a menace. Earlier Jehanne had demanded that Fulk not ride, as Sperling had a distinct fear of mounted men. Fulk had agreed to leave his courser nearby. Even without a horse, the knight would dwarf the shepherd.

"That is Fulk de Galliard, Sperling. He will not harm you while he is here."

The shepherd paused and looked from Fulk to Jehanne. An

expression of profound sympathy filled his dark eyes. He cast his gaze to the ground. A jab of fear caught Jehanne's heart.

"What? What do you see?" The young man was fey, everyone said so. But he almost never spoke. And now he and his dogs began to drive the flock into the narrow lane. "Nay, Sperling, we will not be able to get through!"

The shepherd's expression grew stubborn, and he continued as if he had not heard. Fulk, freed at last by the bellwether's return to duty, marched toward them from the other side of the flock. The sheep grew more agitated, bleating and jostling each other. Fulk looked angry. He was saying something, but Jehanne could not hear him over the din. He began to gesture, jump up and down, point at her, trying to push his way toward her through the surging animals.

At first bewildered, Jehanne quickly realized he was not pointing at her, but beyond her. She turned and looked toward the swift, dark waters of the Leven. A half-dozen riders rounded the bend at a gallop and clattered across the timbered bridge. At their head was a stout warrior, blond hair flowing from beneath his old-fashioned, open-faced helm, like a Saxon or a Norseman. He let his horse run unchecked, and gripped an axe with both hands.

Jehanne froze, her mind churning. She did not have her usual assortment of weapons, only her dagger. Fulk roared, and started picking up ewes, flinging them left and right, making a path toward her that only closed behind him. The strangers were almost upon her.

A hundred sheep stood between her and safety. Jehanne looked at Sperling. Whatever happened, she could not bear him coming to harm. His lips, the only clean part of his face, had paled. Then they moved. "M-milady, the sheep are as a river, filled with stepping stones."

How absurdly poetic. With a smile of gratitude, Jehanne understood and jumped upon the back of a sturdy ewe. "Let us cross, Sperling!" Just as she did along the merlons of the battlements, she ran from back to back, never slowing enough to let the animals' milling make her slip or lose her balance. Sperling, light and agile, followed suit.

Fulk stared, astonishment written on his face. He released the ewe struggling in his arms and caught Jehanne as she was about to leap past him. She fought to free herself.

"Come with me!" He dragged her through the rest of the flock, then took her at a run toward his horse.

"Nay! Will you not fight them while I get my javelin?"

"I will not." Fulk pulled her along by one hand, as if she were a child. Sperling followed, though obviously distraught at leaving his defenseless charges in the lane.

Jehanne tried to yank herself free, to no avail. "So it is true you value your skin above your honor?"

"Think what you like." Fulk threw her upon his courser's back as easily as he had tossed the ewes.

Sperling stood nearby, his eyes wide. He looked alternately from his lady to his precious sheep and the men who were slaughtering them. In a few strides Fulk was upon him. He caught the terrified shepherd by the scruff of his neck and bodily heaved him onto the horse, behind Jehanne.

"Save him, if not yourself, lady," Fulk said.

She looked down into his upturned face. Into his eyes, large and warm. "You would have Sperling take your place?"

"There is no difference between us, in God's sight."

Jehanne glanced at Fulk's left side and realized he had not brought his sword. "There is room. Hurry up and get on!" She held out her hand.

He answered with a smart slap to the courser's flank. By the time she had the animal under control, had pushed Sperling off its rump into the shelter of the forest and galloped back, the blond knight was resting his crimsoned axe upon his thigh.

Fulk stood before him. No fight. No challenge. Nothing but what appeared to be polite conversation. Jehanne observed warily, while the gray snorted and pawed the ground. After a few more words, the strange knight touched the brow of his helm in an apparent salute to Fulk. He gave Jehanne a long look, then wheeled his horse and led his men away, leaving a scattering of dead ewes in his wake.

The sheep, distressed by the smell of blood, moved in a stream around Jehanne, heading back to the fields. She urged the courser forward. Her belly clenched at the sight of the limp animals in the roadway.

"What means this? Some noble friend of yours, come for sport?"

Fulk rubbed his neck. "That, my lady, was Hengist, the Hurler of Longlake. He paid this visit as a courteous—for him—warning, a reminder of our enmity. He takes his example from the earl, who, as you well know, draws every bit of pleasure he can from the fear he inspires. Except it seems Hengist does possess a few polluted drops of decency."

"This—Hengist—might have killed you. Why didn't he?"

Fulk shrugged. "His pride did not allow him to cut down a fellow knight who bore no weapon. There is no glory in it. So I am afraid he took his disappointment out upon your sheep."

The situation crystallized in Jehanne's mind. "Hengist is Grimald's bear-baiter...and you are the bloody bear!"

Fulk closed his eyes. For a moment his face was serene, almost angelic. Then he frowned. "So it would appear," he said, and with a heavy sigh, came to lean against his horse's hip. "I have promised him satisfaction. But not here, not now. I am sorry about your sheep. Are you going to give me back my courser?"

"I can walk home. As for the sheep, I cannot lay the blame for their loss upon you."

Jehanne slid down from the tall horse. The animal promptly reached around with its head and shoved her between the shoulder blades. Fulk stepped forward and she bumped into his chest. She dug her heels into the ground to spring away, but he held her, his hands at the small of her back.

"Did you train him to do that?" She wriggled in vain to free herself. Fulk gave her a negative shake of his head. Jehanne had to look up to see his face, and the trace of a tight smile. He met her eyes. She forgot to struggle. His body, pressed against hers, felt as though his clothing barely contained it.

Of a sudden he was a dark storm, laden with emotion, ready to unleash himself upon her. He was solid, hard muscle—twice her size. His fingers flexed and rose to her waist in a slow caress. Warmth crept from deep inside, up and up, until her cheeks stung and she knew her scar was livid.

Enough of his pawing. Jehanne ducked her head and punched Fulk below his ribs. And again, as hard as she could. It was like beating a side of beef. He continued to gaze down at her, as if he had not noticed the blows, but a now cold light gleamed from his eyes.

"Thrice, now. You do enjoy danger," he said quietly. Too quietly. "You have a voice, woman. Use it instead of your fists."

She swallowed, her throat dry. "Let me go."

Immediately Fulk's weight shifted and his hands left her body. He turned and started to walk away.

Jehanne took a deep breath, and balled her hands to stop their shaking. "Do not ever touch me again...w-without asking."

He halted, his back to her. Slowly, he came about, his palm upon his midsection. "I would make the same request of you, my lady." A short bow later he was striding down the lane. He climbed up the embankment into the meadow, and headed cross-country, abandoning both Jehanne and his horse.

"Where are you going?" she called, feeling angry and foolish at once.

"To have a drink with Sperling," Fulk said flatly. "And to thank him for his quickness on your behalf."

For all your vast experience with women, you have much to learn about me, Jehanne thought. She remounted Fulk's horse and set to helping the dogs move the flock back to pasture. Fulk could have his drink, and talk all he wanted to whomever he chose. But she would not let this attack upon her livelihood go unavenged. Once she had recovered her strength, the troll, Hengist, would pay.

Fulk strode through the fields, his heart racing. *Don't run. Don't run from her.* He kept to a walk, forcing back his anger at Jehanne's incredible audacity. Not only had she been ready to battle Hengist right there in the lane, she had struck *him,* Fulk, her only protector, yet again.

It was intolerable. He had nearly slapped her. The thought horrified him. Never before had he allowed a woman to provoke him to the point of violence. Nor had any woman ever stirred his blood as did Jehanne. She was so very earnest in all the things she did, so idealistic, so...stubborn. He admired her courage, and bemoaned her foolhardiness.

Soon Hengist would return for him. Why, Fulk was not certain. But the Hurler needed no reason, once he considered a man his enemy.

And that meant Jehanne would be in danger again. She should get away from the keep, go upon a quest of some sort, out of reach of the earl and his familiars. Or better yet, he himself should go, and draw Hengist away. But he could not leave her alone. He could not leave her at all.

The realization was like her fist pounding his gut. This wretched place was one big trap, closing about him. And Jehanne was the bait. What an irony. He, who had tasted a great many females of peerless beauty and elegance, was slowly succumbing to the unlikely charms of a warrior-maiden, as used to a sword in her hands as other women were their distaffs.

Fulk shook his head and concentrated on the task at hand, scanning the ground for traces of Sperling's passing. Whatever happened between himself and Jehanne, Windermere needed defending, and all who benefited from the land should participate. The shepherd could not have gone too far in such a short time.

Fulk cut through a hedgerow, and a field stretched before him, divided into strips, some still fallow and others already under cultivation. In those, feathery shoots rippled like a breath of green blown along the dark soil.

He paused to watch the villeins as they broke the crusty, untilled earth with their hoes. Men and women, hard and weather-beaten, their half-naked children alongside, gaped at the sight of the new lord, alone, afoot and unarmed.

"I seek Sperling the Shepherd. Have you seen him?" Fulk addressed a young man who had straightened from his planting. His neck was wrapped in ragged wool, his hands were thick and red from the cold. A tired-looking woman, big with child, stood behind him, gripping a cloth sack. Fulk recognized it as a seed-bag he had brought to relieve Windermere after the siege.

"Yonder." The villein indicated the forest with a brief jerk of his head, and returned to his work. The woman stared at Fulk for a moment. She caressed the bag's rounded sides, then touched her distended belly. Her eyes burned bright with unspoken emotion.

Fulk looked away briefly. How easily death visited the poor. A few grains of oats were all that stood between her and starvation. "Be well," he said. "Send word when the babe comes. Lady Jehanne will want to bring you something, I am certain."

Leaving the couple behind, he made his way toward the wood. He caught a flicker of movement in the underbrush, as one shadow merged with another.

"Sperling? I would speak with you." His patience was rewarded by the shepherd's appearance, like a creature of the forest, hesitant, yet unable to resist the call to light and open air.

"The baroness needs help, Sperling, and I would ask your aid in giving it. What say you?"

Keeping his wary gaze upon Fulk all the while, the shepherd reached within his mantle and brought out a wineskin. Carefully, as if it were a throne, he sat upon a fallen tree, cocked his head, and offered the leather bottle to Fulk.

"Thank God someone has the wit to bring refreshment." Fulk took a mouthful. Whatever it had been, it was not wine now. He could not swallow the vile stuff, and spat it out.

Sperling's laugh was like a rusty hinge. Grinning, he took back the skin and gulped down its contents. He wiped his mouth, his eyes sparkling. "Fulk of Windermere, I am at thy service."

Of Windermere! Fulk coughed. "Right. I thank you. I commend you for showing lady Jehanne a way of escape. Sperling, I have little experience with the creatures in your care, but they mean much to your mistress, and therefore it would behoove me to have some basic knowledge of their needs. I would rather ask you than her."

Sperling nodded and leaned closer, and Fulk was most attentive.

The villeins and tenants of Windermere, though still in mourning, rebuilt their herds and flocks, and worked the fields as the weather allowed. Jehanne rejoiced in the progress of the fief.

The foals were healthy, the bees flourished, but she continued to push herself, whether shoulder to shoulder with her people or striking bargains with passing merchants. By the end of each day she was often so tired that she fell asleep wherever she happened to sit, and Lioba had to undress her and put her to bed.

Jehanne tried to avoid Fulk as she attended the concerns of Windermere. Although he did not approach her except to ask questions, he seemed ever-present. He was fast becoming an integral part of things, suggesting improvements, making himself useful.

It was annoying in the extreme.

He appeared unexpectedly, often when she needed extra hands the most and could not refuse his help. Even during the lambing, Fulk did not seem to mind being up to his elbows in panting ewes and afterbirths. She was mystified at how he, who had lived as far removed from such livestock as anyone could, knew just what to do.

He watched, he learned and he did not complain. More and more he began to offer his own ideas on how the mares should be bred, on which fields to leave fallow, on whether or not to find new markets for the wool. Nothing escaped his attention, not even the kitchens were free of his interference.

Jehanne had seen Cook in fits of rage after Fulk had stopped by. The poor man would throw bread like bricks at the grooms, dump whole cauldrons of soup into the bailey and sometimes hurl the cauldron itself afterward. She contained her own irritation and tried to be grateful for Fulk's apparent good intentions. After all, she had encouraged him. But she did not want a partner and needed no advice. If this continued, soon he would be running Windermere instead of she. And what a beautiful place it was becoming, once again.

The snows had melted early, and the grass grew lush and tender. The first sweet hint of cherry and apple blossoms graced the air, and the lake glowed with the soft colors of spring.

It was mid-March, Saint Zacharius Day, and the winter revels, missed for lack of food or for an excess of grief, were being celebrated at last. All day and into the evening the great hall filled with laughing, boisterous folk, from the lowliest serfs to the would-be lord of Windermere and his lady of pretense.

Though modest, the feast was more food at one gathering than Jehanne had seen in months. She eyed the venison in the trencher before her, shared with Fulk at the crowded, noisy high table. She had been ravenous on her way to dine, but now, with him beside her, a queasy flutter claimed her stomach.

Fulk gazed at her, as one might study a curiosity. His very nearness disturbed her. He threw off an aura of rude good health. And as always, damn him, he smelled better than any man had a right to...of beeswax, and woodsmoke and clean leather.

Jehanne forced herself to concentrate on the meal in front of her. But there he was again—sitting in the seat her father had once occupied as the lord of Windermere.

With a delicacy surprising for hands so large, Fulk maneuvered a bite of juicy meat onto the end of his eating dagger and held it up for her. "Lady Jehanne? You would refuse the fruits of our efforts?"

He quirked a black eyebrow as he spoke, and Jehanne's stomach roiled anew. Indeed, he and his men had worked hard, filling the larders with game. "I—I find my appetite has fled before you, even as must have this stag."

"He did, but you need not follow. If you don't eat, you will weaken." Fulk brought the morsel closer to her lips.

"Nay, I cannot. It is too rich, too much at once."

He redirected the meat to the trencher and gave Jehanne a sidelong glance. "As were the kisses I gave you, perhaps?"

Her heart swelled at the memory. The heat of his mouth had penetrated even her glove. The remembrance of his dark head bowed over her hand, of his gentle but irresistible grip when she tried to pull away, still brought a strange tumult to her breast.

Then in the snow she had nearly given in to the longing to be held...perhaps even protected. But of course Fulk had wanted something in return. Men could not be trusted. Not when it came to women. Lioba had always tried to impress that upon her, and her father and the earl had proven it beyond a doubt.

Jehanne tried to smile, to show she did not care.

"You mistakenly believe me capable of appreciating such courtly attentions, sir. However, it does please me that you saw fit to share this bounty with my people."

"I couldn't eat it all myself." Fulk smiled in his subtle, devastating way. "So, my lady. When will you leave for London?"

"London...?" Jehanne had forgotten her declaration on the night of his arrival. She had not the faintest idea how to present a case before the king. Nor did she know the way to London Towne, or even which turning to take at the very first crossroads outside of Windermere. She lifted her chin. "Oh, within a fortnight."

"Excellent. I shall take the opportunity to escort you, for I too have reason to go forth."

Alarm stiffened Jehanne. "Pray tell me why. Would you abandon these people?"

"Nay, Malcolm will see to their well-being. Won't you, Malcolm?"

"Aye, that I will." The Scot looked at Fulk and Jehanne. "Best not be gone too long, though." He raised his head and sniffed. "There's treachery on the wind." ·

"Ah, my friend, you see enemies in every shadowed corner. Rest your suspicions for a time, and be easy." Fulk leaned back, and his arm brushed Jehanne's. Her traitorous insides quivered, but she kept her gaze fixed upon Malcolm.

"A man in a plaid cannae afford to relax, now can he? He'll save his arse through vigilance alone. Pardon, milady." Malcolm offered her a bob of his head, his hard expression not in the least apologetic. Even now his gaze darted from group to group among the revelers.

Jehanne bit her lip to hide her smile, and nodded in return. The Scot must have been reared in a household fraught with assassins. She looked to Fulk again. He was bound to try to thwart her effort to see the king. "What takes you to the road?" she asked.

He looked down at her, his amber eyes half closed. "Would you like to meet my mother?"

"Nay! You have a mother?" Oh, complete and utter fool that she was, to blurt such an inanity.

Malcolm burst out in a full-throated laugh, and Fulk's grin worked its way around his mouth until he could contain it no longer. He put his hand over his heart. "Most assuredly, lady. I am neither heaven-sent nor devil's spawn nor elfling."

"I meant, I did not know you had a living parent, as I understood you were a ward of the king."

"Be that as it may, she lives and breathes. I would find Celine and leave her in our mother's care, where she will be safest."

Malcolm scowled. "You said you would bring her here."

"I have changed my mind."

"She will never agree."

"She will do as she's told."

"Nay, Fulk. You cannae have your way in everything."

"I can and will have my way in all that means much to me."

Malcolm's smile was almost a sneer. "We will see, milaird. Won't we just."

Jehanne stared at the pair of them, her eyes wide. If any man had dared speak in such a tone to her father, in his own hall, he would have been on his way to a flogging already. She sought to ease the tension between them. "Sir Fulk, no doubt your sister would want to come to Windermere to be with you. Do not force your will upon her—it is the quickest way to foster darkness in a woman's heart."

Fulk's eyes narrowed further. "You speak from experience."

Jehanne twisted the tablecloth in her fingers. Why could she not simply keep quiet? The open discussions Fulk indulged in were too painful. "I—where is Lioba? I would fain go to my rest now—as you would have me do." Her sarcasm was lost upon Fulk, but she did indeed feel faint.

"You do not need Mistress Lioba to lead you about. And you still have not taken enough to sustain a mouse."

Jehanne felt his gaze intensify. Like the sun shining upon a closed bud, to which Lioba oft compared her. But she was never going to flower. Too much had happened. Sorrow had gnawed away at her until there was only enough bloom left to get through each day, on her own fortitude. Hers alone.

If she allowed Galliard too close, she would certainly begin to weaken, to relinquish control in the face of his devious charm. There was the ever-present, awful temptation to melt into his embrace, and bask in his strength. Nay, she must hold tight to what little power she had left.

Besides, it was all a pointless fantasy. Even if he did want her, which she found difficult to believe, she would never conquer her fear of being touched. Of being seen.

"My lady?"

Jehanne started at the nudge of Fulk's voice. "I am not hungry."

His casual manner vanished. He gave her a long, hard look and swung his legs from beneath the table to the bench they sat upon. Instead of continuing to the floor, Fulk used the seat to jump up onto the trestle top. His wine-red surcoat swirled in Jehanne's face.

He took a step sideways so that his booted feet were apart, his weight distributed on the creaking planks. What in Mother Mary's name was he doing, besides ruining her table linen?

"Friends!" The talk and laughter died down, and the faces of Windermere turned expectantly. "I rejoice this day, to see all of you hale and able to partake of this feast with us. But what brings me even greater joy is that at long last, your lady, Jehanne the— Fair, has agreed to become my bride. Indeed, we were betrothed in private this very morn, and the wedding shall take place once the archbishop sees fit to send a replacement for the late Father Edgar. What say you?"

The resultant shouts of glee and thunderous trestle poundings were deafening, especially once the dogs joined in the chorus. Even Sir Thomas, fully recovered from the fever, did not withhold his approval. He thumped his mazer down and offered a loud "Huzzah!"

Betrayed! Again—and by her own beloved mentor. Jehanne tolerated several heartbeats of the clamor before she felt herself slide off the bench and under the table into blackness.

Chapter Ten

Jehanne woke to an unfamiliar roar. She lay in her own bed, beneath the covers, wearing only her shift. The noise was Fulk, bellowing out the door into the corridor.

"Nay, woman, your lady has had enough coddling—she must be taken in hand before she withers away to nothing! Nor shall she leave this chamber until I can see that she is increasing."

The door slammed upon Lioba's sobs and the other handmaidens' wailing. Increasing! Jehanne's throat closed. He could not possibly mean that in the usual sense when applied to a woman. But a smooth, uncontested succession at Windermere was what the king wanted. Perhaps Fulk had decided to follow orders after all.

The bed shuddered as he swung to face her, one huge hand around the corner-post. She sat up, clutching her blankets. "How dare you chastise my maids and force me abed? Get out!"

"Nay, lady. We both shall stay, and you will obey. The quicker you cooperate, the sooner you may leave."

"Fool! You know not what you are up against. You will never break me. No man has." Jehanne bit her lip at her own outburst. No man had broken her, but never had she spoken thus to one and not regretted it.

And for an instant, she was certain Fulk would be no exception. His face stiffened, his eyes lost their warmth and became impenetrable, like fire-hardened oak. Then, as quickly as it had flashed, his anger vanished. She could see it retreat, even as darkness flees the dawn. So completely did he banish it, Jehanne almost doubted it had been there at all. She breathed her relief that he was not going to beat her for her insolence. He moved closer. As he sat next to her legs, Fulk radiated heat and strength. His own words came to her...*like some great, well-favored beast.*

Yet there was something more. Much more. She scarcely believed it, but—at this moment, she felt safe in his proximity. A feeling she never had, except when curled into the tightest ball possible, under as many bedfurs as she possessed, tucked in with all of her maids, and every bolt shot. As if his stern regard was a shield behind which she might find sanctuary. What an absurd idea.

Fulk leaned on one palm, his gaze boring into her. The firelight bounced blue sparks off his hair, and he seemed to fill the whole field of her vision. "I have no wish to break you," he purred, a whisper of steel in his voice. "But bend you I will, and if it takes 'til summer, so be it."

Her sense of security fled. In vain she tried to pull the bed-clothes higher, but his weight held them in place. She strove to speak lightly. "Why? What concern is it of yours?"

"Lady, do you not see beyond your immediate situation? My confining you is as nothing should the earl discover I did not do his bidding. Would you rather he sent another man to finish what I will not? This way, as far as others are concerned, anything might be happening behind closed doors, for good or ill. We will buy time, and no one but you and I will know the truth."

Jehanne sniffed disdainfully, but her stomach tightened. "Why did Grimald not come himself, then? Why send you at all? Do I hold so little appeal?"

Fulk paused, and rubbed his lip. "The earl has no appreciation of a true challenge. He wants his desires met immediately. Be that as it may, you are my responsibility now, and I must see to your welfare."

"This is a fine way to go about it." Jehanne crossed her arms.

"I think so, too." Fulk seemed to relax, and with the subtle settling of his limbs, he filled up even more of the space before her. The masculine timbre of his voice sent shivers through her. There would be no escape from this bed—not unless he willed it.

Jehanne tried to remain calm. "Why did you lie to the assembly? Betrothal, indeed. Everyone knows with Easter upon us no weddings can take place for another forty days. What do you hope to gain?''

He smiled. "I spoke of private vows to protect your reputation."

"But Sir Fulk, do you not realize? We shall be made prisoners of your falsehood!''

"Perhaps it will not be a falsehood for long."

"It will while I yet have breath." She jerked on the blanket.

"Has no one ever taken thy breath away?" He half rose and leaned toward her, his head tilted—as if he meant to kiss her.

"Nay! No one has. N-not the way you mean...that I think you mean." Jehanne took the opportunity to scoot down, and pulled the newly freed covers up to her chin. She hoped he had not spotted her lie. Why did he insist upon tormenting her so?

"Ah, lady, I begin to see the truth in Malcolm's words."

Fulk gazed at her mournfully and sat back.

"I know not of what you speak."

"Never mind. Here." He leaned down and brought a covered tray up from the floor to rest upon her blanketed lap. "I will sit over there, and you may eat or not eat, as you will."

Jehanne caught the scent of fresh bread and made her decision. "Don't watch me."

Fulk strolled to the window seat. He drew his long legs up, hugged them, and resting his chin on his knees, stared out into the night. Satisfied that she had as much privacy as he would allow, Jehanne lifted a corner of the cloth to peek at the contents of the tray. What in heaven had he done? And how?

There were two perfectly browned, fist-sized loaves. A small dish of butter and another of salt. A bowl of warm lentil soup, with colorful bits of vegetable crowning it. A flaky pasty leaked an aromatic juice that made her mouth water. And, beside a deep wooden mazer of spiced wine lay a pair of honeyed figs.

Glancing every now and again to see if Fulk kept his gaze averted, Jehanne nibbled, then devoured the savory food. What at first began as a wish for privacy, ended as a desire to be spared embarrassment at the rapid deterioration of her table manners. She captured a last delicious, greasy crumb from her upper lip with her tongue, and sighed.

"Better?" Fulk drawled, still not looking at her.

"Aye." She felt as stuffed as the bolster she rested against.

"Your cook should be drawn and quartered, for the evil fare he has served up to now—even with the best ingredients at hand."

"Aye. How did you do it?"

"One can learn many things in the company of accomplished women. I have had some skilled instructors." He winked.

Jehanne shuddered to imagine what else they had taught him apart from stew-making and bread baking. "I am grateful—you have my thanks. And my leave to take Cook's place in the kitchens, forevermore."

Fulk's laughter sounded out of place in her chamber, where she had shed what had seemed like rivers of silent tears.

"It is good to hear you jest," he said.

"Think you I am jesting?" Jehanne drew her bed-shawl around her shoulders. The easy intimacy growing between them was dangerous. She felt self-conscious and vulnerable.

"You still want me gone, then." It was a statement, not a question, and his tone was carefully neutral.

"I do not know the half of what I want, anymore." Another lie. She closed her eyes. It would be something, to hear that deep, rich voice of his saying her name with passion. To know his beguiling smile was meant for her alone. To experience the embrace of his warm hands and muscled forearms and powerful shoulders, up and down, the overwhelming whole of him—what *would* she do with a man like Fulk?

"I know."

Jehanne heard the grin in his voice and opened her eyes in alarm. "You know my desire?"

"I know your need, and *my* desire." He stood.

"Beware, my lord. They do not match. Never will they match."

"Think you not?" Fulk came to stand beside the bed, and crooked his arm about the corner-post.

"I *know* they will not." She drew her knees to her chest.

"You are wrong, Jehanne. As wrong about me as you are about yourself." He moved in closer, leaning on his palms.

She wanted to shrink from his nearness, but met his eyes and spoke in as cold a voice as she could muster. "Good though they were, you cannot woo me with vittles, my lord."

"Nor can you fool me with your haughty indifference and your incessant 'my lording'. You need me, Jehanne. Whether you loathe me or not is beside the point. The sooner you realize it the better—for you and Windermere both."

Fulk straightened and stepped back, chilliness closing about him like a curtain, shutting her out. A frisson of unexpected panic trickled through Jehanne. "Don't...do not go."

As a falcon might, he turned his dark head and caught her with his gaze. "You offered yourself to me once. Honor was satisfied. What is it you do now?"

"Forgive me. I did not intend to make demands upon you." She meant it. She wanted nothing from him.

He faced her fully, and spread his arms. "Am I such an awful prospect? And do not say anything unless it be the truth."

Why did he keep turning things round and round? Coming at her from a different angle every time he opened his mouth? But, as long as he invited her to look at him, she might as well.

Jehanne found the subtle tension in his mouth intriguing. The dark slant of his eyebrows most appealing. His combination of restrained force and keen intelligence quite irresistible.

"I warrant you are no more awful than any other man." She prayed he did not notice the blush she felt mounting in her cheeks.

Fulk narrowed his eyes. "I should thank you for that, I suppose. But mayhap there is not much to distinguish me from the gang of suitors the earl supplied you with. Why did you reject them all?"

"Because to a man they were odious and vile, and I cared for them not."

Crossing his arms, Fulk leaned back against the bedpost. It creaked in protest. "I do not believe you."

"Why not?" She could feel the blood creep upward in indignant waves along her scar.

"It is unlikely that the earl would handpick repulsive men when he wished you wed."

"He surrounds himself with repulsive men."

"And you see me as one of them, no doubt. Why did your father not intervene?" Fulk's gaze hardened.

"He did...but his choices were no better."

"Are you so very difficult to please?"

"Apparently." Bubbles of anger began to build in Jehanne's chest. How dare he presume to judge her? He had not suffered as she had.

Then, his eyes, like sunlit ale, grew languid...almost dreamy. His lips curved in the slightest of smiles. "What if *I* were to try to please you?"

Jehanne prayed for forgiveness as she opened her mouth to lie yet again. "I doubt that possible, but, in what way?"

"Oh, it would have to be small things at first. Like not standing upon the table and shouting out betrothals." He waved a hand in emphasis.

"You might have asked me," she said in a small voice.

"Shall I?"

"Don't—unless you wish to be denied."

"You are cruel, mademoiselle. As cruel as you are beautiful." His tone was matter-of-fact, but she thought she saw a flicker of pain in his eyes. How unlikely. And how dare he call her beautiful to her face? Thanks to her father's careless rages, she bore closer resemblance to a quintain's target than a maid's freshness.

"Do not mock me, sir."

"I do not."

"My father..." Again, the linen sheet suffered her twisting hands.

"Tell me," Fulk said softly, and rubbed his arm, the one that she had wounded.

"He—he said that if spinsterhood was my aim, I was sure to succeed, for no man would wed me willingly having once seen this scar." Her hand strayed to her cheek as if of its own volition.

Fulk gave her an earnest look, searching her eyes until she could bear it no more. She turned away. He must feel just as her father had told her. How could he not, when he might have any beauty in the world?

"How did you get such a wound?"

His frank question startled her. "I do not wish to speak of it."

The bitter memories still had the power to reduce her to tears. Struggling to keep them at bay, she held tight to what shreds of dignity she could.

"Come. Get up. I would show you something." Fulk reached down and put his hand over hers.

The contact elicited a shocking surge of warmth. Except in the bath, he had not touched her bare skin before, to her knowledge. Always a layer of leather or wool or linen had been between them. Jehanne knew not whether to snatch her hand away or to throw herself into his arms.

Why did she have such childish reactions to his nearness? Was she as weak as the simpering maids who flaunted themselves wherever he turned? She must maintain control. But he continued to catch her by surprise with his lightning shifts.

"Pass me my surcoat, then," she said, mastering her trembling limbs with difficulty.

Fulk ignored her request and picked up his own dark-green mantle. He held it out, inviting her to step into its folds.

Gingerly, Jehanne slipped from bed, the planks of the floor rough against her feet. Fulk immediately enveloped her within the warm wool, but did not follow its embrace with his own. She felt relief and disappointment at the same time. The garment held his smoky, dark scent, enticing and seductive. She inhaled deeply.

This could not go on.

"Over here." He led the way to the window seat. "Behold."

In a sky as black as Fulk's hair, the moon hung plump and white, surrounded by a hazy circle. It looked lonely, and bruised. As if it ached as much as did her heart.

Fulk gestured widely toward the heavens. "See you how the moon is mottled, and splotched, and flawed? But its beauty is in no way diminished. Its light shines just as bright, and it wears its halo proudly. Were it unblemished, how boring it would be to gaze upon. One could not look for faces, or figures, nor find the marks that are so comforting in their familiarity."

Jehanne looked from the brilliant orb to Fulk, and blinked.

She tried to swallow past the lump in her throat. No one had ever before spoken in such a tender way to her...about her.

And the most bewildering part was that he meant it—or if he

did not, then he was a masterful liar. A king of liars. But she saw no guile in his handsome face. Even so, his chivalry was unbearable. He did not know the half of her scars.

"Sir, I must believe you mean well."

"Aye, you must." He moved behind her, and she looked down at her feet as his upper body gently bumped her shoulder blades.

"You have had many an opportunity to hurt me, my lord, and as yet have taken advantage of none. But there are other qualities of this moon which you have omitted."

Jehanne returned her gaze to the night sky. "It is cold. Self-contained. And though it looks as though one might hold it in one's hands, it is far, far out of reach."

"Is that what you would have me think of you?"

Her eyes prickled, and Jehanne rubbed them with the back of one wrist. "I wish that it were not so. But that is what I am."

"Nay. It is what misfortune has made you resemble. But not what you are." Fulk's hands came to rest upon her shoulders.

She fought the impulse to turn to him, to put her face against his broad chest. With regret, she shrugged free of his touch. Men were not for comfort. They were for fighting, for punishment, for rutting and begetting sons. Fulk had not harmed her. But it was only a matter of time. It was nothing that could be helped, nor could he be blamed. Men were men, just as wolves were wolves....

The moonglow spangled Jehanne with a silver aura, as Fulk stared at the crown of her head. Fine strands of her hair quivered from the skimming of his breath and her small, restless movements. A pulse bounded in his throat and his heart's rapid pace left him giddy, his fingers trembling.

God help him, he wanted to spin her around and kiss her. Not tenderly, as he ought. Nay—he wanted to toss her back into bed and show her what was possible between a man and a woman. To awaken her. To have her clutch him in ecstasy. To make her weep for joy, with his name on her lips. Aye, all that—and to take her, deep and hard. Over and over again.

But beneath her bold front it was plain to see Jehanne was tender and afraid. And he was big, perhaps overwhelmingly so to a woman like her, uncomfortable with herself, let alone a man she scarcely tolerated. Once unleashed, his passion might terrify her. He could not risk it, even in the attempt to give her pleasure.

Putting his hands behind him, Fulk stepped back. "My lady, I—I think it best if I return you to your maids' care. I have been clumsy in my efforts to see you strong. Please accept my apology."

She turned to him, her gray eyes gleaming, her body enveloped in his mantle. It surrounded her, fending off the cold—just as would he, if she only allowed him that privilege.

"Never have I known a man like you, Fulk. I cannot rank you with the others. And for that very reason, you are better off without me. Truly, I might be the unhappy fate some of those evil men deserved. But, if you do not detain me, and my appeal to the king still fails, then so be it. I shall honor our agreement. We must be wed, if only to protect Windermere from his wrath—and your sister from the earl. But until that time, I take your most evident, gracious manner as assurance that you will not violate me."

Fulk looked out the window rather than meet her eyes. She still assumed him brutal. Not only brutal but capable of doing violence to a woman—to her. In truth she must consider him no better than the lowliest caitiff in Grimald's service.

Jehanne was wise, no doubt, to keep him at bay. He was daft to even think of taking her to wife. And unless she wanted him, he never would. But Celine's future happiness was at stake, perhaps her very life. One did not come into possession of a fortress like Windermere every day. Fulk put his hand to his damp forehead.

"Worry not. Sleep now, and I shall send your women back to attend you." He moved toward the door.

"My lor—I mean, Sir Fulk?"

"Aye?"

"Are you ill?"

Fulk stopped in the act of unbolting the latch. He did feel wretched in the aftermath of his attack of lust and guilt. "Nay, though I am weary. Why?"

"Ah...I but wondered. You seem overly warm. I had thought the fevers gone from this place, but..."

"I never sicken. Rest easy, and God keep you this night." His face hot with embarrassment, Fulk slipped out into the walkway, only to confront the unblinking stares of Jehanne's ladies.

"Stifle your wrath and see to your mistress, then. She has had her fill of me." He strode away to the hiss of their whispering.

Fulk ran down the narrow spiral of steps, two at a time. In the great hall, folk dozed atop the tables and sprawled snoring on straw pallets. A muffled giggle, followed by a moan of satisfaction, escaped from one of the darker corners. Fulk ground his teeth at the reminder of what he had done without for so long, and did not stop to investigate. The woman sounded willing enough.

As Fulk passed the central fire pit he nodded to the bleary-eyed guard seated there, an empty pannikin at his feet, and dried blood on his knuckles. Mogg had an apparently endless capacity for ale.

A large, thick man, one who saw things only as black or white. Extraordinarily opinionated but without sufficient wit to convince others of his wisdom, he tended to either drown his frustrations or engage in brawls.

"Get some sleep, Mogg. I will send someone to relieve you."

"Aye, milord," the mercenary replied. With but two words he managed to convey his surly, sodden state. It was late, and Fulk was in no mood for anyone's bad temper but his own. He let his gaze harden until the man looked down. Once Mogg had shuffled off toward bed, Fulk continued through the hall.

Outside, in the back bailey, he sought clarity for his mind and heart. It was a poor choice of destinations. He was beset by the stink of the kitchen midden and in particular of the tanning vat, all overlaid with the piggy odor of stray swine. Before he could escape, Jehanne's hounds roiled happily to greet him.

Though the moon was well on its way to the horizon, it was yet bright. Fulk leaned down to stroke the silky ears of one of his favorites, part gazehound, by the look of her narrow head.

"Galliard."

Fulk spun about at the irate feminine voice. "Mistress Lioba?"

She stood in a shadow cast by the curtain wall, her expression hidden by the gloom, but Fulk had no need to see her face. Meek or fierce, Lioba was always lovely, he knew full well. Tonight, fury crackled like sparks about her. Fulk took a step backward. He could not see her hands, nor what they might contain.

"Why do you torment my lady?" she asked. "Can you not see she wants none of you?"

"I do. But Lady Jehanne can speak for herself. And we have come to a truce, of sorts."

"You have taken advantage, and confounded her—cast a spell upon her. I will not let you do her hurt." Lioba raised her arm. "Warlock! Keep away from her, or I'll—"

Even as she rushed at him Fulk moved in and caught her wrist. Moonlight glinted on the blade of the dagger she held. With some difficulty he took the knife from her and threw it. It thudded into a post and quivered there, at head height.

Lioba struggled in his grip, strong, firm, and full-bodied. Passionate and womanly. Suddenly she stopped, and pressed her warm curves against him. "If 'tis comfort you want, I am yours to do with as you will."

Her hands ran down Fulk's back to his buttocks, then rubbed his thighs and squeezed. Fulk knew it was but a ploy to distract him. Or was it? He inhaled deeply and his words tumbled out. "Lioba—you do to me what you would have me refrain from attempting with your lady. I admire your loyalty, but—Lioba, stop that!"

She had him up against the wall, her hands bold, her breath rasping even as his defiant flesh quickened. "You are quite something, my lord. 'Twould not be a complete sacrifice on my part."

"You attempt to murder me in one instant and seduce me in the next? Thou art perilous fair, methinks." His blood pounding, Fulk thrust her away by the shoulders.

Lioba stayed in the shadows, but her voice betrayed the grim determination surely written on her face. "I will do anything to see Jehanne happy. And her happiness lies not with you, nor any man. I told her so, long before she learned it for herself. The love of men is an illusion."

"You would poison her innocence with your own bitterness?"

"What do *you* know of plighting troth? Or the pain of betrayal? You are a selfish bastard, just like the rest!" Lioba burst into tears.

"Aye. I have never promised to love anyone."

Lioba's sobs wrenched at Fulk's heart. He did not believe she truly wanted to kill him. Women could not help themselves, their emotions ruled their actions. He had spoken to her harshly, when he should have tried to soothe her.

"Come back inside to the fire. Have some wine and calm yourself."

"Nay!" She tore at her clothes, at her own hair, and screamed. She clawed at Fulk and caught his face with her nails. "Nay, milord, please, I beg of you!" Her piteous words contrasted sharply with the decisive strength of her blows.

Fulk then realized her plan. The dogs' barking roused the servants and folk started to gather. Though he had done nothing but restrain her, Lioba's shrieks grew louder.

"I'd not have thought you capable of such viciousness, lady."

Lioba stepped out of the shadows and fully faced him. The added light from the bystanders' torches revealed finger-shaped bruises blooming on her cheek, and blood about her nose and mouth. She had no need to speak. The people drew their own outraged conclusion.

He could not deny it, not when she had so cleverly prepared his guilt. Fulk shook his head and wondered who had obliged her with his fists. She had gone to much trouble for what seemed a minor gain. It was not as though he were vastly popular among the people and needed taking down. Their trust was yet fragile.

It was Jehanne's happiness they had cheered for at the feast, not his. Fulk shouldered his way past Lioba and glimpsed her smile of triumph. His jaw hurt, it was clenched so tight.

A woman threw her hands wide. "A faithless bridegroom. Couldn't he have waited?"

"Aye, he's the Reluctant when it comes to battle, and the Ready when it comes to fair ladies!"

The muttered remarks followed Fulk into the hall. How fitting that the women of the keep did not hesitate to accuse him. He rounded on the taunting crowd. They fell back, stark fear upon their faces.

Fulk spoke in a low voice. "Lioba is the daughter of a knight. But I would no more use a shepherdess than her or any other

unwilling female. Go to bed, all of you. One day, you may b
glad of me.''

The people looked at each other in confusion. No doubt the
had expected to be punished for their censure. But at that mo
ment Fulk could not be bothered with the opinions of servant
and was too angry to trust himself not to do something he woul
regret.

He turned, and lengthening his stride, mounted the stairs an
left them behind.

The moon had set and darkness reigned. Fulk lay upon h
bed still fully dressed, unable to sleep. Malcolm sat hunched lik
a gargoyle upon a chest nearby, wrapped in his plaid.

''Well, 'tis a sad state of affairs, now. Mayhap you shoul
have added your own mark to those Lioba already bore, an
made her less of a liar.'' The Scot drummed his dagger's hi
against the lid of the chest in a steady beat.

''How can you say such a thing, even in jest? Lord, I am sic
of this place. I will leave at first light, find Celine and delive
her to my mother.''

Malcolm coughed behind his fist. ''Shall I go ahead with S
Thomas and recruit lads to train in arms, as we planned?''

He sounded less than enthusiastic.

''Aye,'' Fulk replied, grateful that the Scot did not argue wi
him about Celine. ''Mind you, I want recruits, not conscript
Malcolm. Two willing hands can do more than six reluctant-
oh, *God*.''

That word—his name—Fulk scrubbed his face, as if the actic
could wipe out his evil memories. They leaped out at him, gro
tesque, clutching phantoms, especially at night, when slee
would not come. He remembered too well the day he had foreve
confirmed what he truly was, on a field of war, in France.

It had been years ago, but not so long that the images did n
still sear him like an ordeal by fire. And every time, he can
out guilty, so deeply burned he might as well have been brande
on his forehead for all to see.

He had fought for the king to the point of collapse. Havir
sunk to the ground at last, he had put his head between his knee

nd stared at the red-tinged earth. He had tried to slow his
reathing, but could not.

His face tingled, then grew numb, his hands followed suit. He
vas wallowing, slipping, drowning. One great gasp and yet an-
ther had brought him no relief. Blackness roared closer, and he
itched forward onto the battlefield.

"Fulk!" He heard his name, as if from a distance. It pene-
ated past the ringing in his ears and the moans of the dying.

"Fulk, where have you taken hurt?"

Malcolm. It had been he who had made him stay flat, and
egun to remove his armor. Fulk had no pain. But cold gripped
im, deep inside, even after his exertion. His ungauntleted hand
rifted to his chest. The thick gambeson he wore was sodden.
ticky with blood. He shuddered at the realization he must have
wung his blade at his friend, had not recognized him through
e red haze in his mind.

Another voice joined Malcolm's. "I cannot find his wounds
n this mess. Jesu, he looks as though he just crawled out of his
other!"

"Dinnae move, lad. Let's carry him off the field, Bayard."

The words rippled through Fulk's stupor. It amazed him to
ear tears in Malcolm's voice.

"Nay, I can walk." He opened his eyes. The sky wheeled,
uffs of brilliant cloud swirling in a sea of blue innocence. When
e sat up, he felt heavy, and his clothes were already stiffening.
Malcolm." He looked into the Scot's worried eyes and blinked.

"Aye, Fulk, I am here."

"Tell me...have I turned into a demon?" Cautiously Fulk felt
is head. His blood-drenched hair had clotted into long ropes,
ut there were no horns. Not yet. "Am I still human?"

Malcolm paused in his binding of Fulk's wounds, and fresh
oncern creased his brow. "Aye, you are the same, but—"

"Time will tell. Where is my sword?" Fulk cast his gaze
bout. When he saw his weapon he wanted to vomit. A dozen
r so men lay strewn nearby, and his blade was buried in the
iggest of them. He had cleaved the man's helm—and his skull.
ulk shut his eyes, but the hideous sight remained.

"'Tis broken, Fulk. But the king will honor you with a new

one, and spurs, too, no doubt, for the work you have done th
day. You turned the battle, and Godefroi's knights got through.

He would accept no spurs. Not even from the king. "And n
horse?" Fulk's head felt light, his eyes stung, he already kne
the answer.

"He died bravely...*tha mi duilich.* I am sorry."

Growing increasingly numb, Fulk stared at the crowd
knights and men-at-arms who looked in awe upon him and th
surrounding carnage he had created. A cheer went up, for Fu
de Galliard and his valor against great odds.

Malcolm grinned. "You're a hero, lad!"

Fulk fought the nausea churning in his stomach. Twelve dea
men. Sons, fathers, husbands...*brothers.* He could bear it ⋅
longer. "Nay. My lord father was right. I am an abomination

The words had echoed, their terrible truth a reality that cou
not be undone, not then, and not now. Fulk sat up in bed ai
clutched his head ever tighter, to no avail. His father's conder
nation still scorched like hot iron in his heart, relentless ai
unforgiving.

Malcolm came to sit at the foot of the bed, and was silent f
a moment. "Do you remember what I told you before, Fulk?

"Nay. Your constant instruction does not stay with me. I t
my best not to listen."

"Och, you do, but you willnae admit it. What I said that d
on the battlefield, was that you experienced a taste of *furor,*
the ancients put it. A wonderful, fearless, killing rage, that upli⋅
a warrior until he feels no pain. His strength is tenfold, ai
nothing can stop him. 'Tis a state priceless in battle, but, as yo
learned to your sorrow, dangerous when misplaced."

Malcolm leaned closer, his eyes intense. "You were youn
Rabel irksome, and you lost control. The *furor* came to life, Ful
and took you by surprise. You cannae continue to stuff it awa
as you have done for so long."

Fulk looked at the Scot from behind his fingers. "I am curse
by it. A man on the outside and a devil within. It is wicke
savage blood lust, and you try to make it sound like rapture."

Malcolm shook his head emphatically. "'Tis nae a curse,

you would have it, but a rare gift. It can carry you when all
seems lost. But you must respect it, face it, and learn to use it
properly.''

"Why? It is nothing less than berserking with a Latin name."

"Because, my friend, it hasnae dwindled. It has rested and
strengthened, and one day will strike again—without warning.
'Tisnae a part of yourself you can afford to ignore, Fulk, or you
will walk divided all your days.'' Malcolm crossed his arms and
frowned, his speech evidently at an end.

"I say let sleeping dogs lie."

"Och, you are a useless puddle o'piss. Dinnae tell me I didnae
warn you.''

"Malcolm, you are no doubt exhausted from wasting your
breath. Take your rest in this bed. I will go to the byre and sleep
in the hayloft. That way, when Lioba comes here to harvest my
ballocks, she will have yours to contend with instead.'' Fulk
swung his legs over the edge and pulled on his boots.

"If that is your pleasure, Galliard, so be it." Malcolm seized
a pillow and stretched out with it locked in his arms.

Jehanne took a wet cloth and dabbed carefully at Lioba's
swollen, tearstained face. "He did this? Fulk?" She could
scarcely breathe for the anger and hurt and disbelief welling in
her chest.

Lioba nodded, her eyes downcast. "I chastised him for both-
ering you, and he flew into a rage. Then, h-he...he...''

"Shh, do not speak of it. I was a fool to think there might be
some chance he was different. He will not go unpunished. Fulk
is not yet lord here, and you are the daughter of a noble house.''

Jehanne began to gather her clothes. A sunbeam struck the
ragged tapestry on the wall as daylight rimmed the hills outside.

"Nay, lady—do not—I am happy to see him gone, but do not
try to exact vengeance on your own.''

"What do you mean, see him gone? Is he not here?"

"Well, nay, he rode away in the wee hours, I know not
where.''

"And the Mac Niall?"

"He is out roaming the countryside with Sir Thomas. Please
lady, just bar the gates against him.''

"And lock in the twenty armed men he has left behind? Nay.

I shall go after Fulk. I will not suffer such a betrayal in my own household."

An hour later Jehanne was on the high road, sword at her hip and bow at her back. Nothing like the one Fulk had so callously broken, but better than most. Young Corwin rode alongside, bearing her shield, lance and provisions.

Riding hard and fast, they stopped only to enquire if any had seen the distinctive Frisian bearing a dark, broad-shouldered man. Few had noticed his passing, but Jehanne was still able to track his progress, loosening tongues with silver as she went.

They avoided the great oakwood, infested as it was with robbers and thieves, and kept to the open fields. Two nights later, nearing exhaustion, they heard a stallion's throaty call, and Jehanne's mare answered with a whinny that shook her whole body.

They found Fulk in a meadow on the outskirts of a walled abbey. As Jehanne watched from the shadows, he sat before a small fire, knees up, his head resting upon his crossed arms. The Frisian nickered, then using his mobile upper lip, played with Fulk's jet hair.

"Stay back, Corwin." Jehanne stepped forth into the small circle of light, sword in hand. "Fulk de Galliard, stand and be challenged."

He looked up. Shock registered briefly on his face, then he put his head back down. "Bloody animal betrays me for the sake of a female," he muttered.

Jehanne ventured closer. Mud from the bad roads coated Fulk's boots and legs, and it appeared he had brought nothing with him, neither food nor drink nor a spare tunic. But why should she even take notice of that, much less care about his comfort?

She straightened her shoulders. "You have abused one of my own, and I cannot let it pass."

Fulk met her eyes. "I grieve for Lioba, truly. She is an unhappy woman. But I did not beat her, nor gift her with myself, nor would I do so with any woman if she did not emphatically desire me."

"Gift, indeed! You are but too lazy to get up and fight."

"Jehanne, you weary me beyond all reason. I am entering the abbey now. You may follow me and risk expulsion for bearing arms against me on holy ground, you may rest and eat within or await me out here, as you will. But you will not return home without proper escort.''

Jehanne did not know what to think. Fulk was not behaving normally, and certainly not as though he was guilty of assaulting Lioba. It was as though he did not care about himself anymore.

"What are you doing in this place?" she asked. "Are you joining the priesthood?" The thought provoked an unbidden spark of protest in her heart.

Fulk smiled, and Jehanne bit her lip at the sight. He nodded in the direction of the abbey. "It is a nunnery, my lady. I am but stopping on my way to Celine. I will bring her here, if they will take her." He kicked out the fire, and became a dark shadow, nearly invisible against the even deeper black of the Frisian.

"I thought you said you wanted to leave her with your mother."

"So I did." He led his horse toward the gates.

"Wait—you must allow me to avenge my handmaid!"

"You have my full permission to do so, once she speaks the truth about who used her so ill."

Jehanne stifled her growl of irritation. Never had she known a man more frustrating than Fulk. She could not see well enough in the dark to fight him, in any event. It would just have to wait.

And if he felt safe from her inside the abbey, then so would she from him. She turned to the horseboy. "Come, Corwin. Let's see what he is up to in this place."

Chapter Eleven

Fulk eased onto his knees in the chapel of the Sisters of Thornton Abbey. The joints still ached. He frowned and tried to concentrate on his prayers for the well-being of Celine, his mother—and Jehanne. He heard an urgent exchange of whispers from somewhere behind him, but did not turn his head.

The nuns were aflutter, it seemed.

The prioress had taken one dismayed look at him, ushered him into the candlelit chamber, and begged him to lay his sword on the floor. She had scurried away without another word. He did not know what had distressed her more: his unexpected and filthy appearance, or the fact that it was near midnight and she would have to awaken Sister Brigitta, whom he had asked to see.

He should not have come. But Celine was a great responsibility. The keep at Windermere was still far from recovered. If the crops failed or the sheep were taken by the bloat, it would be another hungry winter next year. It was best that he bring her to Thornton Abbey, safe from Hengist and Malcolm, too.

Fulk continued in his attempt to pray, but his mind filled with thoughts of Jehanne. The stubborn, pigheaded girl. She had followed for revenge, but when that failed, she might decide to pursue her appeal to the king for his expulsion.

Should she gain an audience it would only serve to draw more disaster upon herself. Of course she had not believed his warnings. There was no arguing with the king.

Fulk jumped at a light touch on his shoulder. He turned and the warm, loving gaze of Sister Brigitta caught him. He had not seen her in years, and her smile was a balm to the dreadful ache in his chest. Still on his knees, he bowed his head to one side and threw his arms around her black-robed legs. If she blessed him, he might be able to look her in the eye again.

"Ah, Fulk, my beloved, you have come at last. How I have longed to see you," she whispered. Her fingers ran through his hair, tenderly combing and smoothing it. With a great wrench of his heart, he attempted to prostrate himself before her, but she stopped him with a gentle hand.

"Nay, son, do not treat me as a holy relic. I am still your mother. Let me see your face, Fulk." She put her palm to his scratched cheek as he regained his knees. "You must have a clumsy tonsor. You are much too lean. What is amiss, that you should starve yourself? And for the love of heaven, get up off the floor!"

Fulk still could not speak. How could she talk of such trivialities in the face of his guilt? But he was immensely grateful that she did not revile him. He found his voice. "There is nothing amiss, my lady. It is you who deserves concern, locked away here."

He kissed the backs of her fingers and pressed them to his brow.

"What sweet nonsense. Please Fulk, stand. Let us go to the refectory. You must sup and talk and I'll not take my eyes from you."

Unashamed of his display of emotion, Fulk crossed himself before the Virgin, then rose and followed his mother to the dining hall. Smiling, she served him a bowl of soup, bread and hard cheese, assuring him all the while that she was well. A few swallows of the hearty fare dulled his hunger and he took her hand in his.

"Madame, why do you stay in this place? Why do you not come away with me, and claim your rightful seat as Baroness of Redware?"

"You know full well I have no wish to return to such a worldly life. I know this is not why you are here at this late hour. Is it Celine?" Brigitta tipped her head, just as lovely as Fulk had remembered her to be.

He closed his eyes briefly. "Aye. Your daughter fancies herself a woman, capable of making her own decisions. She has no idea of the dangers facing her, nor of the measures necessary to keep her safe. She should come here and be with you, if you will not go home." He stirred the lukewarm stew in slow circles with the horn spoon.

Brigitta wrapped her fingers over his. "Fulk, she *is* a woman, no matter that you still see her as a babe. What desire of hers has come into conflict with yours?"

"I fear the Earl of Lexingford will break his word and marry her to Hengist of Longlake." Fulk looked down at his hand, still entwined with his mother's. "And, I fear that Malcolm the Fierce will win her and carry her away."

"Ah, the Gael. He loves her?"

Her voice held a decided note of interest, instead of the disapproval he had expected. "Aye, he does."

"Then wed her to him."

Fulk stared into Brigitta's calm eyes. "How can you suggest such a thing? The Mac Niall is wild, too—too full of—"

He waved his hands in a futile effort to find an inoffensive way to describe Malcolm's raging desire. A state with which he himself was becoming all too familiar.

"Full of what? Passion? Think you Celine will break beneath the furor of a man in love?"

That word again. And in such a context! Fulk looked around to see if anyone had heard, but they were yet alone. Once Fulk had explained his purpose, Jehanne waited outside in the courtyard with Corwin, refusing to enter until he had had time alone with Brigitta.

"Madame, you shock me."

She laughed, and the bright sound echoed off the soaring stone buttresses overhead. "I? How can that be? I have shocked, yea, and disappointed many, but you are quite shocking yourself." Smiling, she reached up and caressed his cheek.

"You believe such gossip?" Gently, Fulk took her hand and put it back to the tabletop. An impossible lump formed in his throat at the reminder of those years of torment, trying to bury his anguish in the flesh of eager women. "How can you ever have forgiven me?" he whispered, and searched her eyes.

There was a flicker of pain, then the pure, loving warmth returned. "Ah, Fulk. You might as well ask how God ever forgave me. What happened was not your fault."

"It was no one's fault but mine. Father died blaming me, and he was right. I am a brute. I should face the fact that is all I am fit to be. I have wasted so much time. If I had gone to war again I might have gained much glory by now, and wealth to see to your comfort as well as Celine's. Not to mention her dowry."

Brigitta took Fulk by the shoulders. "Look at me, son. Rabel died because it was God's will. If it had not been your hand, it would have been someone else's, for just like his father's, his tongue was sharper than any blade. I know you never meant for him to die."

Fulk rested his elbows on the oak planks of the table and held his head in his hands. No matter what she or anyone said, it *had* been his hand, his alone. His subsequent attempts to make amends by living without bloodshed had failed to ease the painful jabs of the demon of guilt still within him. And the anger was yet there, too, suppressed beneath a carefully polished manner of imperturbability.

"If only he could have struck me back. Taken his dagger and—"

"Nay, Fulk! Not another word. How could I prefer the loss of one son over the other—or both? You tell me to take my place as baroness, yet you yourself refuse to accept the privileges that are yours by rights." His mother jerked the ends of her wimple tighter about her shoulders.

"But Father disowned me. The lands and title still belong to Rabel."

"Rabel is dead, boy. What of your responsibilities? Think you the king's man is a benevolent master of Redware? Go to the king, Fulk. Ask him to reinstate you as lord of Redware. Show him you are able and true, strong and loyal. For you are all these things, Fulk. You can be no other way, no matter how you try to deny yourself."

He looked into her eyes. "Come away with me, then. Leave this place of silence and help me with Celine. She needs you, now more than ever. Do this, and I will speak to the king."

"And what of the Gael? I liked him well, Fulk, and what I saw in him will not have changed over the years. He has a stout heart, and he will need one with my daughter. She would drive a sedate man to ruin and madness, I am certain. Celine must wed one who is a match for her spirit—one whom she might have cause to restrain, and therefore think of restraining herself as well."

Fulk sighed. "It is a risky slope you would have them scale, Madame."

"Aye. But see how Celine receives him, then decide."

"So be it. I bow to your greater wisdom in such matters."

Brigitta smiled wryly. "If I did not know it to be impossible, I might think you mocked me, Fulk."

He looked at her fondly. "Nay, *Maman*. I love thee too well for that."

"Son, let us sleep, and pray for guidance. Come the dawn we may find clarity in our hearts."

Fulk paused, putting a hand on Brigitta's arm. "My lady, there is someone I would have you meet ere you retire."

She raised her brows. "By all means."

He ran to the door and caught the eye of one of the abbey servants, hovering near the outer entry. The man disappeared and in a moment Jehanne came inside, her cheeks bright from the cold, her hood thrown back, revealing her golden hair. Before Fulk reached her he heard his mother's soft step behind him.

"Ah...she is lovely, Fulk." The older woman gave Jehanne a glowing smile.

Jehanne's face grew even redder. She went to her knees and kissed Brigitta's hands. "Milady—"

"You children astound me. Never have I been treated with more respect when I deserve it less. Please, rise. You must be famished! For shame, Fulk, to leave her outdoors."

"Nay, milady, your son merely respects my wishes not to intrude. And he keeps me well fed, have no fear." She frowned at Fulk. "I am Jehanne of Windermere."

"Sir Alun's daughter? I have heard tales of your recent sorrow—in fact, a young man took shelter with us not long ago. He described the cruel siege and starvation of your people by some crazed knight who broke with the Earl of Lexingford. What do you know of this, Fulk?''

Brigitta drew Jehanne to her bosom and looked at him over the top of the girl's head. Fulk swallowed and opened his mouth, but no words came. It had to be that imp, Thaddeus, telling tales.

Jehanne pulled away from the lady's embrace. ''Fulk did all he could to set right the devastation wrought by the earl's man.''

Fulk closed his eyes briefly in thanks.

His mother continued, ''I am glad to hear it. According to Father Gregory, there is quite a hue and cry arising to take vengeance upon the greedy rogue for the foul murder of Sir Alun. But praise God you have emerged safe, my dear.''

Fulk felt the blood drain from his face. *Murder?* Folk thought he had *murdered* the FitzWalter?

Jehanne shot him a glance before responding to Brigitta. ''Thank you, milady. Please, say a paternoster for my father, it would ease my mind. He was not shriven before he died.'' Jehanne bowed her head. ''But, the besiegers did not kill him. He perished from a fever....''

She paused, as if there were more to tell, but remained silent.

Fulk stepped to her side, anxious to change the subject. ''I am escorting *Baronne* Jehanne to beg an audience before the king, to right the injustices done to her and her family.''

Oh, even half lies were like quicksand. Jehanne stared at him.

Brigitta smiled. ''Then it is settled. You shall petition for Redware to be restored to you. And now to bed. Wait here, young lady.''

Fulk bowed to Jehanne, and she inclined her head to him as his mother led him to the male guest quarters. After kissing his cheek, Brigitta left, closing the door.

Fulk settled to the straw pallet on the floor. Resting his head on his arm, he gazed at the red shimmer above the coals in the brazier. Despite his concern over the mischief Thaddeus was up to, his heart warmed. His mother had not said nay to leaving the convent.

Once the place was thriving again, he would convince her to come to Windermere and watch over Celine, and mayhap even give Jehanne a bit of comfort. In the meantime he would try to do Brigitta's bidding, to regain his family honor and estates.

The irony struck him. What he wanted from the king was exactly what Jehanne did, too. But he feared if she got her desire he would lose more than Windermere, and more than his freedom from Grimald. He doubted the earl had ever intended him to live so long.

Malcolm had put it rather well. To wake beside the same woman, day in and day out. But Jehanne would see it as a prison. One of honor, which she would view as stronger than any of stone or iron. She would never complain. Nor would she ever love him.

Brigitta's recounting of Thaddeus's story echoed in his mind. He had played right into the conniving young man's hands, by bluffing and telling him to convey to Sir Alun that "we will take his head." Had no one but Fulk himself believed the story of Sir Alun's treachery?

God, what a fool he had been.

Why had Grimald wanted Alun out of the way? Had he been privy to some secret evil? Fulk knew he himself was a painful reminder to the earl of a humiliating past in which Fulk's father had played a large part. And it did not help that Grimald resented Fulk for the excessive admiration women tended to bestow upon him.

His death at the hands of the king's executioners—or perhaps Hengist had been given the task—would simply be a bonus to the earl. Jehanne would be rid of him. And if she did not want him, he could not stay at Windermere. All the more reason to free Redware.

Fulk let his eyes close. He could afford no more nights of lying awake in restless exhaustion. Sleep began to overtake him, but a small creak snapped him back to alertness. He felt for his dagger. The planks of the floor vibrated beneath him as someone came to the door and eased it open.

Jehanne poked her head around its edge. Her hair fell loose in a shining, brassy curtain, lit by the glow from the brazier.

Fulk winked at her formidable glare. "What, lady? Are you cold? Come, lie with me."

"Nay, assassin. I am warmed quite enough by my anger." She stood, her arms crossed over her walnut-brown leather tunic.

"I would rather not face another round of accusations." Fulk sat up, nevertheless.

Jehanne's booted foot tapped the floor. She stared at him and chewed her lip.

At least her scar was no darker than usual. Perhaps he would be spared another beating at the hands of a beautiful woman.

She looked down her nose at him. "I see Lioba scratched your cheek."

"Aye."

"You do not deny being that close?"

"I disarmed her, and she...advanced upon me."

The toe tapped a little faster, then stopped. "Did you rape her or not?"

Fulk faced Jehanne squarely. "I did not."

Jehanne searched his eyes with her own. Her body seemed to relax slightly. "Someone did."

"In my opinion she had 'someone' make it appear that way."

"How dare you suggest such a thing! I know Lioba. Her weeping was not contrived."

Fulk's stomach clenched. "Her tears were genuine, born of the hatred she bears me. But, I am telling you, I did not do her harm."

"Oh, nay, a man like you, with a thousand conquests under his belt, would not see it as harm. You are a *gift,* are you not?" Jehanne's gaze did not waver in its harshness. "Well do I remember the women at the Duke's tourney. So many you had to satisfy."

Fulk worked a kink out of his neck and wished he were far from her accusing eyes. "You grossly exaggerate both my capacity and my cruelty. Most of those ladies imagined far more than they ever actually experienced with me. But if, as you say, I am so legendary, why should I force myself upon anyone?"

Jehanne studied him a moment longer, then sank to the floor. She crossed her legs and rested her chin on her palm. "I do not know. I suppose it is possible Lioba may have lied and arranged your guilt. But she is extraordinarily proud and stubborn. She will insist it was you."

"Do you doubt me?" Fulk stirred the red coals in the brazier with a piece of kindling.

Jehanne sighed heavily. "I want to believe you."

He cut his gaze to her. "Indeed?"

She unfolded her legs and hugged her knees. "I would not be alone with you in this chamber otherwise."

"Well, you have my word. In your chamber, only three nights ago, did I not promise to leave you alone?"

"Nay. You said 'Worry not.'"

Fulk reached around and pulled his sword from beneath the pallet. Jehanne sat up straight, her eyes wide.

Fulk left it sheathed, but placed his hands over the pommel and knelt before her. "I swear to you, Jehanne of Windermere, before Christ and His apostles, that never did I have carnal knowledge of Lioba, with or without her permission. Nor did I beat her. Furthermore, I shall treat you as I would my mother or sister, even should we be wed, if that is your desire. So help me God."

"We shall see if your word is good, Galliard. You do not live by the sword—how can you swear by it?"

Fulk stared at her, and his fingers tightened about the sword hilt. "If I had used that crucifix up on the wall, no doubt you would say the same. What reason have you to mistrust me? What have I done to deserve your ill will?" He thrust his weapon back under the bed.

Jehanne stood and went to the door. "It is not what you have done, Sir Fulk, it is what you *are*."

"And what am I?"

"Nothing more, or less, than a man." With a last flash of her eyes, she slipped out of the cell.

Fulk bounded up and not caring who heard, shouted after her, "There is no bloody hope for me then, in your eyes, is there?"

Pale and slender, she turned in the dim corridor. "None at all."

The way to London from the abbey seemed exceedingly round-about to Jehanne. This turning, that crossing, all melded into a confusing hash of lanes and byways. After hearing several conflicting reports from other travelers on which way to go, she had decided to ride by the sun. If she kept it to her left shoulder in the morning, and the right in the afternoon, she and Corwin should be on course.

But now the sun hurtled toward the horizon, and the spring weather had deteriorated back to that of a month before. A great bank of clouds lurked like ruined castles along the craggy edges of the fells to the east. The wind rose with a moan, bringing the promise of a long, cold night ahead, far from home.

Heavy, dark wings of loneliness swooped to claim Jehanne in a familiar embrace. She was the last of her proud line unless she took a husband—and gave him Windermere. Unless she bore him a child...Jehanne shook her head in vain as Fulk came to mind and would not leave.

He was blessed with a mother, indeed. One who was virtuous and beautiful and who adored him. Jehanne had not been prepared to see such love for a man blazing from a nun's eyes, son or no son. An unconditional love that absolved him of all wrongdoing. Fulk must have done something awful, something that had wounded Brigitta terribly.

His every gesture, his deference, told how he still begged her forgiveness even though she had already given it. But in truth it was his own forgiveness he needed. Jehanne knew that of him, as surely as she knew it of herself. And just as surely, she knew it would never happen.

Some acts were simply unforgivable.

A faint rumble, more felt than heard, prickled Jehanne's skin. Her breath stilled. Hoofbeats. Coming fast and getting louder on the road behind her. She hefted her lance, leveled it and turned her horse to face the danger. At her nod, Corwin moved his mount into place at her flank.

A horseman approached at a canter, his shape outlined by the golden glow of the lowering sun. Should they stand or flee? She looked to Corwin.

He blinked his thick-lashed lids. "'Tis Fulk, milady. I know the pattern on the Frisian's brow band."

"Ah." Jehanne raised her lance-tip. Relief fought apprehension. The knight would be furious, no doubt, that she had not waited for him to accompany her from the abbey. Her fear was realized when he neared enough for her to see the daunting look on his face. He brought his horse neatly to a walk alongside hers.

"Lady Jehanne. I thought we had come to terms. What are you doing out here with but a boy for escort?" He glared at Corwin as if it were his fault, then turned back to her. "Are you completely stupid?"

Jehanne lifted her chin. "Nay, not completely! I thought it best to leave you in the safety of the abbey, as it appears you are being hunted as a miscreant. I decided to make haste to Henry's court."

Ignoring her, Fulk turned to Corwin. "How could you be party to such folly? There are any number of rogues and murderous folk out here, just waiting for someone like you to pass."

Corwin's defiance was less convincing than Jehanne's. "I—I follow my lady's orders. She needs no more protection than I can offer."

"Do not be so bloody cocksure about that. What could you do against a company of armed men? Go back a few paces, I would speak to her in private."

Corwin ducked his head and did as he was told.

"Do not presume to chastise me or mine, Sir Fulk. I am yet free of your command." Jehanne thudded her lance-butt to the ground.

"What offal. You may reign supreme at your keep. But on the road you will follow my lead."

"And if I do not?" she asked his back, as he reined his horse around.

"Well, if you do not, you will find yourself at Grimald's castle in Blackburn, for the road to London was the last forking to the right." Fulk gave her the smallest of smiles over his shoulder.

"Oh! Oh, dear." Chagrined, Jehanne urged her horse to fall into step beside the Frisian.

Fulk glanced down at her. "What *are* you doing with that spear?"

"The same as anyone. I carry it to fend off enemies."

"Indeed." Fulk sounded dubious.

"You don't believe me capable?"

"Capable or no, it is not fitting for a lady to ride about loaded to the heavens with weaponry."

Jehanne threw him a withering look. "I hear that given a choice, *you* would prefer not to bear arms. If neither of us did, what then?"

Fulk narrowed his eyes at her. "I need not explain myself to you. But I take no joy in spilling other men's blood. I did once, but no more. It is a pleasure too dearly bought."

"As I have said before, duty does not imply pleasure." Jehanne sat forward and guided her palfrey around a low spot in the road, boggy with half-melted ice. "But you are a sworn knight. How can you avoid bloodshed and still maintain your honor?"

Fulk reached over his horse's neck and with nimble fingers disengaged a burr from its long mane. "What do you want? Have you a champion to challenge me in the lists? Or would you still rather go at me yourself?" He flicked the burr away, set his jaw and stared straight ahead.

Jehanne sighed. "I would not provoke you, sir, it is but the way I was raised. As my father desired a son more than anything else, I strove to meet his approval in all things martial. But, in the end, my attempts to please him failed, so that—" Jehanne's throat tightened at the memory of her father's wrath.

"So that...?"

Fulk's voice had turned soft again, creating within her an unaccountable desire to hear him say her name in that same velvet tone. She took a deep breath.

"I came to realize that neither a son, nor a proper daughter could I be. I am so far past the sweetness expected of a maid, and fall so short of the prowess required of a warrior, that I can only act as steward of my family's honor. My father was a perfect knight. I cannot add to his glory with great deeds of my own, but I can, and will, fight to protect what is left."

"So you have convinced yourself. But, my lady, there is no such thing as a perfect knight. Your admirable ambition leaves little hope for a life of your own."

Jehanne balked at the seed of doubt Fulk's words created, and resorted to yet another of her maxims. "There can be no life without honor. At least none that I care to lead." As if to emphasize the point, a dull ache started below her belt, and she shifted in her saddle.

Fulk rode on, oblivious to her discomfort. "True. One is generally better off dead than disgraced."

"You sound most sincere, sir. But, why then, did you forfeit your honor, that day at the Duke's tournament?" She could see his back stiffen at her question.

"You mean with Grimald?"

"Aye. Have you forgotten the hail of rubbish the crowd threw at you? I have not. Never did I see a more unhappy state of affairs—all those weeping women—"

Fulk raised his hand. "Never mind them. Wisely, the crowd was anxious to satisfy Grimald's lust for my humiliation. I bear them no malice. But I did not forfeit my honor. Not on that occasion, at least."

"But I saw you—"

"You did not. By the merest chance, *I* saw Grimald's girth had been nearly cut through, by one of his faithful retainers, no doubt. If he had met me with impact, he might have broken his neck. At the very least taken a hard fall."

Jehanne's heart suddenly felt a great deal lighter. "You saved your enemy, at the cost of victory?"

"Well, once I had stopped, and he realized what was amiss, he accused me of tampering with his girth and threatened the heralds. They did nothing to disabuse the onlookers that I was not simply backing out for my own safety, considering the tip on his lance. I would have truly covered myself in shame had I protested at that point."

"You chose not to win with an unfair advantage, yet he held you captive ever since?"

"Aye. Grimald has no respect for fair play."

Jehanne no longer wondered at Fulk's frequently troubled expression.

He continued, "But as you well know, one cannot always think of one's own pride. As long as there are those who need my service, I must keep body and soul together."

Jehanne gave him a pointed look. "Your mother and sister?"

"Aye." His eyes glowed with the warm color of burnt earth. "And you."

She swallowed, and surveyed the forest-clad hills rather than meet his intense gaze. "Tell me of Celine."

Fulk heaved a sigh. "She is delicate, and sweet, and dark like a wood violet. Those who meet her cannot help but love her. And she returns their love with grace and innocent, joyful affection."

His voice took on a note of devotion, even of reverence. An awful stab of new pain struck Jehanne within, stopping her breath momentarily. With a start of dismay, she recognized it for what it was. Envy. Celine must be a precious doe of a girl. And Jehanne herself was a bloodthirsty lioness by comparison. Not anything Fulk could ever love.

But since when did she want to be something he might love? And after all, lions could defend their lairs, roe-deer could not. Her sigh was an echo of Fulk's. "I should very much like to meet her."

Fulk gave her a pleased grin. "You will. You can help me guard her honor until I find her a suitable husband."

"I shall guard it as I do my own," Jehanne said flatly, drawing a sharp glance from Fulk.

"Then I have no worry on her behalf. But your honor is safe with me. You need not exercise such vigilance."

Jehanne stroked her palfrey's warm neck, and wound a bit of mane around her finger. Perhaps Fulk spoke the truth. Perhaps she was nothing more than a nuisance to him. But to her he was a large problem of brawny, beautiful, incomprehensible male. She decided not to reassure him. "When will the lady Celine come to Windermere?"

"As soon as I fetch her from where she is fostered."

Jehanne took another deep breath. If he was willing to talk, she might as well ask. "Why, sir, in truth, are you called 'the Reluctant'?"

Fulk kept his gaze aimed between his horse's ears. "It is a long, sad story."

His tone told her the subject was closed, so she took a different approach. "But, and I mean no offense, you seem more suited to be a cleric than a knight, from what I have seen."

"What have you seen?" He looked at her from beneath thick brows.

"You show too much mercy to be an effective knight. You feel the pain of others."

"I but feel my own pain, reflected. If you think me merciful, others think me a coward."

"What are you like when you are angry, then?"

"Pray you never find out, my lady."

Jehanne had already prayed to that effect, though she had not let him know it. There was another sharp twinge of pain in her abdomen, accompanied by a heavy ache. With a sinking feeling she realized that her courses had started.

They had stopped for some reason during the siege, and she had not missed them. But now they came with a vengeance. It had to be the cursed full moon. The twinge turned into a stab, and a warm wetness spread beneath her. Her saddle would be ruined.

"Sir Fulk, I must stop a moment, over here."

"Shall I dismount, or will you be quick?"

"Call Corwin and keep your back turned."

Half-doubled, Jehanne took the small bundle Corwin handed her and retreated to the shrubbery. She had brought a gown to wear before the king. A sorry rag it was, too, compared to what the court ladies wore. But it was comfortable. She would don it and shed her sword belt. She pulled her undertunic off over her head and eyed it. The sleeves could be replaced, she decided, and set to cutting them off.

A short while later, a bit more comfortable, she emerged. Corwin knew exactly what the trouble was, Jehanne could tell from his sympathetic grin. He had six elder sisters.

Fulk appeared baffled at first, then colored and glanced away. Without a scrap of sympathy for him, Jehanne took her reins and accepted a boost from Corwin.

At a flurry of beating wings, she glanced up from adjusting her stirrup. Past a bend in the road they had come down, a flock of birds burst into flight from the trees.

In the dusky lane Fulk looked over his shoulder, his attention riveted on the empty roadway. Then he turned, and in one smooth motion threw his leg over his horse's neck, slid to the ground and grabbed Corwin's arm. "Men are coming, with heavy horse. Run into the forest and hide."

"Nay. I won't leave my lady."

"Oh, for the love of Christ, there is no time!"

Jehanne cried out as Fulk backhanded the boy. Corwin fell to the ground insensible, his nose pouring blood. Before she could arm herself Fulk dragged her from her palfrey.

"What are you doing?" Blind panic filled her. Her body took over, nothing but instinct and terror moved her limbs. With all her might she kicked and punched at Fulk. Her chest tightened as she fought his powerful arms.

His features blurred into what could have been any enraged man's face. He had become a complete stranger—or rather, the embodiment of the brute she knew every man to be. Exactly what she had expected he would reveal himself as, sooner or later.

"Shut up, lie down and do not move." Fulk shoved her off-balance toward a grassy patch and drew his dagger. Hard-eyed, he advanced upon her.

Jehanne froze. Despite her dark expectations, she had secretly hoped—but here was a world turned nightmare. Reason fled and her wildest fears roared to life in a crimson wave. He would murder her, blame it on evildoers and be free. This was it. All that he had held back when she had attacked him, everything she imagined he would inflict upon her once his true masculine nature broke loose.

She clutched her own dagger. "Nay, Fulk. Touch me and I'll kill you where you stand."

Fulk's eyes were cold, his jaw bunched with muscle. He glanced over his shoulder. "Can't you understand? You are dead! Get down!" He pushed her harder and she fell to the grass. She tried to stab him but with a deft twist he wrested the knife from her and straddled her hips. Sweet Mary, he was huge.

Jehanne fought the urge to close her eyes. If she was to die, she would do it facing her enemy. The terrible, handsome Fulk, who had turned on her at last.

"Bastard! Let me go, give me a chance to fight back, you big disgusting animal!" She could think of nothing else to call him.

"Play dead, you stupid, stubborn little she-ass!"

"Hah! I will never—" Through the earth at her back Jehanne felt the pounding of hoofbeats. She raised her head and squeaked at the sight of armed riders skidding to a halt behind Fulk. Their mouths opened in apparent surprise at the spectacle of him atop her, then they grinned as one.

Fulk clamped his left hand over her mouth and before she could blink his dagger was on its way toward her throat. With all her strength she writhed beneath him. He winced, and blood spurted—his blood. She had spoiled his aim, at least.

"Poxy bitch!" he snarled, loud enough for the strangers to hear, but his pained look did not match his words.

Jehanne's stomach lurched as Fulk wrapped his hands around her neck. He smeared his hot, rich-smelling blood all across her throat and down her front. Quickly he slid down to her knees.

"Must I knock you senseless, too?" he hissed. Dragging up her skirts, he forced her legs apart despite her fierce resistance. "Raise your hips. Do it!"

A wail of agony escaped Jehanne. Not for her body, but for the shame and torment Fulk caused her already ravaged soul. She would rather die than be treated thus. Her inferior strength made pitifully obvious. Her ability to fight and defend herself lost. Her dignity stripped away by his savage force.

In that moment she hated him, with a consuming, bitter rage.

"Please..." he whispered.

Even as she was about to spit in his face, Jehanne saw the desperation in Fulk's eyes, the fear—and an apology. He begged in silence for her trust. With a stunning, painful jolt, she realized Fulk's concern was for her, not himself.

What in God's name was he doing? If these riders were his enemies, why did he not let her up that they might fight them off together, as friends in arms? This was a coward's way out.

Horror crawled in her gut. But some instinct told her to obey him. She lifted her bottom just in time, for his blade grazed the inside of her thigh as he rammed it into the ground between her legs, under the cover of her skirts. She let her head loll and lay still.

Through half-closed eyes she watched Fulk rave and curse like

ne possessed. He jerked the dagger free as though he had just
hrust it into her.

"Filthy, lying whore of Satan!" He lurched upward and stag-
ered back a step, then spat upon her body before turning to face
he contingent of horsemen.

"Woman trouble, Fulk?" the fair-haired leader drawled, and
is thick lips curled into a smile Jehanne would have given good
ilver not to have witnessed. Hengist of Longlake. "It seems
ou've made the wench pay dearly for marking you."

"Aye." Fulk clutched his slashed forearm, which still bled pro-
usely. "I have paid her, and then some."

Hengist stilled. He peered at Jehanne, and frowned.

She wanted to swallow, to blink, but dared not move. Under-
tanding flooded her. Fulk had struck Corwin down, knowing the
ad could not defend himself against men like these. She had not
poiled Fulk's aim—he had cut himself to create the illusion that
e had slit her throat. Then he had feigned her mutilation so this
vild knight and his warriors would not be tempted by her female
lesh. A living woman or a dead one, they might not be particular.

An overwhelming desire to jump up and challenge them
gripped her. Then the enormity of the situation sank in. There
vere too many for the two of them to fight alone. Too many for
nalf a dozen men to fight.

Abruptly Hengist bellowed, "Galliard, you murdering swine!
You've slain Alun's daughter! She refused you after all, did she?
Well, I'd best finish what she started." The Hurler spurred his
norse forward, sword raised to cut Fulk down.

Jehanne's throat closed. Never had she dreamed a man like
Hengist would mourn her passing. For a hideous moment Fulk
ust stood there and stared. Breathing hard, with his left wrist
pressed against his chest, the red stain growing larger.

Hengist bore down upon him and still he did not move. At the
ast possible moment Fulk leaped aside and Hengist's blade whis-
led through the air. Carefully, Jehanne released the breath she
nad been holding, as Fulk drew his sword. Hengist wheeled his
mount and jerked it onto its haunches, brandishing his weapon.

Jehanne's mind raced. Her palfrey stood just by the gorse patch
at the roadside. Her bow was tied to her saddle. She lifted her

head a little and glanced left and right. Hengist's men watche
the fight, apparently satisfied with the entertainment their lord an
Fulk provided with no danger to themselves.

Fulk might hate her for it, but she had to help him. Still on he
back, Jehanne began to ease herself toward her horse.

Chapter Twelve

Fulk drew a deep breath, fighting the nausea and dizziness threatening to engulf him. God's face—what was wrong with him that even now he hesitated, with Hengist ready to mow him down? He tightened his grip on his sword. His thoughts raced into their familiar pattern of litany and rebuttal.

This is not Rabel. This is a man I have every reason to slay.

Nay, this is a man, created in God's image. This is a body, with a touch of the divine giving it life, that you would render into pieces.

Nay, this is a demon, who would gladly defile the bravest maid in England....

"'Tis true, Fulk. Your cowardice is greatly understated. Look at you, quaking as you stand, ready to puke, too frightened to do anything but wait for me to take your head!'' Again, Hengist dug his spurs deep, and the destrier bounded forward.

Fulk swallowed, and let the red roar building within him rise and emerge as a snarl. A feral, beastly sound. One of rage and terror, for he caught sight of Jehanne, worming her way closer to her horse.

Even as he swung his blade at Hengist, Fulk prayed Jehanne would have the sense to mount and gallop away. But he knew she would not, no more than would any valiant warrior.

Steel sparked as Hengist's sword sheared down Fulk's, the tip racing toward his throat. Rather than fight the weight of both knight and horse, Fulk ducked and spun. Hengist nearly lost his seat with the sudden lack of resistance.

"Bloody stoat! Stand still and die like a man!" The blond knight heaved himself upright, and with a motion of his head, summoned the rest of his men to the fray.

With joyful whoops they descended upon Fulk. At the sight of so many eyes, gleaming with blood lust, Fulk forgot that the men behind them had souls. Forgot that he would have preferred his own death to that of another. Forgot Rabel, and his own searing guilt at the surge of pure, wicked, pleasure the crunch of his fist had brought when it splintered into his brother's arrogant face.

All that mattered was that he prevent these men from harming Jehanne. His *furor* rose to claim him. It gave his body a speed and power that toppled the closest of Hengist's men.

Fulk swung with all his strength and felt his sword bite flesh, over and over again. His attackers' glee turned to wails of pain and death, and still he slashed at them, well beyond reason.

The terrible force he had hoped was dead burned bright, flourishing with every stroke of his blade. Enemy blood flowed, and Fulk gloried in it, for its own red sake. *An abomination.* So had his own father pronounced him.

"Lord God, oh Rabel, forgive me!" Clarity returned too late to Fulk's mind. The ground shuddered as Hengist raced toward him, howling. Fulk gasped as steel sliced into his upper arm.

Someone smote his head with a lance-butt, and black danced on the edges of his vision. One knight rammed him with his horse's shoulder, and another caught him with his destrier's rump. The riders forced their stallions together, so that as each animal kicked at the others they struck Fulk, trapped in their midst.

This was a beating the likes of which he had no experience. His body was no match for the massive horses' pounding. Their hooves were turning his legs to pulp, breaking his ribs.

Fulk felt himself slipping toward darkness. He had to remain standing or they would trample him unto death. He had no room to swing, and as distasteful as it would have been to cut a horse, he would have, given the chance to survive. But the heavy battering was killing him.

He could not draw breath. He could not see. But he heard a loud hiss and a solid thud. Then another, and another, and with the sounds, men began to fall from their saddles. Arrows pro-

ruded from their bodies, some buried all the way up to the peacock fletches of the ashwood shafts.

Surprise and fear etched the faces of the men who remained.

Through the blood streaming into his eyes Fulk could just make
out Jehanne, readying yet another shot. But Hengist and the remaining warriors kicked their mounts and galloped away. Their
mail could not withstand a fast archer at close quarters.

With a sigh of bittersweet relief Fulk let himself sink to the
ground, his head resting upon the thigh of a fallen enemy. He had
proven to himself once and for all his own evil was marrow deep.
A part of himself he could not eradicate. On this occasion, because
of his *furor* he had overcome his enemies, with Jehanne's help.

But she would never be safe with him. Next time, the terror he
had seen in her eyes at the sight of him might be warranted.

Now, to his amazement, she knelt at his side, her cool palm
stroking his cheek. With her skirt she wiped his face, and her eyes
glinted, as if loaded with tears. Then, to Fulk's utter astonishment,
her lips touched his, as lightly as a leaf floating on water.

"You fought well." Jehanne's voice brimmed with admiration.

"My lady..." He wanted to tell her it was not something of
which he was proud. He looked into her shining eyes, and knew
he must remain silent. The warrior maiden would not understand.
Fulk took a breath and pain streaked through his chest. He tried
to sit up and found agony with the slightest movement.

"Corwin, is he—"

"Shh, be still. The boy is in one piece. Thanks to you, they
did not bother with him."

Another soothing touch to his sweaty brow. "You have both
saved and shamed me, my lady. And although you have my gratitude and thanks—"

"Be quiet."

"—I would rather die than be rescued by the hand of a
maiden." At the moment, such a gentle hand.

"You can still die, and by my hand, if you wish. Now hush,
or I will see that it comes to pass."

Those same small hands possessed surprising strength. Jehanne
mopped and bound Fulk's wounds with strips of her undergown.
She forced him to his feet.

He looked about, his knees threatening to buckle, and his heart nearly stopped. The magnificent Frisian was gone. It was enough to make a man weep. His legs wobbled. "They have stolen my horse."

"Do not worry, you will have him back one day."

Fulk did not want to dispell her confident prediction. Hengist would probably eat the Frisian out of spite.

Jehanne helped him stagger to her palfrey and mount. Once she and Corwin were seated upon the lad's horse, they led Fulk into the forest, down a lane thickly strewn with brown, crackling leaves.

The farther they went the narrower it became, until the thread of a trail opened onto a clearing, echoing to the chirps of small birds sorting out their roosts for the night. There in the deep blue light of evening sat a cottage, in ill repair, the thatch gone in places. Nearby was a great, blackened stack of timbers, set on end.

"What is this place?" As if indeed he cared.

Jehanne sighed. "Well, it would seem I have been going in circles all day, for this is the charcoal-burners' hut. The fever did not reach here, but still they fled, for they thought if God were so displeased with us at Windermere, He might be more so with them, for they do still practice pagan ways."

"I see." Barely, for one eye had swollen shut.

Slumping between Jehanne and Corwin, Fulk lurched into the single room of the cottage. They bade him lie down on the bare planks of a bench, built against one wall.

"Do not move," Jehanne said unnecessarily.

Fulk did not, could not move. His limbs rapidly stiffened and swelled. His head felt barely attached to his body. Thirst raged in his throat.

Jehanne rummaged, and he heard the clang of tin.

"Corwin's off to the brook."

He could only grunt in reply. When the boy returned, Fulk gulped down the water. "I am sorry I hurt you, lad."

Corwin replied softly, "No matter, sir. I understand. One day I will know how to fight as you did."

Fulk could not respond, for his attention was fully claimed by

Jehanne, who, with careful fingers, examined his legs through the rips in his hose.

"Ow."

"I should think so. You have great horseshoe-shaped dents in your thighs, cleats and all. It will be a sennight at least before you can bear weight," she pronounced grimly. "You will be black and blue down to your ankles. I have seen legs lost for bruising this severe. And if we do not get these wounds properly stitched and plastered you may bleed to death."

"I feel much better knowing that, my lady."

"What possessed you to take on the horses as well as the riders?" Jehanne frowned at him as she snugged the bandages tighter around his upper arm and wrist.

Just like a woman, to scold under such circumstances. Fulk squinted through the slit his swollen eyelids allowed him. "I could hardly challenge one without the other."

"You should have demanded that they either dismounted or waited for you to mount."

"Think you they would have complied, just for my asking?"

"A few were knights. They should have dealt with you honorably and fairly."

"Aye. I wish to God they had." As bad as his reputation was, he would never live down a female coming to his aid. Especially a lovely, naïve lass such as this one.

"I was surprised to see you draw your sword at all."

And more so a lass who despised him. "Why would I carry it, then? Did you expect me to go down on my knees and beg for mercy?"

Her color rose to a charming pink, encompassing her cheeks and her scar, barely noticeable of late. "Well, I—"

"Listen, lady. I had little enough honor before you saved me. Now I have next to none. How and if I choose to defend it is up to me. But when it comes to your well-being, there is no question of holding back."

She did not meet his eyes, but fiddled with his lacings, loosening his boots. "Why is it shameful for me to help you, but not the other way round?"

"Because you are a woman."

"Corwin, go gather some firewood." Once the boy had gone, Jehanne continued dryly, "You noticed?"

"Frankly, despite your best efforts, it is hard to miss."

"I saw how you kept looking toward me during the fight. It seems each of your roving eyes needs a separate target upon which to focus. Good thing they are not too far apart."

"My eyes, or your targets?" The objects he referred to were not a foot distant from him, and brimming most provocatively at the edge of her bodice.

"Sir, were you not already sorely beleaguered, I would slap you for your impertinence."

Fulk took a deep breath and stifled his resultant moan. "When I am better, you can throw down your gage before me."

She stopped, boot in hand, and stared at him. "Will you pick it up?"

"Oh, aye. Gladly. I will win, too, with one arm tied behind my back. Perhaps both." He failed in his initial attempt to smile.

"That will not be necessary. Rules are rules, and you will have your choice of weapons."

"Ah, true. I shall have to think about that."

"Mace, sword, lance or axe?" Jehanne sounded quite serious.

"Mmm...I have something else in mind."

Her eyes widened, as did Fulk's lopsided grin.

"You *are* a dreamer, sir!"

"Aye." Fulk caught her hand and dragged it toward his mouth. Her back pull was powerful. He gradually relaxed his grip, and with that her resistance waned. He kissed the first knuckle of her thumb. "There, was that so bad, this time?"

"You have three and ten more joints to go, Galliard. On that hand," she added, and he saw the first glimmer of a smile in her eyes.

"I will save them for later. God knows they have seen better days. And the taste is awful."

"It is your sweat and blood, not mine!"

"You used to smell of mint."

"That was before." She looked away.

"Ah, mayhap you thought to entice me?"

"What rot. Its smell is not sweet, it was a balm for my illness.

Lioba anointed me with it. You need to rest. You're talking nonsense.'' Jehanne drew her mantle over Fulk.

He was not cold, but he did not stop her. He gazed at her increasingly blurry face, and tried to chase away his grogginess by talking. "It is pleasant here, is it not? You and I, alone with night coming on. Have no fear of the dark, my lady, I shall keep you safe. And warm—until either I fade or the dawn arrives....''

"Oh, Galliard. I fear for your mind. Even were we—that friendly—you could not so much as lift your head, never mind your—''

"Don't say it.''

"I can hardly bear the thought, much less give it substance by uttering words on the subject.'' Again, she blushed.

"It is indescribable, in any event.'' Again, he grinned.

"That I do not doubt.'' Jehanne rolled her eyes.

Exhaustion won and Fulk closed his. Physically, he was in more pain than he had ever been in his life. Merely to breathe was torture. "I am going to die.''

"So shall we all. You will get no sympathy from me. How many's the time I have heard such tales from lovesick men.''

There was an unexpected, tiny quaver in her voice. But he could not hide the truth from her, no matter how distressing.

"If I fall asleep I will not wake again.'' That did not seem such a terrible prospect, considering how he felt.

"Then open your eyes! Now!''

Fulk wondered at her fierce command. When he did open his eyes, she spoke softly.

"I shall remove you to the brook. You can lie with your legs in the cold water.''

He groaned. "Oh, nay, I cannot budge. I do not want to wallow in any brook. I do not swim!''

"At this moment you are a simpleton, sir. I hereby relieve you of all decision-making on your own behalf.''

Fulk did not know when Jehanne had begun to sound like Sir Bayard, the king's master-at-arms, who had frequently attempted to beat Fulk into submission when the latter was a squire. It was most disconcerting. "As you wish,'' he said, resigned to his fate.

She did not fail him. With Corwin's help, a horse was soon

dragging him on a makeshift sledge, assembled from a half-rotte
cow hide lashed to the bed planks. Fulk gritted his teeth ove
every bump, and by the time they reached the water he wishe
he could indeed go to sleep and not awaken. The ice-cold strea
water turned his legs blessedly numb, but he began to shiver ur
controllably.

Jehanne sat on a stone and calmly watched him suffer.

"Why do you not go home, lady? You do yourself no goo
here. If Hengist returns he will have both our heads. You can sen
someone for me. Or not. Windermere will be yours again."

Her lips twitched into a rare smile. "When I best you it sha
be on equal terms, not by deserting you when you are half dead
And those men shall not venture here, not after dark, at least."

"Too many evil spirits?" Fulk scoffed even as he shuddered

"There certainly are. When the pagan gods are abandoned an
no longer receive offerings, they turn vicious. Stragglers in th
woods are a favorite prey." Jehanne slanted her gaze to him from
beneath dense golden lashes.

"Ah, well, we must appease them, then."

"With what? They want skins of ale, and eggs and bread, no
promises of good behavior. Besides, it would be unchristian. Bu
if it makes you feel better, I shall leave some barley from m
saddle bag upon the hearth."

Visions filled Fulk's head, of himself and Jehanne in a fore
meadow, energetically appeasing the gods in a thoroughly paga
fashion. Most certainly not good behavior. Curse his mind for th
things he thought of when his body could not follow through. B
he was dreaming, in any event. "Jehanne, I am merely makir
conversation. You need not take me so literally."

Lord. If only she would.

"I think you should be quiet. I am taking you back to th
abbey. You have lain in that water long enough." She rose an
stood before him, straight and slender, her arms akimbo.

"Oh, sweet Jesus, spare me. Another move and I shall wee
I swear it." He slapped the water in frustration.

"Go ahead, I will not tell anyone. But we cannot tarry her
You need proper attention. Once you have warmed by the fire,
am going to put you on my horse, one way or another."

The "way" turned out to be painful. She and Corwin got Fulk onto a stump, and he was able to slide into the saddle. But every step the palfrey took felt like a jab from hell in his ribs.

It was a long ride back to the convent.

They rested there three days, and Brigitta showed Jehanne how to make herb poultices useful on both humans and horses. But Fulk could not lie still as Jehanne applied them. He squirmed and writhed and caused himself a great deal of avoidable pain.

"Why do you torture me with those stinking bags of vegetables? And why rub me with salty dough? Am I some joint of meat you are preparing to roast?"

Jehanne gave Fulk a look of long-suffering and continued to massage his swollen thighs, no matter his groans. "I do not understand why your mother puts up with you. Such an ungrateful sod! I should leave you to the care of Sister Agatha, the one with whiskers and hands the size of hams. She will set you to rights with none of your nonsense. Then you would be more appreciative of my ministrations."

"Oh, little do you know how much I appreciate them, lady. And Sister Agatha is a honeycake, quite unlike you. Please. Just give me my clothes and I will ride home without complaint. In a bloody cart, if you insist."

"Will you obey my instructions with regard to your wounds?"

He nodded, each motion aggravating the pain in his shoulder, which had not hurt all that much before. In fact, every part of his body hurt more than it had at first, and he could barely move.

But soon he was bedded down on a thick pile of straw in the back of a curtained, horse-drawn wagon, on the way to Windermere. To be carted thus was humiliating, but he had no choice.

Jehanne rode most of the afternoon. Occasionally she jumped down and climbed into the wagon without asking the driver to stop. *Solely for my torment,* Fulk thought. She sat opposite him and watched while he pretended to sleep.

Except to tend his bandages she never once touched him, and rarely spoke. Just watched, her gray eyes like storm clouds flickering with lightning. And he lay there, his heart pounding, wanting her to curl up beside him and put her head upon his chest.

From her corner, Jehanne kept a careful eye upon Fulk. It wor-

ried her that he slept through the jolts and rumblings of the
wagon's progress. She had ordered that they drive on, stopping
only to rest and feed the horses. Fulk had grown increasingly pale
as the journey continued, and she feared he was bleeding inside,
where she was helpless to stop the flow.

He lay so very still. An image of her father's once-powerful
body flashed before her. Motionless. White-faced.

Stone dead.

Jehanne waited until the pain in her heart eased, then crept
closer to Fulk. He was not one who snored, and between the
jarring of the road and the murky light, she could not see the rise
and fall of his chest. It would reassure her mightily to hear him
breathe.

On hands and knees, she moved slowly, so that she would not
be accidentally thrown against him by the lurching conveyance.
Stretched out beside him, Jehanne attempted to listen, but the
creaks and rattles of the wagon made it impossible to tell by that
means if Fulk yet lived.

She thought of pinching him, but rejected the idea, in case he
proved himself alive by lashing out at her. Only a fool would
chance a blow from fists that size. Nay, a bolder path was needed.

She skimmed her hand over his chest. There were no openings
in his clothing through which she might feel his heartbeat. Quickly
she withdrew, and blew on her fingers to make sure they were
not cold. Then she slipped her hand higher, to his neck, where
she had seen the throbbing of his lifeblood. On several occasions,
in fact.

Delicately Jehanne pressed where his jaw and neck met. The
skin was warm and damp, partly smooth, partly stubbled. Straining to keep her balance, and her weight from bumping him, she
held her breath. There. She could feel the pulsing movement.
Slow, full and heavy. She bowed her head in relief. But even as
she lingered, the blood's pace quickened, bounding beneath her
fingers.

"Would you throttle me as I sleep, little one?" Fulk's hand
captured hers.

"In a trice," she countered, startled, but did not attempt to pull

way. He was in no condition to do more than hold her hand, she
ssured herself.

"I thought as much. I had best keep this where I know it can
do no harm."

"What?"

"You heard me." Fulk wrapped his long fingers about her
and, pressing it to his chest. Jehanne knew her error, for now,
ven through the layers of his tunic and surcoat, there was no
mistaking the potent thud of his heart, vibrating onto her palm.

"I thought perhaps you had died," she said, wishing she had
tayed in her corner.

Fulk chuckled, coughing a little. "I don't believe I shall die so
quietly after all, my lady. I hope I have not disappointed you."

At the timbre of his voice, as palpable as his heartbeat, a wild
urge raced through Jehanne, an irrational thrill. Never had she
ain so close to a man, even like this, fully clothed. And to lie
ext to such a one as Fulk, to experience the leap of—what?
Desire? Lust? She did not have a name for it.

But her discovery that the mere sound of his voice at close
quarters, the mere contact of his skin to hers now triggered waves
f heat and dizziness, was more than alarming. He was dangerous.
And she was a fool, just like all the other women he had charmed
o the detriment of their eternal souls.

"Nay, you have not disappointed me. Not yet." Who had put
uch words into her mouth? Fulk had bedeviled her. She was
ossessed by some pet demon he had at his command. She never
hould have touched him. Especially not when she wanted to so
adly.

"Let us hope that I never do." His languid gaze drifted over
er face, then focused on her lips. "Hmm. A kiss, perhaps?"

Jehanne's stomach collided with her heart. "What?"

"A small test only, to ease your mind. As you are most likely
oing to become my bride—if I live—you have a right to some
xpectation of proficiency."

"I have heard more than enough testimony in that regard. I
ave no doubts about your...proficiency."

"Ah, but what pleases some does not please all. There is noth-
ng like firsthand experience. You, *Baronne,* may instruct me ac-

cording to your preference and desire.'' Fulk gave her hand
little squeeze, and rubbed his thumb against her palm.

''Oh, Lord,'' Jehanne moaned. ''But I know nothing about kiss
ing.''

''Truly?'' Fulk's voice held genuine interest.

She thought about it. ''Well, apart from the one you stole from
me in the snow, I have kissed the Bishop's ring, the sweet hea
of Mary the Proud's babe, my father's cheek, and once Thaddeu
pushed me down and thrust his—'' Jehanne stopped, unwilling t
elaborate.

''Don't be shy. Believe me, I am aware of every possible per
mutation of such activity. You cannot possibly make me blush.'

Jehanne frowned, not at all reassured by Fulk's avowal. Sh
had already made him blush at least twice since they had met.

''Well, he said it was a greeting common among the French
But to me it seemed a most unnatural and distasteful invasion.'

''Invasion of what?'' Fulk asked carefully.

''I shudder to think of it. I am too embarrassed to tell.'' Th
memory of her cousin's sticky fingers and greasy lips and probin
tongue was one she took pains to keep at bay.

''Then it is certain he did not do it properly. There is a knac
to these things, eh? After all, he is a mere stripling, one canno
judge his technique too harshly.''

''You seem to know more about the matter than I do, when
have not even named the where or how of it.''

''Then kindly do name the where and the how of it.''

''His tongue. In my mouth. I bit him. That was all.''

Fulk's bark of laughter ended in a groan. ''Oh, my ribs. Yo
bit him? Good for you.''

Jehanne propped her head on her free hand. ''Of course yo
will never try anything like that with me.''

''Assuredly not. The Reluctant takes no unnecessary risks.''

The devil prodded Jehanne again. ''But...what if I swore a
oath not to bite?''

''That would be another matter entirely. In such an event,
might be persuaded to show you how *I* would do it.''

''*It?*''

Fulk's voice dropped to a husky murmur. ''How I would tak

an ordinary kiss—an affectionate greeting, that is—and move it beyond the commonplace, into the regions of honey and fire...of thrust and parry...of burning and quenching.''

Jehanne trembled. His words were like a warm, silken veil being drawn slowly across her naked skin. ''Show me,'' she whispered, dismayed at her own audacity, but unable to resist his offer. ''On my honor, I swear I will not bite you.''

''Come closer, then.''

She shifted up, leaning across his chest.

''Ah, sweeting, not there...ow, nor yet there—''

She freed her hand from his grasp and sat back. ''I don't mean to hurt you. Where, then?''

''Forgive me. For this demonstration to work, as much as I would like to embrace you properly, it is you who must embrace me.''

''How?''

''Well, you may not want to do it. You may find it most unseemly and offensive.''

Kneeling beside him, Jehanne put her fists to her hips. ''Galiard, you have started down this path, you must see it to the end. Cease this stalling! I will not be left the most ignorant maiden this side of the Narrow Sea!''

Fulk smiled. ''Very well. Straddle me. As you would to ride.''

Jehanne faltered. ''Where, exactly?''

His eyes gleamed, whether with amusement at her expense, or anticipation, she could not tell.

''You have seen my bruises, my wounds. Where, exactly, am I untouched?'' Fulk's tone was all innocence.

Jehanne gulped. *Mayhap you should remain untouched,* she thought, but said, ''How much weight shall I rest upon you?'' She raised her knee and began to cautiously position herself astride his hips, without actually letting her bottom meet his...more sensitive, but uninjured area.

''Keep most of it on your knees and lower legs, and put your hands to the straw, on either side of my chest. Then you may rock your weight forward or arrears, as you will.''

The image these instructions evoked left Jehanne breathless. ''My God, sir! What is it you have in mind, after all?''

"I told you you would find it offensive. You can certainly leave off, if you wish," he said amiably.

"Indeed not. You will not best me in this, Fulk." She braced her arms and let her weight rest upon her hands and knees. The fact that this left her rump up in the air did not soothe her ruffled dignity, but she was not about to back down.

The position left her feeling a peculiar mixture of dominance and vulnerability. Thank the Lord this was only a test, as Fulk said. Merely the clarification of a matter of etiquette she would have learned long ago, had her father sent her to be properly educated.

"Just so. You have excellent form, my lady." Fulk's rich voice bathed her in approval.

"M-my thanks, sir."

"Mmm...very well. I will put my hand on your arm as a guide for once our lips meet I cannot speak to direct you. If I pull, come closer. If I push, fall back. If I squeeze, then do what I do. And when I touch you like this..."

Gently, he rubbed from her shoulder to her wrist and back again. Her elbow nearly buckled beneath his warm caress. "Aye?" she managed to say, fighting the urge to flee the wagon and seek the safe, stolid company of Corwin and her horse.

"Then it is your turn to guide *me*. Ready?"

Jehanne nodded, unable to trust her voice.

He pressed the back of her arm. "Forward, easy does it."

The wagon bounced in a rut and Jehanne froze in place, her muscles taut, suspended between fear and curiosity. She had to admit, disgraceful as it was, fascination for this man churned in her, as well as a good bit of admiration.

She stared into Fulk's eyes, as they shifted from dark gold to molten copper in the swaying lamplight. Looked upon his sculpted cheekbones and strong, shadowed jaw. Wondered at his waiting lips, curved in the slightest of smiles.

With a small flash of triumph, she realized that in this moment, he was hers. He wanted her, but his legs were still swollen, his wounds too fresh, he was weak from loss of blood. He could not easily overpower her, nor chase her...nor could he escape. There was nothing to stop her from taking charge of the situation.

Nothing but her own dismal lack of experience. Then, quite unexpectedly, Jehanne felt him draw his knees up behind her. In the obvious grip of pain, Fulk clenched his jaw for a moment, then relaxed once again. She eased her weight off her palms, and found her back supported by his thighs, her bottom resting upon his flat, hard belly.

"There, my lady, now you may sit without fear of making me stiff." He grinned shamelessly. "Where were we?"

"Oh, Galliard, how do you spin such magic? Not three days ago, I was ready to cut you to ribbons with my sword. And now, I...I know not what to do with you."

"I am trying to show you what to do, lady, if you will but give me your attention. And your mouth."

Jehanne bent to meet him. She did not await his instructions but followed her own, springing from deep within her body. To touch his lips was like being struck with fever. Heat and dizziness. She melded her mouth to his. Her tongue did not hesitate to venture into unknown territory. He tasted faintly of anise, and she smiled at the feel of his smile mirroring hers.

Fulk met her with restraint at first. He nibbled, stroked and nuzzled. But his ardor quickly overran her burgeoning response. He caught her nape and locked her in a one-armed embrace. In one moment he inflicted small bites and nips on the skin of her neck, only to soothe them away in the next.

When Jehanne returned the favor, he growled low in his throat. Before she could regret her boldness, his aggressive kisses shifted into an exquisite dance of passion and tenderness. The spark of fear he had ignited with his vehemence gave way to a melting, liquid warmth.

Fulk softened the rhythm of his tongue's forays between her lips. The tension in her muscles eased. He would never force her, Jehanne knew it in her bones, now.

But seduce her he could, she knew that right to the aching of her breasts, and the desire beginning to burn between her legs. Desire that rapidly overtook rational thought. Without conscious intent, she rubbed herself against him, matching the flowing movement of his tongue. The instant response of Fulk's body sent a wave of wild, ravenous heat surging to her core.

He grew—and grew hard. A groan escaped him, between shallow, ragged breaths. Jehanne shivered with the shocked awareness of the effect her wanton act had on him—and of the immense satisfaction she took in her newly discovered power.

The trouble was, she had started a fire without knowing how to quench it. Nor, indeed, how to feed it. His fingers tightened at her back. His hungry kisses slowed and moved from her mouth to her cheeks. Then he buried his face against her neck, in the thick fall of hair he had managed to unbind single-handedly.

"Do not do such things, Jehanne," he ground out. "At least, not until I am better, and you are ready for the consequences. Get off of me. *Now*."

Jehanne's budding delight shriveled, and mortification at her own disappointment took its place. "With pleasure, sir. I find your presumption intolerable."

Fulk gazed at her, looking quite ravished. "I am sorry. You took me by surprise. I was not prepared for such untutored skill. You have left me with a great...discomfort."

Aflame with embarrassment, Jehanne made her way back to her corner and wrapped her arms about her knees. She would not leave, as much as she wanted to. But nor would she have anything to do with his "discomfort." He, the expert, should have been prepared for any eventuality. He, who considered himself the veritable master of love, should have had better control.

"Be assured it will not happen again," she said.

"Ah, but you speak a falsehood, my lady. It *will* happen again. I know it, and you know it. It is only a matter of time. But then you will not be so indifferent to my suffering. You will wind up on the rack, right along with me. And I shall make certain you find it a delectably sweet torture."

Jehanne could only stare, speechless in response to his outrageous claim. An arrogant man, that he surely was.

But, deep, deep inside, past her pride and beyond her fear— she hoped he was right.

Chapter Thirteen

Celine, the Wild Rose of Redware, the only daughter of the late *Comte* de Galliard, kicked the heavy leather ball out of her friends' reach and with a gleeful shout ran after it. The other girls, also fostered at the household of Lady Greyhaven, chased her, laughing and breathless. The ball tumbled downhill, rolling along the common, faster and faster toward the River Aire.

The waterway paralleled the road, which Celine often watched with longing. Travelers passed, and horses pulled barges loaded with wood, stone, hides and all manner of trade goods. All moving toward great cities, new people and ideas. Exciting places.

But through the line of tall, swaying alders there were no boats in sight this day. She ran up to the bank just as the ball plopped into the water and slowly sank out of reach, the current tumbling it away. Celine threw up her hands, amidst the groans of her companions.

At the sound of a horse's trot she turned, the ball forgotten. The horse was stout, skewbald, and it picked up its feet in an energetic rhythm. The rider looked heathen, quite strange, yet vaguely familiar.

His dark-red hair flowed in long tangles away from his face. Deep-set eyes flashed from beneath what looked to be a habitual scowl. Beneath a leathern jack, armored with horn plates, he wore a saffron-colored shirt. An outlandish, checkered blanket was belted about his waist, and while a good portion of it draped over one shoulder, the lower part barely approached his knees.

"Celine, come away! 'Tis a wild hill-man! Please!" The girls pulled at her sleeves. "Oh, we never should have gone beyond the gates!"

"My friends, go if you must. I would hear what this hill-man might tell me of faraway lands." Celine stepped to the edge of the greensward and smoothed her kirtle of wine-red wool.

The horseman slowed, then halted before her, his blue eyes fixed upon her face. Celine's companions cried out in dismay.

"Nay! Oh, Prissy, go tell the baroness that the Lady Celine is up to her tricks again!" With small shrieks of fear, obviously laced with the anticipated pleasure of seeing Celine scolded and locked in the buttery—yet again—the young women retreated to a safe distance while the fleet-footed Prissy raced away.

Celine gazed up at the dark man. He looked like a hawk, sharp and fierce. She nodded toward her companions. "They fear you."

He did not take his gaze from her. "'Tis only natural." His voice rumbled in a thick accent.

She eyed him critically, then smiled. "You are a Gael. A Scotsman! Your knees are naked. Do they not get cold?"

He chewed his lip for a moment, as if the reply required some thought. "Aye, they do. Dost thou not recognize me, lady?"

"Nay...you know me?"

"Aye." He slid from his horse. Drawing his sword, one of the long, double-handed type, he knelt and laid the weapon upon the grass before her.

"Lady Celine, I am Callum Mac an t-Sealgair, Clann 'IcNèill. I have come from thy brother, Sir Fulk, who sends his warmest regards, to escort thee to him without delay. There are those who would do thee harm, lady, and I am here to see that it disnae come to pass. My sword, my life and my heart are thine." He bowed his head.

"Oh!" This was too wonderful. Her very own champion, come to take her to be with Fulk—*Sir* Fulk! "My brother is a knight at last? Kallam-mackant-shelker—I am sorry, what is your name?"

"Malcolm, son of Hunter," the man amended. "Fulk calls me Hunterson, betimes. And aye, he now has his spurs."

"Lovely! But, Malcolm son of Hunter, have you a token for

me, from my lord brother? He will be most angry if I do not ask, though I mean no offense to your honor.''

''Of course, forgive me.'' The Scot reached within his shirt and withdrew a parchment, tied with a leather thong.

Celine unrolled it and recognized Fulk's bold hand, and his seal at the bottom. She smiled at the blotchy decoration he had put near the salutation of the letter. He was not the artist in the family.

''Have you read this, sir?''

''Nay, I have no such skill.''

''Well, Fulk praises you most thoroughly, says the blood of kings flows in your veins, and that I am to obey you fully, as if you were he.'' Celine quirked an eyebrow at the Scot. ''Perhaps I should not have told you that.''

''I expect full obedience, once thou hast placed thyself under my protection.''

Celine gazed at Malcolm. A hard man, and even on his knees, not one to be taken lightly. ''You are a lord and a knight as well, no doubt.''

Malcolm gave her the slightest of nods.

''I thought as much. Well, I must tell the countess Greyhaven so she does not worry. Come along and dine with us.''

Malcolm got to his feet. ''I will not be welcome at your English lady's table. 'Tis now we must be going, lass. I ne'er thought to find thee like this, and 'tis a grand sight simpler than scaling walls. Fulk's letter or no, 'tis thee alone who must decide if I am worthy of thy trust.''

Celine looked into his eyes, shining with some intense feeling with which she was not familiar. He reached out and gently put the backs of his first two fingers against her cheek.

Leather, wet wool and horse sweat. The smells of the road. Of adventure. Of an opportunity that might never come again.

''Let us away, then, Sir Malcolm,'' she said.

The Scot mirrored her smile, and his face lost its harshness. ''Art thou certain?''

Celine nodded, fascinated by Malcolm's mixture of manners and audacity. He had given her a choice. That meant more to her than any number of pretty promises.

''A braw lass. Fulk's sister and none other.'' He mounted,

pulled her up behind, and gave her the upper half of his blanket to drape over her shoulders. Her friends, abandoned on the common, wept and hugged each other.

Celine waved at them. "Farewell! I am off to my brother's care. I shall write to you and tell you everything!" She put her arms around Malcolm's hard middle.

He put his hand over hers, and the powerful haunches of the horse bunched as it sprang forward, bearing them down the road, toward wonders she had only imagined. Now, she would see them for herself.

That evening, as their small fire popped and sparked, Malcolm drank up the sight of his lady squatting before it, sucking her fingers clean without remorse.

"A good, fat tunnie, was it not?" he asked. The river had been generous.

"Aye, my lord Malcolm, a fish beyond compare. I was starving." Celine wiped her rosy mouth and tilted her head back, exposing the long, pure line of her neck. She pointed to the sky. "There is Ursa Major, the Great Bear."

Malcolm could not reply, for his heart was in his throat.

She came upright again and studied him. "I was given to understand that Scotsmen resemble great bears, with red fur covering their bodies and faces, so that all one sees is blue eyes peering out. And any unfurred skin they paint with woad, to terrify their enemies. So I was told by Leith the Dogboy."

Celine tilted her head and raised her brows, as if to ask why *he* was so tame.

"Master Leith must be a man of vast experience, for even I havenae encountered such a one."

She sighed happily. "Aye, Leith knows everything. But what of my brother? Why has he stayed away so long?"

Malcolm played with a bit of twig, rolling it between his fingers. "Well, he has found himself a lady, on a lake called Windermere."

Celine clapped her hands. "Truly? And we are going there? Oh, I cannot wait to meet her!" A small crease formed between her fine, black brows. "He has wed her and not invited me?"

"Em, they're not wed."

"They live as man and wife, then? Handfasted?"

"Certainly not, lady. She keeps him at arm's length. Fulk captured her keep, and her along with it."

"You jest."

Celine's smile did things to Malcolm's stomach he had never thought anything but a good fight or a breakneck gallop could do.

He managed to mutter, "'Tis true. I was there."

"She is his prisoner?" The girl was incredulous.

Malcolm grinned. "Rather, he is hers."

"Ahh, how delicious. But, tell me, does Fulk have a noxious plan for my ultimate good, involving some crusty old man?"

Malcolm poked at the coals with his twig. "He would see thee safely wed, to a man noble, wealthy and circumspect."

"And whom might that be?"

The twig burst into flame and disappeared. Malcolm looked at his hands, dark from the sun and still smelling of fish entrails.

"He has yet to be found."

"I shall run away if Fulk gives me to someone I do not love."

Malcolm's heart lurched again. He swallowed, then blurted, "What if someone loved *you,* and burned for you, and would risk his life for a mere glimpse of your face?"

Celine gazed at him, her lips slightly parted, her green eyes wide. Then she blushed and bowed her head. Her jet hair shimmered down in loose waves, hiding her expression.

Malcolm cursed his lapse into informality. "Forgive me, lady. I beg thy pardon for my indiscretion."

"You are honest and speak your mind. I much prefer that to mealy-mouthed courtiers who spout all manner of compliments and then laugh behind one's back."

"I shouldnae be leading thee astray. Fulk is right. Thou hast need of a good husband."

"Do I?" Celine gave him a direct look. "What if I decide to enter holy orders so that I might draw and paint all day? What then?"

Malcolm choked, briefly.

"Or," she continued, "what if I become an acrobat and learn

to juggle? I should like that. A new town every few days, new sights and the camaraderie of the troupe. What a life!''

Malcolm frowned at her severely, his blood pounding in his ears. ''A randy, flea-infested life of connivin' fools and bloody thieves! I willnae hear of it!''

A dimple appeared in her cheek. ''Indeed.''

Malcolm suddenly found breathing difficult. He did not know whether he ought to kiss her or put her over his knee, but he did know he was lost for certain.

''Right,'' he growled. ''Put this betwixt thee and the ground.'' He handed her a thick, rolled-up fleece. She spread it out and settled upon it, but he saw she still shivered. ''I came for thee in too much haste. I didnae think to provide for thy comfort.''

''Do you know what, Sir Malcolm?'' Celine murmured.

''What?''

''You could lie behind me, and wrap me in that blanket you wear. Then we would both be warm.''

Malcolm closed his eyes, prayed for strength, and cursed under his breath. ''Lady, Fulk would kill me—slowly—should he learn of such an arrangement.''

''He disnae—does not have to know. He is so ridiculously overprotective. He treats me as if I have no sense, as if I were a child. We are here, he is not. We are cold, therefore we must remedy the situation.''

''Och, lady.'' Malcolm put his head into his hands.

Celine continued, undeterred. ''What if I catch the ague? Would not the delay from that be worse than your having to endure sharing your blanket with me?''

'''Tis not only a question of endurance, but of propriety.'' Malcolm stood, shook out the upper end of his plaid and proceeded to cut off a good length of it with his dagger. His hauberk provided warmth, but it was too stiff to sleep in, so he would be cold. But better that than risk falling to the temptation of the lass's innocent invitation.

Celine rose onto one elbow. ''Oh, nay, sir! That is not what I would have you do!''

''I dinnae believe you have the slightest notion of what I would do, were I a different sort. Now take this, close your eyes, and go to sleep.''

"You have my thanks, sir." She smiled, snuggled into the heavy piece of wool, and was asleep within moments.

Malcolm stared into the fire. His heart felt like lead in his chest, now bare but for his linen shirt. He understood at last why Fulk wanted his sister wed to someone of stature, of age and respectability. She needed a wealthy man to indulge her, to keep her agile mind occupied. But she also needed a man willing and able to curb her waywardness, gently but firmly.

If she were his—he hardly dared allow the idea into his head—and he took her home to his island, Barraigh, she would joyfully become a wild thing and have no idea it was wrong. He could never fetter her, neither body nor spirit. She would be in danger, too, for he had his own enemies. Then a devastating thought struck him.

He might as well have slept beside her. They were alone, on the high road, with no chaperones other than his honor and her innocence. Those were enough for Fulk, he would warrant. But they never would satisfy any lord of consequence. And he could not allow anyone to...inspect her...to determine if she were intact. Malcolm shuddered, part from cold and part from revulsion. Englishmen. He looked at Celine again, at her dark lashes, thick against her cheeks.

He would simply get her to Fulk as fast as he could.

Jehanne watched from the gates of Windermere as Malcolm and the fabled Celine approached, with the girl riding pillion behind the Scot. And no one else as escort. She raised a brow at Fulk, who remained stony-faced beside her.

"It was a plan conceived in a hurry, and few to trust," he muttered.

His clipped response was typical of their exchanges since the return to Windermere, a fortnight before. As his body slowly mended and his wounds closed, it seemed to Jehanne that Fulk himself withdrew, further and further. He had not been the same once it became apparent that he would indeed survive. She did not understand why winning a fight, even at such cost, would distress him so.

It was as though now, after the heat of battle had faded, he was ashamed of his victory, a feat other men would take pride in. And his dark mood was not caused simply by the fact that she had come to his aid. Nay, it went much deeper. Right to the marrow of his guilt, whatever that was about.

Fulk found killing distasteful, Malcolm had told her as much. But he still had the capacity for it, he had proved that well enough. Whether he liked it or not mattered little. If he could use his sword to good effect when necessary, that went a long way to raise his estimation in her eyes.

Jehanne nodded in the direction of the new arrivals. "Malcolm looks half dead, though your sister appears quite happy. She is even more beautiful than you profess."

"Aye..." Fulk began to limp toward them, apparently unable to wait.

Malcolm halted his horse. The girl slid down and ran full tilt to her brother. Though she was far from small, Celine all but disappeared into Fulk's embrace. He kissed her cheeks, her eyelids, her hair, and she clung to him, her arms entwined around his neck. Then she touched the fading bruises on his face, making comforting noises all the while. Jehanne and Malcolm exchanged a mutual look of exclusion from the reunion.

At last Fulk disengaged himself from Celine and brought her before Jehanne. The girl curtsied, stunning in her fresh beauty. Clear, ivory skin, wide, tear-dewed eyes and hair just like Fulk's, except, loosely bound at regular intervals, it hung to her knees. Nor was Jehanne much surprised to find that the young woman was taller than many men.

Celine studied Jehanne in turn, then astonished her by throwing her arms about her as if she were a long-lost friend. Jehanne found herself stroking the maid's silky tresses, and murmuring soothing words as Celine wept upon her shoulder. Her own eyes began to burn, though she knew not what she and Celine were weeping about.

She threw a questioning look to Fulk, who passed it on to Malcolm, who shrugged and shook his head. At that moment Fulk seemed to notice the Scot's half-clad state, and his face darkened. He turned to Celine, who had recovered and was wiping her eyes.

"Was the journey arduous?" he asked, in an ominously quiet tone.

"Oh, nay, we had a jolly time! The first night we slept right out in the open, and only woke when wolves began to howl around us. 'Twas ever so exciting. The next we spent in a haystack. Simply heaven, until that bull stuck his nose into our faces. But Malcolm frightened the beast off with terrible curses in the Gaelic, English and French, too, for good measure. And last night—"

"I have heard enough, Celine," Fulk said, his voice deadly calm.

"But I am not done. Sir Malcolm is so clever! He found us shelter at a brew-mistress's house, and I had bowls and bowls of hot mead. You cannot imagine how delicious it was, after a lifetime of ale and watered wine. I was quite dizzy for hours." She smiled adoringly at Malcolm, who looked near to fainting.

Fulk appeared ready to explode.

Celine blithely ignored him, and turned back to Jehanne, who was making a truly heroic effort not to laugh. Celine's eyes radiated kindness, and Jehanne found she did not mind the girl's open scrutiny.

She lightly stroked Jehanne's scarred cheek. "If ever I saw a lovelier lady, more fitting or more worthy of my lord brother, may God strike me dead on the spot."

Jehanne's throat tightened, and she knew not how to respond.

"He undoubtedly shall strike someone dead, very soon." Fulk glared at Malcolm.

The Scot straightened his broad shoulders. "I brought her safe to you, Galliard, and I havenae slept a wink these past three nights."

"That is supposed to reassure me? What were you doing, if not sleeping?"

An uncomfortable silence fell.

Fulk looked from Malcolm to Celine, then to Jehanne. He shook his head. "I am outnumbered. She seems well enough. My thanks."

Jehanne was relieved to see the men clasp hands.

Celine beamed at them, then turned to Jehanne. "Fulk is so stuffy," she whispered. "He worries too much."

"I do not blame him, sweet. You are his jewel, and he wants you safe."

Celine linked arms with Jehanne as they started back to the hall. "Milady, I believe you are the rarer gem, and at least as precious to him."

Pleased astonishment surged through Jehanne. For all her artless candor, the girl was neither stupid nor a flatterer. Jehanne glanced at Fulk, only to find him looking at her, his expression serious.

Whatever his faults, no man who loved his sister so emphatically could have attacked Lioba with such cruelty. She could lay to rest any lingering suspicions of Fulk in that regard. Jehanne offered him a smile, of apology and understanding.

He did not smile in return, but the heat in his gaze flared to a penetrating intensity, until Jehanne felt naked before him.

Oddly enough, the sensation was not altogether unpleasant.

Days went by, and Jehanne watched uneasily as a nearly tangible passion grew between Fulk's sister and Malcolm. When Celine was in the Scot's company, she claimed his entire attention, and vice versa. The way Celine blushed and Malcolm stammered, it was a wonder they ever exchanged two coherent words. Jehanne took great pains to discreetly ensure that they were not alone together, but she knew Celine slipped away to meet Mac Niall whenever Fulk was not about.

Not often, but enough to cause Jehanne a great deal of worry. And Fulk himself was no small part of that concern. Nor was he a fool. He knew what was going on as well as did she, and his moods grew blacker day by day.

Her dogs tangling around her legs, Jehanne descended the stairs to seek out Sir Thomas and get his advice, from a male perspective. But there Fulk sat in the great hall, staring into the fire, as was now his habit for hours on end. The servants and villeins stayed as far from him as possible. Likewise, a pair of the mercenaries, arriving to take the watch, warily crept past.

Fulk did not spare them a glance. Jehanne's gazehound bitch
osed his hand, and he leaned over the side of his chair to stroke
er fine head. Of late, the dogs and horses were the only recipients
f his attention, which was excessively gentle.

Indeed, Fulk never shouted, never beat anyone, nor demon-
trated displeasure in anything. But his seething malcontent
eeded no violence to make itself apparent.

Jehanne strode across the hall, intending to leave Fulk to wal-
ow in his gloom, but his voice stopped her.

"Where are you going?"

"To find a knight who will talk to me," she replied truthfully.
'rom long experience with her father, she knew sometimes only
oading would bring a man out of a dark hiding place.

"I am a knight. I will talk to you. What is it you want to hear?"

Jehanne turned to face him. Fulk's jaw was shadowed with
everal days' worth of beard, his tousled black hair was likewise
ntended. The only well-kempt thing about him was his sword,
vhich he now wore almost constantly, except to bed. When he
vas not wearing it he polished it, or sharpened it, or merely gazed
t the firelight reflected in its smooth, silver surface.

"I would like to hear your plans, sir. Do you intend to sit here
orever, fondling that blade?"

Fulk looked up from the weapon lying across his lap. "I am
eady, my lady, as you would have me, to fell any threat to your
eaceful demesnes."

"Ballocks," Jehanne replied. "You are ready for nothing of
ne sort. You neither ride nor practice nor scout my borders."

Fulk smiled thinly, eased himself to a standing position, and
autiously twisted at the waist, sword in hand. "My ribs no longer
rind when I move, so perhaps I should sally forth."

Jehanne winced at this reminder of his suffering. "If you had
ot refused to wear the binding, you might have healed faster."

"Of course you are right. As ever. Tell me, have you seen my
riend Hunterson about? And my fair sister, is she available to
ike the air with me?"

"If you would know, seek them out for yourself. The last I
aw Celine was this morning when she and Lioba went fishing

by the lakeshore. And Malcolm has ridden off in search of some
herb or earth that your sister needs to mix her paints.''

Fixing Jehanne with a baleful stare, Fulk placed his hand upon
the pommel of his sword. ''I do solemnly swear, o Lady of Windermere, that if I catch him with so much as a naked finger upon
her, I will lop it off.''

''You cannot fight love, Galliard.''

''I can try.''

Jehanne shrugged. ''Then you had best go find her a husband
of whom you approve, instead of standing about making threats.''

Fulk groaned and rubbed his brow. ''She will hate me. But she
is incapable of sense. I must do what is best for her. I will make
the journey to Henry, explain that I did not murder your father
and ask him to grant me title of Redware for Celine's dower.
Once word gets out, I will have my choice of suitors.''

''Apart from making her life a misery, and giving away your
land, what of the earl's enmity? He sent Hengist to kill you once,
he may do so again. Besides, I thought you were out of favor
with the king.''

''I am.''

Jehanne wondered what made Fulk suddenly think Henry
would grant him any boon. ''Then I should accompany you, to
verify the truth of your innocence.''

''Not to demand my removal from here?''

She studied her booted feet. ''I am no longer certain that is
what I want.''

''Well, well. Of course, what you want must be the cornerstone
of everyone else's life.''

''How dare you speak to me thus? I do not seek personal happiness, I have only the welfare of my people at heart. You have
proven to be a capable strategist and swordsman. I am therefore—''

''You are therefore prepared to sacrifice yourself. How noble.
How righteous. You have not changed a bit from the first night
you offered me your body, have you? Ever the practical, self-
serving woman of prowess.''

Jehanne stared at Fulk, stunned, wounded to the quick. He must have recognized her pain instantly, for his expression became one of regret, and he came to her, an apology tumbling from his lips.

"Forgive me, lady, I am sorry, truly...."

She turned her back on him and walked out the door.

Chapter Fourteen

Over the next several days Jehanne immersed herself in Celine's companionship. Fulk still claimed he was going to Henry soon, and she did not want to have to think about the potential consequences of his audience with the king. Apart from marrying Celine to the wrong man, Fulk might never come back, for any number of reasons. She could scarcely admit that the thought dismayed her, particularly after his rudeness.

For part of what hurt the most was that he had been right. She *was* selfish. She prided herself on nobility and virtue, when in truth she owned neither quality. She hid behind a shell of indifference, not daring to risk the appearance of weakness or caring.

Was that an act of bravery? Should she be proud of her coldness?

Nay. But what could she do about it?

Practice, a small voice told her. Sir Thomas always said, if one found a maneuver difficult or frightening, the only remedy was practice. Make it a part of oneself. Second nature.

Jehanne trembled. From her perch atop the battlement she breathed in the scents of mown wheat and warm soil, giving way at last to the cool evening air. Tonight presented an opportunity to share something of herself.

May Eve. Bonfires and laughter and moonlight. A time when seduction was the rule, and virtue the exception. Maids and young men would dance around hilltop blazes to the beat of tabors and lilting flutes.

The night promised to be splendid. Splendid, at least, for those who gave themselves over to the wild spirit leaping from heart to heart between lovers in the darkened fields and dells.

Jehanne could not help a wistful sigh. Never had her father allowed her to participate in village celebrations, he insisted all were beneath her station. As a girl she had watched the merriment from a distance.

While other maidens wove flowers into their hair and embroidered their kirtles for the festivals, she had sat atop the curtain wall. She had fletched arrows, honed her dagger, and mended the grip upon her father's shield.

Now the people looked to her for protection, or they had before Fulk's arrival. A barefoot lass skipping about with her tresses flying free was hardly an inspiring figure in that regard. So, it had been exceedingly awkward when Fulk approached her and made a ridiculous proposal.

"I would make amends and extend an invitation to you, lady, to meet me in the outer bailey, alone or in company, as you will, as soon as the moon rises above the gatehouse."

He had given her one of his skewed half smiles, leaving her wondering if he was jesting or in earnest. Lioba had begged her not to even consider such an assignation. Jehanne saw his overture as a challenge, except that she did not know for certain what manner of confrontation he had in mind.

But, many...*raw* sorts of things happened on Beltaine. There were always lots of babes born the following winter. That was reason enough to stay right where she was. Especially if it was Fulk she would avoid. She might be betrothed to him, but she was not yet his.

A lustrous sliver of moon edged its way up behind the gatehouse, getting bigger and brighter by the moment. Remembering how Fulk had compared her to it, Jehanne sighed again. She turned her back on the sight and made her way to her chamber. What was the point? She could not possibly enjoy a wanton roll in the hay.

Could she?

She did not know. Nor was she ready to find out. Their encounter in the wagon had been a mistake, that much was certain. Fulk would just have to go without her. In the dark, one female was as good as the next, she would warrant, to someone with appetites like his.

Determined to remain unswayed, Jehanne settled upon her bed, sewing in hand. Lioba had agreed to keep an eye on Celine, and Jehanne had dismissed her women, seeing how restless they were to join the others.

But for her hounds, indoors the only sound was the hiss and pop of the fire. The lurchers sprawled among the rushes, snoring heavily, chasing creatures in their sleep.

Jehanne jumped as the candle flames wavered, and the shadows with them. Fulk leaned in the doorway, arms crossed, gazing at her with his amber eyes.

She stared back. "What are you doing here?"

He twiddled something between his fingers. "I've brought you some Saint John's wort." Fulk stepped closer, and offered her the leafy stem. "Have you any rosewater?"

Jehanne shook her head. He wanted her to play the game of sprinkling the herb with rosewater, and if she found it still fresh on her pillow in the morning, so would she find true love.

What nonsense. "Put it in your own bed."

"You disappoint me, lady." He chewed on the end of the sprig, eyeing her all the while, then curled his hand in an impatient gesture. "Come."

"Do not even think about snapping those fingers at me," she said. She would not betray her nervousness.

He smiled. This time, a rare, wicked smile that turned her insides to jelly. Then he spoke, his voice smooth and resonant.

"Oh, nay, lady. They will do much more than snap, if only you will wait and see." Fulk approached her bed, and placed the herb carefully upon her pillow. "There."

Jehanne pressed her lips together. "You will go too far, one day."

"I fully intend to do just that. This very night. Put whatever it is you are wasting your time on aside, and come with me."

"You have no reason to—"

"I am beyond reason." Fulk took her sewing and tossed it away, caught her by the hand and hauled her out the door.

Her feckless dogs did not even raise their heads, much less try to stop him. Fulk walked too fast for Jehanne to keep up without running, even had his legs not been so long.

Along with the surge of anger in her breast came an unexpected thrill, the promise of unknown, forbidden pleasure. There was something different about Beltaine, no matter how Father Edgar had tried to convince her otherwise.

Her hand felt comfortable within Fulk's. Indeed, had she really wanted to, she could have pulled free. So, instead of her normal course of beating him with her fists, she asked, "Where are we going?"

"Why, May-riding, of course." Fulk turned and cornered her on the stair landing. As if he had planned it, a moonbeam shot through the arrow aperture and lit the small space. He trapped her with his body, close but not touching, leaning one palm on the wall behind her.

She looked up at his shadowed face. "Truly? Have you a white horse for me?" Tradition dictated that for the riding a lady be borne by a milk-white steed, the lord a black one.

"Nay, I have a mount that is a mixture of dark and light, even as we are."

His presence seemed to enlarge and encroach upon her, though he did not move. Jehanne shivered. To go May-riding at all was to cast caution to the wind. To do it with Fulk—and on but one horse—was to invite disaster. Indeed, he exuded an aura of basic, urgent energy.

He wanted something. Wanted it badly.

She cleared her throat. "You have turned aggressor, sir. I like it not. Stand aside."

Fulk's hand drifted upward and cupped her cheek, the delicacy of his touch at odds with the fierceness of his gaze. He stroked her temple with the pad of his thumb.

Jehanne allowed her eyes to close briefly, and savored the caress of his palm against her skin. Just that sensation, by itself, without thought of whose hand it was, or of anyone's pride or loyalty that must be upheld.

Just she and Fulk. In the end she could not separate him from what he gave her: a vision of herself with a man. Of herself with no one but Fulk. Not dueling, but drowning with him, writhing in the throes of ultimate, loving intimacy—

"It is a beautiful moon," he murmured, though he looked not toward the sky.

Jehanne snapped her eyes open and tried to sound matter-of-fact. "In the eye of the beholder, you mean?" Her cheek felt cool when his warmth first left it, then burned at his knowing wink. Her lips tightened. Let him think he might get somewhere. This could be just the chance to put him in his place.

Nay...practice!

She tried to block out the nagging voice.

Fulk led her down and out until they reached the bailey. There stood his courser, bridle jingling, a front hoof pawing the ground, its sturdy back free of saddle or cloth. Without consulting her, Fulk swept Jehanne up and onto the horse, then put himself behind.

A surge of craven panic assailed her. Be he charming or otherwise, she could not physically stop Fulk from doing exactly as he pleased. She hated that knowledge. At the same time, a confusing, inexplicable sense of sanctuary accompanied his touch. He was warm, confident, sure in his actions.

But that, no doubt, was because she gave him no indication he might not succeed. Twisting, she readied herself to swing her leg over the gray's withers. "We are too much for this horse, methinks."

A perfectly reasonable excuse to get down.

But the animal immediately moved forward at Fulk's command. "He could easily bear four of you, Jehanne, or two of me."

It would be better to be plump, she thought angrily. Then she might not be so easily tossed about. And yet, she relished the solid feel of Fulk's powerful legs and body cradling her.

But she was not ready to let him know that. "For the last time, tell me precisely where you are taking me."

"To heaven. Where else?" He squeezed her between his thighs and the horse walked even more briskly toward the gates.

Jehanne shook her head. "Saints, listen to the man! You are quite confident of your destination."

Fulk slipped his arm around her waist. She dared not try to

wiggle free. He would only use it as an excuse to get his hands on the rest of her.

Perhaps she *should* wiggle.... Quickly she squashed the shameful thought.

"Mmm. Indeed, I know exactly where I am going," Fulk said.

His remark spoiled any possibility in Jehanne's mind that this outing was at all spontaneous. To Fulk this was a campaign. A well-rehearsed series of moves. With but a single objective.

"Well, do not count upon sprouting wings and flying with me!"

"We shall see, my lady."

Jehanne considered jabbing her elbow into Fulk's no doubt still-sore ribs and jumping from the horse, but as they cleared the curtain wall the courser leaped forward into a canter.

After a short stretch of road they clattered over the great stone bridge to the other side of the river. The darkness was unbroken but for the fires dotting the ridges and knolls. Sweet, smoke-tinged air rushed past Jehanne's face, bringing an exhilarating, disembodied sensation of speed and flight.

Fulk guided the gelding unerringly, heading straight for where the oat-grass meadow gleamed pale against the edge of the woods. The soft earth kept the horse's hoofbeats quiet, and Jehanne saw no one else about.

Fulk halted and slid down, bringing her with him.

It was the exact spot where he had caught her in the snow, the winter before. As her toes met the ground apprehension regained its foothold in her chest. She waited while he hobbled the courser.

"Fulk, I—"

"What?" He came to her and swiftly brought his lips to hers, in a bold, searing kiss.

She forgot what she had been about to say. The waiting was over. She was with him, alone in a field, on Beltaine. The one night of the year when a lapse of control might be excused. Not only that, but expected.

It was all so new. His textures, his taste, his manner. No longer the courtier, no longer the man of words. He captured her wrists. He slid his hands around hers and interlaced their fingers. With a small sound she pressed against his length.

He tightened his embrace and kissed her again. Slow and lingering this time, his lips soft and firm at once, his teeth smooth and straight to her instinctively questing tongue. Her palms slid up Fulk's muscled back. He smelled like sun and blue sky, left over from the long, hot day.

Amidst the roiling sensations of pleasure he evoked in her Jehanne was only vaguely aware of him cradling her bottom. He hoisted her to ride on his hips and carried her to a patch of unmown grass. He knelt with her, laid her down and put himself alongside, all without breaking the contact of his lips to hers.

With both arms Fulk locked her against his chest and stomach and thighs, while he continued his delving exploration of her mouth. At last, he allowed her to take a dizzying breath, and she could not think why she did not have the smallest urge to slap him.

Whatever was the matter with her? He brought forth things in her she had not known were there. Heat and aching desire.

Things that gave him power over her.

"Do you still want to run away?" he murmured against her neck.

As if she could, with him pinning her to the ground.

"I run from nothing. But truly, Fulk, it is wicked of you to tempt me. I am baroness here, not a country wench good for a tumble in a field."

What a righteous sentiment for one who felt as wanton as she did at that moment. At least she assumed the tingling, hot surges in her body were wanton.

"I tempt you? That is something I shall have to boast about in the barracks." Fulk made a tut-tutting sound, the same as he did with her kestrel. "Don't feel guilty. There is magic here tonight...and I am your conjurer."

"You are many things, but certainly not that."

His breath skimmed behind her ear and onto her throat. "Say the word, and I will be anything you desire."

She had to at least try. "Begone, then."

"Nay. You don't mean that."

"An obedient suitor you are not, Fulk de Galliard."

"That is because I know you better than you know yourself."

"How can that be?" Her fingers were poised to slide into his thick hair, already grown as long as her middle finger.

But even as she hesitated, Fulk's hands coursed over her body, starting from the top. With but a thin layer of cloth between his flesh and hers, he stroked her breasts, never yet touched by a man.

How dare he make so bold!

Before she could squirm away, his thumbs brushed her nipples. To her shock, a completely separate part of her body responded. She gasped as warmth rushed from deep in her belly to between her legs, and shot to the soles of her feet.

Fulk's strong fingers slid farther down. Across her ribs and into the small of her back. Along the way his mouth caressed her throat, making her take shallow, rapid breaths.

Never had she experienced such an onslaught of sensations, so powerful they threatened to overwhelm her. He pressed her to the earth, which still held a remnant of the sun's heat. She could not understand why, here and now, she was not afraid of his touch.

It was as though he were an elemental force of nature, impossible to resist. It seemed that to do so would be wrong, somehow. Jehanne looked beyond Fulk to the heavens, thick with stars, and began to feel part of something larger than herself.

Larger, even, than Fulk.

A blaze of heat surged through her body. Just as Lioba had warned her it might on Beltaine, an unholy urge to shed her clothes seized her.

Nay. Not hers.

His.

With a small growl Jehanne jerked and tore at Fulk's tunic.

He chuckled. "Ah, little one, you feel it, too, am I right? Those old gods who wanted appeasing are making their demands upon us now." He lay back, reaching up to smooth the hair from her face. "With your cooperation this night, Windermere will be more fertile than any other fief in the land."

"Are you saying it is my duty to lie with you? To make the crops grow?" Jehanne gave up her struggle with his shirt at the notion of such a duty...and a pleasurable one, at that.

"It couldn't hurt. But certainly it is *my* duty to help you get this irksome garment out of the way.'' Fulk had his tunic off in a twinkling.

It was madness and pure joy to lie in his arms, her cheek to his naked chest, and listen to the powerful thud of his heart. The sound pulsed against her skin. He was so very human, after all.

He was, after all, a man.

The thought echoed. The stark reality of her position, of her vulnerability, clicked back into place in her mind, like fetters on a hostage. The same skillful hands that made her thrill to the subtleties of their touch could turn against her in the blink of an eye.

No one's fault, but a simple fact of nature. She could not bear for Fulk to see her fear, nor discover just how deep her scars went. She pressed her palm against his shoulder. ''I have behaved improperly, Fulk.''

He exhaled slowly and loosened his hold on her. ''You have not, sweeting. But we can lie here just as we are, until you want to go home. I will not force you.''

''I—I know.''

Fulk raised himself on one elbow and smiled down upon her. ''I never thought to hear you say that.''

''Nor did I.''

Nor could she resist the sultry timbre of his voice.

Despite all her intentions otherwise, Jehanne reached for him. Pulled him closer, to let him fit his mouth to hers again. To run his hands over her curves and to cup her breasts. To touch her as he willed, not just with his body, but with his very heart.

Fulk's embrace was pure and tender, honest and without guile. It swallowed Jehanne in loving warmth. It made her want to weep with relief. At last she might surrender and perhaps let go of her pain.

With his gentle urging she followed where he led. She stroked his back, his flanks, and thrilled to the bunching of his muscles beneath her fingers.

Moment by moment, the rising pitch of Fulk's excitement carried Jehanne just as fast and far, like a floating twig caught in a torrent. The moon soared over his shoulder as he shifted, putting her beneath him. Magic.

It *had* to be in the air, in the night, for her to allow him such liberty. But, Jehanne realized, most of the magic was in Fulk himself, and he shared it with great generosity. So generous was he that she scarcely comprehended what was happening, or why she felt so odd and breathless.

She was wonder-struck to discover that she enjoyed not only the emotions he evoked, but the actual feel of him. His weight. The scratch of his whiskers on her skin. His broad, bared shoulders under her palms, and the sound of his voice whispering to her. His impossibly hard manhood, pressed against her thigh.

Aye, even that. It was all so very base and wicked, yet exquisitely right. For the first time, she felt womanly and was glad of it. There *was* power in being a female, after all, and she wanted to test its limits. On Fulk.

The one who had made it happen.

His breath too came faster as he deftly unlaced her tunic. He spread the edges of cloth and slipped his hand onto her damp skin beneath. The heat of his mouth met the hollow of her throat and moved down, scorching her breasts.

Instinctively Jehanne pressed her upper back to the ground, preventing Fulk from touching her there.

Undaunted, he ran his other hand up her thigh, to where the top edge of her hose ended. There was nothing but bare skin beyond.

"You are wearing no braes, my lady," Fulk observed thickly.

Jehanne grew still, despite the heat blossoming between her legs. She was not ready, would never be ready. She sniffed.

"Well, nor do you wear them, I warrant," came her inane reply.

"My God..." Fulk whispered. "You are beautiful, Jehanne. Do not hide from me. Don't make me suffer from longing to behold you. Even if you never allow me possession of your body, let me gaze upon it, just this once...."

"Nay—"

Again, his kisses cut off her reply. Again, the urgency of his body straining to meet hers, swept away all sensible thought. His passion, so far held in check by a mere word or gesture from her, was about to break free. She knew it. He was doing his best to make her lose control before he did.

And Fulk's best was marvelous, indeed.

He rubbed along her thigh, to her hip. Gradually he raised the edge of her tunic, kissing his way up each leg, skimming her woman's place with a feathery touch of his hand. She trembled in an agony of helpless need, and a wordless, animal sound escaped her.

"Shh, it is all right, petal, for you are with me...." He reassured her with murmured endearments, brushing her abdomen with his mouth. He traced up the center with the tip of his tongue, then back down again. So enraptured was she by his touch that bit by bit, her self-consciousness began to slip away, and she gave herself over to Fulk's most delicate ministrations....

A moan sounded. She was fairly certain she had not uttered it, for she was biting her lip to keep from making too much noise.

"What was that?" Fulk raised his head from her nipple, now jauntily exposed to the smiling moon.

Jehanne dragged herself out of her daze to listen. Faint drumming, distant laughter and something not unlike the sounds she and Fulk had just been making. "Lovers in the field, no doubt."

"Nay, it cannot be. I thought I heard—"

"Oh, Malcolm! Oh!"

The name was unmistakable, uttered in a passion-drenched, throaty voice.

Celine's voice.

Fulk stiffened in Jehanne's arms.

The spell broke. Alarm rushed through her body as she sobered into cold awareness. Not because the Scot must be nearby with Celine, but because she realized just how close she had come to letting Fulk see her completely unclothed. Be they wed or unwed, he could have his pleasure when the time came, without her having to endure his gaze, his inevitable disgust, or worse yet, pity.

Thank God Malcolm's lust had interrupted them.

"I will kill the bastard!" Fulk jumped up. "Celine!" He pulled his tunic back on, grabbed his sword, and abandoning the warm nest he had made of Jehanne, took off toward the sounds.

''Nay, Fulk, wait!'' Jehanne straightened her clothing and ran after him unshod, even as was he. ''Fulk, don't hurt him!''

By the time Jehanne caught up, the men had faced off, circling, swords gleaming in the moonlight. ''Fulk!''

Celine alternately wept and screamed at her brother. ''Leave my dearling be!''

Fulk kept up a steady litany of curses and gory promises to Malcolm. ''I swear to God I will plow this field with your face. I will turn you into the biggest bellwether Sperling ever had. I will—''

''Fulk!'' Jehanne shouted.

At last he paused and turned to her. ''You knew of this.''

''Nay, of course not, but—''

''You said you would protect her honor as your own. And by God it looks as though that is the case!''

Jehanne's outrage rose and burst. ''What is that supposed to mean? That it is *my* fault you have been trying to seduce me?''

Fulk gave her a look of long-suffering, then turned his attention back to Malcolm and Celine. The Scot stood at the ready, intent, perilous, his shirt hanging open, handsome as a devil.

Fulk glared at his friend and beckoned to his sister. ''Celine, get over here. Now.''

''Nay.''

He caught her by one wrist and dragged her, struggling, to his side. ''Has he compromised you completely?''

Celine jerked in an attempt to free herself, and kicked at Fulk's shins. ''Aye! I will say aye, be it true or no, for 'tis what I want! I long to be big with his child, dear brother. How does *that* suit you?''

''I trusted you, Mac Niall!'' Fulk released Celine and lunged after his friend. Malcolm skipped backward and Fulk's sword sparked as it clashed with the Scot's.

Fulk raged on in Gaelic. ''You are a damned *stràiceil meirleach*, a *sèapair, a*—''

Celine ran after Fulk and grabbed at his shirt from behind. With a speed born of alarm Jehanne jerked the girl back before her brother inadvertently beheaded her.

''Hold!'' Malcolm called out, and threw down his weapon. He

stood quietly before Fulk, who took his time lowering his own sword.

Celine shook her finger at him. "Malcolm makes me happy. He understands me. You will not come between us. Besides, we are handfasted."

"Wretched son-of-a—*handfasted?*" Fulk turned to the Scot, who had resheathed his blade.

"Aye, Fulk. She is mine for a year, wed or no."

Fulk loomed over Malcolm, despite the latter's own substantial size. "To what village full of approving kinsmen have you made this declaration public? This is not Scotland. You have ruined her!"

"Stop moaning, Fulk," Jehanne said. "Your best friend and your dear sister love each other. That is a *good* thing."

"Good? To see her bound to a madman like him? Tell me, Hunterson, how would *you* react if I took one of your sisters to a meadow on Beltaine and filled her with my seed?"

"Well, you had best be asking whichever's husband that question, Fulk. I dinnae need your blessing. I would like it, but I dinnae need it."

Fulk planted his sword violently into the soil, and sat down with his arms on his upraised knees. "I never should have asked you to bring her here."

He sounded so genuinely miserable that Jehanne put her hand on his shoulder. "Can you not be happy for them, Fulk?"

"Nay, I cannot." He wiped his face with one hand.

Celine pulled Malcolm closer and dropped to her knees before Fulk, bringing the Scot down with her. "I love him. You understand that much, do you not?"

Fulk shook his head. "Ah, Celine, the pity of it is that I love the filthy swine, too. Your happiness is all I have ever wanted. What have you to say for yourself, Malcolm? Are you proud of what you have done?"

"I am, at that, Fulk. The least attention from Celine does me more honor than ten victorious battles."

"Jesu. You are hopeless. I shall return to my bed and pray that when I wake in the morn this never happened."

"When I wake, it still *shall* be happening! My Malcolm has

that much prowess.'' Triumphantly Celine linked arms with the Scot, who frowned and put a finger to her lips.

Fulk got to his feet slowly, as if he were an old man. He fixed his gaze upon the couple before him.

Malcolm coughed. ''Now Celine, there is no call to torture your brother. He has suffered us very lightly, in fact.''

Fulk sighed. ''I have a good mind to never forgive you, Mac Niall. But if I am going to allow you to live, you two shall be wed as soon as may be. At least our mother approves of it.''

He turned away as if the matter were settled.

''I will not marry Malcolm,'' Celine declared, chin high.

Jehanne stared at the girl, as did her dearling. The only one who did not seem surprised was Fulk. He remained silent and crossed his arms, waiting.

''I will not. Not unless you wed Jehanne at the same time.''

Jehanne's mouth dropped open.

Fulk took a step toward his sister. ''Celine, you are in no position to issue ultimatums. Unless you cease, your new husband will no doubt give you the hiding you deserve. And if he will not, I will.''

''Nay!'' Jehanne leaped to stand between Celine and Fulk. It was unthinkable. ''If ever either of you raise your hand against her, I will make you wish you had never been born as men.'' Jehanne was so intent upon Fulk that she jumped when Celine touched her shoulder.

''Lady Jehanne, pray calm yourself. My brother ever makes such threats when I vex him. If he did not, I might worry that I had lost his love.'' With a new edge to her voice, Celine added, ''But he would sooner cut off his right hand than raise it against me.''

Jehanne retreated, embarrassed to have interfered.

But Fulk stared at his sister as if he had never seen her before. His anger vanished like a hot coal dropping down a well. ''You would say such a cruel thing to me, Celine?''

She put her hands to her cheeks. ''I—I had to make you stop. I am sorry, Fulk, please forgive me.''

Fulk shook his head. ''Malcolm, put the women upon my

courser and take them back to the hall, will you?'' His voice was flat, his movements efficient as he brushed his sword free of soil.

"As you will, Fulk. I will just bring my horse from over there." Malcolm waved in the direction of his grazing palfrey.

"I'll get him. You have my thanks for the loan of him." Without sparing any of them a glance, Fulk strode off, his white tunic gleaming in the moonlight.

"What will you do?" Jehanne called. She struggled as the Scot prevented her from following Fulk, who did not reply.

Celine clasped her hands. "He is going to find us a priest. I would wager my maidenhead on it. Oh!"

As if realizing for the first time the enormity of what she had done, Celine hid her face.

Malcolm gathered her into his arms and smiled at Jehanne over the girl's head. "Och, an angel hast no need for modesty, Celine, *mo luaidh.*"

Jehanne's heart twisted at the beautiful sound of Malcolm's endearment. Even the hard-bitten Scot had allowed himself to be changed by the love of a woman. But, had not Fulk had been about to use her just as he had used so many other ladies, each of them far more accomplished and wealthy and beautiful than she?

For him, there was nothing special about yet another seduction. His tenderness had been her delusion, a silly maid's fantasy. He had forgotten her and left her half-ravished in the dirt, all because of his obsession with Celine's virtue.

A black desire for solitude claimed Jehanne. Over Celine's protests she turned and began the long walk back to the hall, even as she caught a glimpse of Fulk on Malcolm's horse, cantering down the road.

Go, she thought, *I shall bar your reentry. I shall retake my keep. I will let no one in. I shall rely on myself, as I have ever done.* But even as she repeated the words to herself, Jehanne knew she too had been changed this night, no matter how it had ended.

There was no question of her barring Fulk's return.

She recognized the terrible ache in her breast at the sight of him riding away. He had succeeded in making her see it, feel it, whether she liked it or no. She loved him, with a deep, sweet agony of longing.

Painful as it was, she could not give it up for any treasure in the world. It was there to stay, until her breath parted from her body, whether he felt the same or flitted to another woman.

Fulk de Galliard. What a creature for God to have loosed upon the world.

Chapter Fifteen

"*O*yez, *oyez!* Our lord His Grace King Henry's magistrate the most excellent and honorable William of Paxton is arrived to do justice in the matter of one Fulk de Galliard and his assumption of rights as lord of Windermere!" The herald's announcement, all in one breath, shattered the morning calm.

Upon hearing his name so rudely shouted, Fulk opened his eyes and lifted his head from his pillow. Paxton. The selfsame ass who habitually turned a blind eye to the earl Grimald's steady acquisition, by means both violent and subtle, of lands not his own. Including Redware.

Fulk threw back the covers and rubbed his face with the sheet. His memories of the previous week's wild encounter with Jehanne still caused him to wake up each morning in a sweat. As did the thought of Celine, handfasted. As a common village girl might be, with only a declaration of love binding Malcolm to her. He drew a great breath and tried yet again to accept the fact that it would take time to find a priest willing to come to a place so recently ravaged by disease and a siege.

The chamber door creaked, and a moment later the curtains surrounding the bed jerked apart, exposing his bared skin to cold air, bright light, and the blazing eyes of Jehanne. She stood there looking angry, sleep-tousled, comely in her loose tunic, and not in the least moved by his discomfort.

"Ah, it is my precious bride-to-be, come to take mercy upon me at last." Fulk bestowed an invitational grin upon her, to no avail, though she colored prettily.

"What are you doing still abed?" she demanded. "That horrid, unctuous man is outside, asking to see you. Get rid of him, sir! I need no maggot of an official to regain what is mine."

Taken aback by her display of temper, Fulk drew the bedclothes up to his waist. "Is it your time again? Or are you simply mad? You have gone to such pains to get the attention of the king, and now that he has sent his representative, you would have me chase him off? This is your chance, lady, to be rid of me. I cannot believe you will not embrace it wholeheartedly."

The uncomfortable, strained expression on Jehanne's face, and her hesitation, made Fulk wonder. Perhaps her feelings were not all they once had been. Perhaps she did not despise him so very much.

Or perhaps she despised him more. But who could hope to understand a woman like her? With the May-riding he had confirmed the full-blooded passion he had suspected she possessed. But ever since, she had been like a pot about to overboil.

And he felt little better.

Jehanne dropped her gaze and spoke in a low voice. "I am loath to do anything to distress the Lady Celine. Whatever you may be to me, or not be, she is my dear friend."

"If, as everyone insists, she is no longer a child, then she must learn to face the truth, as we have. I will tell you something, lady. I do not want to be here any longer."

Jehanne looked at him and her eyes widened.

Fulk crossed his arms. "I have my own concerns, believe it or no. Redware, its lands and people, who are suffering even as we speak. Why should I spend my time and effort here, where I am not wanted?

"I am tired of fighting uphill. I have been patient with you. I have been polite. I have been sorely injured, embarrassed, accused of heinous crimes, and for what? I get more gratitude from your sheep than I do from you."

"You do not feel appreciated?" Jehanne rested her palms on the edge of the bed, and her bosom swelled as she leaned forward.

It was not much under ordinary circumstances, but more than enough for a man on the brink of utter frustration. Fulk swallowed, held on to the edge of his quilt and raised his knees for modesty's sake.

Apparently unaware of the havoc she was wreaking, Jehanne continued, "Am I supposed to thank someone who simply showed up one day to take for himself what I have cherished my whole life through? Who would have killed my father in order to get it?"

"I did not intend to kill him. And you know damn well I am here only for Celine's sake."

"Aye. She must be wed straightaway. Then you can leave! I am more sorry than you know that there is no priest within twenty leagues."

Jehanne tossed her hair and pushed a stray lock behind one ear. With that careless, feminine gesture, something in Fulk snapped. He caught her by the hand and pulled her down against him. "It is you I want, not your land or anything else you possess. Just you," he growled.

"Swine. Liar." She struggled in his arms. Her body, warm and lithe, was like a cat's, writhing to be free. "In your state you would be happy to rut with anything female, no doubt."

"That is not what I meant."

But it was, though not in the bestial way she probably imagined. Fulk held her tight. Her heart thudded against his chest. Her hips pressed against his loins, increasing his ache. He stroked the back of her head with his free hand.

How badly she needed gentling. She could be so much happier if she would only let him love her. Just a little.

Jehanne paused in her efforts to get away and snarled, "So, think you this display of refined manners will bring you your desire?"

"Jehanne..."

Her teeth met his naked shoulder.

His fingers squeezed a handful of her silken hair. Gently, but allowing no chance of her escape, he tipped her head back. Her up-tilted eyes were still fiery, but something else was there, too. A trace of weariness, of yearning, perhaps, to give up her endless battle.

Fulk returned her gaze, and her wolf-at-bay look softened even as his own intensity of feeling increased. His mouth curved into a smile, and she blinked. His hand relaxed on her hair.

Jehanne's eyes darkened, smoldered, until Fulk's breath stopped. Her lips barely parted and the softest of sighs escaped them....

The door banged open and Malcolm burst in. "Well! Fulk is courtin' the lass in the time-honored fashion of his savage forebears, I see." He grinned and spread his arms wide as he bowed. "Kiss her quick, before she bites you."

"Get the hell out, Mac Niall!" Fulk released Jehanne so abruptly that she had to steady herself by leaning on one of his still-tender areas.

"Nay, Malcolm, wait. I will leave with you." Jehanne shrugged herself back into a semblance of order. "I did not ask for you to do that, Fulk."

"Aye, you did. Not in so many words, but you were ready. And I don't care who knows it."

"I never want to see you unclothed again! Shameless bully. Flaunting yourself before a maiden." She turned to the door.

"Aye, a maiden who storms a man's bed before he is half awake."

"Oh, you were fully awake, don't deny—I did not storm your bed!" Hands on hips, Jehanne had recovered all her anger.

Fulk smiled sweetly. "You had best go, before I give you the pleasure of seeing my bare arse again. You just might lose control next time."

Jehanne clenched her fists, then marched out of the solar, chin high.

Malcolm rolled his eyes. "You have lost your touch with women, Fulk. What a pity. You're randier than a tomcat, these days."

"Did you come up here to tell me what I already know?"

"Nay. The Paxton is below. He is under the impression that you and Lady Jehanne murdered Sir Alun together."

"Still an inspired man, I see." Fulk jerked his hose and tunic on. He pulled a heavy surcoat over his head, strapped his dagger about his middle, and jammed his feet into his deerskin boots. He felt his chin. He had not been shaved in days.

"How do I look?"

Malcolm grinned. "A bloody mess, lad. But good enough for the likes of Master William. Heaven knows what the lady Jehanne sees in you, though."

"Don't remind me. Let us deal with this rogue and be done."

"Hmm. Hmm, hmm..."

William of Paxton's nasal opinion did not vary from the one syllable he used. His crusty, deeply bagged eyes watered profusely as his gaze drifted from Jehanne to Fulk and back again.

"But, my dear lady, the evidence of your father's murder was plainly given by several witnesses. Why you wish to defend his killer is certainly beyond me, unless, of course, you were party to the offense. With an inheritance such as yours, a great deal is at stake. And at Smithfield, most definitely will be!"

He guffawed at his own feeble joke, and his attendants carefully echoed him.

Jehanne fought the ripples of panic in her stomach. Smithfield. London's convenient, well-used site for hangings and burnings. The nasty creature had mentioned it apurpose, to remind her of his power.

"Lord William. I too am a witness, and I am telling you my father died of fever, along with many others."

"As a female, your word must be corroborated by that of three worthy men. Bring them forth, and I will be satisfied."

"But I do not have three men, worthy or not! He died in my arms...and I—I hid his body. I told no one of his death, in the hope that our warriors would stay and help me defend this place." She would not shame her father's memory by revealing how his men, terrified by the pestilence sweeping the keep, had abandoned him long before he reached the point of death.

Paxton shook his head sadly. "Such wickedness! For you to treat your father so, even were it true. Ah, me, perhaps I shall take Sir Fulk into custody until this is sorted out."

"Nonsense!" Jehanne exclaimed. "Where is the warrant, or the sheriff?"

William smiled. "Oh, not far."

"Nay!"

"Lady Jehanne, please do not trouble yourself on my account." 'ulk's voice was mellow. "Paxton knows very well he has no ight to detain me. He enjoys tormenting young women, is all."

"You misjudge me, Fulk." The magistrate's tone had changed ɔ that of a sulking, pouting wench.

Fulk motioned in the air with his hand, as if flinging the man's mpty words to the winds. "Then, William, what is it you truly ame for? You have never been a champion of justice, and there s no gold nor silver here, nothing but wool, and little enough of aat."

William smiled thinly. "*You* are here, Fulk. A disgrace, but a ɔrce to be reckoned with, nonetheless. And *she* is here. A virago, ut also heiress to a large holding. Verily, though the king is most ngry about the whole shameful escapade, the question of whether ou slew the FitzWalter lawfully or not is Grimald's problem, not iine."

He leaned back in his seat, and looked down his nose at Je-anne.

She could barely contain her shock. The *king* was angry? But ccording to Grimald, Henry had wanted her father put down. If e had not, then perhaps the hue and cry Fulk's mother mentioned ad not only been embodied by Hengist, but sanctioned by the ing. And that could only lead to a dire end for Fulk.

William continued, "Sir Alun is dead. No matter how it came ɔ pass, there is no help for it. But, under certain conditions I iight be able to persuade Henry not to seek your early demise, ialliard."

"What conditions?" Fulk asked quietly.

"As the wedded lord of this lady, you will see to the well-eing of the bridge over the Leven. You will collect tolls from very merchant, every knight, every villein and crofter who sets ɔot upon it in either direction. As a show of faith, you will remit treble tithe of each year's income from it. For Henry, of course."

A wave of dismay swept Jehanne. Tolls would break the back f Windermere's recovery. No one could afford them, least of all ie peasant folk who needed access to the mill and the village aarketplace.

Muscle bunched along Fulk's jaw. "Now it makes sense. Wha
is the alternative?"

"Instead of casting doubt upon the story of your murderou
encounter with Sir Alun, I will reinforce the king's conviction tha
the earl Grimald is justified in his pursuit of you."

"You win either way. Why make me an offer at all?"

"Your brother had a particularly vicious wit. I will always b
grateful that you silenced him." William's gaze slanted back t
Jehanne, and she frowned, thoroughly confused.

Fulk rose, menace in his every movement. His eyes turned th
color of cold flint. His lips whitened and he took a deep breath
which made him seem yet larger than he was already.

He stepped up to Paxton, forcing the man to tip his head bac
in order to look into his face. "William, I invite you to reconside
what you just said."

Jehanne could smell the fear flowing from Paxton.

"I...I...beg your pardon."

After a long, tense moment, the shadow of Fulk's fury passe
and he raised his right hand. "Granted. Now, explain to me wha
my marrying this lady has to do with any of the king's interests
Can she not hire a bridge-keeper, and collect tolls herself?"

The magistrate sniffed. "The lady Jehanne is well known fo
her headstrong ways. She needs a husband to guide her in th
management of this fief. To allocate its resources wisely."

"To fill Henry's coffers, and yours, too, you mean. I ha
thought Jehanne's petition must have undoubtedly been eloquer
to get such a quick response, but I will warrant it was no desi
to aid her that sped you here."

"Well, the king has need, and 'tis your duty to contribute. Wha
petition?" Paxton added.

Fulk threw a questioning look at Jehanne.

Even as she shrugged her shoulders, the bottom dropped out o
her stomach. Fulk could read, scribe, cipher, speak English, Latir
French and Malcolm's bewildering tongue as well. Never woul
she admit to him that although she could read—slowly—she coul
not so much as sign her name. "Mayhap it went astray," sh
offered weakly.

Fulk rasped his hand along his chin. A thoughtful cast came t

his expression, and he turned to Paxton. "I do not believe the
king knows you have come here at all. Am I right?"

"What?" The magistrate paled.

"I will wager I could keep you here indefinitely and he would
not notice. He might even thank me. Am I right?"

"Nay, Fulk, don't you dare speak to me in that manner. Your
head could easily be the next to ride a pike on London bridge."

Jehanne strode forward. "Stop this! Are you not Christian men?
You speak of heads and imprisonment and robbery in my hall—
aye, it is still mine, Lord William—and I will not have such talk
here."

She turned to Fulk. "You sir, have shown yourself to be capable of reason, so use it now. Paxton has a large contingent of
knights outside, had you noticed? They are helping themselves to
my oats and my ale and no doubt soon to my milkmaids. I want
them gone. And if it means I have to wed you to be rid of them,
so be it!"

Fulk stared at her. "Oh, you flatter me, lady, indeed. Fine. As
you will. Are you satisfied, William? The lady's word is her
honor, by God." He jammed his thumbs into his dagger belt.

"Splendid! Hmm, I do so love weddings." Paxton sighed and
dabbed at his brow with his sleeve. "'Tis better this way, lady.
You do not know the half of what Galliard is capable, when his
ire is up."

"If that is true then you are a fool, William, to speak thus
within arm's reach," Fulk said.

"Ah, but you are the Reluctant, are you not?" William's eyes
narrowed to slits and the sound he made was more bray than
laugh.

Fulk's voice stayed low, his hands gradually unclenched. "My
lord, you had best hope so."

Jehanne stepped to Fulk's side. "Do not worry, Lord William,"
she said. "I will see to it that Fulk does you no harm." She
scoured her brain for a convincing reason, and the thought came
to her that there was still plenty of work that needed to be done.
"He will be too tired," she blurted.

Paxton roared and slapped his thighs. "Now that will be a first,
Galliard. For the girl, and you, too!"

Too late, Jehanne realized her mistake. Fulk turned a dusky red, and looked as embarrassed as she felt.

"Leave while you may, William," Fulk said. "If Henry wants his tithes, tell him he had best keep Grimald on a tight rein."

"Thank God they are gone!" Jehanne brushed her palms together, as if that would speed Paxton and his men upon their way. Fulk sat near the fire circle, frowning at her, his arms crossed. She frowned back. "What are you looking like that for?"

"He was right. You do need a man to guide you. With a tongue like yours trouble is only a matter of time. So, when do you want to be wed?" He tossed the question to her like a bone to a hound.

Jehanne stared, her hurt and anger rekindling. *This* was how the great lover offered himself? "Think you I was serious? It was easy to fool a lecherous old sod like him, but you? Celine is now safely here, Malcolm is pledged to her, there is no need for us to be wed."

She turned, ready to march out of the hall. Out of Fulk's presence. Out of his sight. Out of his reach—

"You are forgetting something."

Fulk sounded so sure of himself. A sinking feeling hit Jehanne squarely. "I am?" Slowly she came around to face him again.

"Certainly. I announced our 'betrothal' weeks ago, remember? Your people are overjoyed. They feel their future is secure, that your marriage will bring them stability and prosperity. They love you, Jehanne. You are their hope. I am merely the vehicle to supply you with babes and to stay your enemies when you cannot. But if you can accept me, they will be all the happier."

"I need no one to supply me with babes."

"Indeed. Planning a virgin birth to further your line, are you?"

"Blasphemer!"

"If you do not produce an heir, Windermere will one day revert to the crown."

"I will fight it!"

"Listen, Jehanne. Whatever you can offer Paxton is but a pittance compared to Lexingford. William will take all he can from you and still do whatever Grimald wants. The king is busy with his politics and the earl is not rational. He is set upon revenge.

upon satisfaction, and it is only a matter of time before he tries again. So it matters not whether we strike a bargain with William or anyone else.''

"Then nor does it matter whether we marry, he will destroy me anyway,'' Jehanne insisted stubbornly. She wanted Fulk to desire her for her own qualities, not take her to wife because of a protective urge toward a weak female.

"Nay. I will not allow it. And whether we wed does matter, for once you have brought Windermere completely back to life, made it profitable again, then a ruthless man might simply take possession of both you and it, unless there is someone like me to stop him.''

"Hah! Someone like you, who prefers not to fight?''

Regretting her outburst, Jehanne looked into Fulk's eyes, and what she saw made a chill shudder through her. A deadly light, like ice, so cold that it burned.

He smiled, a thin, grim smile. "But I do love to fight, my lady. I relish the sensation of my blade biting flesh, of hot blood spurting over my face, the smell of another man's fear and his moans of pain as he dies. Did you not know? How could you have missed it, that day on the high road with Hengist?''

Fulk stood, and at the coiled tension in his movement Jehanne's alarm grew.

"Is that not what you admire in a man?'' he continued. "The capacity to kill without regret, for honor or for glory? Well, if that is what you want, you have it in me. There are many who discovered firsthand the reason for my ultimate reluctance. And they are long dead.'' His voice was more cutting in its softness than if he had shouted at her.

Jehanne swallowed. "I am sorry, sir, that you find your duty painful. So would I, no doubt. But, I have never killed anyone.''

"You slay *me,* lady, with every single day that passes.'' With a final glare, Fulk turned and stalked off.

Jehanne watched him go, unwilling to consider what he meant by his parting words. But the other things he had said—cold crept along her skin. He loved blood? Other men's pain?

It could not be true. And why did he think she would admire such an admission? Did she seem so heartless to him, so proud?

She shook her head. It did not matter what he thought of her. Did it? Her hand rose to her cheek, and she ran her fingertip along the shallow ridge of her scar. Her chest tightened. God help her, it had come to matter a great deal. And here she was, belligerent, willful, ugly—everything a man would not want, except for her land.

Fulk had had his pick of women. There was no reason for him to choose her, except that with her came Windermere and his freedom from Grimald. What prudent man would not stifle his disgust in order to gain both?

Jehanne shook herself. She had no business wallowing in self pity. There were crops to plant, cattle and sheep to tend, folk who needed her encouragement and care. Ever it came back to the same thing. She was lady of Windermere, a place she loved more than life. And the thought of giving it to anyone else was simply unbearable.

She went to the window embrasure and gazed out over the land. Lofty clouds soared, backlit and glorious in their brilliance, and her heart flew with them. Their shadows rippled in a mad dash over the hills and fells, purpling toward the horizon.

Fulk might appreciate such beauty and share her joy in it. More importantly, marrying him might keep him safe from the king's wrath. But at what cost to Windermere from tolls and tithes?

Jehanne turned away from the light. She could not yet decide. There was something that must be done first, and she had to do it alone.

Fulk left his horse at one end of the bridge and climbed down toward the river's edge. He would see for himself what condition it was in. Tolls. What an unhappy idea. It would require a whole hierarchy of enforcement. A sheriff, bailiffs, collectors, guards for the takings, penalties for those who could not or would not pay.

And the tithe, even trebled, would never be enough. They never were, no matter who demanded them. Always, barons were pushed to their limits by the crown. And always, it was the villein and peasant folk who bore the brunt of it, sooner or later. This was exactly what Jehanne feared most. How shameful that her humane management of Windermere would not be rewarded.

She never asked too much of her people, they saw that she worked just as hard as they did, and she used her wealth for the betterment of everyone. She had no jewels, nor chests full of silks and velvets. Nay, she had sheep and cattle, and the goodwill of all. Little wonder she had not wanted to wed any man the earl had on a leash.

Fulk made his way down the slope until he was at the base of the massive pilon. He ran his hand over the stones' roughness, which gave way to a mossy cushion on the damp underbelly of the span.

The river's voice echoed against the bridge, and the water rushed past, swift and dark. Here and there, cracks and moisture had weakened the rock, and he was able to pull it away in pieces. Even so, it would be many years before it needed serious attention, barring a great flood.

Damn Paxton and his meddling. Fulk started back up the embankment. He would charge no tolls, nor pay any tithes, not in goods nor in silver. Let the collectors howl at the gates. By that time, Windermere would be ready to welcome them as they deserved.

Scrambling up the last steep bit, out of the gathering mist, he approached his horse and was startled to find Jehanne there as well. She was pale, drawn, still too thin. With her hair bound back in a tight plait she looked more waifish than ever. Holding the reins, she passed the leather back and forth between her hands.

"How does it look?" she asked.

Fulk stepped closer to her. "It is a great, stout bridge. It will be here long after we are dead and gone." He reached to take the reins.

Jehanne ignored him and proceeded to lead the courser along the riverbank. "Think you Paxton is concerned about the structure?"

Fulk watched the water as it rippled and eddied past the bridge, flowing into a wider, deeper part of the river. "Mayhap his worry is that not only can we charge tolls, we can block anyone from crossing. Anyone—be he peasant or king. They would be forced to go leagues out of their way when the water is high."

"We cannot afford to offend the king."

"I agree. But nor will I force people to pay for what should be free passage." Fulk put his hand on her arm and stopped her. "Did you truly come out here to discuss the bridge?"

Jehanne gazed up at him, her expression serious and unhappy.

"I owe you an apology. I behaved abominably. I should not have burst in and shrieked at you this morning. I should not have bitten you. And I should not have said what I did about you preferring not to fight." She looked down at her hands. "It is not the truth. I saw you go after Hengist. I do not know what makes me so cruel."

The breeze picked up, bringing the smell of reeds and wet stone, of moat and woodsmoke. Fulk inhaled the familiar scents and breathed away his flare of pain at the memory of Jehanne's hard words. Words she had every right to utter.

"I deserved your teeth, my lady, and your censure. A hesitant warrior is no warrior at all." His old wounds, deeper than the physical, began to bleed anew.

"But, Fulk, you are not a coward. I think it is insight, knowledge and God's love that holds you back."

"Nay, lady. It is shame and the bitterest regret. I am just as crippled by them as if I had but one arm."

"By all that is holy, Fulk, what happened?"

To his greater dismay, her eyes began to well with tears. "I have already told you as much as I can bear to tell anyone. Please do not trouble yourself. I promise you, as your husband, I will defend this keep to the best of my ability."

Jehanne stroked the gray's long neck as she spoke. "I can ask nothing more."

"You should. You should expect more, and demand more."

"Now it is your turn to err, sir. I expect little, and demand less. Eventually I will learn my place in the marriage, as other women have theirs."

Fulk caught her shoulders. "I am not looking for your defeat, Jehanne! I do not want to conquer you. Why do you insist upon seeing me in that light?"

She gazed up at him, her eyes full of pain and longing. "Because to think otherwise is like trying to stop a cock from crowing or the sun from rising, for that matter. Expecting or desiring them do anything else is useless. It is simply a matter of time until ou manifest a violent need to dominate, for all men do, even-ually. But believe me, I will not hold it against you. I know that en cannot help what they are.''

"Lioba has truly warped your vision, Jehanne. I cannot listen o any more of this.'' Fulk took the reins from her. "Did you valk all the way down here?"

"Aye. Now I have offended you again.''

"You astonish me, lady, is all. I see I have a great task ahead f me to convince you of my sincerity.''

She shook her head. "That has nothing to do with it, I tell you! incere or not, being a man carries with it an indelible imprint of ertain qualities that are simply bound to emerge, sooner or later.''

Fulk stopped walking, and stared at Jehanne. "And what of vomen? Would you agree if I were to say that I expected you to ne day lose your apparent virtues and become a coquette, or a hrew, or behave like a nagging fishwife?''

"I—I cannot say, from my perspective. If that is your experi-nce, then perhaps it is so. Perhaps I am already showing some f those traits.''

"Enough. Get on this horse.''

Jehanne raised her chin, and one eyebrow.

Fulk ground his teeth. "Kindly mount, mademoiselle. I would ake you back to the keep before I turn into the ravening beast ou believe lies within me.''

"Aye, I can hear it growling already, milord.'' She flashed him wry smile as she climbed into the saddle. Fulk considered riding ehind her, but decided it best to stay afoot and lead her home. hat way there would be no temptation either to reach around nd touch her breasts, or to wrap his hands around her sweet neck nd shake some sense into her.

And there it was. She was perfectly correct in her concerns. He ad not yet conquered his *furor*. It could leap out of control gainst anyone who provoked him. Even her. For her own sake e should leave, as soon as the recruits Sir Thomas was training vere capable of defending the fief. But every day that passed nade departing more of an impossibility.

This warrior maiden touched him, as no other woman had done, vith her idealism, her striving to do right. She was a pearl, and ike all pearls, would do best with frequent handling....

Chapter Sixteen

"But, Jehanne, you cannot leave now. The priest is on his way, we are all to be married within the week!" Celine paced before the fire in Jehanne's chamber and wrung her hands.

"Come, tighten this strap for me." Jehanne indicated the side buckle of her *cuir-bouilli* breastplate. Several days had passed since Paxton's departure, and she would wait no longer. Whether bride or spinster, she had made a vow the day her flock was savaged, and she would see it through. "I shall be back in good time, have no fear. It will be a lightning strike."

"I fear not so much for that as for what Fulk will do when he finds you gone!" Celine struggled to fit the buckle's tongue into the proper hole of the strap.

"My thanks. But that is why I do what I must now, before he has the right to tell me nay."

Celine knelt and caught Jehanne's gauntleted hand. "Let me come, too. I can be your shield-bearer, your squire, your groom, whatever you need."

Jehanne smiled and kissed Celine's brow. "Please, stay here and do not fret. God will grant me this small victory, I have no doubt. Honor must be served." She adjusted her surcoat and looked around the chamber for anything she might have forgotten.

"But, to avenge sheep, Jehanne? Is it not beneath you?"

"I will not suffer being robbed for sport by a good-for-nothing like Hengist of Longlake."

Celine staggered backward. "Oh, my lady. You did not say it was him you were going after. Forgive me, but I must tell Fulk."

She made a run for the door, but Jehanne caught her hand. "Shall I be forced to bind and gag you?"

Celine straightened her shoulders. "Not if you take me along."

"You are not a fighter, and I will not risk your safety. I am even leaving behind my women who have ridden with me before." Jehanne crossed her arms. "Besides, what of Malcolm? Do you wish to incur his wrath as well as Fulk's?"

"He is not truly my master yet. But neither of them will punish me." Celine's eyes sparkled. "They will be too happy to have me back."

Jehanne could not help smiling. She shook her head. "Now I know why Fulk gnashes his teeth over you. You are enough to try the patience of a saint."

"So I am told."

"Do you promise to obey orders without question?"

Celine put her fist over her heart. "I swear, milady."

"Then I hold you to your word. I command you to remain here, but do not relate my plan to Fulk unless he asks you directly. I will not have you telling falsehoods. It will be dark in a few hours, I must go. Corwin and Sir Thomas await me."

"Nay, Jehanne! I beg of you—"

Leaving Celine still protesting within the chamber, Jehanne closed the door and strode down the corridor. She did not like playing on the girl's sense of honor, but to bring Celine along simply because she sought adventure was sheer folly.

Nay, this was about far more than sheep. Hengist had abused Fulk unforgivably the day of the ambush. The beast needed to be taught some knightly manners.

Hengist raised the bowl of steaming mead to his lips. Before gulping it down he breathed deep, inhaling the liquid's heady aroma. It was his twelfth draught. The hall had begun to sway and drift pleasantly. It was like lying in a cradle and being rocked to and fro.

Like putting his cheek to the breasts of a big, beautiful woman...

He grunted, opened his eyes and found that his head rested upon no female bosom, but his own arms. He sighed. His men lay sprawled about the hall, as drunk and bored as he. What a tedious place was Redware. The villagers crept about like mice. No one challenged him any more. It was no life for a man of prowess. Aye, Grimald had called him that. *Un preudhomme.*

But where was the girl? Fulk's sister. And the other one, a prize, indeed! A saucy lass, whom he had thought so wastefully slain until she fired upon his company. Even that he would forgive if he thought he had a chance to win her.

But Fulk had the women. All of them. And that had been the way of it for years. He hated Fulk for it. The earl hated Fulk for it. Even Fulk's brother had hated him for it.

Women and Fulk. It was damned unfair.

The night was moonless, as thick and black and warm as a fresh blood pudding. What should have been a journey of dread toward all the unknown terrors the darkness held, felt to Jehanne like an evening jaunt with friends.

Once on the road they had made good time, though Jehanne did not wish to hurry. She wanted to enjoy every moment of freedom, savor every bit of anticipation. And she would have were it not for Sir Thomas's endless scolding.

"I accompany you, milady, only because my duty forbids me otherwise, not because I bear the slightest approval of your intent. And I do not stop you, only because 'tis time you learned the hard way your will is not always the wisest course."

"You have ever been faithful, Thomas."

"Aye. Make certain you have that carved upon my headstone." Jehanne laughed. "Most assuredly, sir."

"You are in a fine mood, considering what may come to pass. And to drag young Corwin into such folly—"

"Please, Thomas. Corwin, am I dragging you into folly?"

"Nay, milady. You couldn't beat me away from this noble endeavor." Corwin too was in fine fettle.

Sir Thomas snorted. "She could not. But think what Fulk de Galliard will do to the pair of you, no doubt. You are unwise to provoke him, Jenn."

"I am satisfying honor, not provoking him. Besides, it is a test of his love." Jehanne sighed contentedly.

"Of what else d'you think I speak?" Sir Thomas waved a hand n emphasis. "Would your outrageous actions anger him if he did not love you? Nay, he would welcome them as an opportunity to rid himself of a madwoman!"

"We shall see, then. And since you are so angry, I thank you for your love as well, Thomas."

"Confounding female!" The old knight fumed and muttered for quite a while, then pointed. "There, is that not the place?"

Across the fields and woods, atop a hill, Jehanne saw the faint flicker of torchlights. "We have come at least twenty leagues since yesterday. Redware is the only fortalice in this region. That has to be it."

"How do we know the Hurler is in residence?" Corwin asked.

Jehanne lifted her chin. "He is there. I can smell him, even at this distance."

The night eased into dawn, and the wild countryside gradually gave way to neat fields and cottages, each with a thicket-fenced garden attached. No one emerged to challenge their passing. So this was Redware, Fulk's lost inheritance. A well-kept village, decent woods, good pasturelands, and an easily defensible keep, set upon an ancient Norman motte, so it appeared.

Hardly worth the earl's notice, Jehanne thought. But Grimald took more interest in the amount of pain it would cause the rightful owner to lose a thing, than the thing's actual worth.

It was odd, though, how no one emerged to mark their passing. The wattle and daub buildings were like tombs, but for a shutter of the alehouse window someone hurriedly clapped into place. The folk were unfriendly, or more likely, frightened.

The small party splashed across a shallow stream and approached the iron-studded gates. Once there, Jehanne thumped the palisades with her lance-butt. "Hail, Hurler of Longlake! I am Jehanne of Windermere, come to take my due!"

There was no reply. Jehanne threw several stones at the small gatehouse which jutted above the wall, but that too brought no result. "What does it take to gain entry here?" she demanded of no one in particular.

"What dost want?" a rough voice shouted from within the bailey.

"An audience with thy lord, Hengist, if he be so disposed."

"Be you a wine-merchant?"

"Nay."

"A jester or a bard?"

"Nay."

"Off wi' ye, then!"

"I am a purveyor of fine manners, my friend." At Sir Thomas's pained expression, Jehanne merely smiled and continued. "Your lord will have great need of these, if he wishes to impress the kings of this world. Believe me, Sir Hengist will not thank you for barring my entry. And when he finds you have kept me waiting, he shall be most displeased. Here is a penny for your trouble." Jehanne tossed a silver piece over the wall.

The gates creaked open. A bleary-eyed man peered out from his hood and showed a gap-toothed grin. "'Twere openin' time, anyways. But there's how the Hurler best impresses folk."

The man indicated a post set in the center of the yard. Currently unoccupied, it was fitted with chains and manacles. A flogging post, much like her father's had been before she burned it. But this one had some adornments. Jehanne rode closer, then drew back in disgust.

"Ears?" Corwin wrinkled his nose.

"Aye," the gateman said. "Them as don't listen the first time get no second chance."

Jehanne suppressed a shudder. "Where is everyone?"

"Well, they ain't at Mass, that's the truth. Our Hurler was celebratin' last night, just as he does every night. He'll be delighted t'have visitors of quality, though. If anyone dares wake 'im."

After a brief argument and not a few threats, Jehanne finally had to order Sir Thomas to leave off his attempts to prevent her from meeting Hengist alone. She wanted her foe to see she was not afraid, that she felt no need for guards.

Leaving Corwin and the old knight with the horses, she climbed the stairs to the foyer, carefully stepped over the snoring watchman, and passed between the parting of a thick tapestry curtain to enter the hall.

The dregs of knightdom and various men-at-arms shared the

ables and benches in noisome sleep. The keep was indeed old, and still had a floor of beaten earth, spread with rushes in need of freshening.

An obviously more recent addition was a beautiful round stained-glass window, but it had had something thrown through it, bending the lead and leaving a jagged hole. The Hurler's work, no doubt.

A broad man raised his head from his arms and stared at Jehanne, his pale blue eyes made small by the puffiness around them. He sat up, ran his fingers through tangled blond hair, and blinked a few times. Then he rubbed his neck, and worked his shoulders in circles.

Jehanne swept him a bow. "Sir Hengist?"

He frowned and looked left and right, as if to make certain she meant him. "Aye. Who're you?" Without awaiting an answer, Hengist rose, went to stand at the nearest window aperture, and sent a formidable yellow stream arcing into the outdoor air.

Jehanne coughed into her fist until she had recovered her composure. That was one manly art she would never care to master. "I am the Baroness of Windermere."

Hengist stilled, then turned toward her, smoothing his surcoat into place. He rubbed his eyes, stared and took a step closer. "Why...I do believe you're right!"

Jehanne had not realized just how thick was the Hurler. "Aye. You owe me satisfaction, sir, plus three and twenty sheep."

"Sheep?" He laughed unconvincingly, like an overconfident urchin caught thieving. "I owe you *sheep?*"

"And satisfaction."

Hengist's smile faded. "Fulk has sent a woman to avenge his hurts? You, who helped him slay my men?" His eyes narrowed in an unpleasant way, lending his face a predatory cast.

Jehanne swallowed. What had she been thinking, to saunter into this beast's den? She locked her knees to stop their sudden shaking. "Fulk knows nothing of this errand. But it was on my behalf he suffered your attack. You set a dozen warriors upon him, so I had no choice but to come to his aid. And before that, it was my ewes and their unborn lambs you slaughtered."

"You have come alone?"

"My men are outside."

Hengist threw a questioning look to one of his servants, who stepped out and returned quickly.

"Only a stripling and his grand-da, milord."

Hengist crossed his arms. "What's to stop me from keeping you so that Fulk must come for you himself?"

A dense array of dark, rusty stains were splattered over the front of the big knight's surcoat. Fulk's blood could very well be among those spots. But Jehanne forced that thought from her mind. Here was where she would either succeed or fail in her scheme.

"I count upon your knightly honor, Sir Hengist. Fulk has told me you are possessed of a greater sense of fairness than ever was the earl Grimald. Sir Fulk is many things, but not a liar."

At Hengist's look of startlement, Jehanne hurriedly continued. "My father was a great man, and I would do his name no honor by carelessly placing myself at the mercy of a knight of vicious mind, no wit and little grace. Therefore I assume you are not possessed of these faults, and desire to demonstrate your virtue and nobility. Perhaps your assault was the result of a misunderstanding between yourself and Fulk, and my sheep happened in the way, that first time. But as a loyal subject of the king, I appeal to you for compensation in this matter."

Hengist's men had begun to wake, yawning and scratching themselves into alertness. They watched her with decided interest. Jehanne fidgeted, swept by an urgent desire to run away rather than be the object of their combined attention. Hengist was quite bad enough on his own.

He puffed up his chest and stuck his thumbs into his belt. "Er, of course. I would not have it said I lack largesse. What shall I bestow upon you? I have cattle, salt, a bolt of red samite—"

Jehanne took a deep breath. "There is but one thing that will satisfy me, and that is the return of the black horse, the Frisian."

Hengist grunted. "You place a high price on a few slabs of mutton and some bruises."

"Honor is at stake, sir. You can appreciate that."

He advanced yet again, to stand directly before Jehanne. It took all her will not to bolt, not to turn her face from his rancid, sour-wine presence.

"The horse is yours, milady. But will you not stay awhile? Break your fast with me...and play a game or two of chess?"

Jehanne blinked, speechless at the contrast of Hengist's words against his belligerent posture. For the merest instant she felt sorry for the man. Perhaps he truly was trying to better himself, unlikely though it seemed.

If he wanted what she could not give, but forebore wresting it from her by force, then he was a bigger man than she had thought. But whatever the case, she could not stay a moment longer in his company.

She met his hungry gaze. "You are gracious, sir, but there will be other opportunities to exchange hospitality. I have matters of importance awaiting me at home."

"Fulk will not be pleased at our alliance," Hengist said.

Alliance! "Well, since you offer me peace, mayhap he will see a benefit where before there was none. I bid thee farewell, and thank you, sir." Jehanne's feet began backing her away before she finished speaking, but Hengist followed.

"One of the lads can bring the horse round for you. Are you certain you will not stay?"

"Aye, my regrets. God be with you." Jehanne gave the knight a brief nod and turned toward the curtained entrance, walking as fast as she dared.

"Are you quite, quite certain?"

Jehanne stopped dead. The gravelly voice came not from behind, nor did it belong to Hengist. The tapestry before her parted, and there stood Grimald, Earl of Lexingford, poised to enter.

Chapter Seventeen

The lord strutted in, wearing a floor-length velvet robe that rivalled Fulk's for opulence. He pulled a rope, and Celine stumbled after him, leashed like a dog, her hands bound before her.

A sickening wave of fear and disbelief washed over Jehanne.

"I have brought you something, Hengist." Smiling, Grimald jerked the cord and the girl fell to her knees.

Her clothes—formerly Thaddeus's, Jehanne saw—were torn and soiled. Celine was white beneath the dirt smudged on her face, and seemed terrified beyond any ability to defend herself.

Jehanne felt weak, ill and more afraid for her young friend than she thought possible. This is what Fulk suffers, she realized, as anger mingled with her fear. A pox on the blessed girl for trying to follow!

Addressing Hengist again, Grimald pinned Jehanne with his gaze. "Have you trapped this other vixen for me, Hengist? How thoughtful."

The knight stood straighter. "She is not a prisoner, my lord, but a lady of rank who has entrusted me with her safe passage."

The earl stared at Hengist. "Good God, man. What has she done to you? Do not tell me she has bewitched you into thinking she believes you capable of chivalry. Or worse yet, that you believe it yourself?"

Hengist opened his mouth, then closed it.

Jehanne raised her voice. "Not everyone is as base as you, Lexingford. This knight has discovered the finer side of his nature. You, however, simply do not possess such a side. Unhand my friend. Sir Hengist does not want an innocent to suffer indignity in his hall.''

"Is this bitch now your mouthpiece, Hengist? Does she speak for you? Mayhap even think for you? What else does she do in your stead, eh?''

"Enough, Grimald. Give me the girl!'' Hengist's face darkened. He lunged for Celine's rope, and the earl allowed him to take it.

"Ahh, that is the Hengist I know and love.''

Ignoring Grimald, Hengist stared at Celine. The knight ran his tongue over his lips, quite unconsciously, Jehanne thought.

Celine tried to pull away from him. Her struggles grew increasingly wild and she began to choke as the leash tightened. Hengist drew her in like a fish on a line, until he was able to wrap one beefy arm about her middle and hold her tight against his body.

"Do you know whom you embrace, Hengist?'' The earl took a seat by the fire, and his minions arranged themselves in close order at his back. He held out his hand, and one of the men hurriedly brought him a mazer of wine.

"She...she resembles Fulk,'' Hengist breathed. His stubbled chin was touching Celine's hair, and his cheeks grew shiny.

Grimald sneered. "My, your powers of perception are magnificent! Indeed, this is his sister, just as I promised, for Fulk has not kept his end of the bargain. Nay, by all reports he could not stomach our Jehanne, and she is intact, though *this* sweetmeat is far from fresh.'' The earl drew a gloved and beringed finger through the air to indicate Celine, and two great tears slipped down the girl's cheeks.

Icy sweat broke out between Jehanne's shoulder blades. Her heart blazed in pain. She unsheathed her sword and brandished it. "Filthy bastard! What have you done?''

"Whatever I pleased.'' Grimald yawned as his men rushed toward Jehanne. "Mercy, wench, you do bore me. Lady Celine, on the other hand, is quite an intelligent and entertaining little slut. She knows when to surrender.'' He took a sip of his wine.

"Celine, do not listen to him. Think of what Malcolm told you. You are an angel. Remember it!'' Jehanne slashed at the earl's vanguard, but they were many and well-armed. She took a stunning blow to her temple from a lance-butt. As she swayed, the men wrested her sword and dagger from her.

Celine moaned and closed her eyes. "Malcolm tried to save me, Jehanne." Her voice was barely audible. "I no longer care what happens, for he is dead."

"It was only a matter of time, lady," the earl said. "The king is on his way here to see for himself the ruin Fulk has wrought, and His Grace wanted the Scot brought to justice, anyway. These rebels—so many, and so few hangmen to accommodate them."

Jehanne slowly let go of her throbbing head and squeezed her nails into her palms. Rage and anguish surged at the thought of Malcolm, cut to pieces, and Celine, having to watch and suffer Grimald at the same time. No doubt he had played upon their love to further his amusement.

"God will punish you for this, Grimald, as surely as the sun will rise on the morrow." She took a deep breath and prayed for strength. "Leave Celine alone. Let me take her place."

The earl jumped from his seat. Before Jehanne could duck he cracked his fist across her face, and his ring gouged her cheek.

She reeled, but her father had taught her to endure such blows. Grimald caught the back of her neck and forced her to look at him.

"I weary of your righteous indignation, lady. I should cut out your tongue and nail it alongside those ears out there as a lesson to all nagging women. You, take *her* place? You, so repulsive that your only courtiers consist of a pack of mongrel dogs?

"Nay, spare me. I want you to go to Fulk and tell him what has come to pass. From now on, each time he sees you, whenever he hears your voice, he will remember me—and the loss of his bold friend and dear, sweet sister. He will know that her fate is your fault as well as his own, by virtue of your wayward example, and his failure to keep you under control."

Tasting blood, Jehanne staggered backward as the earl thrust her away. She stifled a groan as the horror and truth of his words penetrated her heart. Fulk would never forgive her.

Hengist stood by, watching Grimald with narrowed eyes and a sneer on his face, like that of a dog ready to snap. He still held Celine close, as if his life depended on her being next to him.

The earl gripped Jehanne by the arm and swung her toward the anteroom so hard that she tumbled to the floor. "Away, bitch! Tell Fulk. Let him come and dare demand justice of me and the king."

Celine, now sagging against Hengist, raised her head. "Nay! Lady, please tell him nothing! I cannot bear to lose Fulk, too. I would rather let them use me, then die, so I might meet Malcolm in heaven."

"Ah, my innocent friend." Jehanne's voice broke, and from her hands and knees she met Hengist's gaze. "Celine, I leave you in the care of the mighty Hurler of Longlake, Sir Hengist. He would sooner give his life than see you harmed and thereby tarnish his newfound, sterling honor. Hengist, may God help you if it is not so!"

The knight blinked hard and nodded without uttering a word. Then he thrust Celine behind him, turned and hurried her up the stairs.

Grimald laughed aloud. "Begone," he snarled, giving Jehanne a final shove as she got to her feet.

She stumbled out of the hall, down the steps and into the bailey, fully expecting to find Corwin and Thomas's corpses lying on the ground. But the pair were merely tied to the fly-blown post, otherwise unharmed. The earl's squires stood by with their own horses and barely paused in their conversation, so unconcerned were they.

Thomas's mouth thinned into a grim line. "I will not say I told you so."

"Say nothing at all." Jehanne untied their bonds with shaking hands, then headed for the stable. When a groom stepped into her path, she fixed him with her gaze.

Carefully, he backed away.

She addressed him and the rest of the horse-boys. "I am taking the Frisian to his rightful owner, Fulk de Galliard, who also happens to be your rightful lord. Sir Hengist has released the animal to my care. Do not hinder me."

They scuttled to obey. The stallion was cross-tied in a narrow stall, and Jehanne spoke soothingly to the horse as the grooms led him out. He nickered to his stablemates from Windermere, and seemed well enough. Jehanne tried to concentrate on the small tasks at hand, so she would not fall down and weep for Celine and Malcolm. At least she could bring Fulk something he cared about. He would take no pleasure in her own return, seeing what she had just cost him.

They mounted, Sir Thomas leading the Frisian. Once they had passed through the village and were out of sight of Redware, Jehanne halted. "Corwin, ride the stallion back to Windermere quick as you may, and warn Sir Fulk that Celine is in danger. Thomas and I will stay here and think of a plan."

"Um..." Corwin looked as though he had something to say, but thought better of it. "At once, milady." He switched his cob's saddle and bridle to the big black.

Jehanne watched the young man canter the Frisian down the road. "A fast horse is his only chance, without a weapon."

Sir Thomas's lip curled. "And ours is to retreat to the wood, and await Fulk."

"Malcolm? Jehanne? Celine! What the hell is going on?" Fulk had been gone but a day, at first to cool his anger, then in a futile effort to find a bowstave of seasoned yew worthy of Jehanne's impeccable scrutiny. Now no one was about. He stormed across the bailey in search of Corwin, only to be met by Lioba. Her curls streamed in disarray, and her red cheeks shone with tears.

Dread flowed into Fulk's heart at the sight. "What has happened?"

The woman put her palms together and dropped to her knees. "Please, sir. Beat me or turn me out for my past transgressions against you, but keep my lady safe, or I promise before God, my shade will haunt your dreams and remind you that I loved her well!"

"Why does Jehanne need to be kept safe? Where is my sister, and Mac Niall?"

"All gone!" she sobbed. "My lady left with Sir Thomas and Corwin, yestereve, and has not returned. Then, though she was strictly forbidden to do so, the Lady Celine followed her. Then, though I begged him to wait for you, the Gael rode after them both. Ah, sir, forgive me for the pride and hatred I have fostered in Jenn's heart!''

"Jenn?''

"Aye, my lady's milk-name.'' Lioba wiped her eyes.

Fulk bent down and helped her to stand. "You nursed Jehanne?'' he asked gently.

"I had a cruel husband...he did things...I—I was widowed at three and ten, and my babe was stillborn, even as Jenn's mother died.'' Lioba clutched Fulk's hands and burst into fresh tears.

"Shh...'' Fulk led her to the steps of the chapel and made her sit, with himself beside her. "Lioba, I know what it is for a mother's heart to be broken. But right now it is mine that is breaking, for I know not where Jehanne and the others have gone.''

"Why, to Redware, to Hengist, to avenge the wrongs he did you and the sheep.''

Fresh, black rage descended upon Fulk as he ran for the armory. Women! He should have kept the pair of them locked in a tower.

He rode the gray at speed toward Redware. The road rose before him, and from the other side of the hillock a horse and rider bounded over the top. About to collide with them, Fulk pulled his courser to a halt, ready to lay into whomever had slowed him down. Then his eyes widened at the sight of his beautiful Frisian, white with lather and near exhaustion. Corwin, barely upright, perched upon his back.

"Where did you leave them, boy?'' Fulk demanded.

"A league or so outside of Redware.'' Corwin wiped his brow and leaned on the Frisian's neck with one hand.

Fulk shook his head but made no comment on the state of the animal. The lad would never have ridden him so hard without good reason. "Corwin, go home. Slowly, mind you.'' Noting the boy's lack of weaponry, Fulk held out his dagger. "Here, take this. I shall be sending your lady back to join you shortly.''

"Sir, I think you misunderstand.''

"Then explain.''

Corwin frowned and squirmed a bit as he slipped Fulk's dagger under his belt. "Milady has already spoken to Hengist. Sir Thomas is with her. 'Tis the lady Celine who did not come away, and Malcolm Mac Niall is...well, I know not where he is."

Fulk's body grew numb, his heart stilled. "Celine is *alone* with Hengist?"

"Nay, milord. The earl Grimald is there, too."

Fulk closed his eyes and cursed the day he had come to Windermere.

Jehanne's stomach tensed at a distant jingling, the rhythmic snort of a horse in a steady lope. With a glance at Thomas, still dozing in the shade, she urged her palfrey out from the cover of the oakwood and trotted to the road. She held her ground as a knight in battle array headed straight for her. It must be Fulk, for it looked to be his gray courser.

But she had never seen Galliard thus. At the tourney he had been helmed and in full harness, but there had been a festive air that day. Now he was completely formidable, seemingly a stranger, potentially without mercy. He circled, trapping her with his horse's quick moves. Her palfrey squealed a bit and pawed the earth, but offered no other help.

"Fulk? Is that you?" Jehanne managed.

"Aye, and damn your foolhardiness, woman." Shaking his black hair free, he dismounted and strode toward her, helm in hand.

Jehanne slipped down from her horse and forced herself not to back away as he neared. "Fulk, I—I am sorry. You know that, do you not?"

"I know exactly how sorry you are. And how sorry you will be!" He threw down his helm and it clanged into the dust of the road.

Jehanne caught the tang of the oily coating on Fulk's mail, and the sharp essence of male fury.

He began to pace, two strides in each direction. "Listen, take heed and obey. Do you understand? Can you follow that simple sequence?" Fulk stopped, the yellow light in his eyes burning darker as his anger focused upon her.

"Aye." Jehanne felt she might shrivel beneath his scorching

gaze. For the first time in her life, she thought perhaps this once she did deserve a beating. But she prayed it would not come from Fulk. She could never forgive him that, no matter how foolish she had been.

"Please, I have spoken to Hengist, and believe it or no, I think he will protect Celine from further insult by Grimald, but I know not for how long."

"*Further* insult?"

Jehanne stared at him and the words would not come. Fulk paled. He knew. Oh, he knew full well. He clenched his fists and bowed his head. His anguish bored into Jehanne. Her tears, held in check for so long, began to spill. "Oh, Lord, I commanded her to stay at Windermere. I cannot fault her, but I did try."

"Speak no more of it." Slowly, Fulk picked up his helm and wiped it on his surcoat. Now expressionless, he fixed his gaze upon her. "Who struck you about the face?"

On the surface he seemed in complete control once again, but it was as though his emotions were a wild river, flowing unchecked beneath a thick layer of ice. Jehanne rubbed her cheeks and looked at her feet. She had forgotten Grimald's fist, though the vision in her left eye was yet blurred from the blow his guard had inflicted.

"I fell. The moss on the keep's stairway is slippery."

"You are a pitiful liar, my lady. I asked who did it."

"There are more important concerns, Fulk."

He regarded her in stiff, painful silence.

Jehanne took a ragged breath. He could not hate her any more than he did already. "Celine s-said Malcolm perished in his effort to save her."

"Where? How?" Fulk's voice was cold and sharp, a blade's edge cutting through the thick, warm air.

"I know not. I think perhaps on the road."

Fulk swung back onto his courser. "I will believe him dead when I see his body. Mac Niall's slipped out of a noose more than once."

Jehanne almost reached up toward Fulk, but put her hand to his horse's damp shoulder instead. She had no right to expect his forgiveness, or even to ask for it. But she could not bear his anger. "I want to help," she whispered.

She could scarcely believe it when the rough leather of his gauntleted fingers slid over hers. Leaning toward her, he enclosed her hand with a gentle squeeze. Jehanne clung to the moment, hoping beyond hope that he might not condemn her after all.

"I know you want to help, Jehanne. But go back to Windermere. Lioba needs you. If I fail to return, Sir Thomas has—"

"If you fail to return?" The thought appalled her, was beyond bearing.

"I will not come back without Celine. But I shall do my best to return. I promise, sweeting."

"Stop!" Jehanne blinked back the fresh stinging in her eyes. "You need not pretend to be kind. Please. I will do whatever you want. My own will has brought only disaster."

Fulk released her hand. "Now you understand."

Wearily, she climbed onto her palfrey. She understood, but too late. "Tell me, Fulk. Why do this alone, when you have men at Windermere?"

He gazed at her, then looked out over the hills. "I would not leave your keep undefended. Nor risk other men's lives on a quest of no concern to them. And I alone want to be responsible for bringing Grimald to his knees. I shall slay him and every man who tries to stop me."

Jehanne gathered her reins, her heart breaking at the fatal tone of his voice. Chances were he was going to die even if Grimald did, too, but Fulk did not care. And she could do nothing to stop him. "God speed to you, then, my lord."

"Jenn."

In her misery it took a moment for her to realize he had spoken the name only Thomas and Lioba had ever used. "What?"

Fulk tilted his head, and there was a ghost of a smile on his lips. "I never pretend kindness. Ask a wish of me, as the ladies of old did when their lords left them behind."

Jehanne looked up into the amber eyes she now knew so well. "There is nothing I want but your swift return."

"Prove it."

Keeping her gaze locked with Fulk's, Jehanne leaned to meet

him, mouth to mouth. She closed her eyes and kissed him, melted into him, was ready to die with him, or for him. Then her horse shifted, pulling her away.

Fulk collected his reins. "I thank you for that, Jenn, truly. Adieu."

He saluted her, the same way he had the gallery full of ladies at the tourney, so long ago. But this time, the elegant gesture was for her alone. Jehanne watched him go, her throat getting tighter and tighter, the salty taste of him still on her lips.

She could not let him ride alone toward death. "Thomas!"

The old knight rode out from the wood, looking tired and cross. "You are going to break your word," he said, disgust evident in his voice.

"I did not give my word."

"Oh, you did as much and you know it! What next?"

"We must return to Redware. Fulk cannot best them on his own."

"What good are two more, without swords or pikes, against dozens?"

"There is a whole armory full of weapons there. All we need is a diversion. And, I forgot to tell Fulk that Grimald said the king is on his way. We might be able to make a plea."

Thomas raised his hands, as if in supplication to heaven. "And we might lose our heads. Why, Lord? I should be resting by a fire, telling tales to my grandchildren, my great-grandchildren, not flitting off on the whim of a foolish maiden."

"You live for this, Thomas, just as you taught me to."

He gave her a rueful smile. "True enough. The Reluctant has a good enough start. Let us follow him to grief."

Chapter Eighteen

Corwin led the Frisian, whispering apologies to the beast all the while for having used him so hard. The horse nuzzled the lad's shoulder, as if to say he was forgiven. "We'll stop in a bit, and mayhap find a patch of clover for you in the shade."

Corwin scanned the roadside. The sun beat down upon his shoulders, and insects hummed. There might be gooseberries in the hedgerow, or a stream nearby to quench the horse's thirst, as well as his own. Through the tall grass a patch of bright yellow caught his eye. The Frisian snorted and pulled on the reins as they approached.

"Easy, lad."

What was left of a garment hung from a bramble, the shredded cloth for the most part stained a dark red-brown. The Eirelanders and Scots all wore similar saffron-hued shirts. His heart heavy, Corwin touched the stiff linen with his fingertips, then carefully disentangled it and wadded it into his tunic. The Lady Celine would want this remnant of Malcolm, however awful its implications. But where was the rest of him? Such a man should not be left for the crows and foxes to dine upon.

With a start Corwin realized this was the same part of the road where Hengist had attacked Fulk, a perfect place for an ambush. It must have been here that Grimald caught Celine. And over there was the trail leading to the charcoal-burners' hut.

"We cannot go home just yet, my stout-heart," Corwin said to the stallion, and remounted. It was worth a look, just in case.

The path was overgrown now that it was nearly summer, but

still passable. But for birds chattering overhead the woods seemed deserted. Not a deer nor squirrel to be seen. Leaves rustled in a breeze that did not penetrate to the stillness of the forest floor, and the warble of the brook grew louder as they approached the clearing with its tumbledown cottage.

"Mac Niall!"

The name echoed, and the birds went silent. Shadows between the tree trunks seemed to shift in subtle movement, then grow still. A shiver raced through Corwin's body as he remembered the pagan gods, the fairy-folk and tree-spirits, just a breath away, lying in wait for the unwary. The Frisian stamped a forefoot.

Then, a female face appeared at the door of the hut, with blackened skin and a wild tangle of hair. She eased out into the open, her body thin and raggedly clothed.

"Hallo, goodwife...nay, wait, don't run off!"

The woman tried to dodge past him but from horseback Corwin caught her arm.

"Nay, my prince, nay, I am but a poor, wretched woman!" She shrieked and wept and clawed at his hand, but he held her fast.

"Then you have naught to fear from me. Have you seen a slain or wounded man with hair the color of these stains?" He pulled out the shirt. The woman hissed and rolled her eyes.

"Aye, my prince, we found 'im. He were far gone. He said unless we took him to a priest afore he died we would be accursed, and food for the devil, and that Lord Fulk would hang us by our own entrails."

Corwin's heart leaped. "And?"

The woman shuddered. "My man was afeared, so we did the best we could and all of us together helped move 'im. We carried 'im in his own cloth, like a shroud and left 'im more dead than alive outside that place of holy women."

"Thornton Abbey?"

"Aye. We watched from the trees. They took 'im without a scrap for us, nor a kind word," she said bitterly.

"But if no one saw you..."

"Them as has powers should know!"

"Aye, well, the lady Jehanne knows. She left a gift of barley for you when the iris bloomed. Did you find it?"

The woman's manner softened. "We took the barleycorn as a good omen, that we might come back here to live."

"And so it was. You will receive your reward in heaven and on earth, for your aid to Mac Niall."

"He were terrible t'behold." She wiped her nose with the back of her wrist.

From the almonry purse Jehanne had given him, Corwin handed the woman a few coppers. "More shall be forthcoming once my lady returns."

The woman put a bony claw on Corwin's knee. "My prince, we have no use for such as these," she said, indicating the coins, which she held tightly anyway, "but a brace o' pigs would do us nicely."

"Very well. I shall see to it."

Corwin rode away, leaving the woman with her hands clasped to her breast and a grin as black as the rest of her face. Once back to the dusty road he turned the stallion toward Windermere. If Mac Niall was dead he was in the right place for it, and if not, he would have no better care than with Sister Brigitta.

Fulk rode as though the devil himself chased him. The courser's stride lengthened, and urgency flowed between man and horse and back again. The devil was behind Fulk, before him, within him—*he* was the devil. It was time he faced it, used it, and let it burn, until either it was gone or he himself was consumed.

He came upon Redware fast. Charged through the open gates. Raced past the astonished squires in the bailey and rode his horse up the stone steps and into the hall. What might have once been his hall.

Guards jumped to bar his way, their long pikes crossed before the gray's chest. Fulk had intended to hew them down, but a new, cold voice within him bade him stay his hand. *Save it for Grimald.* He clenched his sword as if it might leap from his grasp, while a fury as painful as boiling oil raged within him.

Grimald sat at his ease before a trencher of stew, and with one raised finger checked his men. Only a tic in his cheek betrayed

:hat he felt anything other than mild irritation at being so dis-
:urbed.

"Welcome home, Galliard."

"Grimald, with you here I would sooner see it in flames. What
greater dishonor can you hope to bring upon me and mine than
you have already?"

The earl shrugged. "I am finished with your sister. I find her
endless tears quite tiresome. But they do not bother Hengist at
all."

Fulk struggled to keep from spurring his horse forward and
cutting the man short. Literally. *Wait.*

The earl smiled, the cultured, insincere smile of a man used to
having his slightest wish anticipated. "But, do you really want
her, Fulk? She can no longer be sold to the highest bidder."

"Grimald, if all that remained of Celine was a last sigh from
her lips, I would still fight you to the death in order to hear it."

"To the death, eh? Well, we need no fight to bring that about.
Hengist, my lusty fellow! Come down, and bring the girl with
you, if she is not too weary." The earl narrowed his eyes at Fulk.
"If you want her in one piece, get down from that animal and
hand over your sword, you ungrateful cur. Anything you are, anything you have, is due to my goodwill and forbearance. Let me
see you on your knees."

"To hell with you!" Fulk swung hard as he urged the courser
forward. His blade severed three pikes and was on its way to
Grimald's head when he heard Celine's voice.

"Oh, Fulk, nay!"

The earl dove for safety under the table, and Fulk's blow splin-
ered the heavy oak planks. "Seize him!" bellowed Grimald.

Fulk fought as one possessed. His horse nimbly dodged and
pirouetted without guidance, as Fulk slashed at his attackers. He
felt part of a nightmarish dance, each move an irrevocable con-
inuation of the last. His sword struck true, as if he were able to
aim at his leisure. He and the blade were one. It was an extension
of his body, of his mind.

But something was different. This was not his *furor* at work,
beyond control, but desperation. He could not summon the *furor*
at will, any more than he could subdue it once aroused. And

Celine's presence acted like water on fire. To subject her to another display of his killing passion, no matter how justified, would scar her forever, he was certain.

But without that all-consuming, blinding rage behind his skill it was not enough to overwhelm Lexingford's guards. They scattered and regrouped, surging and ebbing like wolves, patient and persistent.

Then the gray reared, and one of the Danes stabbed the animal's underbelly. At the courser's terrible groan of pain, Fulk hesitated and in that instant the earl's men swarmed to pull him down.

Even as he tried to beat them off he knew the truth. He could do Celine no good. Malcolm had been wrong. His *furor* could not be both contained and useful. It was all or none. He had never been a born warrior. And no matter how much blood was shed or whose, it was selfish to continue down a hopeless path for honor's sake. Grimald wanted his complete humiliation. It was the least Fulk could offer in an attempt to save Celine.

"I yield!" he shouted. The awful words tasted bitter in his mouth, and he felt the remains of his soul turn to dust.

"Oh, Fulk!" Celine's outcry dissolved into a sob.

He gave up his sword, and one of the vanguard led his wounded horse outside. The others proceeded to strip him of everything else, until he stood barefoot and barechested, in only braes and leggings, his wrists bound before him.

Fulk stared at Celine and prayed for her to be strong. Slender and graceful, she descended the steps, dazzling despite her bruises and muddy attire. Hengist followed, more like a devoted dog than a man who had just spent his lust on a beautiful young woman. Perhaps Jehanne had been right, after all. He could but try to reach the great ox with his words.

"Hengist, for the love of Christ, get her out of here!"

Fulk's plea was cut short by a paralyzing blow to his back. He fell to his knees, gasping. Just as he managed to draw air, another blow came, and another, each carefully placed to overlap the one before, until his body howled with pain.

"The flat of the sword, eh Fulk? Wasn't that what they gave you after you killed Rabel?" The earl's breath rasped faster as he exerted himself. "Something reserved for disobedient animals—

serfs—criminals—and men like you.'' He punctuated each word with a resounding stroke of the blade.

''Stop, Lord Grimald! I will do anything you ask!'' Celine wailed.

''Do you hear that, Fulk? Ever do women step in for you. Do you want mercy? You will have to beg me for it. Lady Celine, though you are wondrous fair, I can take whatever I want of you without giving up *this* pleasure. But your brother knows as long as he stays on his knees, you are safe from my loving attentions.''

Fulk was beginning to see bursts of white each time the steel met his skin. Through the haze of his shame and rage he wondered if Grimald intended to beat him to death on the spot. And why?

It came to him then, the remnants of whispered tales from when he was a boy—a hostage of the English. Grimald and the Chateau Galliard. Richard the Lionheart betrayed and the castle lost to Fulk's own father, through Lexingford's treachery. Good reason for the earl to hate Fulk, a bitter reminder of his own cowardice.

But Fulk could not die like a dog, leaving his sister to her fate with the vision of his ignoble end forever burned into her mind.

What would he have her witness, then? The sight of him killing the earl with his bare hands? He could do it, bound or not, with one blow between the bastard's eyes. Nay, not again. He would not choose that particular death for any man, no matter the provocation, and never with Celine looking on, for she had seen him do it once before. Gritting his teeth, Fulk took his beating in silence, without moving, except once he lifted his gaze to her.

Weeping loudly, she kicked Hengist's shins as he prevented her from descending the stairs. Fulk's mind flashed to when he had first glimpsed her. Squalling, wrapped in swaddling clothes. Her tiny, toothless mouth had clamped ferociously about his finger. He had rejoiced in her strength. She had survived, as so many babes did not. She had a will to live. And God help him, so did he.

He lurched to his feet. Blood lust did not claim him. The *furor* did not rise. Instead, a searing wave of love struck his heart. Love for the pure, sweet bloom in a child's cheek, for a mother's tears shed in joy for her newborn, for a thousand things that Grimald despised and would never understand. Love, for Jehanne of Windermere.

He would see her once more and ease her torment, and tell her to her face that he loved her. Summoning all his strength, Fulk spun and kicked his attacker, hard. His foot landed on Grimald's chest and throat. A disgraceful blow. But well placed.

The sword fell as the earl clutched his neck with both hands. Choking, purpling, he gasped and writhed upon the floor.

"Hold!" Hengist roared, and released Celine.

The earl's remaining guards halted their charge and stood as though stunned, looking in disbelief from their fallen master to Fulk. The Hurler's men bristled closer to Grimald's, and after a short tussle the Danes faltered. Pushing past them, Hengist knelt at the earl's side, and Fulk backed toward Celine.

The Hurler stood. "Grimald will die, I think." His voice held a trace of awe, but he made no move to help his lord further. He crossed his arms and turned to Fulk. "You will have to answer to the king for this. He is on his way here, y'know."

"Nay, I did not." Fulk looked to Celine, and she nodded, her face pale and drawn. He went to her and she untied his hands. Then he held her, stroking her hair until her trembling lessened.

The earl's breathing settled into a noisy rasp, and he lay still. Fulk wondered if the shame of being kicked might be worse than the man's physical hurt.

"I am going to have to put you in chains, Fulk. I don't see any way round it." Hengist smiled, as if he wondered whether starting with Fulk's ankles or wrists would give the greater enjoyment.

"You might ask me not to leave, one knight to another." Fulk sank to sit at the bottom of the stairs, and kneaded his aching foot. Anything to distract himself from his beleaguered back.

"But that will not impress the king as much as seeing you subdued," Hengist protested. "He might think the less of me for allowing you freedom."

"I will hate you if you do not allow it!" Celine declared, bringing a worried frown to the blond knight's face.

"The king might think the less of you for not giving him the chance to put me in chains himself, Hengist. I would imagine William of Paxton is along for the ride, and has sung a pretty ong all the way. I shall be bound for the block, unless he decides o shame me by hanging me instead.''

"Nay!" Celine looked horrified.

Even Hengist seemed dismayed. "Who will I fight in future, if ou are unavailable?"

Fulk prayed for patience. "Ask God and He shall provide."

"Provide what?"

"Just let Celine go, Hengist. I will stay, I will take any blame or what has come to pass."

"Do not tell me what to do, Fulk." Hengist waved his arm at he remnants of the earl's vanguard, who milled about nervously. ulk's sword had taken a heavy toll.

"See to the earl! D'you want His Grace to find him like that?)r..." Hengist looked as thoughtful as he was capable of looking. 'What if we toss him down the well?" His gaze turned to Celine. 'Nobody would ever know.''

Fulk got to his feet. If there was the slightest question in the Iurler's mind, it must be put to rest.

"Nay, Hengist. There will be no bargaining, no lies. Celine is lready betrothed to another. If I have killed Grimald, I am not orry. Let the king come and do what he will. But, Hengist, if ou value my respect, and that of Lady Jehanne, if you want my ndying gratitude, allow Celine to leave. At the very least, hide er until Henry is gone. She is not a bone to be fought over.''

"Already betrothed?" Hengist was crestfallen.

Celine caught Fulk's arm. "You will leave with me, or neither f us goes!" she whispered fiercely. "I will tell Hengist 'twas Malcolm to whom I was promised, and keep his hope alive so hat he has reason to please you.''

Fulk fixed her with a hard gaze. "Your troth is not broken until see for myself that Malcolm is dead. Think you Hengist is a big uppy you can lead about on a string? He is an animal, Celine, hat much is true. So never trust him not to bite you. Do not play vith his affections.''

At that moment a fair-haired boy wearing Grimald's colors ran nto the hall, stopped, his mouth agape, and stammered, "They pproach, the royals approach. Oh, my lord, what has happened?"

Wringing his hands, he stared at the earl, whose clothes were splashed with Fulk's blood.

Grimald opened his eyes and tried to sit up, then gasped for breath and sank back. The boy seemed transfixed, as did Hengist

Fulk wondered at the peculiar mix of emotions reflected on Hengist's face, as the burly knight met the lad's gaze. Confusion dismay, and oddest of all, concern.

The page came to life and dashed back outside. His cries o "Murder! Foul murder!" were audible for some time.

Jehanne watched the king's retinue with its slow-moving line of carts, filled with his favorite comforts of home, she knew, and whatever he happened to take a fancy to in the markets of the towns through which he passed. No one dared deny him credit And no one dared complain if payment did not arrive.

Carefully, she and Thomas approached one of the knights riding arrears. Jehanne made certain he saw them coming, so he would not be startled into an attack. He was fully armed, prepared for anything, and regarded her coldly, his hand upon his swordhilt.

Jehanne nodded, afraid her voice would squeak.

He looked her up and down. "State your business, or begone.'

"Sir, I have news for my lord king. I would be most gratefu if you let him know I am here." She told him her name and he father's name.

The knight raised a bushy red eyebrow, made a face of resig nation, then rode ahead with the message to one in the king's own circle. That man, none other than William of Paxton, easily iden tified by the peacock plumes in his hat, leaned to speak with Henry Fitzempress himself.

Without looking back the monarch raised his gloved hand and crooked a finger.

Jehanne swallowed. "Wish me luck, Thomas."

"Indeed, milady."

She trotted up the line and approached her sovereign, his grea white horse bedecked in more jewels and finery than a bride. He sat well in the saddle, his own attire simple but elegant. A blood red surcoat of heavy, lustrous linen, fine ibex skin boots and mantle lined with purple silk. Chestnut hair curled to his broad

oulders, and he turned his head, catching Jehanne with a pierc-
g blue gaze.

She bowed from the waist. "My lord? I—I am—"

"Alun's girl?" He eyed her. "Ah, *oui*. I know you. Mixed
ith a rogue, eh? A tremendous disappointment to your noble
ther, were you not? And he died rather unexpectedly, so I hear.
/hat have you to say for yourself?"

Without giving her a chance to reply, he continued. "*Mon dieu,*
w did he raise you, that you should bear such a scar? And a
lack eye! Have you been brawling? William, this is what comes
f not taking a second wife, or a third, if need be, to train one's
ffspring." Henry turned in the saddle and looked to his courtiers.
As one they shook their heads in disapproval at Jehanne.

With an effort she kept the anger out of her voice. "I have
othing to say on my own behalf, sire. I have learnt the error of
y ways. I would intercede for Fulk de Galliard, if there be any-
ing I might offer for his sake. Windermere..."

Henry's eyes lost the faint look of amusement they had held.

Hope leaped in Jehanne's heart that she might trade her lands
r Fulk's life.

The king stroked his beard. "You would give up your beloved
ef for him, eh? I have heard of this sort of thing before. The
ptive becomes enamored of the captor. But do not speak his
ame aloud to me. I go to this hold to meet with Earl Grimald,
t to reacquaint myself with one I washed my hands of years
0.

"Both you and he had a duty to uphold, a chance to redeem
urselves. You failed to carry it out, and therefore I will marry
u to one of my own. Galliard will hang for your father's death,
d that is an end on it. There will be no bargaining with me!"

"My lord, my lord, please, I swear, there was no murder, no
atter what you have been told. And besides, I—I have already
ed Fulk."

Paxton rolled his eyes. The king stared at her and a spark of
terest returned to his expression.

"Have you, now? There is a sweet irony. He had the adoration
the cream of my court, left a trail of broken hearts across the
ngth and breadth of England, caused me no end of trouble, then

went out of his mind and became utterly useless to anyone. Now
you say you have taken Fulk, after William here told me the man
killed your father by order of Grimald?'' Henry roared with laughter. ''That is rich, indeed!''

His mirth stopped as abruptly as it started. ''I do not believe
word of it. Speak no more, girl, lest you find yourself in true peril
Paxton needs a wife, and Windermere needs a proper master, a
do you. If you are soon to be a 'widow', the solution is easy.''

''Oh, sire, that is not possible—''

''Do not presume to tell me what is possible! If you cannot b
silent, return to your keep while it is yet yours and prepare t
receive me in a few days' time. And Fulk had better be there, c
I will hunt him down. *Allez!*''

At Henry's shout Jehanne wilted, and Paxton's crafty smil
made her belly churn. Her hands sweated so that the reins ke
slipping. The king resumed his conversation with his courtier
and the journey proceeded in agonizing leisure. Jehanne fell bac
to the end of the column, but her entire being screamed at her t
gallop on to Redware.

Eventually the party came in sight of the village. A boy ca
reened toward them, running headlong down the road, crying, the
promptly fell facedown in the dusty lane.

''Move on. One of you fetch that child.''

Despite the king's order everyone continued forward, leavin
the boy where he lay, apparently assuming someone else woul
see to him.

Jehanne slipped down from her palfrey and patted the lad'
cheeks. ''All is well, you are but winded.''

He gripped Jehanne's surcoat. ''Is it true, is he dead?''

''Who?''

''My lord the Earl Grimald.''

Jehanne felt the blood drain from her face. ''Is Fulk de Gallian
at the hall? Did you see him, or the Lady Celine?'' She stroke
the child's blond hair back from his forehead.

''I saw a great man, all bloody, and my lord earl upon th
table, and Sir Hengist, and a lady weeping, and a wounded hors
in the bailey.''

''Come. We shall sort this out.'' Jehanne helped the boy moun

ehind her. With Thomas leading Corwin's cob, they continued
ollowing the royal entourage onward to the village. Then she
aught a movement in the hedgerow ahead, and squinted to see
etter.

A bedraggled pair of villagers emerged to walk the road toward
hem. Half-naked and streaked with blood, the taller of the two
wayed, and his companion steadied him. At first glance Jehanne
hought them both to be men, then her breath caught.

Two dark heads. Fulk and Celine. Even as she readied herself
o rush forward, she stopped. To draw attention to them might be
isastrous. Even as Jehanne willed her to do so, Celine shoved
ulk off the road into the shade of an oak.

Jehanne slowed her horse, lengthening the gap between herself
nd the king's party. Before her palfrey came to a halt she vaulted
rom the saddle and ran to Fulk.

"What have they done to you?" Jehanne caught his shoulders,
nd gasped at the sticky warmth on her fingers. She wiped his
lood onto her surcoat and fought the apprehension trembling
hrough her hands.

Fulk's exhausted gaze slid from her to the departing cavalcade.
"Thank God you are safe, Jehanne. But cover me," he whispered.
"I would not have you see me like this."

Jehanne unpinned her mantle and threw it over his back. He
vas shaking, in spite of the warm day.

She turned to Celine. "Are you all right?"

The girl nodded, her eyes wide.

"Have you...taken the earl's life?" Jehanne asked Fulk.

"No doubt I have," he replied, his voice flat.

"Why are you out in the open? You must hide!"

Celine put her hand on Jehanne's. "The earl was alive when
e left. Hengist began to babble about honor and knightly virtue
nd allowed us to depart, saying he would weave some tale to
xplain the incident, though I doubt he has the wit to accomplish
hat. Fulk wanted me safe, but insisted upon going to meet the
ing, so—"

"Pardon, milady, but I suggest we make haste back to Win-
ermere, please, afore the king has us all strung up at the nearest
rossroads," Sir Thomas said emphatically.

"Right. Boy, will you return to your lord or come with us?" Jehanne addressed the child, still sitting upon her horse.

"I do not want to go back," came the reply.

"Then get up behind Sir Thomas. Fulk, take my horse. Celine you will ride with me on Corwin's mount. Let us be off."

"I should go and face Henry," Fulk said.

"Not now. Face him later, for he is coming to Windermere We have much to do before he arrives." Jehanne surprised hersel by the cool way she ordered Fulk about.

And he surprised her further by not arguing. But a clatter o hooves on the road behind her explained why.

The flame-haired knight from the column halted his horse an raised his right hand. "I am Bayard, the king's master-at-arms sent to provide you escort, Lady Jehanne. What is this rabble here?"

He scowled at Fulk, then his eyes widened. "I beg your pardon Galliard. Pray do not take offense at my words. Forgive me, it i my duty to see that the lady arrives at Windermere in good time."

Jehanne knew this was the king's man's way of saying he ha been told to make certain she did not get "lost." She hid he surprise that he and Fulk were not only acquainted, but apparentl on good terms.

Fulk clasped the knight's proffered hand. "It is good to se you again, Bayard. You are most welcome to join us. I, too, wis to make haste."

They had put several miles between themselves and Redware Jehanne let her horse amble on a loose rein, giving the animal chance to rest. Both Fulk and Celine had kept quiet on the jour ney, and Jehanne was afraid to ask the details of what had take place with Grimald.

But the ongoing silence was hard to bear. She cleared he throat, wondering how to broach the subject of Henry's ire wit Sir Bayard present, but that same knight spoke first, bringing hi horse alongside Fulk.

"So, Galliard, do you plan to leave your lands and people i Grimald's hands, or request their return from Henry?"

"They were never mine to begin with." Fulk's tone was grim. "They are Celine's once she is of age, or wed."

"You will not ask for their stewardship, as your mother wishes?" Jehanne asked carefully.

"I might, but only for Celine and Malcolm's benefit. Except he is at odds with the king, just as am I."

"Malcolm Mac Niall?" Bayard asked. At Fulk's nod, the knight began to laugh.

Jehanne was amazed to see the tough, unsmiling warrior transformed into such a handsome, charming man.

He added, "That Scot has stuck to you through thick and thin, has he not?"

"Aye, he believes me incapable of looking after myself."

Bayard's grin widened. "In truth, Fulk, Henry has probably forgotten Mac Niall's offenses. Be assured that I will not remind him."

"My thanks, Bayard, you were ever a faithful friend. But Henry has a long memory. He forgets nothing."

Celine, riding to the left of Fulk, stared at him, her face white and her eyes blazing green. "You ever speak as though Malcolm is alive. I saw his wounds. They were many and deep—"

Her voice broke and she turned her face away briefly before continuing. "You are most generous, my lord brother, to speak of gifting me with lands not yours, but I have decided to join Mother at the abbey. I have no wish to be some returning crusader's reward from the king. Or whatever it is he has planned for me."

Bayard cleared his throat.

Jehanne leaned toward him and said, "Take no heed, sir, the young lady has no idea what an honor such a match might be." She sat back in the saddle, surprised at herself. She was a fine one to be defending the idea of marriage by command.

He shrugged. "I cannot be offended by that winsome lass, so obviously without knowledge of the world. But, when I marry, it will be to a woman of my own choosing, not the king's. I have lands enough, I need not depend upon an heiress for income."

"You are indeed fortunate, then, Bayard," Jehanne replied.

Celine hastened to make amends. "I meant no insult, sir, 'tis just that I have heard so many tales of Henry's lusty knights and painted ladies and—''

Fulk interrupted. ''My dear sister, you have never been to court, you have no idea what goes on there. It is not the cesspit of vice you might imagine.'' He coughed and glanced apologetically at Jehanne before continuing. ''Henry would not use you as a concubine for his favorites, in spite of what I said to Hengist, not even to punish me. If it is Thornton Abbey you want, so shall we go there.''

''But—'' Jehanne began to protest the loss of her friend.

Fulk gave her a telling look, and she fell silent. No doubt he knew what he was doing. But apart from wanting Celine to come home with her, Jehanne was anxious to return and satisfy herself all was well. ''I hope Corwin is safe. Is there any point in searching for Malcolm as we go?''

Fulk stared between his horse's ears toward the horizon. ''I looked for him as I came, but I rode straight through the night. Knowing him, if he had breath, he would not lie by the roadway awaiting succour. He resembles more a creature which goes into hiding to lick its wounds.''

''I understand,'' Jehanne said. Too well. She was relieved to see that Fulk's gaze had not turned in her direction. Perhaps he had not caught the unintended bitterness in her tone. Then he did look at her, and she read sympathy and concern in his warm eyes.

''Jehanne...''

She trotted her horse ahead. He was too clever by far. He saw too much. Cared too much. Expected too much. And even should he forgive her for Celine's dishonor at Grimald's hands, she was still not ready for Fulk.

They arrived at the abbey just as night claimed the valley below. The scents of lady-slipper and ripe strawberries filled the air, conquering even the sweaty aroma of their group. Jehanne dismounted inside the gates, vastly grateful when a servant stepped forward to take her horse.

Celine caught Jehanne's hand. ''I am afraid!''

''But your mother will be overjoyed to see you.''

''She will know. She will see my impurity.''

Jehanne sighed and slipped her arm around Celine's waist as ⸱y walked. "Your love of Malcolm is pure by definition, and ything else that happened...was not your fault." The thought Grimald still made her furious.

"I have done many things willingly, against Fulk's wishes, ainst my better judgment, by following my heart." The girl ⸱bed at her eyes with her wrist. "I am not repentant, but nor I want to give my lady mother cause to be displeased with me ⸱en I am come to join her in sisterhood."

"Celine, I have heard your mother speak of delicate matters ⸱arding guilt, when your brother—"

Fulk loomed out of the darkness. "You were listening at the ⸱or that night?"

"And were you eavesdropping just now?" Jehanne demanded. "Certainly not."

"Then go and ask for a bath, before you fall asleep on your ⸱t." Jehanne wanted to ease Fulk's weariness and pain, but she ⸱ld not fuss over him in front of the others.

He grumbled and departed without making a comprehensible ⸱mment. Jehanne waited until he was inside the cloister. "I was ⸱ing, your mother is very understanding. She will not presume judge you in any way. Besides, she could not know, unless you ⸱ose to tell her."

"She is very wise. But what if I am already with child? You ⸱d me that kissing a man is just as risky as lying with him. If ⸱t means a kiss is enough to start a babe, then I am guilty of many of those with Malcolm, I could be *full* of tiny babes by ⸱w. I will have a whole litter!"

Jehanne could not help laughing. "My sweet Celine, I assure ⸱u that is not the way of it. I meant kisses are a starting point, ⸱ich lead to...the other. That is why, outside of marriage, one ⸱st not allow any kissing at all, unless one is prepared for carnal ⸱wledge."

Celine's relief was evident.

Jehanne would not raise her concern of what might result from ⸱imald's having taken Celine by force. She squeezed the girl's ⸱d. "Come, I hear Sister Brigitta chastising Fulk. Let us not ⸱ss it."

They entered the hall to find Fulk on his knees yet again, bei lectured by his mother in a voice soft yet cutting, as a variety nuns looked on.

"...and furthermore, it is beyond my understanding how grown man can be so foolhardy as to ride alone into the midst an enemy's guard and expect a civil welcome."

"My lady, I expected nothing of the kind."

"But look at you, Fulk! Jehanne and I spent so much effort t last time to see you back on your feet, and now you return beat and battered again. Do you have so little regard for your ov health?"

"Forgive me."

"Maman?"

At the sound of Celine's voice, Brigitta put her hand to h mouth. Fulk groaned and sat on the floor. As mother and daughte embraced and wept, Jehanne went to Fulk. She pulled him to h feet, supporting him with the competent help of a nun, Sist Agatha of the Large Hands, as it turned out, and took him to t infirmary.

There were several double beds but only one was occupie Jehanne led Fulk to a cot beneath a torch, where she could s better. His back was striped with a sorry mixture of deep cu livid bruises and raw welts.

The flat of a sword, no doubt that was what had been used. N wonder he had not wanted anyone to see. Her stomach churne She knew exactly how agonizing such treatment was for bo body and spirit. She made Fulk lie facedown, then gently washe salved and dressed his wounds.

He was silent, his eyes closed for the duration. His breathi grew deep and even. To Jehanne's amazement he was asleep by the time she finished.

Sister Agatha smiled. "I had best fetch a pitcher of ale an some food for when he wakes. Himself'll be starving and dry a stone. Shall I bring a drop and bite for you as well?"

"I thank you, Sister."

The good lady winked and strode away, her clogs clattering the stone floor. Jehanne returned her attention to Fulk, whose fa was extraordinarily sweet in repose, though it retained its streng

f bone and character. As ever, she wanted to stroke his brow,
ad as ever, did not.

"What's all the bloody noise in here?"

The complaint came from the other patient, and Jehanne started
olently. "As I live and breathe, is that you, Mac Niall?" She
n to see, her heart in her throat.

"Nay, 'tis the ghost of Mac Niall, a mere shadow, the feeble
eature left waning by the evil ministrations of these wretched,
oly *hags!*" He shouted the last word, and it echoed around the
amber.

The Scot was pale, with a ghastly green undertone. His chest
as loosely wrapped in bloodstained bandages, as were his right
m and his head, leaving only one eye visible.

Jehanne knelt at his bedside, tears already warming her cheeks.
Quiet, you blessed son of a—"

Malcolm reached out, and with one hand at the back of Je-
anne's neck, pulled her close and kissed her mouth soundly.

"Stop that, sir! Phew! Has something died under your bed?"

"Nay, 'tis just myself that is rotting here. I am but glad t'see
ou, milady. Have you brought my wee *mhuirnin?* I have held
ody and soul together just in case."

Malcolm's grip abruptly fell away even as his voice failed, and
hanne realized the effort it had taken him to put on his show
jollity. He fixed his one-eyed gaze upon her.

"What did they do to my sweet, pure heart? Does she yet live?
failed her miserably, but when next I meet the Earl Grimald I
all leave him a changed man," Malcolm snarled through his
vn tears.

Jehanne sat on the edge of the cot. "Nay, Mac Niall, you did
l that anyone could, I am certain. But Fulk has left the earl in
bad way, already. And Celine is very well, except she believes
ou dead, and has come here to join her mother. She loves your
emory more than any life she could imagine without you."

The Scot threw his good arm over his eye. "Let her go on
inking as she does. 'Tis likely enough to be the truth before
ng. She should not be given hope only to have it taken away,
ow that she is resolved in her course. But it warms my heart to
now that Grimald has taken hurt, even if not by my hand."

"Celine would hate to lose even one moment with you. An
she will never forgive me if I allow it." Jehanne started to ris
but Malcolm caught her hand.

"Please, lady, I beg of you. I cannae abide being wept ove
Dinnae force me to lie helpless before her, unable to offer h
comfort, unable to make her any promises. Just let me die know
ing she is safe."

"You underestimate your lady, Malcolm. She needs no prom
ises. She wants only you, however you are. Why can men n
understand these things?"

The Scot moved his arm from his eye and a slow smile raise
his moustaches. "Och, I see! You have taken to Fulk. Nay, dinna
turn your face. Admit it. He's more than meat and bones, is h
not?"

Jehanne took a deep breath. "Aye. He is a whole banquet."

"Then you had best have a taste before it gets cold."

"What do you mean?"

"Fulk will only take so much nay-saying. He has never bee
one to stay where he is not wanted, when it comes to women.'

"Malcolm, I thank you for your advice. I shall consider yo
request to deny Celine knowledge of your living presence, but i
all likelihood she will be at your side within the hour, whether
tell her or no. She will ferret you out."

"You are a hard, cruel woman, Jehanne of Windermere."

"I know. Take your rest." A thought occurred to her. "Th
king always has a surgeon with him. He could undoubtedly hel
you."

"Do you want to see me dragged behind a cart and flogge
hanged, then—"

"Whatever have you done to merit such attention?"

"What have I not done, is more the question. Suffice it to sa
His Grace will be pleased to see me, that he might enjoy my pai
Have no doubt—he will make me scream like a woman in chil
bed."

"Good lord."

"Aye. I want no surgeon. Leave me with my maggots, the

will do me more good. They dinnae mind the smell, nor charge any fee." Malcolm grinned ghoulishly.

"Oh, Mary. I think I had best go. God bless you, Mac Niall. I will return anon." Jehanne put a hand to her stomach and hurried away to see to the comfort of Thomas and Bayard.

Chapter Nineteen

Fulk joyfully raised the blade high. His muscles bunched as he put his weight and power into the racing arc of steel.

Smiling, Jehanne looked up from her needlework, then screamed as his sword met her flesh. He faltered and dropped the bloody weapon. He felt her agony burst upon him, her terror, and her scream became his...

Fulk opened his eyes, his heart hammering. Sweat chilled his skin, and he lay absolutely still. It must be a dream, only a dream. But that demon dwelt within him still, and the price he paid to keep it at bay was killing him. *I will live in shame the rest of my days....*

He lifted his head, wincing at the spasm the movement caused across his shoulders. Carefully he pushed himself up to a sitting position, and waited for the spinning sensation to stop.

Recollections of the events of the day washed through him in a sour tide. He shuddered at his own folly and slid his legs off the cot. His bare foot, still aching from its encounter with Grimald, met with something heavy. Jehanne was asleep on the floor. She stirred and yawned even as he watched her. Gratitude warmed him, that she was safe and at his side.

"Sir?" She blinked, her gray eyes soft with sleep.

"Are you cold, mademoiselle?" How he wanted to warm her!

"Aye."

"Let's go to the brazier, then." He held out a hand for her to take.

"Malcolm is just over there, did you know?" Jehanne sat up

hout accepting his aid and got to her feet. "I think he sleeps,
should not disturb him."

ulk buried the small sting of her rejection and followed her
e. Brushing past her restraining arm he hurried to the Scot. In
flicker of torchlight Malcolm looked waxen, like an effigy of
allen knight.

'Does he live, truly?" Fulk's throat closed and his eyes burned.

"I spoke with him earlier. He was rude, misbehaved, and felt
te sorry for himself," Jehanne whispered.

"That is good. Very good. I hope these nuns have prayed over
n enough. Mercy, what a stench."

"Let us leave before he wakes."

Fulk allowed Jehanne to lead him back to the opposite side of
infirmary, where there was a bowl of ale waiting, with warm
ad and cheese. He downed the brew at once but ate slowly,
ile she picked at her food. Fulk closed his hand over hers.

"Jehanne, hear me out. We can be wed, come the morn, and
lcolm and Celine, too."

She stared. "How?"

"There is a priest visiting here to hear the sisters' confessions
d give the sacraments. He will do it."

"But—"

"It is the best thing for all concerned. We have come too far
gether. Perhaps you do not feel especially...drawn to me, but
might still make Windermere a thriving place. And if you find
unbearable, well, I will leave you in peace. But Celine must
wed now, without delay, even if Malcolm is not expected to
e, in case she is carrying his child. If it comes to that I will
irney to his people in Scotland and tell them what has hap-
ned."

"What if she is carrying the earl's babe?"

Fulk's blood chilled. "I need to speak to her about that."

"Surely not. She is only now recovering her composure."

"I must know for certain what happened. But for now, consider
at I have said. I will not broach the subject again. I shall be in
chapel at dawn. If you meet me there, I swear I will try to
ng you joy."

Jehanne met his gaze. "I do not know how to bring anyone

joy. How can you want me, after all I have done to deserve y
wrath?''

"Jenn, you speak as though you are the only one in the wo
to have ever made a mistake. If you will not have me then y
will have no one, and you need my right arm.''

"Perhaps.''

"Let me put it another way.'' Fulk rubbed the back of her ha
Jehanne's smoky eyes widened. He drew her close, but she
mained stiff in his embrace. "Will you never surrender?''
asked, as gently as he knew how.

"Not until it is the only choice I have left.'' Her voice w
low and tight with pain.

"I will checkmate you yet, Jehanne.'' Fulk let the stubbo
female go without kissing her. He started back to Malcolm's be
side despite Jehanne's urgent whispers to refrain from doing
"I will not leave him.'' Fulk settled himself uncomfortably on
floor.

Jehanne crossed her arms and leaned against the wall. "He h
maggots in his wounds, so he told me. Should we not clean the
out?''

Fulk raised his brows, and a glimmer of hope awoke in
heart. "Perhaps you have not seen what can happen when m
are left for dead, and blowflies settle upon their wounds. There
some magic in the creatures. Mark me, by tomorrow he will
better.''

"I hope to God you are right. Shall I allow Celine to come a
see him? He asked me to keep her away.''

"It will be hard on her but Celine had best face the truth.''
Jehanne nodded, and Fulk watched her depart. She moved d
cisively, square-shouldered and proud. To have her turn her ba
on him in love, or in life, would be too much. Still, he pray
that he was not about to make a terrible mistake. Or two terrib
mistakes, one for himself and another for his sister.

When Celine came he would find out exactly what state s
was in.

A thin sunbeam slipped through the chapel window, a spear
light impaling the dawn air. Silent nuns were assembled, includi

'ulk's mother. Sirs Thomas and Bayard stood as witnesses. No
owers adorned the brides, there would be no feast. The young
riest stumbled over the words.

Jehanne still could not believe she stood next to Fulk, about to
ecome his wife. His chattel, pledged to honor and obey him.
'ear and resistance gripped her throat, even as a secret joy burned
eep within her heart. She looked down at her slender wrist,
ound to Fulk's thick one with a strip of cloth.

A tearful Celine was attached similarly to Malcolm, who had
nsisted he could keep standing as long as it took to wed his
nhuirnin. He had indeed improved overnight, but his state was
recarious. Jehanne could not decide who looked worse, Fulk or
he Scot. They both seemed ready to topple.

An elbow bumped her ribs. "What?" she asked, startled.

"*Do* you?" Fulk demanded.

Everyone's eyes were on her. Jehanne felt her cheeks redden,
nd the familiar tickle of blood along her scar. No more pretend-
ng this was not happening. She would go through with it, for the
ake of her people. For Windermere.

Nay, in truth she desired it for herself. From the day Fulk had
aught her in the snow a part of her had wanted to belong to him.
Now, with two short words, she could make it so. He would own
er, but she would also own him.

"I do."

With the cleric's final pronouncement their fates were sealed.
Malcolm pitched forward, taking Celine with him, for the priest
ad forgotten to remove their marriage bonds. Fulk lunged to
atch his friend, and Jehanne followed, jerked after him as if they
vere playing crack-the-whip.

She slammed against the Scot in time to support one side as
'ulk helped Celine with the other. Jehanne was grateful Malcolm
lid smell a bit better.

"Honey?" she asked, panting with her effort.

Fulk stared at her over Malcolm's lolling head. "Indeed. An
xcellent suggestion."

"I sent for some yestereve," Brigitta informed them. "I will
ring it."

As the priest genuflected, the nun rapidly untied all the involved wrists. "Bless you, children."

"My lady mother, you have our gratitude. Celine, here is a grand opportunity to fulfill a loving wife's duty. It is time to evict your beloved's tenants." Fulk half carried Malcolm back to the infirmary, and leaving him there with his bride, returned to Jehanne. He stood before her, much as he had that day so long ago in the bailey of her keep. Tall, powerful, with beautiful eyes of surpassing warmth, a half smile upon his lips. He was familiar to her now in many ways. But not intimately. That was yet another ordeal to be faced. An ordeal? A great many women seemed to feel otherwise.

Perhaps it would be one for him, instead of for her. She swallowed. "Will you wash?"

Malcolm's wounds had been generous to them both, after all.

"I will if you will."

"You first." Her voice broke and she bit her lip.

Fulk rolled his eyes. "Jehanne, do you imagine I am going to scrub myself in holy water and then throw you down in the nave to exercise my husbandly rights?"

"I am certain that is within the realm of possibility. But your rights would be short-lived." In her nervousness she waxed defiant despite her intent to cooperate.

"Jesus God, woman, is gelding me all that you can think about? We must put Malcolm in a wagon and leave tonight. I do not want Henry to get to Windermere ahead of us, nor risk him finding Malcolm here, undefended. I am going outside to the well. Tell the nuns to keep their eyes on their crucifixes while I bathe."

Gelding him! That was not what she had meant. Apart from his purposely misunderstanding her, Fulk had not even kissed her yet to seal the marriage pact. "Shame on you to suggest yourself as a temptation to these good women!"

"You are so naïve, Jehanne. Perhaps you had best avert your eyes, too." He stalked away.

In spite of her pique, Jehanne found herself wanting another look at him. She had seen most of his body when she had removed her blindfold after his bath in the solar. And again, briefly that day when she had woken him, upon Paxton's arrival.

He was lean and dark and took up a great deal of bed space. She had had no proper protocol of a family member inspecting him to make absolutely certain he was as healthy as a groom ought to be. But she had no doubt of Fulk's health, wounded or not.

Jehanne hurried through her own cold-water scrub. She wandered into the courtyard with a fluttering in her chest, and met with disappointment. A sheet held up by Sir Thomas and a servant screened Fulk, except for his head.

"One cannot be too careful." Fulk grinned at her, his wet hair a dense, glossy black.

Seething at his knowing arrogance, Jehanne retreated into the comfort of readying her horse for the journey home.

They set out as the sun lowered and the frogs began to call. The earl's pageboy remained at the abbey, and Brigitta had sent a message to his parents. Celine rode in a wagon with Malcolm. A lantern swung from each corner, and insects battered their wings against the glowing horn panes.

Fulk and Sir Bayard were in front, while Jehanne stayed arrears with Sir Thomas, who had perfected the art of dozing in the saddle. She felt out of sorts. The lane was too narrow for three abreast, and the men were engaged in conversation. At least it was cool, and Malcolm would not suffer as much.

Celine had bravely ousted the "tenants," as Fulk had termed them, and the honey she substituted was doing its healing work. But in spite of her joy at Malcolm's survival, Jehanne's irritation grew when she heard a giggle from within the curtained wagon.

"My lady!" Fulk beckoned for her to join him as Bayard dropped back. The knight winked as he passed. Jehanne refused to acknowledge it. She had no doubt they had been discussing *her*.

"I think Malcolm is feeling better," she offered, her horse falling into step with Fulk's.

"Aye. He is inspired now that Celine is with him." Fulk took a deep breath. "Do you want to know what she told me?"

"If it is not of too private a nature."

"It is extremely private. But also a bit late for the earl to object."

"The earl?" Jehanne squirmed in her saddle. "Must I hear?"

"I think you should. My mother will not leave the nunnery, so you are the one Celine looks to for guidance."

"Go on, then."

Fulk cleared his throat. "On the road that day, Grimald did not ravish her in front of Malcolm or anyone else."

Jehanne stared. "But, it was obvious. Her weeping, and the way he spoke of it. Boasted, rather."

"Exactly. According to Celine, he dragged her into the wood, tore her clothes, beat her when she resisted, but when it came to the point of violation, Grimald was limp as an unbaked loaf. He was desperate to take her, she has no doubt.

"But he was so embarrassed at his failure, he threatened to kill her and me if she breathed a word of it to anyone. She was to act the victim or suffer the consequences."

"Oh!" was all Jehanne could utter. Her relief was so great that tears started in her eyes. "Praise God." She looked at Fulk carefully, but he maintained a neutral expression. "Is that why he hated you? Because you are...popular with the ladies, and he was inadequate?"

Fulk shrugged. "I do not imagine that circumstance endeared me to him. But, I swear, I did not do half of what the court gossips say I did."

"Half was more than enough, I trow."

"And what do you know of such things?"

"Only that unchaste men have nothing of which to be proud."

Fulk was silent for a moment. "Chastity is a noble virtue. But so many women are starved for..."

"Aye?" Jehanne prodded. Such delicate hesitation was unlikely in one so sought after, she thought.

"For what their lords deny them for months and years on end, because they are too busy drinking or warring or being unfaithful to pay their ladies proper attention. And not just the physical."

"I am certain you filled those voids admirably, sir. Was it all done out of charity, or did your heart ever get involved?" Jehanne held her breath. She did not know what would be worse, to know he had truly loved other women, or that he had simply met a mutual need with each.

"You embarrass me with your questions."

"Forgive me. But answer."

"I cared deeply. I bore them genuine affection. I protected their ᵣutations and I made them happy for as long as possible. And ᵣaught a few husbands some manners. What of you?"

"I beg your pardon?"

"Come, can we not be frank, now that we are wed? Do you ᵣr feel...well, that you lack something?"

"I have everything anyone could want. A good horse, a strong ᵣce and my honor intact."

Fulk laughed into the night. "My lady, you are rich, indeed."

ᵣt was not a reaction Jehanne expected. Nor did she find it ᵣasing. "You mock me."

"Indeed I do not. I admire your simple needs. Would that mine ᵣre so few."

"The fewer the needs, the fewer the disappointments."

Fulk cocked his head. "Ah. That may be true, but I prefer to ᵣk myself than remain apart from loving, female warmth."

"As will any dog risk a shower of sparks to be near the fire."

Fulk glanced over his shoulder to the wagon creaking behind ᵣm, lit by the swaying lamps. "What of a moth, Jehanne? It ᵣes not seek comfort from the lantern's heat, it goes to its an-ᵣilation in pursuit of the light. It sacrifices itself for beauty, for ᵣerfect moment of clarity. It becomes one with the flame."

"You do not qualify as a moth, Sir Fulk. You have singed ᵣurself in innumerable flames, but by your own admission you ᵣve never been annihilated."

He fixed his amber gaze full upon Jehanne. "I would like to ᵣ, lady. To burn and burn and be forever changed. I reserve that ᵣst for you."

Jehanne could not bear the intensity of his eyes. "You speak ᵣ though an inquisitor has addled your mind," she mumbled. ᵣesides, by the time a man—or a moth—like you is done burn-ᵣg, there will be nothing left of the lantern, either."

Fulk smiled and shook his head. "Shall I take that as a com-ᵣiment? Or do you despise love?"

"It is a mystery to me. I do not know when to believe fair

words, so oft have they been used in attempts to obtain what own, rather than my heart.''

"We had best do something about that when we get home."

His casual words brought her up short. Windermere was hi now, down to every last grain of wheat in the fields. She bit h tongue to keep from crying out a protest. But hadn't she tried buy his life with her property, not two days ago?

To her wonderment it was not the handing over of her belove lands that hurt. Nay, today she would not hesitate to give hi anything she possessed. But to think that she must give him he self, that was going to be difficult.

"What do you mean to do, then, at home?" she asked.

"About your misgivings in regard to my poetic exposition c small, winged creatures?"

Jehanne nodded, and refrained from sighing in exasperation.

"Well, that depends upon you and your willingness to learn."

"You do not know everything! I too have things to teach you.

"I can't wait." Fulk grinned.

"I mean husbandry of the fief."

"What of husbanding the husband?"

Jehanne lifted her chin. She could not retreat from such a cha lenge. "I can take whatever you serve. With one hand tied behin my back." At Fulk's blank look of surprise it was her turn smile. "Remember, you said you would pick up my gage?"

"Oh, my lady, will I ever have peace with you?"

"Just do not push me, my lord."

Fulk inclined his head in a gracious nod, but his eyes gleame languid and sensual. Jehanne felt an unbidden thrill speed throug her feminine center. He was no moth. He was a man, *hers* now with a burning lust that she was duty bound to satisfy. She woul not shirk that duty, though it required her physical surrender, he complete loss of dignity.

She would meet Fulk bravely, for within her woman's bod beat a warrior's heart.

The next afternoon found them within sight of Windermere. breeze skittered over the long lake's surface, and lush, heavy topped marsh grasses rippled in echoing swells along the shore

Fisherfolk waved, and men and women in the fields dropped their work to watch them pass. Fulk found it a beautiful sight, and a fitting tribute to Jehanne that the people were strong and well once again.

At the gates Lioba stood, her arms full of flowers. She threw them at Fulk, the better to embrace Jehanne, who had jumped down the moment her horse stopped. Fulk dismounted and gathered up the red-hued poppies before Jehanne's palfrey could eat them and colic.

Celine clambered out of the wagon and skipped over to join Jehanne. Fulk let the women chatter on for a while, then put his hand upon Jehanne's wrist.

"Forgive me, I would settle Malcolm, take a mouthful of supper and go to bed. I must have a few hours of sleep and time to prepare before Henry arrives."

Jehanne merely nodded and led her horse toward the well in the inner bailey.

Lioba glared at Fulk. "You have gall, sir. You have come all this way, spent all this time, finally wed my lady as was your original intent. Now you neglect your bride? A groom who wants to sleep? Pah! What more useless thing can be imagined?"

Fulk rubbed his brow. His back ached and burned and itched, and he was reeling with fatigue. He had spent yet another night wide awake, too close to Jehanne for any possibility of rest. No one had promised it would be easy.

"That is quite a change of tune for you, Lioba. Do not concern yourself. I shall attend my lady when she wills it. Kindly see to her comfort. And mind your tongue."

Fulk saw that Bayard watched their exchange with interest. At last Lioba noticed the knight. She stared at him, curtsied, then hurried into the hall like a doe fleeing a hound.

With that Fulk summoned bearers to carry Malcolm within the keep. He accompanied his friend while Jehanne's ladies made much of her and Celine's return.

From the stable, Corwin loped to Fulk's side. "I found Sperling, and all is well. Glad to see you among the living, Mac Niall, sir." The boy grinned at Malcolm, who had bits of straw in his hair and still appeared decidedly the worse for wear.

"Aye, for a time I wasnae certain I wanted to be among the living, for the feast I was providin' certain others."

Corwin looked puzzled, and Fulk distracted him by thumping his back. "I shall fall down soon if I don't find a bed. Malcolm here has lazed and dozed his way from pillar to post in ease and comfort, with a lovely woman at his beck and call. He will be able to advise you should the need arise. And Sir Bayard is ever willing to be of service."

Fulk decided to forego food and headed straight for the solar. A basin of water and clean sheets were all he desired in the world at the moment. Or almost all. He paused at the landing and looked down.

Between the two great open doors of the hall, Jehanne stood backlit by the glow of the afternoon sun. Her hair had fallen loose and shimmered around her. She was greeting her people, embracing them and being embraced. He had not misspoken. She was rich, indeed.

That evening, her heart pounding, Jehanne took Lioba aside. "You owe Sir Fulk an apology, as you do me, for the lies you told. I understand you thought to protect me, but it was still wrong to tarnish the honor of such a man."

Lioba's eyes welled with tears. "Forgive me, my lady. I have already asked him to do so, for your sake. But I brought shame to your house, and I regret my actions."

Jehanne could not bear to see Lioba suffer further. "I know you are sincere, for you have ever had my best interests at heart. Let us put it behind us, and speak of it no more."

The young woman nodded, and as Jehanne put her arms about her, Lioba said, "The ladies will attend you, now. It is time you embraced the fact that you are a woman, wed to man who has...much to offer."

With that she led a reluctant Jehanne to the women's quarters. The door opened to reveal their smiling, ribald glee.

Jehanne was appalled. After all their staunch defense of her virtue, now that she was wed it seemed her women could not wait to see that she lost her virginity as rapidly as possible. Even Celine, whom Jehanne thought would show some sympathy, was enthusiastically weaving ribbons and wildflowers into her hair, making remarks kindly intended, but exceedingly embarrassing.

"Now, you are not to be afraid, my dear sister, for although Fulk would be the last to admit it, he is the perfect knight. A lion and a lamb in one. 'Tis up to you to bring out whichever side of him you prefer in bed."

Jehanne found the resultant giggling of the young women unbearable, but could not bring herself to spoil their joy. She kept her shawl around her shoulders and tried not to think about what was to come. She realized she did have a question, after all.

"Em, ladies, I have heard it said that it is important to *pretend,* that there is some element of play-acting involved in this business, of what, I do not know. I was always told by Father Edgar that a decent wife should lie still and pray for the good of her soul that she not prove to be her husband's downfall into excess."

The women looked at each other. Young Ellie was clearly baffled. Lioba, Celine, and the others barely contained their mirth.

Lioba was the first to brave Jehanne's deepening glower. "Milady, with such a man as your husband I doubt there will be any need for pretense. Though I am sure none of us know exactly what was meant by what you heard." She threw a quelling glance to Celine. "And lying still might indeed be the wisest course, at first. Worry not. All will become clear in time."

Jehanne bowed her head. It would. Every last hideous scar she bore would be clear to Fulk. He had been adored by the noblest, loveliest women in the land. The king himself had said so. No doubt once he made her a mother, he would find some excuse to return to one of them. Perhaps he would even were she not ugly. She shook her head.

Self-pity was unseemly. It was time to be bold.

Chapter Twenty

Shortly after sunset, having made dire threats to her maids should they try to follow, Jehanne ventured into the solar. The bed loomed big and dark, like a cavern that might hold a wild animal set to devour her. Or worse, look at her unclothed. She shivered and glanced out the window.

Pale wisps of cloud drifted along the horizon as the sky deepened from blue to black, and bats flitted above the torches in the bailey below. Jehanne pulled the shutters closed and prepared to face her husband. If the silent lump under the furs was indeed Fulk, perhaps he was still asleep. Perhaps she could quietly turn around and leave him thus.

"Jehanne?"

She jumped. "Aye?"

"I cannot see my hand before my face. I will keep myself covered if you wish, but light the candles."

It was not quite so dark as he said. There was more than enough light for him to do...what he needed to do. "It is I who will remain covered," she whispered, coming no closer than the corner-post of the bed.

Fulk sat up and leaned forward, resting his arms on his knees. "Why? I long to see you." He found her hand, and gently drew her to him.

"Nay, please...I cannot." Jehanne could not bear the thought of his inevitable hesitation, his dismay, when he discovered what he had for a bride. The fact that his good manners would keep it a fleeting pause only made her feel worse.

She plunged into her excuse. "It is immodest. You seem to have an idea that the marriage bed is for pleasure. But this is no moonlit night of magic in a hay-field."

During the brief silence that followed, Jehanne could just make out Fulk's expression of consternation. She wished she could insist upon him wearing a blindfold, as she had once worn.

"Hmm. My lady, I think this is one arena in which I am the better qualified. Allow me to guide you." He touched her knee. "Unless you mean to continue to thwart my efforts."

Jehanne took a step back, then flattened herself against the bed-post. Fulk's shadow shape rose, brushed past her and went to the door. When a sliver of light struck him she saw his naked body from the side, and did not avert her eyes.

He was lithe and graceful, every muscle of his torso and legs clearly visible, but without grotesque bulges or knots. She bit her lip, and drank him in. Fulk returned momentarily with a burning splinter, with which he lit a pair of tall candles beside the bed.

She saw the still-livid evidence of his encounter with Grimald. She winced to think she had once envied him his smooth back. Thanks in part to her, it was no more. "How are your wounds, Fulk? If they pain you, there is no need to—"

"I am fine. Your careful attentions will speed my recovery."

He made Jehanne sit on the mattress and settled next to her, his presence a surprising comfort in spite of her nervousness. Carefully she examined her hands, turning them over and inspecting each nail. Anything to avoid a close-up view of the heart-stopping man beside her. Her lord. Her husband. And soon, her lover...

"Look at me," Fulk said softly.

Slowly, Jehanne raised her head. The hazy golden light caught his big body's curves and angles. His skin gleamed, as did his black hair, which these days nearly met his shoulders. He was utterly magnificent, with a lean, sculpted beauty of which he himself seemed completely unaware, in spite of his reputation.

"Now touch me."

At his gentle command her mouth went dry.

"Please." He tilted his head.

"Where?" She tried to swallow.

"Anywhere you like. Just pick a spot and touch it."

"Oh...I cannot." Her fingers crept to her mouth and she began to chew her nails.

"Jehanne, stop that. I will not maul you, I promise. Think of Beltaine. You enjoyed what we did, until we were interrupted, am I right?" Pulling the sheet up to his waist, Fulk leaned on his elbow and lay on his side.

She nodded. God help her, it was the truth.

He gazed at her, his amber eyes seemingly lit from within. "Have you ever tamed a horse?" he asked.

Jehanne blinked at this shift. "I have helped the avener, on occasion."

"Pretend I am a horse and you are gentling me. No one has caught me, no one has ridden me, and I am afraid, for you are a creature with whom I am unfamiliar."

Fulk's sultry voice made her feel part of a dream. He held out his hand. "Here, start with this. It is not so fearsome, is it?"

"Well..." Gingerly, Jehanne placed her palm over the back of Fulk's hand. It was warm, his knuckles rough. He did not move or respond, leaving it up to her whether to continue. Going higher, she met the heavy bone of his wrist, and the smooth, dark hair on his forearm. The same hair that on his chest served to define his beautiful form. Jehanne winced again at the sight of the scar near his elbow, where her arrow had pierced his flesh.

Why was he doing this? She should not play this foolish game any longer. But, she found herself relishing the illusion Fulk allowed her, that she had power over him. She liked the feel of his skin, and the weight of his hand as she picked it up. He had never once raised it against her in anger. How long would that last? She began to tremble.

"What is it, love?"

"I—I do not know. Let me go, Fulk. I cannot be a wife to you. I am so sorry, but I—"

"Shh..." He engulfed both her hands in his. "I will not let you go. Ever. So there is an end on it. But, Jehanne, whomever you are is what I want. I know you are afraid—"

"Of course I am not afraid!" She made fists, still between his palms.

"Then why do you tremble, and your eyes fill with tears?"

"All right, I am afraid." Jehanne held herself stiffly, her stomach muscles rigid.

"Of me?"

She thought she heard disappointment in his voice. But the truth could not be helped. "Aye. Of you. Of what will happen when you...when we..." She had to stop the shameful welling of her eyes, and rubbed them dry on her arm.

"Tsk, but such fear is natural. It is my responsibility to ease your worry." He drew the backs of his fingers along her cheek.

As much as she wanted to enjoy his touch, the caress only made her turn her face away. Oh, why did she torture herself? He had best know her heart before there was no going back.

She took a great breath and met his eyes. "I fear your reaction to me as I truly am. I fear that I will never be able to produce a living child. And even if I do I am afraid I will die as a result, as my mother did after fifteen years of trying!" There, he had it, the whole ugly story. Or nearly the whole of it.

"You fear I will see you as a coward for that? Or that you are not good enough breeding material, am I right?"

"I am not a coward."

"Of course not. Very few women are capable of cowardice. But think you that every warrior believes courage is about being stoic and hiding what he feels? I will tell you, Jehanne, the finest examples of chivalry among the bravest, most skilled warriors I have known, were those who wept when their friends died, or for that matter, when their horses died. And, on occasion, when they had slain a worthy enemy. It is not so simple as you would have it. Not all men have stones for hearts."

"I am aware of that."

"Good. Come, sleep beside me." Fulk's smile was both sweet and sensual. "Or in your own chamber, if you prefer," he added gently.

"I am not sleepy, and...I have a duty to perform."

Fulk sat up. "Do not speak to me of duty. I want you willing or not at all."

Jehanne was not prepared for his challenge. "Wh-what of our heir?"

"He will come when he is ready. Let us stop talking." Fulk frowned and punched his pillow. The seam burst, sending eider-down floating like snowflakes into his hair. He looked absurd. And incredibly handsome. He sat and waited, his only movement a visible pulse throbbing in his neck.

A little spurt of panic rushed through Jehanne. "I am not ready to stop talking." She turned her back on Fulk, to collect herself.

Then, his hands settled upon her shoulders. Heavy, warm and still. Only the thin linen of her chemise between his skin and hers. With strong fingers, he began to knead her tight muscles. Jehanne closed her eyes and allowed herself to relax a bit.

She would enjoy his touch while it lasted. Soon. Soon he would know. And she would know what manner of man he truly was. From behind, Fulk untied the narrow ribbon that secured the front of her shift, and slipped the garment off one of her shoulders. Then the other. He paused, and kissed her bared skin.

Jehanne felt a shiver start deep inside. It worked its way up through her chest and beyond, until her teeth chattered from sheer, mindless reaction. His fingers deftly worked through her hair. One by one, he removed the flowers and ribbons.

"You need no adornment, Jenn."

She could not respond to his sweetness, knowing he was about to discover her shame. Quickly she leaned over and blew at the candle flames. Only one went out. She held herself still.

Fulk's hands skimmed down her spine. Stopped. Retraced their path upwards. And stopped again. Then he sighed, his breath warm upon her naked back. A heavy sigh. He had seen the scars. Touched them. They revolted him. She revolted him. The marks were thick and would be there forever. She tried to pull away.

"Jehanne, nay. Stay with me. Stay."

Fulk cradled her against his chest, and she hung her head, afraid to speak. She wanted to remain in his embrace and never move again. But the memories of her father's rage swept through her like wildfire, even as she gripped Fulk's hand and clung to him.

He squeezed her fingers and held her yet closer, bringing her back from the nightmare. His grim voice vibrated from his body to hers. "The FitzWalter did this to you."

"Aye," she whispered. Fulk tightened his embrace so that Je-

nne could scarcely breathe. But she said nothing in the face of
e mounting fury she felt coursing through him as he spoke.

"I wish he were still alive. I would take my sword and run it
rough his heart. Had I known, I would have put him to death
ng before the fever saved him from my hands."

"Oh, do not say that. I could have prevented it. It was the
ages of my disobedience. I spurned the earl."

Fulk pressed the side of Jehanne's neck with his scratchy cheek
d relaxed his grip on her. "That was no reason to treat you
us." He reached over and relit the taper she had just extin-
ished.

Jehanne turned to face him. It was still not too late for an
nulment, should he wish it, after hearing what she had to say.

"I loved my father. But I hated him, too. Ah, my lord, I am
wicked. I used to wish him dead. Prayed for him to die. Imag-
ed killing him with my own hands. I went to the priest to confess
y dark thoughts, and he reviled me. Then the fever came, and
ather *did* die. In agony, just as I had once wanted."

"There is no need to confess to me, love."

"But there is. You must know the full extent of my evil."
hanne spoke faster as her throat began to close, threatening to
ep her guilt inside. "During his fever Father begged my for-
veness, over and over, and in the end I denied him. *'Ask it of
od, not of me.'* Those were my words." She choked back her
ars.

Fulk cupped her chin with his palm. "Listen to me, Jehanne.
our feelings were natural, not wicked. No one suffers torture
adly unless they are either true saints, righteous fanatics or sick
d twisted within themselves. If you have since forgiven your
ther, you may be sure he knows it. And if you have not, I am
rtain he understands and accepts that he was wrong. The rest is
r him and the Lord to sort out."

"What about his forgiving me?"

"There is no question of that."

"You sound so convincing, Fulk. Are you sure you are not a
iest yourself?" Tentatively, Jehanne rubbed the dark center of
s chest, between the firm, rounded muscles, and played with the

gilt cross nestled there. She was surprised when the pulse in Fulk
neck bounded at her touch, and his breathing quickened.

He smiled wryly. "A priest is one thing I am sure I'm not.
is only that I have sinned so greatly, I know more than most abo
guilt and forgiveness."

"C-can you bear me as I am? Forever marked as a remind
of my stubborn willfulness?" Jehanne felt foolish and vain f
asking, but she needed to hear his answer.

Fulk held her shoulders and gazed into her eyes. "I will lo
you all the more for your scars. Every tear you shed, each mome
of pain you suffered brought you closer to me, though you kne
it not. Your father called it stubborn willfulness. But in my vie
you were steadfast and true to yourself, Jehanne. You allow
none of them to claim you. Your strength has made me happi
than I have any right to be, for I am the one fortunate enough
be your husband, and I admire you, so very much...."

Jehanne could not speak, so unexpectedly tender were Fulk
words. The way he looked at her melted her heart. He had bee
telling her he loved her, in so many ways, for a long time, s
realized. What a callous, selfish fool she had been.

He kissed her cheek, and the inside of his thigh rubbed her hi
sending fresh shivers through her.

"What is important is that you are willing. God *knows* I am.
he said, and Jehanne heard his smile. She held her silence, baski
in his embrace. Fulk spoke into the thick hair at her nape. "F
knows, too, that I can wait until you want me, however long th
takes."

"But I want you now! I simply feel so..."

"What?"

She turned to face him. "Old. Used up. I am like a—a chewe
upon shoe. It retains some virtues of basic form and function, b
no beauty. Nothing to excite a man's desire." *Nothing a man li
you deserves.*

"Let me be the judge." Fulk pulled her against him. "Wou
I do this if I did not find you beautiful?" He kissed her earlob
tenderly, ran his lips up and down her neck. "And, would yo
find me in such a state if you were not desirable?"

"What state?" she breathed.

He drew her hand beneath the covers, and placed it upon the state in question. "Oh! Good lord."

"Aye, He is. See what you do to me?"

"I am afraid to look. Is all that for...for wanting m-me?"

"Aye, all for you. Rest easy, love. It will only hurt a little, for just a moment."

Jehanne gulped. She had forgotten about that. "I would like to give you joy."

"You do already. And what I feel, so shall you."

A rash urge to defy fate came over her. "I would like to give you a son." She hesitated, her heart pounding. "Or...a daughter."

"Either will do." Fulk tilted his head in his charming way.

Gladness filled Jehanne's heart at his reply. "I am certain it will be one or the other."

He smiled. "You would take that risk for me?"

She tried to sound brave. "Aye. Go ahead. Do what must be done."

"You are looking forward that much to my full attentions, eh?" He quirked an eyebrow.

"Well, Lioba says—" Jehanne began.

"Lioba has never been to bed with me."

"Aye, we have settled that."

"It was not for want of her trying."

"Sweet liar."

"Mmm..." Fulk rubbed the underside of her jaw with one finger. "You know, Jenn, there is a simple way to avoid begetting children. The church calls it an 'unnatural act,' but to my mind there is nothing wicked in merely withdrawing bef—"

"Nay. I do not want to hear about it, and I do not want you to sin on my behalf." Jehanne did not know of what he spoke, and did not desire any clarification.

"But—"

"Nay! We are in God's hands."

"You are in my hands, and I am in yours."

His breath warmed her shoulder, in the beginnings of a nibbling kiss. "Fulk, you are an arrogant, spoilt—what are you doing?"

He slid her shift down until it was around her waist. He caressed her neck, then sifted her hair through his fingers. "Shh. This will be my greatest pleasure, and I will make it yours, too."

"Ah, Galliard, I do wish I resembled you." With her finger, Jehanne traced the powerful curve of bone from the hollow of his throat to his shoulder.

"Heaven forbid there should be two of me loose in this world."

She batted at his chest. "I meant you are not shy or afraid of me looking at you unclothed, after all."

"Of course I am not. You have no one to compare me with." He grinned shamelessly. "For all your limited experience, my body might be perfect in every way."

"I am afraid that indeed it is, Fulk. And here I thought you did not know it."

His expression grew serious. "I know only what you tell me."

His voice was soft and thick, like the hair curling at his neck. Fulk's gaze dropped to her breasts. Jehanne's eyes widened. He was pleased with her, that much was obvious. Or at least with *them.*

He lay on his side, and gently drew her down with him. "As far as I am concerned, you are my first, as I am yours."

Cautiously, she slid her arm around his waist. It felt right. It belonged there. She settled herself more comfortably.

He stroked her hip, for her leg had somehow draped itself over his. Impulsively Jehanne grasped Fulk's hair in two fistfuls and pulled his mouth to hers. She kissed him lightly, still not daring to give rein to the rising excitement within her.

Fulk shuddered beneath her questing fingers. Jehanne looked into his eyes, now dark with desire, and felt his rising passion call to her. Only a complete coward or an utter fool would stop now. She pressed his hands to her aching breasts.

Fulk was rocked, clear to his soul, it was plain from the expressions that coursed over his face. Surprise, joy, and gratitude. And shining through them all a look of untrammeled love. Not a saintly love, by any means, but one heartfelt and true.

He spread his fingers to encompass her, and his thumbs brushed the sensitive skin of her nipples. She fought her instinct to flee, as the magical sensations surged through her body. This was not wrong.

This was how lovers touched each other, and sometimes even husbands and wives. Had not Lioba once admitted as much? Fulk had every right to do whatever he pleased with her, no matter how she felt. Jehanne stopped herself. This was not about him. She was the one who must learn to surrender, to accept the goodness he offered and enjoy it.

"Let go. Relax." Fulk's whispered entreaty filtered through her thoughts. "Jehanne, let me love you." He nearly moaned his plea, and she tried to be calm, letting her weight sink into the feather bed. Fulk came closer, looming over her. "You be the horse, now," he said.

She braced herself, expecting to be mounted, literally. But instead, he knelt at her side and pulled her shift completely off of her body. Jehanne trembled in embarrassment at being so exposed, even in such dim light, but she was amazed to see frank appreciation shining in Fulk's eyes. He began to rub her ankles. The soles of her feet. Up and down the length of her legs, her hips and stomach, over her chest to her shoulders and along her arms. Jehanne's skin tingled with the pure joy of his touch, even as she tensed, unused to such sensuous familiarity.

Fulk leisurely surveyed her nakedness as he worked, and his blatant approval was so pleasing, she tried harder not to hold herself like a plank. But it took a great deal more rubbing before her muscles fully relaxed. Fulk's hands moved over Jehanne's body like the ebb and flow of a warm tide.

With every retreat she felt a loss, and each advance brought a renewed surge of pleasure. How had she survived without him for so long? His touch was like a feast of many courses for her starving soul, presented with elegant, loving care. He had never done this for anyone else, it was not possible. Not with this much skill and restraint. She could not bear to think otherwise.

He turned her and started again on her backside. Her neck, back, waist, the insides of her thighs. Such hands. Strong and large, capable of inflicting more pain than she could possibly bear. Yet she felt only love and the utmost care in his touch. Fulk handled her as if he were an artisan and she were a piece of fine clay he wished to model precisely.

Gradually she stopped feeling ticklish as the rhythmic strokes slowed and deepened. Then the hands rested, and his mouth took over where his fingers left off.

Twisting to face him, she shivered beneath his kisses and could not stop. He lingered over her breasts, drawing each one to rapt attention with slow suckling. Apparently satisfied that they were content, Fulk left them behind with a last brush of his lips for each, paying no heed to Jehanne's archings and small cries. He reached her mouth at last and stayed there, slipping between her lips with his tongue.

Fulk kissed her, devoured her in such a provocative manner that Jehanne responded in ways she could not have imagined possible, mere weeks before. Her legs began to ease apart of their own accord. The caresses she showered on him in return redoubled his ardor. For every exquisite sensation he drew from her body, she discovered she could mirror his actions and bring him similar pleasure.

She wrapped Fulk in a fierce embrace and writhed against him. She wanted to be close to him. Very close. To blend and merge and burn with him. He no longer sought permission to touch any intimate part of her, for it seemed he knew exactly what she wanted and how far he might go. With each sweep of his fingers he brought her nearer a state of readiness. Of heat and melting, hollow desire. Then, with one hand he lifted her while the other slid a pillow beneath the small of her back.

"Now," he growled, a smile playing upon his lips.

Oh, sweet heaven. No possible retreat. Fulk looked to be unstoppable. But Jehanne did not want him to stop.

He recaptured her full awareness by rubbing her again, *there*...in that certain spot. She gasped at the intense sparks of sensation.

"Do you want me?" he asked thickly.

She drew up her knees and tugged on his shoulders. "Fulk, stop talking."

He obeyed. Fully and at great length. He carried her past the fleeting pain, then with increasing urgency pushed her beyond all control. Caught in Fulk's primal rhythm, meeting him at every thrust, she flew to a peak of physical rapture, of complete, joyful

render. He gave her unbearable pleasure, brought her to an
possible state with his sorcery. She would not survive.

No one could experience such love and heat and ever be the
ne again. Jehanne moaned as she raced toward the edge of an
vss. Desperate. Helpless. About to die in flames, and oh, so
ling to perish.

'Look at me, Jenn," Fulk begged.

She was gasping. Breathless. On the rack with him, just as he
predicted. She opened her eyes to meet his. Intense concen-
ion. A tender, raw gaze, and Fulk buried himself again within

Her ecstasy exploded, creating a brilliant fire, thundering
ugh her in wave after blissful wave. She could not help but
out, so loudly that the dogs in the bailey began to bark. Some-
cheered, drunkenly. Jehanne did not care who heard.

She was the Iron Maiden no longer.

Fulk had remained silent, but for a strangled hiss through
nched teeth. He shuddered into stillness. After a while he
fted his weight and lay on his side, holding her tight, stroking
hair with his free hand.

She jammed her head under his chin and listened to the rapid
mmer of his heart. "That *was* a great effort." Her eyes closed,
I she inhaled the warm, earthy scent of his body.

"Aye," he rasped.

"Can it ever happen again, or was that a miracle you just per-
med?" Jehanne hardly dared hope for another similar experi-
ce in future. Perhaps such bliss was only reserved for new
des, a once-in-a-lifetime occurrence. Unless... "Tell me, did
I cast a spell to make it so?"

Fulk choked on his laughter. "It can happen as often as you
h it to, sweeting. That much I promise. But I cannot explain
w."

"In truth, I do not know if I could bear it a second time," she
nitted.

His hand stilled on her hair.

"Oh, nay, Fulk." She reached up and laced her fingers through
. "I mean, I might die of happiness. No doubt the pagan gods

are very pleased with us, but they may become jealous if we enjoy
each other too much.''

"To hell with them, then.''

Jehanne smiled and whispered against his chest, "I never
dreamed a man's body could bring me such pleasure.''

Fulk responded with a kiss of surpassing tenderness, which no
longer surprised her, but brought tears to her eyes all the same.
She looked at their interlinked hands, then to his closed eyes, and
the dark fans of his lashes against his cheeks.

"I am glad it was mine bringing it,'' he said.

Jehanne fitted her curves as close to Fulk as possible. He
wrapped her into his arms and rested his head between her breasts.
She smoothed the damp tendrils from his brow, pushed him back
against the bolsters and rolled on top of him. His stomach muscles
bunched as she touched them, his hipbones were hard under her
thighs. She felt his flesh stir beneath her. Jehanne smiled. "Let
me cast the spell, this time.''

Chapter Twenty-One

hanne descended the stairs the next morning with Fulk's warm
nd at her waist. They were met by smiling, expectant faces. The
lagers, her ladies, the peasant folk—the backbone of Winder-
re—all had gathered to congratulate them. Fulk's mercenaries
od grinning and elbowing each other, even her dogs wagged
mselves into a frenzy.

She felt herself blush and looked to her husband. He smiled
evolently, and his fingers tightened around hers. Jehanne gazed
the group of well-wishers. Their sincerity evoked emotion so
ep it rendered her speechless. Never before had she felt so loved
so many.

But the prince of her happiness stood behind her. His warmth,
strength buoyed her. That she had once fought the notion of
ning herself to Fulk seemed insanity in retrospect. There was
loss, no relinquishing of power. She had lost her heart, that
s true. And she was weak with the after-effects of his love-
king, of baring her soul and having it held and cherished as if
vere a newborn babe, innocent as the dawn.

He had given her much more than she had ever dared hope to
ceive. His acceptance, his faith, his love. A whole new world
experience. It was her sworn duty not to fail him. More than
t, it was a sacred trust.

With all of her brimming heart, Jehanne smiled back at the
hering of people. A boisterous, collective shout arose, and joy-
mayhem erupted. She watched for a moment, then turned and
Fulk gather her into his arms.

"You have pleased them mightily, Jenn," he whispered, holding her close.

"No more than you have me, sir."

"I could not help but make the attempt or die trying."

"After last night, a mere glance from you will be enough set me alight, remembering."

"That is just as well, lady, for you have worn me out."

Jehanne heard his grin as he spoke, pressing his cheek to h hair. "When you have taught me more, mayhap I shall exhau you less," she suggested.

"Aye, well, even I learned a few things by placing myself your hands, believe it or no."

"It was divine inspiration, my lord, nothing less."

"Do not pray for further inspiration if you want me to surviv the summer," Fulk admonished her sweetly.

Jehanne sighed and wrapped her arms more tightly about h body. She would be content to stand like this the rest of the da

"Come, Jenn, let us greet the morn."

Fulk linked his fingers with hers and led the way through th thronged hall. Food and flowers filled the tables as the people spirits continued to rise.

Bride and groom wound their way out of the bailey, across th drawbridge and out onto the common, with a trail of curious ch dren following. Jehanne inhaled the sweetness of the air and a mired the brilliant hues of sky, forest, and lake as if she had nev seen any of it until this day.

As if she had only just come alive.

Fulk stood before her, holding both her hands in his, and raise his face to the heavens. "I can breathe, Jenn, without my hea hurting. It still aches, but only for your presence. My eyes longer burn, except to behold you. I am more tightly fettered th I have ever been in my life, yet I feel free. Do you understand"

"Aye, Fulk, I do. And I am glad of it." Jehanne looked wi satisfaction upon his handsome, sun-bronzed face and was gl of that, too. Then, she heard a faint chorus, growing louder a more distinct by the moment. Men were singing as they cam and the children ran toward the music.

"What is that?"

Fulk shaded his eyes and looked down the hill to where the
alky lane threaded its way from the village to the keep. He
inned. "Some gleemen have found us. God knows how they
ard of our wedding. Unless, of course, they heard *you.*"

Jehanne felt a blush mount in her cheeks as the singers drew
arer, playing lutes, flutes, and beating drums. Their bawdy song,
mething about a brave cockerel and a thorny hedge, embar-
ssed her almost as much as Fulk's remark.

It was a marvel how such groups appeared overnight, like
ushrooms, on any occasion that might merit their musical tal-
ts. Such was the power of gossip and travelers bearing tales,
rtainly not the result of the ecstatic noise she had made—she
ped not, anyway.

"Let us go see Malcolm and Celine," she said. "After all, it
is their wedding night, too."

Fulk grunted. "They had theirs already. But, aye, we must at-
d them."

His mood seemed to darken with the mention of Malcolm and
s sister. They reminded him of Grimald and Hengist and the
ng, no doubt, just as they did her. As she walked back to the
ll with Fulk, Jehanne could not help but feel cheated. One night
bliss, a single morn of newfound happiness, and already shad-
/s crept to darken her heart's blossoming.

After a short search, they found the wayward couple in a sun-
enched corner of the battlement walkway. Malcolm lay dozing,
s head pillowed in Celine's lap. Her fingers flew as she plaited
s hair into narrow ropes, weaving in buttercups at regular inter-
ls.

"Does he know what you are doing, Celine?" Fulk asked
tly.

She grinned and whispered, "Nay. 'Tis a surprise."

Jehanne suppressed a giggle. "You are wicked. I wish I had
ught of that! Except Fulk's hair needs more length for me to
aid it properly. I will just have to be patient."

"Do not even consider it, Jenn, or I will have my head
aved."

Jehanne stuck out her tongue at him.

Malcolm opened his good eye and reared up, then grimaced

and sank back into Celine's arms. "Och, I thought you were
troll, Fulk, standing there so disgruntled-like. Now I have taken
fright I cannae well afford."

"I remind you of your guilty conscience, *brother*."

"Well, it had to happen sooner or later. Grateful you will b
one day, when a dozen hulking nephews stand before you, awai
ing your slightest command. 'Tis a private army you will hav
Fulk, betwixt my bairns and yours."

Jehanne and Celine looked at each other, then at Malcolm.

"What have I said to deserve such baleful stares?" he asked

"After we go to all the trouble of bearing sons—and daugh
ters—you would risk them in some foolish battle?" Celine de
manded.

"What else are they good for? Besides, there will be plenty
spare. Ow!" Malcolm grinned as Celine beat him about the hea
with her fistful of buttercups. "Fulk, your sister lacks the manne
befitting a lady. I want my bride-price back."

"Please, spare me the knowledge of what you consider to b
the bride-price. In any event, I promised *you* would be paid, r
member?" Fulk asked mildly. "As you well deserve," he adde

When Celine's jaw dropped and her eyes grew wide, Jehann
interrupted. "He is teasing, dear heart. Shame on you, Fulk."

"In truth," Fulk continued, "Malcolm still has a great de
coming to him. He is looking forward to it, I am certain, po
deluded man."

"Wait 'til I am on my feet again, Fulk, then you may challeng
me and we will have it out to your satisfaction."

"Take your time, Mac Niall. I will not forgive you any da
soon."

"Good. 'Twill inspire me to quicker health." Malcolm ease
himself to a standing position, and offered his hand to Celin
"What is this?" he exclaimed as the firm, beflowered plaits h
wife had fashioned slapped his cheeks. His face colored, an
frowning, he ran his fingers down one braid.

"The first of many future payments, Mac Niall. Do you beg
to understand?" Fulk inquired, his voice like velvet.

"Oh, Lord," Malcolm gazed in helpless adoration at his wi
"No trodden ground, Fulk? No quick kill?"

"Nay, brother. Where Celine is involved it is strictly slow tor-
re. And it will only get worse, believe me."

"Whatever are you talking about?" Celine's cheeks glowed,
d her eyes flashed with temper.

"They are referring to what one gladly pays for something that
beyond price," Jehanne said.

"Thank you, my lady. Well put." Fulk kissed her hand.

"Fulk."

"Aye, Malcolm?"

The Scot stared out through the crenellations. "Henry rides a
nite horse, does he not?"

Unreasoning panic assailed Jehanne as she rushed to see. Power
proached, bringing with it the potential for the death and de-
uction of all she held dear. "Fulk, get Sperling to move the
ck onto the bridge, as you and he discussed. Alert your men, I
ll get my bow, we can hold them off, and—"

"Jenn!" Fulk grasped her shoulders and held her firmly. "That
madness. We will not attempt to fight the king, unless you want
die, and see every last person here slain as well." He searched
r eyes.

How could Fulk be so calm? Jehanne felt like a bird fluttering
a net. Always she had found a way to fight back. "You are
t afraid. But I am. I cannot bear to lose you! Not now."

"Listen, Jenn. In what do you believe? Honor, loyalty and fair
iy, am I right?"

She nodded, blinking back her tears.

"Henry is our liege lord. He is imperfect, just as we are, but I
ıst submit to him with dignity, come what may, just as you did
me. Even had I a whole host at my command, I would not use
Do you see why?"

Jehanne shook her head "no," her throat so tight she could not
eak. She had done this. Out of her own wilfullness she had
ated a situation where Fulk had been forced to come to her,
ıs trapped with her, and would now die as a result. Not to
ntion Malcolm. She had no fear for herself. Whatever hap-
ned, nothing could be worse than losing Fulk.

He sighed. "You are one of the proud and courageous, Jehanne.

But sometimes great courage means holding absolutely still. Yo
know that, better than most.''

He understood. He knew how she had survived her father
wrath. She could only look up at him, as her tears overflowed.

"Nay, Jenn, do not weep, please, I cannot bear it.''

Summoning all her will, Jehanne took a deep breath an
scrubbed her face with the heels of her hands. "There. How
I look? Fit for a king?''

Fulk's strained expression relaxed into a wry smile. "Ay
sweeting. Good enough to eat, I'll warrant.''

Jehanne smiled, too, forced thought it was. She sensed a da
layer beneath Fulk's light demeanor. He was holding somethin
back. The truth struck her, then, like a hammer on a smithy
anvil.

"You will let the king do as he will with you because you fe
so much guilt over the knight you felled, Henry's favorite. Is
not so?''

As Fulk gazed at her, his vital presence seemed to recede in
the distance. He closed himself off, locked himself behind shutte
of icy calm. The warm amber of his eyes turned opaque, stonelik

"As you have confessed to me, so will I to you. The man
murdered was named Rabel. My own brother, Jehanne. My f
ther's heir. Over a lady, can you believe it?''

He flung the words at her.

Jehanne looked at Fulk in horror. He spoke truly, she could se
it in his face. He had turned on his own flesh and blood. For th
sake of a woman, he had killed his brother.

The desperate hardness of his gaze increased as she stared. Sh
realized what her expression of dismay did to him, but could n
change it. "You did not find his name worthy of mention, in
this time?'' she whispered.

"It is difficult for me to speak of it.''

"It is difficult to hear of it, my lord.''

Malcolm coughed. "You have left out a great deal, Fulk.''

"There is no time.''

"There damn well better be time, for if you dinnae explai
she will ne'er understand the why of it. Anyone in your pla
would have done the same.''

"I am not just anyone."

"You have *that* right. You are a bigger bloody fool than most!"

Celine began to wail. Malcolm pulled her against his chest, wincing and murmuring to her even as she pounded him with her fists.

Despair swept Jehanne and she shook her head. It had all been so good to be true. Poor Celine, to have lost one brother at the other's hands. No wonder she wept at the mere mention of the tragedy.

"Never mind, sir. I must go down and greet the king, and reassure the people. I will turn this place over to him, if it will keep you safe."

"You will do nothing of the kind." Fulk's voice held a cold, hard edge. He turned his back to her and looked down upon the approaching party. Royal banners flew, dozens of lanceheads glittered in the sun, festive and warlike at once. "I would not have brought this upon you for all the world, my lady."

"I know."

Malcolm put Celine aside and caught Jehanne's elbow. "I will tell the tale, even if he willnae. 'Twill take but a moment."

Jehanne jerked her arm free. "There is no need. Fulk must have had a reason for his action."

"But you will always have a doubt, now, won't you?" Malcolm glared at her, his expression tight and angry, then his mouth curled into a scornful sneer.

She stared. What was wrong with him? Why did he not leave well enough alone? The Scot brought his hand to her face, and with the backs of his fingers slapped the underside of her chin, hard, so her teeth snapped together.

In the first instant of shocked disbelief she looked to Fulk. He stared, watching as if transfixed by horror. A savage, red wave of rage seethed through Jehanne. Malcolm's act was an unforgivable affront to her dignity. Her father would have struck the Scot's head from his shoulders.

Men! Hateful, useless creatures. All of them.

She charged Malcolm, drew her fist and knocked him down onto the allure. His head hit the stones with a dull crack. He lay stunned.

Celine screamed like a wildcat and shoved Jehanne away.

Deep regret coursed through her. "What have I done?"

Malcolm lifted his head wearily. "Exactly what Fulk did, m
lady. Except he delivered a blow so powerful Rabel never wok
up."

Jehanne put her hands to her cheeks. "You are a fiend to in
dulge in such play-acting!" she told him bitterly.

"I am not acting now." He rubbed his jaw. "But, listen to m
tale. Imagine yourself a strong young man, the glorious winner
an important tourney. Afterward, a lovely Spanish princess loo
your way, one of several ladies showing you interest.

"Your elder brother, whom you love and respect even thoug
his wit has caused you endless public torment, has had his ey
upon the lady all day. You decide to help his cause. In priva
you speak to the lady, though your Spanish is limited, and arrang
a rendezvous later, between her and your brother."

Jehanne glanced at Fulk, who now sat in the walkway, his hea
in his hands. Celine huddled beside him, her cheek resting again
his shoulder, her eyes tightly closed.

"Continue," Jehanne said.

Malcolm fixed her with his intense, one-eyed gaze. "Imagin
that you bring your brother to the appointed place to introduc
him to the lady before you yourself depart. She arrives with he
handmaidens, looks from you to your brother, and runs to yo
instead of him. She wants nothing to do with him. She has mi
understood and thought the assignation was betwixt the two
you.

"Your brother, your elder, is offended, outraged and believe
you have been busy behind his back, no matter what you say. H
is the king of sarcasm, of belittlement, just as you are king
courtesy and charm. He names the lady a tease, you a cur. In fro
of her and her companions and your sister, who has foolish
followed, he calmly chucks you, just as I did a few moments ag
How did it feel?"

"Unbearably humiliating," Jehanne admitted. "I would hav
preferred a beating. For an instant I—I wanted to kill you."

Malcolm stood and dusted himself off. "So it was with Fulk
But once having thrown the blow at Rabel, he could not take

back. When he lost his brother, he lost everything else he cherished as well. And he has never made excuses for himself over it. He has ever taken the full blame upon his own shoulders. So, aye, he will submit to the king's pleasure. And so will I.''

Malcolm moved with surprising speed to the stairwell and disappeared down the spiraling steps. As one, Fulk, Celine and Jehanne jumped to follow, calling after him.

The four of them, plus Bayard and an unusually subdued Lioba, waited at the gates for Henry. Jehanne hugged herself, stiff with apprehension. She prayed for a hole to open up and swallow the royal cavalcade, and to swallow her, too.

Fulk was right. There was no such thing as a perfect knight. She had pretended her father was one, in her desire for him to be all she longed to admire. But there were men who pursued ideals, who sacrificed themselves for honor in ways not obvious to outside observers. Fulk had forgone glory to do what he thought proper. And she had thought the less of him for it.

She looked up at him, standing at her shoulder, his solid presence a comfort beyond words. She could not imagine how she had ever been afraid of him. Now she could not imagine life without him.

''Jenn, turn and make obeisance to the king,'' Fulk murmured.

She whirled about. Fulk dropped to his knees beside her, as did Celine and Malcolm. It was the only thing to do, and Jehanne followed their example.

Henry leaned forward in his saddle, heavy brows drawn together, his eyes narrowed, and kept a painfully long silence before speaking. ''Fulk de Galliard. You proud beggar. You, who refused to be knighted by my hand. You, who slew the noblest champion I had. I loved you like a son, and you repaid me in pain.''

Fulk met the king's gaze. ''I carry only sorrow and regret for my actions, sire. In your wisdom and grace you forgave my father his victory, and I treasure the memory of the love you bore me. I throw myself at your mercy, for I have slain yet another of your lords, the Earl Grimald.''

''And pray tell me why the Reluctant has seen fit to carry out such an act?''

"Sire, when Lexingford used my sister ill, he forfeited his right to life."

Henry looked at Celine, who had assumed an attitude of prayer but peeked through her fingers. "This dove is your sister?"

"Aye."

The king regarded her with interest for several moments, then returned his gaze to Fulk. "Did you put Alun FitzWalter to death?"

"I was sent here to carry out that task. I accepted the commission. I did not complete it."

Jehanne chilled at this admission. She had believed Fulk when he had first said he would not have taken her father's life. But then, he had been sore pressed. She cleared her throat. "Sire, Grimald threatened Celine if Fulk refused, and—"

"Therefore," Henry intoned, cutting Jehanne off, "you are as guilty as if your hand had done the deed, just as a man who lusts after another's wife is guilty of fornication, even should he never know the woman."

"Sire!" Jehanne spoke again. She must bring the king's anger back toward herself, no matter the cost. "My father knew of the earl's treachery long ago in France, when Galliard was lost, and did nothing! He—"

"Jehanne, no more!" Fulk commanded.

"Nay, I have known of this and kept silent, just as bereft of private honor as my father before me in the matter. He was guilty, and therefore even if Fulk had killed him, it was his due. I will take any punishment my father earned, Your Grace."

She got to her feet, stepped forward and held out her wrists, ready to be bound.

"He did it for you, Jenn."

"What?" She turned at Sir Thomas's quiet voice.

"Alun protected you from Grimald the only way he knew how. His silence kept you from harm. He made certain you hated the earl, did he not, by pushing you toward the man against your will? And he made you tough, did he not? So that you could withstand all manner of pain? Even that which the earl might inflict upon you, should you ever find yourself in his hands?"

Agony stabbed sharp within Jehanne's breast. She moaned and doubled over. Fulk caught her in his arms and held her tight.

"He loved you, but he was wrong to hurt you, no matter his motive. Wrong, Jenn," Fulk whispered.

"I cannot let them take you."

"I need no more rescuing, Jenn."

The king growled, "What of this tale, Galliard?"

Fulk straightened and gently released Jehanne. "I know nothing of what Sir Alun knew or did not know. My father mentioned the Earl Grimald from time to time in scathing terms, and I but recently realized the truth for myself."

"What am I to do with you, then?" the king roared.

"As you will, sire."

"*As I will!* What in God's name is wrong with you, Fulk? You are alive, yet you behave as one dead."

Fulk stared at the king's feet, his fists clenched at his sides.

Henry pressed on. "What of Redware? Are you not going to demand the return of your patrimony, for your sister at least? I hear Hengist of Longlake has been somewhat heavy-handed of late."

"Redware never belonged to me, therefore I am in no position to make demands, sire. As for Hengist, he only follows orders. And now he may change, with the grief of his lord's demise so heavy on his heart," Fulk murmured.

"I can well imagine. If his grief were similar to my own, then he would indeed be reformed. But, I hasten to assure you, Fulk, Lord Grimald has not yet departed this world. He remains with my surgeon at Redware, though he cannot speak to tell his side of things."

Henry swung his gaze to Jehanne. "I am hungry! Let us eat first and dispense justice later."

Fulk spoke again. "Sire?"

"What now?"

"My courser, at Redware, will you have your surgeon attend his wounds?"

"You and your bloody horses!" Henry glared at Fulk, then dismounted and strode to him, deep blue robes swirling in royal indignation.

Fulk dropped back to his knees. The king frowned upon Fulk's earnest, anguished face as if trying to decide whether or not to strike a blow, then clutched his own forehead. "Get up."

Fulk regained his feet, slowly.

"You would do better to look out for your own neck. But the surgeon is doing what he can for the beast. Such an animal is worth ten Grimalds."

"If the courser returns to health he is yours, sire."

"Nay. I need no more mouths to feed. Now, girl, lead us to table." With a scowl for Malcolm, Henry put a heavy hand upon Jehanne's arm and firmly steered her toward the keep.

Having fed the king and his entourage with as much decorum as she could summon, Jehanne was exhausted from the hours of strain, awaiting his determination of their fates. He was a hard man, capable of cold-blooded decisions without regard to pleas for clemency. But he was also her kinsman, however distant the relationship.

He sat in the place of honor, in her father's great chair, rubbing his beard and slanting his gaze from culprit to culprit. Fulk, Jehanne, and back again.

Jehanne looked at the stony, merciless eyes of Henry's knights, and her heart plummeted. It struck her, though, that they *all* seemed to know Fulk, not only Bayard. Their hard expressions never wavered, but she caught subtle exchanges nonetheless. They knew Fulk. And respected him.

The king startled her when of a sudden he turned to Malcolm. "Who are you, and why are you here?"

Malcolm bowed low and introduced himself in Gaelic, to the king's displeasure. Then he switched to English. "I have wed Sir Fulk's sister, Celine, Your Grace. As much as I love her, I vow I willnae see Fulk condemned without offering myself in his stead, for the many times I have broken the laws of your most noble personage's kingdom."

"Nay, sir!" Fulk pounded the table. "Take back those words or I shall ram them down thy most stubborn, gallant throat! Your transgressions are as nothing compared to mine. If one of us is to give his life for the other it will be me." Fulk leaned forward with a belligerent stare for his friend.

"I have poached the king's game!" Malcolm shouted, gesturing dramatically. "Stolen oakwood from the king's forest! Clipped silver from coins of the realm! Assaulted the king's loyal subjects! Are you making note of my crimes, Paxton?"

The magistrate could only goggle at the Scot. For once Celine remained silent, though she twisted her veil into knots. Jehanne watched in dismayed astonishment as Fulk, in the king's presence, jumped up and headed toward Malcolm, for all the world looking as if he would do him violence on the spot.

Henry observed the proceedings, his expression gradually shifting from anger to amusement as Malcolm's outrageous list grew. When Fulk neared Mac Niall, the king raised a hand.

"Galliard, if the Gael is made to regret his outburst it shall be by my will, not yours." He turned to the Scot. "Malcolm Mac Niall, well do I remember your part in the battle that made Fulk a legend in my court. You, at least, accepted adubbement from me. I made no mistake in so honoring you, and you will prove it to me from this day forth, I am equally certain."

"I will, my lord." Malcolm bowed deeply to the king.

Henry gazed at him for a moment, then added, "Besides, how could I, in good conscience, hang a man who resembles nothing so much as a merrily bedecked Maypole?"

Malcolm's expression grew fierce and he growled, "That is easily remedied, my lord." He began tearing out his buttercups.

Henry nodded in Jehanne's direction. "Fulk, this baroness wishes to intercede on your behalf. She claims to be your wife. What have you to say about that?"

Fulk looked at his bride with gleaming eyes. "The Lady Jehanne has suffered a great deal, Your Grace. She has nothing to do with any of this. She has deluded herself. She is—"

"I am with child!" Jehanne blurted, surprising herself. All heads turned to her. "And so beneficent a king as you, sire, could not possibly see fit to deprive an innocent babe of its father, a loving wife of her lord and husband, a devoted sister of her only brother, a good friend of his boon companion, a pious mother of her beloved son—"

Henry shook his head. "Yet again you tell me what is and is not possible! No doubt the hounds and hens and beasts of the field will also begin to plead for Fulk before long. He could charm a nun out of her wimple."

He threw a hard look to Fulk, who had turned quite pale.

"Let us see this child when it comes," Henry continued. "Then I may believe such a fairy tale of fecundity, and be satisfied that Windermere is going to be properly looked after."

Henry scratched his head through his hat. "Pull yourself together, my lad. Turn your attention to this keep, and your heir."

Fulk did not speak, and the heartbeats thudded by in Jehanne's breast. He must accept the king's largesse. If he did not she would be as one cast into hell, utterly damned.

Fulk met her pleading eyes and found his tongue. "You have my thanks, sire."

"Do not thank me, thank the fact that I believe I can still make use of you," Henry said gruffly. "Oh, and as for the Earl Lexingford, whether he is guilty or no, or lives or dies, you shall pay the wergild for his injury and disablement. You will go without your bloody books a good while longer, Fulk, mark me."

Before anyone could stop her, Celine rushed to Henry. Steel hissed as the king's personal guard drew their swords. Their expressions of menace softened into bewilderment as she threw herself into his arms, hugged him as if he were an old friend, and kissed his lips.

Jehanne could not tell who was more shocked, king or onlookers.

"Mac Niall!" Henry bellowed. "Contain this female! Ah, but she is sweet. You are a fortunate fellow. Overly amorous natures must run in Fulk's family." He patted Celine's cheek.

"Aye, milaird, and I thank God for it every day." A bit unsteady, Malcolm gathered his lady and took her back to her seat.

Henry thumped a fist on the table and frowned at Fulk. "Well, what are you waiting for? Do you think I believe for one moment the wild claims of Lady Jehanne? Even you could not have got her breeding so quickly, at least not so that she would know it. There is little of import in this kingdom that I do not find out about, sooner or later. And the priest who married you was only too happy to enlighten me.''

''As you will, sire.'' Fulk bowed, and Jehanne curtsied, blushing furiously. He took her hand and led her up the stairs, amidst a sea of grins.

Chapter Twenty-Two

Once they had gained the privacy of the solar, Jehanne was fair to bursting with happiness and relief. She wanted to let Fulk know straightaway just how glad she felt. But he went to the window and sat on the stone ledge, staring out over the rolling hills of Windermere. His visage was shadowed, brooding, anything but pleased.

"What is it, Fulk?"

He did not reply, nor did he seem to notice she had spoken.

A wretched sort of anger clawed at Jehanne's heart. Long had she suffered the foul moods of men. "Do you attempt to humble me with your silence, my lord? Have I offended you somehow?"

Fulk turned to her, sunlight slanting across his lean face. It caught his eyes, increasing their brilliant, golden depths, revealing an anguish she had not seen in him before.

"How could I be offended by you, Jenn? You, who so zealously pursues honor at such great personal risk. *You,* who are skilled at arms, possess the courage of a lioness, champion the oppressed, are generous and chivalrous and fair. You, my lady, are the perfect knight I never believed could exist. And once again you have saved me."

Jehanne was dumbfounded. *She* was a perfect knight? His words were like a dream come true and a nightmare in one. The virtues he had named comprised her highest ideals. And he, a better judge of character than anyone else she knew, had just told her she possessed each of them. But that very declaration caused him obvious pain.

"What would you have had me do? Allow you to be kicked to death? Bleed to death? Hang from a gibbet?" Her words were harsh but she spoke them gently, for the suddenly the very timbers beneath her feet seemed fragile and tenous. As though something she had just begun to count on and cherish as a reality might dissolve and fade away.

She began again. "My husband, if it pleases you I will try hard to be more womanly, to behave as befits a lady. I will give up my dueling and learn to scribe, I will even wear—"

"Nay, Jenn, do not change. Do as you have always done, for that is who you are, and I love you for it. It is I who should have done things differently. From the day Grimald forced me to my knees before the altar I have made a mockery of knighthood. Nay, from the day I slew Rabel I have avoided facing it. I do not see how a person of your standards has borne my presence for so long." Fulk rose and gazed about as if he were a caged animal looking to escape.

God above! He loved her for her selfish, wicked obstinance that had nearly cost him his sister, his best friend, and his own life? "Galliard, please, there is nothing about you that I do not adore. You must believe me, for I would not lie to you," Jehanne pleaded. "Deep inside, I have ever felt safe with you, even when first we met. I cannot say that about any other man of my acquaintance."

Fulk looked narrowly at her, then out the window. "Aye, betimes I am no threat to anyone. I am like a sharp blade wound round with silken cloths, captive of my higher nature, yet slave to the foulest sort of blood lust one can imagine. A hesitant knight is utterly useless. A knight beyond control is a menace to both friend and foe. They would have done better to dub you instead of me."

"But you confuse bravery and discrimination, Fulk. You do not hack blindly. The king's guard downstairs are men of valor to the last. Each one of them looked upon you with respect. Does that mean nothing to you?"

Fulk smiled grimly. "Do you know what I did to earn their respect, lady? How many lives I took, in a manner so joyously

brutal as to defy description? Ask them, and see if you are not
sickened by what you hear. If that sort of valor is what you truly
desire of me, I cannot satisfy you and live with myself. For all I
know, the next time my *furor* takes me you will be in the way,
or someone else with whom I have fallen in love.''

Jehanne's eyes widened. After all that had been said and done,
how could he be so callous as to speak of future infidelity? Then
she saw that his sad gaze rested upon her still-flat belly. She grew
desperate to find words to put him at ease.

''There are many gentle knights, Fulk. Scholars and men of
God who uphold their vows with no unnecessary violence. Why
can you not be one of them?''

''I told you once before, Jenn, perhaps you did not hear me.
There is a demon within me that exists only for the chance to
spill blood. Once I am possessed by it I become a berserker, like
the Norsemen of old. And woe to anyone who tries to stop me.
Rabel knew not what hit him. None of them did.''

Fulk gave her a telling look as he spoke, and she knew he
meant that she should not stand in his way. He stalked about the
solar, gathering his gambeson and sword and gauntlets.

''What are you going to do? Where are you going?''

He stared at her as if he himself did not know. Then he returned
to lacing up his gambeson. ''I will go to the Holy Land, where
wanton killers are needed and admired, and I shall kill and kill
and kill, until the demon is gone from me. Then I will return. If
you still desire what is left.''

Jehanne could not believe her ears. Her throat tightened until
she could barely speak. ''Have I driven you to this, Fulk?''

''You opened my eyes, Jenn. Thank God it was sooner rather
than later.'' He turned and strode toward the door.

No goodbye kiss. No sweet request for a farewell wish that he
might grant her. He thought himself evil. He must be made to see
how wrong he was in that. How important he was to her.

Jehanne steeled herself to hurt him.

''I will not take you back, Fulk. If you leave I shall bar the
gates against you. You shame me before the world. Everyone will
see I am such a failure as a woman that I cannot keep my husband

ven for a sennight. And the pity of it is, you rush to do battle
gainst yourself, Fulk. No one but yourself.''

Fulk stopped and slowly faced her, his expression stricken.
What else can I do? I am tearing apart inside.''

''Love me again, Fulk. Show me what I mean to you and let
e show you the same. Then...go if you must.'' As she spoke,
er body trembling, Jehanne tugged the laces of her overgown
ee.

By the time Fulk closed his mouth she had dragged her shift
ver her head. She tossed it aside, shaking with the effort it took
ot to pull her hair over her breasts, nor to cover herself with her
ands.

She stood naked before him. For the first time in broad daylight.
ot the kind, golden light of candles and hearth. Every bit of her
as exposed to his sight. All of her womanhood, as well as every
car and welt she bore. ''Do you know what I fear the most?''

He swallowed. ''My gaze. My disappointment. My pity.''

''Aye, and if I can conquer such fear through loving you, then
kewise can you learn to put your demon to sleep.''

When he made no move toward her, Jehanne bowed her head.
er trust was her ultimate offering. If Fulk did not want it, did
ot appreciate it, she had nothing left to give.

The moment drew itself out, a silent cry echoing in the prison
f her heart. A bittersweet prison that yet held her captive. It was
till as it had been on Beltaine. She remained helpless in the face
f her love for him. It did not matter if he could not return it now.
he would go to her own annihilation before she would deny him
nything of herself.

Fulk's sword clanged as it hit the floor.

Jehanne looked up. The very sight of him caused her to shiver,
emembering...

He stared and groaned and dropped his gauntlets at the same
me. ''Oh, my sweet, brave wife. How lovely you are.''

She blushed, and heat spread downward. Her breathing grew
apid and shallow. Biting her lip, she continued to hold still, to
llow his warm gaze to sweep her from head to toe and back
gain.

She fought the need to close her own eyes, to slip into the

safety of the hiding place in her mind. He wanted her. He love
her no matter how she looked...didn't he?

Fulk took a step closer. When he reached for her Jehanne dare
to edge backward, toward the bed. "If you desire me, you mus
prove your love and devotion."

In silence Fulk advanced, shedding clothing as he came.

Her heart pounded wildly before the ravenous intensity of hi
gaze. He was powerful. Dark. A magnificent, mysterious, dan
gerous animal, as the Creature had said.

But Jehanne had no time to admire him, for he pushed he
down onto the mattress and trapped her wrists with his hand
Desire burned through his eyes. She felt it streak across her ski
like sheet lightning over the fells. His growling words confirme
the anticipation fluttering deep within her.

"At the moment, Jenn, I have no devotion. I have no tende
ness. Only unbearable heat and a great deal too much blood cours
ing through my veins."

Never had she imagined him capable of such a frank admissio
But she had asked for him, come what may. And she wanted hin
come what may. She took a deep breath, ready to lose herself i
his all-consuming passion. "Put it to good use, then."

Fulk took Jehanne in, trying to slake his thirst for the sight c
her, fully bared to him as God and nature surely intended. Wh
did she want to hide her body? Everything about her was perfec
from the sheen of moisture on her breasts to the subtle curves o
waist and hip, and the long, elegant contours of her legs.

He ran his hands up those same limbs, caressing them like th
priceless treasures they were. A powerful convulsion gripped hi
heart, a feeling of tender, protective possession that brought hin
to his knees.

For him to harm her, even when filled with madness, would b
an impossibility. Not when his flesh had known her touch, nc
when her skin flushed beneath his fingers, and her pink-budde
breasts filled his hands.

There was so much more to share, to explore with her. But fo
the moment he was in thrall to an urgent need, clamoring fo
satisfaction. She alone could fill it.

Almost with regret Fulk covered Jehanne with his body. He

ershadowed her, swallowed her in the storm of his own hunger.
e bent his head to her neck and savored her fragrance, the tex-
res of her skin and hair. He longed to capture her sweetness,
r generosity and passion, and greedily hold it all to himself.

And he wanted to make certain every last bit of her womanly
rm sang with pleasure. Already she melted at his touch, arching
ward him. Fulk pulled Jehanne closer, swept her body with an
mbrace that only increased his own ache.

She had asked him to show her what she meant to him. Holy
other, if only he could. Physical intimacy would never be
ough to express what he felt, but for now it would have to do.

Fulk prayed he could keep his hands gentle, when he yearned
clutch her to his breast, mold her against him so tightly he
ared she might not be able to breathe. He prayed he could keep
s need at bay, even as her small moans and artless kisses made
m frantic to take her.

She rubbed her lithe body along his. Dragged her nails up his
anks. Gently bit his lower lip, then opened her mouth to him.
lk deepened his kiss and she wound herself around him. Arms,
gs, heart and soul, without hesitation or reserve. He felt his blood
ce ever faster, his control slip further.

"My beloved," she whispered against his cheek, and reaching
wn, wrapped her fingers about him. Undone, he could wait no
nger.

And, God bless her, nor could Jehanne. In the warmth of the
nlight flooding the bed, she surged against him. She gleamed,
ecious and golden, silky and hot. She took all that he had to
fer with a wild abandon that matched his own.

He had lied. He held more devotion for her than he could bear.
nd he was helpless to prove it except by driving into her. Again,
d again. Harder. Faster.

She cried out and rolled with him in a joyous tumble, her un-
ecked enthusiasm a delight. With every beat of Fulk's heart,
ith each breath, he poured his love into his effort. At last it
turated him, and overflowed into her.

Even as he soared, Jenn's cry of release made Fulk smile. She
as an honest woman. No pretending, no holding back. There
as nothing shameful about the whole kingdom knowing of her

joy. He soothed her with more kisses, on her breasts and ne
and lips. She tightened her legs about his hips and would not
go.

"Don't ever leave me," she begged.

With that soft entreaty Fulk vowed he never would. "Jenn
belong to you. We are wick and candle, burning as one."

Nothing was more important than her happiness. Not pride, n
honor, nor even his fear of the *furor*. She had said if he depart
he would only go to fight himself... "Mayhap you are right. N
demon is not a demon after all, but a place where I go in n
mind, where all is blood and power and forgetting. I have but
go elsewhere. To you, whom I love as I have no other."

Jehanne curled into his arms and smiled. "I welcome you,
I have no other. But you already know you can overcome th
violence, for I have provoked you many times, and never ha
you gone berserk."

Fulk kissed her temple. "Not within sight of you, at least. B
if I feel that state coming on, I shall hasten to yon lake and jun
in, until the fire is quenched. Think you that a worthwhile n
tion?"

"Aye, once I have taught you to swim, certainly. But do n
go alone."

"I won't. I want us to go together. I want to drown with yo
In you, again. And yet again." He pulled her to him, fitting h
hips to his, slipping his hair-roughened thigh between her smoo
ones.

Jehanne caught her breath as he began his slow rekindling
her desire. Her breasts swelled to meet his mouth's cares
Bloomed to the nibbling of his teeth. Flushed with the lapping
his tongue. And the rest of her turned to liquid fire at his touch

"Aye, Galliard. Easy, now, these are deep waters. Wait, na
That is not fair. Beast! Oh, my God..."

His clever fingers performed exquisite acts. Things she wou
never have dared conceive of herself. Then he replaced thos
impostors with that unique part of himself she had grown to a
preciate so much. He filled her. Stretched her. Stroked an
plunged within her until she flooded yet again in ecstasy. H
quick breaths turned to gasps and incoherent cries.

"Now," Fulk growled, "be thou well content with me?"

On the brink, Jehanne quivered beneath him. Open, helpless
d panting. "I can teach you nothing of my desire...that you do
t...already...know. My lord, do not stop now, I pray you!"

"I am yours to command, lady."

A moment later, in the courtyard, the lurchers bayed again in
ll-throated unison.

Epilogue

With the celebration well underway, the feast's main course wa
delivered under the flourishing direction of the French steward,
man obsessed with all things courtly and fashionable. Jehann
hardly knew what to expect of him from one day to the next.

Fulk lounged beside her, apparently absorbed in conversatio
with the new parish priest on his left, but beneath the tableclo
his hand rubbed along her thigh in a most provocative way.

Malcolm cleared his throat. "Why are you sitting all wrappe
up around yourself, lady? You are twining like a grapevine. A
you ailing?"

His convincingly worried expression made Jehanne's eye
bulge in irritation. She did not want attention drawn to hersel
"Nay." She stopped squirming, but her cheeks were already ho

Celine smothered a giggle. The priest looked puzzled. Liob
with Bayard seated beside her, paid no attention at all, engrosse
as she was with his attentive, affable silence. Jehanne slid h
gaze to Fulk. He regarded her sublimely, with half-closed eyes.

He knew very well why she twined, the great lout.

He smiled, all innocence. "But, my lady, it is early, not ye
tierce."

Jehanne bunched her fists and leaned to whisper in his ear, "
I were a man, and *you* were my beloved wife, there would be n
question of the time."

Fulk immediately rose and with an apology, excused himse
and Jehanne from the company. Amidst murmurs of concern, h

gripped her arm, hurrying her none too gently out of the hall and up the stairs of the farthest corner tower.

There was a moment of strained silence. Malcolm cleared his throat and with a stern glance willed Celine to remain demure. He raised his chalice. "To the king!"

Nodding and saying "aye," the guests drank.

"To Windermere!"

All drank again, with a fresh chorus of "ayes".

"To the success of Sir Fulk at the Duke of Warrick's upcoming journey!" This brought forth much table pounding and a round of "huzzahs." Encouraged, Malcolm continued in his attempts to distract the assemblage.

He toasted several more people and events, including the imminent arrival of his own firstborn child, and expressed the hope that Fulk's lady too would soon be fruitful.

Almost as Malcolm mentioned her name, Jehanne's broken cry echoed down the stairwell. Near the fire, her hounds twitched their ears, yawned, and went back to sleep.

The cleric had jumped to his feet. "Is the lady ill, after all?"

Malcolm hastened to reassure the man and prevent him from climbing the stairs. "Nay, Father, 'tis of no concern. Sir Fulk has confided in me that he has been much too lenient with the young baroness. She needs frequent, em, firm attention, to curb her tongue and improve her behavior."

"Oh, dear."

"Och, 'tis taking some time, but I can already see the change in her. Watch, when she returns to the hall, she shall be soft-spoken and sweet as a Beguine's daughter. Just as is the Lady Celine, here." Malcolm gazed with affection upon his glowing wife, who was fair to bursting with laughter, as well as with child.

The cleric scratched his tonsure and sighed. "Naturally, he must do his duty as husband, and I suppose if he spares the rod it will be to his lady's ultimate detriment."

Though he had led him to it, Malcolm nearly choked at the innocent priest's choice of words. "Of course. Please, make no mention of it when they return. Sir Fulk would not want the Lady Jehanne to feel any embarrassment. She prides herself on her stoicism...and he never leaves a mark on her."

"Ah, well, that is most considerate. I hope she is properly grateful."

Arm in arm Fulk and Jehanne reappeared on the curving stair.

Malcolm winked at the bewildered priest. "Och, indeed, she is."

Jehanne looked up and caught Fulk's winsome smile. His presence was her bastion against the world. Nothing mattered but that they were together. And he had turned out to be such a satisfaction.

"Enough, my lady?" he drawled. "Can you sit out the rest of the meal now and behave yourself?"

"Aye." She sighed and wanted nothing more than to go with Fulk back upstairs. But this time to their bed in the solar instead of the dim turret alcove they had just left. It was a wonder she had not left her body's imprint scorched upon the wall.

Still shivering from the last remnants of passion, she composed herself as Fulk accompanied her to the high table. He seated her and took his place at her side, a regal and imposing figure. How very fortunate she was.

She looked at the assembly. Young Bryce, now *Sir* Bryce, regaled his dining partner with a thrilling account of his latest exploits. Beside him, dear Thomas discreetly nodded off. Lioba blushed prettily before the ongoing courtesies of Bayard. Celine basked in Malcolm's newfound state of mellow contentment.

And the latest marvel, Hengist, struggled valiantly to master the manners Jehanne had been attempting to teach him. Even now she saw the effort it took him not to wipe his hands on the tablecloth. A passing hound's furry rump received the bounty of sauce instead.

Aye, she was rich as Croesus.

"Do you feel better, milady?" the priest asked, with a significant look to Fulk.

Jehanne beamed at the cleric. "Oh, indeed, Father. I have learned to allow my husband to remedy my small complaints. He knows just what to do with me. When, where, and in what measure. I am truly blessed."

The priest smiled and nodded, apparently satisfied with her response.

Fulk leaned toward her. "One day, Jenn, when that young man as heard enough confessions, and has himself been tempted and umbled, he will think back on this feast and know at last what ou are talking about. Then he will no doubt demand a full accounting from you. And a penance."

"Why from me and not from you?" she demanded.

"Because, sweeting, he will know I cannot help myself, that I m ever at your beck and call, a lowly slave to your will and idding, powerless to resist your charms—"

"All right, husband. Cease your litany and I will give you respite."

"Don't you dare!"

"That is one command of yours I shall take to heart."

Fulk grinned. "See that you do."

Beneath the table, Jehanne squeezed his hand, and gave silent thanks for the cherished comfort of this particular son of Adam. For Fulk, her perfect knight.

* * * * *

*Be sure to look for
the next thrilling romance from
Elaine Knighton
and Harlequin Historicals in February 2005.*

FALL IN LOVE WITH
THESE HANDSOME HEROES
FROM HARLEQUIN HISTORICALS

On sale September 2004

THE PROPOSITION
by Kate Bridges

Sergeant Major Travis Reid
Honorable Mountie of the Northwest

WHIRLWIND WEDDING
by Debra Cowan

Jericho Blue
Texas Ranger out for outlaws

On sale October 2004

ONE STARRY CHRISTMAS
by Carolyn Davidson/Carol Finch/Carolyn Banning

Three heart-stopping heroes
for your Christmas stocking!

THE ONE MONTH MARRIAGE
by Judith Stacy

Brandon Sayer
Businessman with a mission

www.eHarlequin.com

HARLEQUIN HISTORICALS®